The
Orphan's
Secret

BOOKS BY SHIRLEY DICKSON

The Lost Children
The Outcast Girls
Our Last Goodbye
The Orphan Sisters

SHIRLEY DICKSON

The

Orphan's
Secret

bookouture

Published by Bookouture in 2021

An imprint of Storyfire Ltd.
Carmelite House
50 Victoria Embankment
London EC4Y 0DZ

www.bookouture.com

ISBN: 978-1-80019-881-4
eBook ISBN: 978-1-80019-880-7

For my lovely three daughters, who I am blessed to have.

PROLOGUE

November 1953

Joy Radley's small hands covered her face.

'Seven, eight, nine...' she called out.

She peeped between her fingers. She could see Dad, sitting in the comfy chair in front of the fire reading the Sunday newspaper.

She heard creaking noises coming from the staircase.

'Ten!' Joy took her hands from her eyes. 'Ready or not, Freddie, here I come.'

She looked up as a sound came through the ceiling above.

Leaving the kitchen, Joy headed for the carpeted stairs, treading on the sides so they wouldn't creak. On the landing she crept to the back bedroom and opened the door, stepping inside. She gazed around her bedroom at the bed with its pretty pink eiderdown, and the white chest of drawers in the alcove by the cast-iron fireplace – but there was no sign of her younger brother.

Hide and seek was Freddie's favourite game, and his idea of fun was to pounce out of his hiding place and give his sister the fright of her life.

She checked behind the chest of drawers and behind the

curtains, then made her way across the landing, dim in the light of a snowy November afternoon, to Freddie's smaller bedroom. Stepping over the scattered books, toy soldiers and handmade wooden cars, she went to the bed and sank to her knees, pulling up the overhanging bedspread and staring into the blackness.

No Freddie.

Joy chewed a thumbnail in consternation. Then, flicking her chocolate-brown pigtails over her shoulders, she stood and made for the front room. With its cream wallpaper peppered with bunches of pink flowers, and despite the large and heavy-looking wardrobe, the high-ceilinged room with its tall window looking down on the street below had an airy feel.

She eyed the unmade bed and Daddy's brown overalls slung over a chair, then her attention was drawn to the open compact and face powder strewn over the dressing-table top. It took a moment for Joy to register the squeak from the wardrobe door. A spooky feeling enveloped her. Freddie was inside. She crept stealthily towards the wardrobe, grasped the ornate metal handles and flung the doors open.

'Caught you!'

But apart from Dad's suit and coats, and the frocks hanging from the rail, there was nothing to be seen at first. Joy stared at the clothes, sniffing a faint smell of perfume, and saw the arm of one of the coats move. She looked down and spotted feet below the coat, small feet wearing black scuffed shoes.

Freddie.

She pulled the coat aside, then recoiled as a ghostly white face stared at her.

'Boo!' Freddie yelled.

'It's not funny,' Joy said indignantly.

Laughing fit to burst, Freddie emerged from the depths of the wardrobe. 'You should've seen your face.'

Joy frowned. 'You think you're funny now but wait till they find out you've been playing with the powder compact when you're not even supposed to be in here.'

That stopped Freddie laughing. 'You won't tell, will you?'

Joy, older than her brother by two years, considered herself smarter. Like now, when she had a brainwave. 'Only if you promise never to scare me when we play hide and seek again. And I'll help you clean up the mess you've made with the powder.'

Freddie looked glum. 'I promise.'

Joy wasn't sure he was to be trusted. 'Cross your heart.'

'I said, didn't I?'

She raised an eyebrow at him.

'Oh, all right,' Freddie said begrudgingly.

It was then that Joy's attention was drawn to what looked like a blanket he was holding.

'Where did you find that?'

'On the bottom shelf of the cupboard.' Freddie's tone was cross and Joy knew it was because he hadn't got his own way.

She looked at the blanket in his hand. It was made up of different coloured squares of material stitched together. One of the squares showed what seemed to be a flag while another had flowers embroidered on it.

Freddie clutched the blanket protectively.

'You can't keep it,' Joy told her brother. 'Because they'll know you've been in here.'

Freddie wavered, then, pouting, he handed the blanket over.

Joy felt bad but the real reason she wanted the blanket was to study the squares herself.

———

Later, before he switched off the bathroom light, Joy's dad took a moment to look around the newly built bathroom, taking in the cast-iron claw-foot bath, surrounded by white tiles, porcelain sink, flush toilet, all complemented by a black and white linoleum floor. He gave a satisfied smile; no longer would his family have to traipse down the yard to use the outside lavatory.

Switching off the light, he moved to the half landing and,

looking up the stairs, noticed light shining from the gap at the bottom of his daughter's bedroom door.

He checked his watch. Quarter to ten. Joy should be asleep by now as she had school in the morning. He sighed; his daughter, at ten, was growing up too fast for his liking. It had been many a year since Joy had asked for a bedtime story and he missed that special time with his little girl.

Opening her bedroom door, he expected to see her, book in hand, head collapsed back on the pillow, sound asleep. But instead Joy was sitting bolt upright in bed, staring intently down at something.

She started guiltily, and grabbed whatever it was that had captured her attention, attempting to hide it beneath the bedcovers. 'Daddy, I'm sorry. I should have asked but—'

'Joy, lights-out time was ages ago.' He walked over towards the bed. As he came closer he could see better what she was clutching and, recognising the patchwork material, he clapped a hand over his mouth in surprise and shook his head.

'What is it, Daddy? I've never seen this blanket before.'

He slowly slid his hand down from his mouth. He owed Joy the truth. 'It's not a blanket, sweetheart.'

'What is it then?'

'A memory quilt.'

Her brow crinkled. 'What kind of memories?'

He studied her face: those cute bow lips, her snub nose and brown, questioning eyes. He didn't want to continue this conversation for he knew where it would lead. 'Usually treasured memories. People choose a theme before they start: people they love, or happy times.'

Joy's troubled eyes looked at him. Anticipating what was coming next, his stomach clenched.

'Who made it?'

He knew the time had come to reveal the secret he'd kept for so many years. He took a deep breath. 'Your mother.'

Joy's eyes grew round in astonishment.

'Let me explain, sweetheart.' He sat on the edge of the bed.

As Joy snuggled down to listen, he began telling the story, and he knew it would irrevocably change his relationship with his beloved daughter.

1

North-east town of South Shields, early March, 1940

Lily Armstrong finished speaking, inhaled deeply, and waited for the onslaught from Mam.

It was Monday. The pair of them had finished the weekly wash and, the tub emptied, backyard swilled, they were now warming their red and frozen hands in front of the range fire.

Mam, as Lily had expected, was outraged. 'Married next week. I've never heard the like. And without a thought to ask your dad.' Her slight body quivered in annoyance.

With a sigh, Lily leant against the kitchen table. 'I'll be twenty-one in two weeks, Mam, and then I won't need permission to marry. Besides, John and I have been courting for eighteen months now.'

Pursing her lips, Mam shook her head in disgust. Moving to the range, and taking a knitted cloth from the mantlepiece to protect her hand, she lifted a bubbling dish of mince that had been cooking all morning from the range oven. Placing the dish on a table mat, Mam picked up a wooden spoon and, stirring the dish's contents, a mouth-watering meaty aroma pervaded the room.

Then she stopped and pointed the spoon, dripping with hot

liquid, at her daughter. 'Everyone knows it's common courtesy for the man to ask the father's permission to marry his daughter.'

Knowing there was no use arguing, Lily tried placating her. 'There was no time, Mam. John says in his letter he's expecting to be posted abroad after his training's finished.'

The letter from John had been lying on the mat behind the front door that morning. Lily had raced to her bedroom where she'd torn the envelope open. Reading the letter's contents, her heart palpitating, Lily had gone weak with happiness.

Sweetheart, I know this isn't the way to go about things. As you well know, I'm not an articulate man romantic-wise, or for that matter on any occasion when I've to express feelings, but I do love you with all my heart, Lily, and want to share the rest of my life with you. The rumour is that after training the battalion is to be posted abroad. I know we've talked this over before but I can't wait to get hitched and want you to be my wife before I go. Please say you'll marry me now and make me the happiest man.

A grin that couldn't be contained split Lily's face as he went on to say:

I want for us to know each other in every sense of the word. I respect that you wanted to save yourself for your wedding night...

This wasn't strictly true. Whenever the couple's petting got to fever pitch, it was the thought of Mam looking over John's shoulder that brought Lily back to the cold light of reason.

John's letter had ended:

I've got four days' leave from Friday. Is it possible, darling, to arrange a wedding in that short time?

Lily had thought about it; was this what she wanted? To forget the dreams of the past where she'd be as good as her brothers, finding a job and paying her way, before settling down? But she loved John and the idea of anything happening to him before they were man and wife was too terrible to bear.

'Anyways' – Mam, now rolling a floury dumpling in milk, plopped it beside the rest to form a ring on the top of the mince – 'what lass wants to be proposed to by letter?'

Before Lily could reply, the backstairs door slammed. Dad, still wearing his brown work overalls and carrying the sticks he'd chopped in the backyard, appeared in the kitchen-cum-living-room doorway.

He looked from one to the other of the two women. 'What's going on?'

Carrying the dish of mince over to the range and placing it back in the oven, Mam slammed the door.

'That John Radley lad has proposed to our Lily and it's without your approval.' She folded her arms over her bosom in a way that suggested, what was Dad going to do about it?

Dad's reaction was typical. Putting the sticks in the hearth to dry, he eased his lanky frame into his favourite wooden, high-back rocking chair with its plumped floral cushion and, taking his pipe from his jacket pocket, he clenched it between his teeth and lit it with a match.

He knew better than to interfere when his wife was in this contentious mood.

'Arthur! Have you nothing to say on the matter?'

His cheeks sucked in and a cloud of smoke billowed from his mouth.

Mam gave a snort of disgust. 'So that's it. You're just going to ignore the fact the lad's got no respect.'

Lily, knowing Mam was gunning for a fight, intervened. 'John isn't like that. He's—'

'Lily, be quiet. This is between your dad and me.'

Lily sighed resignedly. This should have been a happy moment but instead the proposal was causing havoc in the Armstrong household.

Dad glanced at Lily and must have seen her misery. He took the pipe from his mouth. 'Ida, hold your tongue. Lily's old enough to know her own mind.'

'Arthur Armstrong! What kind of man lets some whipper-snapper make a fool of him and over his own daughter?'

Dad's face darkened. 'I don't know what's got into you, woman.'

The terraced upstairs flat in Fawcett Street was usually Mam's domain and Dad was happy to let her get on with it. But Dad ruled the family and whatever he said was law. A fair-minded man, Dad had a short temper, which, normally, he kept under control, but Lily knew that Mam in this mood could drive him over the edge.

He barked, 'That Radley fella's off to fight for king and country and that's enough credentials for me to allow Lily to marry him.'

Lily's parents glared at one another, the atmosphere charged. Then Mam, lowering her gaze, turned and, stomping from the kitchen, banged the scullery door and made off down the stairs.

Dad, heaving a big sigh, clenched his pipe in his teeth. A mystified expression on his face, he gazed off into space.

Dismayed at the ructions she'd caused, it dawned on Lily why Mam was so upset. Though she'd never admit it, Mam would be fretting because, if Lily married, she would have to run the upstairs flat on her own.

Lily was her parents' second child and the only girl out of five children. Harry, the eldest, was married to Jean and lived over the lane. After Lily came Sam, two years later Ian, then Mam had had two miscarriages before Jimmy, now eight, was born.

When Lily left school, Dad had discouraged her from finding work as she was expected to help Mam in the house. For Mam, by then, was struggling, and Lily now understood that having all those babies, plus the work involved in looking after a household full of men, had taken its toll on her health.

As an aroma of dumplings cooking wafted from the oven and Lily set the table, washed the dishes left in the sink and swept the crumbs from the floor, she noticed, as she glanced through the sash window, it was raining. She headed outside to bring the washing in from the line, glancing up and down the lane for signs of Mam – her mother wasn't dressed for such inclement weather as she'd been in her slippers when she stormed out.

Lugging the wicker washing basket up the stairs, Lily knew she wasn't resentful towards Mam about her reaction to John's proposal, but worried and disheartened. For Mam was a proud woman and it would go against the grain to rely on Lily to share the load around the home. Lily knew it would concern her to think her daughter was putting her life on hold for the sake of her family. Lily was at a loss to know what to do.

Plonking the basket she carried onto the kitchen floor, Lily looked over towards Dad, who, after working a night shift at the shipyard, should have been in bed, but was sound asleep in the chair – head lolling and open-mouthed.

It was different for menfolk, Lily thought as she hung a line on hooks screwed into opposite walls of the kitchen. They worked hard but their shift finished when they came home and then they didn't lift a finger for the rest of the day.

As she hung the sodden sheets on the makeshift line, the feeling of being second best returned. Years ago she'd overheard Dad tell a neighbour, whose wife had recently delivered a son, 'A man isn't worth his salt till he's fathered a son.'

'Aye,' Mam, standing at his side, had chipped in, 'you can rely on sons to bring a healthy pay packet in.'

Lily never doubted that her parents loved her and Dad would protect her till his dying breath, but still she couldn't help feeling second best. Determined to prove herself, to show her parents she was as good as any boy, Lily's competitive spirit kicked in and her ambitions went beyond the expectations of most girls, of becoming a wife and mother and what Lily considered a drudge like Mam. Lily wanted more out of life.

But despite that, looking round the kitchen – at the tabletop that Dad sanded and varnished every year, the round-faced clock that had been in the same place on the mantelpiece since her parents married a lifetime ago – Lily couldn't deny the secure feeling of belonging the place gave her.

At that moment, she heard footsteps on the backstairs and a door close. Mam appeared from the scullery, her slate-grey hair wet and bedraggled, dress clinging to her skinny figure.

'Mam, you're soaked through.' Lily hurried over to the range and, grabbing a towel hanging on the range's brass rail, handed it to Mam.

'It's me own fault.' Mam vigorously dried her hair, then wrapped the towel turban-style around her head. Removing her slippers, she pulled up the black ankle-length skirt she wore and, undoing her suspenders, she rolled down her lisle stockings and padded over to the range to hang them on the rail. 'They say pride comes before a fall.' Her grey eyes, serious, met Lily's. 'I'm sorry, lass, for the way I reacted.'

Lily shook her head. 'It was a shock for you and—'

'No excuses, I was only thinking of meself. Then devilment got into me as it sometimes does and I got carried away and didn't think what I was saying. You know what? When I cooled down, I thought of your da's words.'

'What words was that?' Dad's sleepy voice said as he sat up in the chair.

Mam removed the towel and her hair, frizzled curls, framed her thin face. She turned towards her husband. 'Remember Aunty Winnie?'

'Your mam's older sister?'

'She was like a second mother to her siblings. Like you are, our Lily, to Jimmy.'

'What are you bringing Winnie up for now?' Dad shook his head as though he couldn't keep up with his wife's train of thought.

Mam, ignoring him, told Lily, 'She never married. Just stayed at home and looked after your nana.' She pulled a face. 'Your nana had some kind of arthritis in her blood, so they say.'

Dad said, 'As I remember it, Ida, Winne wasn't given a choice.'

Mam nodded. 'She had a caring nature and was put upon.' Her

grey eyes met Dad's. 'You are right, Arthur, it is time Lily had a life of her own.'

'Holy Moses. This is a first. Can I have that in writing?'

A look of intimacy passed between her parents and a catch caught in Lily's throat. They might argue, be at odds with each other at times, but theirs was an enduring love.

Lily was surer now than ever that that was what she wanted for her and John. She wanted to get married, but she also needed to prove herself and have a career – and if that meant putting off starting a family for a time then so be it. John, the dear man he was, who always saw the other person's point of view, would understand.

Mam broke the spell by making a move toward the door. She sniffed. 'The dinner smells cooked. Our Lily, I don't want the mince burning. Meat's another precious commodity these days.' She pulled a disgusted face. 'This new allowance of one and tenpence worth per person' – she folded her arms – 'is barely a pound of meat. It'll go nowhere with three starving men in the house.'

'Aye, but that's not the case if you've the money to splash out on a restaurant meal,' Dad chipped in, his face relaxed now his wife was herself again. 'They can serve meat without asking folk for coupons. Lucky buggers.'

'It's all right for some,' Mam agreed. 'Lily, the lads will be home from work soon. Take the dinner out of the range while I get changed.' She opened the door to the front landing, then turned to face her daughter. 'After dinner we've a wedding to arrange.'

2

First thing the next morning Lily sent a telegram with a single-word reply to John.

Yes! Xx

Returning home from the post office in Mile End Road, Lily was turning the corner into Fawcett Street when she realised she hadn't taken her gas mask with her. Most folk thought the war a nuisance so far, with rules about blackouts meaning curtains were drawn so that not a chink of light was allowed to shine out at night, kiddies being sent to the country for safety, and bacon, butter and sugar rationed. When the annihilation from the air hadn't happened, folk had been quick to call it the 'phoney war'.

Arriving at the front door, Lily entered and took off her coat and slung it over the banister rail. Mam was out getting the shopping in and Lily's two younger brothers were working a shift at the pit, while Jimmy was at school. By rights, the bedroom the lads shared (the two youngest in bunks while Sam had a slim bed of his own) was in dire need of being cleaned, but with stiff and sweaty socks littering the floor and the sniffy smell of tobacco, she decided against mucking out the room today.

Emptying the ash pan in the bin in the yard outside, which they shared with the elderly Simpson couple living in the downstairs flat, Lily filled the bucket from the coalhouse. Heaving the bucket of coal upstairs, she banked the kitchen fire. Then she threw a sheet over the table, and put two flat irons on the hob over the fire to heat.

The scullery door opened and Mam appeared, weighed down on one side with a shopping bag.

'What a carry-on this rationing is,' she declared, removing her hat pin and taking off her hat. 'I stood in the queue that long me legs ache something rotten.'

'Sit down, Mam, I'll put the rations away.'

Mam eyed the ironing. 'You can forget that.' Taking off her worn coat, she sank into the saggy leather seat of a dining chair. 'There's work to be done making a wedding list.'

———

Later, as they sat side by side at the table, cups of tea in front of them, Mam pencil in hand writing in a jotter, Lily realised she hadn't a clue just what it would entail to organise a wedding.

Mam, in her element, made a list of things to do. 'I'll only be mother of the bride once and so, by gum, I'm going to make the most of this wedding.'

She wrote, *see the vicar* (Mam was a keen churchgoer), *flowers, rings, car.*

'Car!' Lily exploded as she peered over Mam's shoulder.

Mam gave an affronted look. 'I'm not going to be a laughing stock by having me only daughter walk to the church on her wedding day.'

'I thought there was a petrol shortage.'

'There is but surely a short drive to the church will be permitted.'

Lily inwardly smiled. Mam would be in her glory stepping out of the house into a motor car for all the neighbours to see.

'What about the expense?'

Mam drew herself up. 'It's the bride's parents' responsibility to pay for the wedding and your dad and me won't shirk our duty.'

Lily's throat tightened and she felt tears prickle her eyes.

'Besides, we've only got one lass to cater for. Dad and I've got a spare bit of cash put by for a rainy day and having your brothers' pay packets in the pot helps.'

There it was again: the reminder the menfolk were the providers. Lily would have given anything to have the chance to work and contribute.

She'd had a job once at the Chichester (Chi for short) picture house, two years ago.

A 'flea pit', Dad called it, when she told him excitedly about her intended place of work. 'I won't have a daughter of mine working there.'

It had been a chance meeting outside the butcher's shop with June Lloyd, a friend from Lily's schooldays, that had got her the job.

June, married and expecting, had been delighted to see Lily. 'What about you? Any sign of wedding bells in the future?' She'd made a point of looking at Lily's third finger for a band of gold.

'Not likely. When am I going to meet anybody? I'm hardly ever out of the house.'

Lily had laughed, even though she was aware it sounded a pathetic excuse. Everyone she knew was getting wed and it was a well-known fact that if you passed twenty-one and weren't married then you were doomed to be a spinster and left on the shelf.

Lily, at the time, wasn't looking for a husband and felt she was only waiting for the chance to begin life proper. Though there was no hope of that with Jimmy only eight, two brothers working at the local mine, and Dad and Harry at the shipyard – the workload was never done. But Lily didn't grumble because working in the mine and the shipyard were considered reserved occupations, which meant Dad and her brothers weren't called up and sent off to war.

The menfolk often worked different shifts, which meant meals had to be served up at all times of day. Lily loved her grub, and couldn't resist a portion when she served each meal. Hence her sturdy and curvy figure, which she despised because up until her teens she'd been a tomboy.

June had said, 'That'll be me never crossing the front step when this bairn's born.' She pulled a long face. 'I did love me job.'

'What did you do?'

'I was an usherette at the Chi. Then when I got in the family way, I had to work nights as a cashier because when I sat in the kiosk me bump didn't show.' She blew out her cheeks in a disgusted fashion. 'Then me mother-in-law poked her nose in and told hubby it was indecent for a pregnant woman to be working and that was the end of that. I finished last weekend.' She heaved a sigh. 'Dick, me hubby, wouldn't hear tell of me working till they found someone else.'

An idea formed in Lily's mind. 'What does the job involve?'

June shrugged. 'Selling tickets and working out the change. Squaring up at the end of the night. *And* taking some lip from cocky males who think they're God's gift. Why? Are you interested?'

'Is it only nights?'

'Yes. I used to stay behind till the last showing to help tidy the place but the manager said it wasn't appropriate.' She made big eyes. 'Honestly, you'd think I had a deformity rather than just being pregnant.'

'Is the post still open?'

'Ask to see the manager, Mr Matthews. Say you're a friend of mine. Not that he's fussy, mind. Working at the Chi isn't most folks' cup of tea.'

So that's what Lily did before she told Dad.

'I've already got the job and the manager says I've to start straight away,' Lily had babbled before Dad could get a word in edgeways. 'I'll make sure everything's shipshape at home and put the milk bottles out.'

Dad opened his mouth to speak.

'Arthur, there's nothing for the lass to do here nights except listen to you menfolk argue over a card game.' Mam folded her arms. 'Where's the harm?'

Dad put on his annoyed face. 'You're just like your mother, headstrong. All right, but on one condition. Me or one of your brothers will come and collect you after you've finished. You're not walking home by yourself in the dark.'

Mam had winked at her.

Now, as they planned Lily's wedding, Mam told her, 'While I'm on about money. When you've a home and husband of your own, make sure from the start you see his pay packet. That bugger, your dad, has never shown me a single pay envelope since the day we wed. I've no idea how much he earns, then there's the overtime. Mind you, not that he's stingy with the housekeeping.'

'Or the Walnut Whip he brings for each of us every payday,' Lily said drolly and they both laughed.

'I could have done worse than your father.' Mam's tone was defensive. 'Many's the man who goes straight to the pub and spends all his pay on drink while his bairns starve. Your dad's a man with principles, no doubt because his own dad was a drunkard. Though he enjoys a pint, your dad knows when to stop. And woe betide those lads of his if they spend all their hard-earned cash on booze.'

There was a moment's silence, then Mam surprised Lily by saying, 'I've been thinking about your wedding dress.'

'How d'you mean?'

'This is the only chance I'll have to be mother of the bride and I've always dreamt me daughter would have a white wedding.' Mam gave a warning look that said, heed what I'm going to say and there'll be no arguing. 'This rationing hasn't affected clothes yet. But I bet it's only a matter of time. Meanwhile, everything's difficult to get and I was thinking...'

'Go on.'

'There's that wedding dress of Harry's wife hanging in the wardrobe and it's only a year old and she's about your build...'

'And?'

'There's shoes and a veil.'

When Lily didn't reply, Mam prattled on. 'Many would have had their wedding attire sold but not Jean, sentimental lass that she is. I suspect she'll be saving her dress for when her first bairn is born so she can have a christening robe made out of it.' Mam's expression softened. 'I wish the pair of them would get a move on.'

Lily made it easy for Mam. 'Do you think I should ask Jean if I could borrow her wedding dress?'

'The whole rig-out,' Mam corrected.

Was it such a bad idea? A white wedding had never been Lily's dream but borrowing Jean's dress would save money and time – which was getting shorter by the minute.

'She mightn't want anyone getting married in her wedding dress.'

Mam's face expressed self-satisfaction. 'You never know till you ask.'

She crossed 'wedding outfit' off the list.

———

Two days later, Lily and Mam were sitting next to one another on the front seat of a trolleybus, making their way up to Mrs Radley's house to inform her about the wedding.

'So, John's dad was a dentist.' Mam's tone held a note of incredulity.

'Yes.' Wearing her Sunday best black-and-white checked swagger coat and pancake beret (which Mam insisted she wear for the occasion), Lily shifted uncomfortably in her seat.

'And it was his own business.'

'So John says.'

Mam's expression was one of reverence. 'Well, I never. Why didn't you let on before?'

'Because you never asked.'

Mam's brow wrinkled. 'So why didn't John follow in his dad's footsteps?'

'He didn't want to.'

'Or he didn't have the brains.' Mam pursed her lips.

'Mam! If you must know, John is good with his hands. And working for a builder suited him better.'

Mam looked unconvinced. 'I bet his folks weren't too pleased.'

Deciding she didn't wish to carry on with this conversation, Lily, who was sitting in the window seat, looked out, hoping Mam would take the hint.

A telegram had arrived from John this morning.

I am now the happiest man. Arrange wedding by special licence. Leave starts twelve o'clock Friday. Tell Mum. Love John.

Mrs Radley lived in a street of large terraced houses off King George Road. Lily had only been to the self-contained house once before, to be introduced to John's mother, a rather nice lady with silver grey, permed hair who called her 'my dear' and dressed smartly in a tweed skirt and white shirt blouse. She had kind eyes and was softly spoken. Mr Radley had died eight years ago from a heart attack. There was a photograph of him on the sideboard. A good-looking man with white receding hair, he wore what looked like a black suit and white shirt and a dicky bow tie (it was the first time Lily had seen anyone wearing one of those) and he had an imperious stare. He looked as though he wouldn't suffer fools lightly.

John wasn't forthcoming when she asked about his dad and Lily didn't like to press him.

The trolleybus, making its way up Imeary Street, passed a chemist then a florist's shop with a striped awning. On display in the window, on different levels of shelves, were various sizes of glass vases filled with foliage and pink tulips.

Mam, bending forward to look out, sighed. 'When we were first courting and your da had a bit of money to spare, he turned up at my house with a bunch of pink lilies.' A faraway look came into her eyes. 'That's why I called you Lily.'

'You never told me that before.'

Mam shrugged. 'Your dad was convinced you were a boy and had his heart set on the name Thomas. Then when you turned up, he insisted we call you Thomasina. I stuck to me guns and d'you know what? To this day the silly bugger still doesn't realise why I called you Lily.'

Lily sighed in resignation. If ever she needed proof that Dad would have preferred her to be a lad, Mam had just confirmed it.

When it was their stop and they'd alighted from the trolley-bus's platform, Lily led the way. They crossed the road where birds tweeted from tall trees and there was a spacious feel about the place – unlike home, where houses in narrow cobbled streets were crammed together without greenery.

Lily slowed as they approached John's house.

Mam stopped and gasped. 'Our Lily, you never told me the Radleys' house was like this.'

'Like what?'

'Big and, you know, posh-looking. You should have said and I would've worn me Sunday best hat.'

'I didn't think.'

The house – in a sweep of tall buildings, with a forecourt garden that had tall bushes hiding a large stone-pillared bay window and a white arched doorway – was simply, to Lily, where John lived.

Lily told her mam, 'According to John, his grandfather helped his dad buy the house when he first went into practice.'

'The whole *house* is theirs?'

Lily nodded.

'Gracious! It pays to be a dentist.'

She stepped forward and rang the brass doorbell, and when Mrs Radley came to the door, she beamed delightedly.

'It's lovely to see you both, do come in.' She stood aside, ushering them through a stained-glass inner door.

Mam, all eyes as she walked along the parquet passageway, passed the front room whose door was firmly closed. Lily glimpsed Mam's disappointed face. They were led further along, past the messy-looking dining room to the kitchen beyond.

'It's snug in here,' Mrs Radley told them, 'as I keep the fire going.' She turned towards Mam. 'Living on my own, it seems sensible just to heat the one room.'

'Oh, I quite agree.' Mam's voice, ridiculously false, sounded as if she were addressing royalty.

'Make yourself at home. I've set the table for tea.'

Mam made no bones about surveying the kitchen. With its red-brick fireplace, slate floor, gas cooker, long wooden table, shabby green units and white shelves surrounding the walls, it was double the size of their kitchen-cum-living-room at home, but despite that Lily noticed everything looked tired and in need of a lick of paint. Through the window the yard outside could be seen with its brick-built washhouse and two doors, presumably the lav and coalhouse.

They took their seats at the table and Mrs Radley, removing a newspaper and some knitting, moved to the cooker and lit a gas ring, putting the kettle on.

'Now then, my dear' – she came to sit next to Lily – 'what brings you here? Not that you need a reason.' Her green eyes, wide with expectancy, looked impatient.

Lily told her of John's proposal by letter and that the wedding would be next Saturday.

Mrs Radley smiled radiantly. 'I guessed the news might be something of the sort, when I received your letter. I'm so pleased.' She told Mam, 'John's hopeless when it comes to expressing himself, especially about matters of the heart. I knew your daughter must be special as he never stops talking about her.' She stood. 'This calls for a celebration and I've got the very thing.'

Switching off the gas, she left the room.

Mam whispered, looking around, 'You've done well for yourself, our Lily.'

'Mam! Behave.'

'I'm just stating plain facts. Did you say John's an only one?'

'Will you shush, Mam.'

'Here we are.' Their host entered the room carrying a tray with three long-stemmed glasses and what looked like a bottle of sherry.

Setting the tray on the table, she poured the brown liquid into a glass and handed it to Mam.

'Thank you, Mrs Rad—'

'I insist you both call me Deidre.'

When the glasses were filled, Deidre held hers aloft. 'To exciting times ahead. Now tell me, my dear, what are the plans and how can I contribute?'

Mam stiffened and told Deidre, 'It's all in hand.'

Lily hurriedly went on to explain about arrangements.

'And the dress? Am I allowed to know?'

Lily explained about her sister-in-law's wedding dress.

'But you must have your own. Let it be my gift.'

'Lily loves the dress and wouldn't want to wear anything else.' Mam's tone was firm.

'But of course, I do understand.' Deidre was as observant as she was wise. 'And where d'you and John intend to live?' While she waited for an answer, she took a sip of sherry.

While Lily struggled what to say, Mam piped up, her chin jutted. 'They'll live in with us until they can afford a place of their own.'

'I see. Only there's plenty of room here and you'd be most welcome.' She smiled benignly at Mam. 'But only if it suits.'

———

Outside, after they'd said farewell, and with Deidre's words of approval about the forthcoming wedding ringing in Lily's ears, the pair of them retraced their steps home.

As they waited at the bus stop, Mam broke the silence. 'Our Lily, of course you'll live in with us where you belong. Then when John goes back to his barracks, we'll carry on as before.'

Although Lily hadn't considered any alternative to living at home, she couldn't help a pang of disappointment. And then she realised her worst nightmare would be being under the same roof as her family when she and John finally made love. She'd heard of families filling the honeymooners' bed with flour on their first night and just knew something of the sort would be what her brothers would get up to. But neither did she want to be moving in here, with Deidre's bedroom probably next to theirs. The very idea made Lily wince with embarrassment.

3

As the train pulled into the railway station, John stood up from where he'd been crouching in the corridor, and, picking up his haversack, he looked out of the window to the familiar scene of his hometown.

The train, belching out steam that wafted in trails past the window, was crossing a bridge and below, in busy King Street, shoppers were playing out their everyday lives. Only today was no ordinary day, as John was home to marry his sweetheart. A temperate man, the rush of adrenalin surging through John at the thought of it made his pulse quicken and a heady feeling of being energised coursed through him.

He made way for a young woman carrying a toddler to pass in the corridor, then bent his head as he followed them through the doorway and stepped onto the platform. Gazing around the busy station, his heightened senses took in the scene: soldiers in khaki uniforms, sailors wearing duffle coats, apprehensive-looking youngsters, suitcase in one hand, gas mask case in the other, following volunteer marshals wearing armbands who shepherded the evacuee children towards a countryside destination. A steam train leaving the station with heavy creaks and squeaks, a whistle piercing the air.

Then he saw her, Lily, and a warm glow of love seeped through his chest. She stood outside the waiting room scanning the compartments of the train. Wearing a long brown coat with sharp shoulder pads, lapel embellished with a brooch, and fastened at the waist by a belt, a floral headscarf covered her blonde wavy hair. As she saw him, her gaze changed to one of beaming recognition and she smiled, showing a row of perfect white teeth, and her transparent blue eyes lit up and sparkled in that special way.

He hurried towards her and, without a word, she stood on tiptoe and embraced him, burrowing her head in the depth of his army greatcoat.

Then she lifted her face and met his eyes. 'Thank goodness you're safely home.' She sagged against him. 'There's been rumours circulating about postings abroad and I've been worried sick you wouldn't make it home for the wedding.'

Powerless to know the right thing to say, John held her tight. 'I'm here now,' he said ineffectually. 'All I want is to be alone with you.'

'Same here,' she sighed. 'But the family are at home and your mam will want you all to herself if we go back to your place.'

With nowhere else to go, they settled for wandering hand in hand down the stretch of Ocean Road and along the coastal path. The sea, under a dull sky, was grey and rolling waves broke in a crescendo of heavy crashes, white spume whirling in the air. As a cold wind whipped up, John gazed out to golden sands beyond the rolls of barbed wire – a defence against a possible sea invasion – then further still to where the arms of the twin piers encircled calmer waters.

He turned to Lily and told her, 'I know it wasn't the best proposal a girl ever had but—'

'John, I wouldn't have it any other way. It's wartime and people live for the day.' She too looked over the sands to Trow Rocks where a concrete pillbox stood on the coastline – part of the war office defence system – and shuddered. 'Folk are preparing for the worst.'

Instinctively, he put an arm around her shoulders and cuddled her in to keep warm. With her body next to his, albeit through layers of clothing, a warm sense of anticipation for the future surged through him.

'What's the plan for tomorrow?' His tone, he knew, sounded husky.

As she looked up at him with beaming expression and glowing cheeks, John's chest expanded. Lily was his girl. How he wished he could tell her all the things he harboured in his heart, but the difficulty of trying to put his thoughts into words struck him dumb.

What Lily ever saw in him he could never fathom, but he thanked his lucky stars she had seen something.

It had been some eighteen months ago, when he'd met up with Dougie, an older man from Sloan builders where he worked, that he'd first clapped eyes on Lily at Chi pictures.

Dougie had been keen to see *Test Pilot*, starring Clark Gable and Spencer Tracy, but his wife, an avid reader, had no interest in seeing the film.

'How about coming with me?' Dougie had asked John one dinner time at work while they ate their bait. 'I'll treat you to a pint afterwards.'

John had nothing else to do that night, so he went along.

'Excuse me,' John had said to the pretty kiosk lass with the blonde hair, 'you've given me too much change. I wanted two tickets and I gave you ten bob but you've given me change of a pound.'

He handed over the ten-shilling note.

The lass's cheeks burnt in embarrassment. 'Thanks for being honest. I'd be for it when the boss cashed up later.' She shook her head with impatience. 'I'm not usually such a dope but I've got this head cold and I feel rotten. I must look a right sight with my red nose.'

The cold made it sound like she said 'dose'.

On the contrary, you look gorgeous, John might have said if he'd transformed into someone else, but, being him, he just stared like an idiot and all he managed was, 'You should be off work, resting.'

She looked at him queerly, as if it was unusual for anyone to care. 'Believe you me, I'll get more rest sitting here than at home.'

He wondered if she was married and had a demanding husband but she didn't appear the downtrodden type. Later, he wished he'd looked down to see if she wore a wedding band, then wondered why he was bothered. He decided there was something about the kiosk girl that drew her to him.

'John!' Dougie hissed and started up the stairs. 'Hawway, man, the picture's gonna start.'

'Look after yourself, miss.'

Her laugh was hearty. 'I'll be fine. I'm just feeling sorry for myself.'

Her infectious laugh had stayed with him all through the film that started off as a romantic comedy but grew more serious and compelling at the end. As he watched, he kept thinking of her, comparing her with the heroine of the film, Myrna Loy. Fresh-faced with high cheekbones, lips curling upward at the sides as though in a permanent smile, the kiosk girl was decidedly more attractive.

The next night, as he stood in the queue outside the Chi pictures, he wondered what the blazes he was doing there – but really he knew she was the reason. She'd kept cropping up in his mind all that day at work.

When he reached next in line at the kiosk, he noticed she wasn't wearing a wedding band and such was his relief the tense-ness in his body relaxed.

When it was his turn to buy a ticket, she smiled delightedly at him in recognition. 'Did you fall asleep last night and miss the end?' she said, and there it was, that catching hearty laugh of hers.

Damnation! Stuck for words, John felt idiotic as he handed over the ticket money.

Then making a decision, the best he'd ever make, John pulled back his shoulders. He blurted, 'I came to see you.'

'Are you serious?'

'This isn't a chat-up line.'

Her features softened. 'Coming from you, I didn't expect it was.' She looked along the line of waiting customers. 'Look – Sam, my brother, is collecting me tonight. But if you come tomorrow night after closing time, you can walk me home, if you like.'

———

'Are you listening, John?'

John, smiling at the memory of how his love had begun, registered Lily's voice.

'Eh! What did you say?'

He took in the seaside surroundings, and Lily standing next to him, a look of frustration on her face.

'I said, all you have to do tomorrow is to be ready for half eleven when the car will pick you up.'

Reality hitting him, John grinned. 'I sure will.' He bent down and kissed her full on the lips. Pulling away, he was surprised to see how pensive her expression was.

'John, have you given any thought about tomorrow night? Where we could—'

'Spend our honeymoon?' John finished for her, heart sinking.

Idiot that he was, he'd been so involved in thinking about the proposal, and the marriage itself, he'd overlooked the most important bit. It was his place to arrange the honeymoon.

'Have you any ideas?' He wished at this moment he was the smooth-talking Clark Gable, who took charge – and knew what women wanted.

'We can't possibly stay at my house with my goofy brothers, who'll get up to no good playing half-witted pranks.' She looked expectantly at him.

He wanted so badly everything to be perfect but his traitorous mind went blank. 'It's a surprise,' he ad-libbed.

She grinned delightedly. 'You tease.'

Later, as they made their way back towards Ocean Road, Lily stopped and looked out to sea, seeming pensive. 'The war's getting closer by the day.' She turned to gaze up at him, a look of unease in her blue, transparent eyes. 'There's been a report the body of a German airman and a rubber boat were washed ashore at Whitley Bay, and two lifeboats were washed ashore at Bridlington.' She shook her head. 'Mam's gone paranoid and keeps all the doors and windows firmly shut.' She smiled and it was as though the sun came out. 'Even though Dad's told her we live in an upstairs flat and he can't see Jerry scaling our walls in a hurry.'

John laughed.

They walked on and, as they broached Ocean Road, passing the tall guest houses on their left, an idea formed in John's mind.

Of course, a guest house would do nicely. Relief flooded through him.

They stopped at a café and ordered at the counter, a mug of Horlicks each. Slipping into an empty booth and sitting opposite each other, as the Horlicks machine made its familiar whirring noise, he watched as Lily removed her headscarf and ran her fingertips through her hair. It fell into soft waves around her face.

'You look gorgeous,' he simply said. 'I can't wait to get you all to myself.' John cringed at his inadequacy with words.

Lily didn't appear to mind. She'd once said she was attracted to him because he was solid and dependable, though he'd interpreted this as meaning boring.

As a waitress brought their hot drinks and put them on the table, he sat back. They thanked her and, after she'd left, Lily told him, 'Dad and the lads have organised a stag night for tonight. They've changed shifts especially. Don't worry about me, I've got heaps to do, though I'd rather be with you.'

John acknowledged that it was good of Mr Armstrong and Lily's brothers to arrange a stag night but time was precious and, like Lily, he'd have preferred to spend tonight with her.

'What have you got to do?' He grinned. Women's beauty regimes were a mystery to him.

'Hair, nails, women's things. A bride needs her beauty sleep if she's to look her best.'

'You won't get much of that on our honeymoon night.' The words popped from his mouth without thought.

'Mr Radley, behave.' Her perfect arched eyebrows raised suggestively and he'd never seen her look so... ravishing. She grinned. 'Or maybe not.'

Meeting her eyes, he too grinned. John was struck how easy it was to be with Lily. He could be himself.

Lily gave a luxurious sigh. 'Imagine, John. This time tomorrow I'll be Mrs Radley.'

'Tell me, Mrs Radley-to-be, what is the dream for married life?'

For a moment her demeanour changed and John thought he saw hesitancy. Then she seemed to recover, and she told him, 'For the war to be ended and to have you safely home.'

'And afterwards...'

The uncertainty was back and, as she observed him, an anxious little frown ribbed her brow. Then the moment passed and she cocked her head. 'I'd like a place of our own where we can shut the front door and just be us.'

John discounted her previous reaction as pre-wedding nerves; he had a touch of wedding jitters himself.

He raised his mug. 'To the future Mrs Radley.'

'To us.' She raised her Horlicks.

His face split into a playful grin. 'And to the little Radleys that follow.'

Was it just his imagination or did Lily stiffen?

4

John's mum, thrilled to see him when he arrived home, had the table set and the fire lit in the dining room.

As he sat at the table, John noticed that the room smelt musty and unused, and he could tell Mum was starved of company as she never stopped talking, which was unlike her as, generally, she was more interested in what others had to say.

'What a splendid idea, John, to spend your honeymoon night at a seaside guest house.' Placing a plate of steak and kidney pie and mash in front of him, Mum gave him a fond smile. 'Whatever gave you the idea?' She sat opposite him and picked up her knife and fork.

'Lily. She wanted to know where we'd spend our first night.'

As she forked up some potato mash, Mum eyed him in amusement. 'What did you tell her?'

John hesitated, abashed. 'That it was a surprise.'

'In other words, like your father before you, you didn't have a clue at the time.'

Earlier, he'd left Lily at her front door and, after a lingering kiss that made his pulse race, John had made his way back to the guest house. With its blue and white striped awning, white front door and windows with shutters, The Sands had a beach holiday feel.

Honest as ever, John told his mum, 'It just hadn't occurred to me to book anywhere.'

'Men!' Mum laid her knife and fork on the plate. 'When we were getting married it was your grandfather who reminded him and recommended a hotel in Newcastle, which was the dreariest place I've ever set foot in.' She took a sip of water from the crystal glass in front of her. A twinkle in her eyes, she added, 'It served its purpose, though.'

John shook his head at her. He was always surprised when she forgot herself and came out with an unguarded comment. *Inappropriate behaviour* were the words Father used on such an occasion.

His father, stuffy and overbearing... John's biggest fear was that he'd turn out the same way. He could never understand what his mother – a caring and otherwise free spirit – had seen in Dad, and he wondered if the attraction was that she had thought she could change him.

Every now and then a feeling of guilt enveloped John for harbouring ill feeling against his dad, who, after all, had never lifted a hand to him or neglected his physical needs. But then, on the other side of the coin, neither had he shown his only son the least bit of affection or displayed any pride in him – all John could remember was his disapproval and disappointment.

John had learnt to keep his feelings to himself for fear of derision, and the habit stuck to this very day.

Never interested in academia, John knew he was good with his hands. With a determination born out of necessity if he was to live a life of his own making, he had told his father his future plans.

'Over my dead body will you leave school and become an apprentice to a bloody builder,' his father had fumed. 'You'll follow in my footsteps and take over the business one day.'

Ironically, it was over Dad's dead body that John had realised his ambition, as his father had a sudden heart attack and died. Afterwards, doubts crept into John's mind, and he berated himself for not having been a better son. And knowing he would never get to prove himself to his dad had become a particular cross to bear.

Mum, reaching over and covering his hand with hers, brought him back to the present.

'Congratulations.' She squeezed his hand. 'Lily's a lovely girl and a perfect match.'

John scratched his head. 'How d'you mean, perfect match?'

'She'll be good for you.'

'In what way?'

Mum gave a gentle little smile. 'Because, son, she'll bring you out of yourself. Lily has a different personality to you – she's more the demonstrative, outgoing type.'

———

John woke with a start. *Today's my wedding day*, was his first thought. The intense feeling of excitement reminded him of when he was a lad on Christmas morning when he'd felt sick with expectancy.

The bedroom was dark, and he leapt from the bed and drew back the curtains. The sun shone through the window, blinding him. He reached for his trousers, folded over a chair, and pulled them on, fastening the buttons of his fly, and a thought struck him. His battle dress was wrapped around the back of the chair and, sliding his hand in the pocket, John checked the condoms he'd been issued with were there.

A knock came at the bedroom door.

'Are you decent?'

'Yes, come in.'

Mum came into the room bearing a blue and white pitcher and went over to the chest of drawers to fill the basin with hot water. All the surfaces were cluttered; John had to make room for the pitcher. *One day*, John found himself thinking inconsequentially, *the house will need to be modernised, with an inside toilet and bath.*

'Breakfast is ready when you are, and proper eggs, mind, not the dried stuff,' Mum said, beaming.

John gave her a grin back. Dressed in a cotton dressing gown, steel curlers peeping from beneath a hairnet, Mum looked adorable. In fact, the room, which hadn't had a lick of paint since God knew when, looked brighter; even the colours on the tired-looking bedspread appeared sharper. With a surge of affection in his heart, he moved over to his mum and awkwardly gave her a peck on the cheek. Mum, face aglow with surprise, remarked, 'John, whatever have I done to deserve this?'

He gave a laugh. 'Nothing. It's just a thank-you for being you.'

Her cheeks glowing pink with happiness, Mum told him, 'You're not even married yet, son, and already Lily's doing you the power of good.'

———

The rest of the day passed in a sequence of magical moments. The black car arriving at the allotted time, taking John and Mum to the church in Mile End Road. Walking down the aisle, aware of people – some of the faces familiar – sitting in the pews smiling delightedly at him. Dougie, his best man standing in the first row, giving him a reassuring, friendly nod. Darling Lily, a picture of loveliness in white, moving down the aisle towards him, cheeks glowing, love shining from her eyes, making his heart hammer. John would never forget the moment when a ray of sunlight shining through a tall stained-glass window touched the tiara she wore, lighting up the crystals, making them sparkle. He was aware of his hand shaking as he placed the golden band Dougie handed him on Lily's finger.

Afterwards, there was a buffet reception in the church hall provided by kindly neighbours and friends helping out by baking, giving up their precious rations and raiding their pantries for bottled preserves.

But the best moment of all was later, when the newlyweds were alone in the guest house bedroom as husband and wife.

Lily beamed as she gazed around the room looking at the four-poster bed, covered with a crocheted quilt, the fireplace with a vase of artificial flowers standing on the hearth and two brown-striped wing-back chairs facing a window, which looked out over cafés and the penny arcade peep show below.

'Clever you, for thinking of a guest house for our honeymoon.' Her words sounded slurred and John put it down to the sherry she'd drunk at the reception.

Changed from her wedding finery, Lily removed her coat to reveal a delightful blue shirtwaist dress with square padded shoulders and nipped-in waist that showed off her curvy figure.

She giggled. 'I feel quite woozy.' She fell back on the bed and looked up at the ceiling.

John gave a fond smile. Undoing the ankle straps on her high-heeled shoes, he placed them under the bed, then lay down beside her. He nuzzled his chin in her neck and she squealed with pleasure.

Facing him, she pulled a sober face. 'John, you know how I've been saving myself till I'm a wife.' Her deadly earnest tone made him suppress a smile. 'The thing is, I feel awkward as I don't have a clue about, you know...' Her cheeks went prettily pink. She shook her head. 'I'm afraid I'm a bit tipsy because I decided I needed Dutch courage – believe it or not, I've drunk too much sherry.' She frowned, quizzical. 'John, where did the Dutch get their courage from?'

He suppressed a grin. Her lipstick now disappeared, he couldn't resist those plump Cupid's bow lips. He gave her a long lingering kiss and, eyes closed, she melted in his arms.

'So,' he said huskily when he finally pulled away, 'you think I'm an expert at...'

'Love-making,' she prompted. She held his face in her hands. 'I do, because you're a man.' She pouted. 'John, I don't know what to do.'

'Then let's learn together?'

'Wonderful idea.' Her eyes squinted at him.

John began undressing, automatically, folding his clothes and placing them over the back of one of the armchairs. Turning, he saw his wife lying on the bed, her cute lips curved into a smile – and her eyes closed. She looked delectable as she slumbered. Resignedly, John pulled the quilt over her.

We have plenty of tomorrows, he thought.

———

Lily woke him during the night.

In the pitch dark, she leant over and whispered in his ear, 'John, darling, I'm ready to learn now.'

At the thought of his heart's desire being fulfilled, John took her joyfully into his arms.

———

It was two days after the wedding, when John was travelling back to his barracks on the train, that the thought struck him: *Damn, I forgot to use protection that first night.* He grinned. *Not that it's likely but would it be so terrible if we started a family straight away?*

5

MAY 1940

There were days when Lily found it difficult to believe her marriage to John had taken place. Especially on a Monday morning when it felt like nothing had changed; there was just the usual endless housework, washing to be done, dinner to make for the family.

These days, Lily, always starving, couldn't resist an extra helping of the meals she served up, invariably vegetable broth with dumplings or stew with doorstopper-sized slices of bread and butter.

'It's contentment,' Mam said when Lily bemoaned the fact she was piling on the weight. 'I've seen it before in a newlywed lass. Once they're married, they couldn't care less about their figures, not when they've hooked their man.'

This wasn't true of Lily. Though she was over the moon she'd married John, she certainly wasn't content with her life. She was a married woman who should have been independent of her family but Lily couldn't see that happening any time soon. She and John had spoken about the future and agreed that even if they could find a home it was pointless as they couldn't afford to pay the rent.

Better to wait until the war finished – and it couldn't go on forever. John could then go back to his old job at Sloan's and, if they lived in with her parents for a while, the couple could save up for a home.

Gazing out of the scullery window as she washed the breakfast dishes in the porcelain sink, Lily smiled at the memory of John telling her, 'I don't care a hoot where I live; home is where you are.'

But she tensed when she thought of his last letter, which had taken ages to arrive. The rumours had been proved true and John had been posted abroad and was now in France. Though he couldn't say much because of censorship, beyond talking about the weather and the grub, he'd said:

Don't worry if I don't write more, as it's busy here. There's lots happening that I can't tell you about. But chin up, Lily, I'm doing fine and think of you every single day. Sorry about this scratty letter but know I love you more than words can say.

Her mind turned to the BBC news broadcast last night when extracts of the new prime minister Winston Churchill's speech had been read out by the newscaster.

'*I have nothing to offer but blood, toil, tears and sweat,*' Churchill was reported as saying, but it was the phrase: '*Poor people, poor people. They trust me, and I can give them nothing but disaster for quite a long time,*' that made Lily feel desperate, thinking of her beloved John in Germany-invaded France.

Lily washed each knife and fork then rinsed them under the tap (Mam was fussy about such things) and as she thought of John's letter her stomach clenched. What did John mean, *it's busy here?*

'Our Lily, I'm away to the corner shop.' Mam's voice startled Lily, and she almost dropped the teacup she was drying in the sink. Mam appeared in the scullery doorway, leaning against the door stanchion for support. 'We're clean out of butter and sugar. I've got me ration book with the coupons in.'

Her face looked pale and Lily saw she was heaving when she breathed.

'Mam, go and have a lie-down. I'll pop out later for the shopping.'

Mam shook her head. 'It's just me asthma playing up. A spot of fresh air might do us some good.'

Mam had had bad asthma for as long as Lily could remember, but it was definitely getting worse. She refused to see old Doctor Porter, saying, 'What's the use of troubling the man? I know fine well what's wrong with me. I've been like this for years.'

There lay the rub. A flash of dissatisfaction struck Lily. She wanted to leave home, forge a new life for herself and John – but how could she ever leave Mam? Resentment washed over her in a selfish tide. When would Lily's own life begin? And why couldn't Jean lend a hand at times? Taking a deep breath, Lily admonished herself; if the situation were reversed, Mam, loving and generous to a fault, would walk on hot coals if she thought it would help her family.

Taking her coat from the peg on the landing door, Mam told Lily as she gasped each breath, 'I won't be long unless I meet someone for a chinwag.' She shrugged her bony body into the coat, then she checked the draining board and clicked her tongue. 'Our Lily, how many times, it's the crockery before the pans to save the water getting scummy.' She shook her head as though Lily would never learn.

After Mam left, Lily began preparing the broth. Putting beef bones in a pan of water, she chopped an onion. As she wiped away the stinging tears with her fingertips, Lily heard the sneck rattle on the door at the bottom of the stairs.

'Yoo-hoo, anybody in?'

'Come up, Jean, I'm in the scullery,' Lily called unnecessarily.

Footsteps clomped up the wooden backstairs, then the landing door opened.

Her sister-in-law appeared wearing a cross-over apron over a floral green dress, her brunette curls fashioned in a victory-roll hairstyle. In one hand she held a string bag.

Lily automatically smoothed her hair back from her brow. 'Gosh. You're a wonder, Jean.'

'How d'you mean?' As Jean closed the door and came into the tiny space, Lily got a whiff of heady perfume.

'Tarting yourself up when you've nowhere to go and only housework to do.'

Jean grinned, displaying a dimple in her left cheek. A year younger than Lily, Jean wore a pleasant, open expression and had both a sensible and practical approach to life. Just what Lily's hot-headed, impulsive brother needed.

'I do have places to go; I see family and friends and, with Harry out at work most of the day, I keep on top of things and housework doesn't take all that much time.'

Lily knew Jean was like Mam – one of the 'Cleanliness is next to godliness' brigade. All the brasses in the house shone, every week she scrubbed a half-moon shape on the pavement outside her front door and you could see your reflection in the gleaming windows.

'Though I do like to see everything shipshape in the home,' Jean conceded. 'I promised myself when I got wed that I'd be the perfect wife and when my Harry came home from the shipyard, I'd have a meal ready in the oven and a happy smile on my face to greet him. I bet you'll feel the same when you and John have a place of your own.'

Lily hesitated, but she'd always found truth the best policy. 'I don't think I will.' She pulled the plug out of the sink and the water gurgled down the plughole. 'This war is changing things. With men being called up there's labour shortages and I've heard tell womenfolk are replacing them in the workplace. Bus conductresses, in factories...'

'You're not going to get a job, are you?' Jean's eyes rounded in scandal. 'Harry doesn't agree with women working after they're wed. He says it's a man's job to keep his family fed and a roof over their heads.'

While Lily's brother was the nicest of men, he had the same

old-fashioned opinions as Dad, and believed a woman's place was in the home.

'I'm not at liberty to look for a job yet, but one day I intend to.'

At Jean's appalled expression, Lily thought it advisable to drop the subject. She moved into the kitchen, poked the fire and put on more coal from the bucket.

Jean followed her. 'Lily, being a housewife is a job.' She plonked down on Dad's comfy chair. 'Men have restrictions too. D'you think any of them want to go down a filthy mine and crawl on their bellies in the dark to dig coal? Or, for that matter, work in all weathers outside in the shipyard? They have no choice. Most of them are only too pleased to have employment, whatever it is. Everybody has their own job and I know I wouldn't swap mine. And if it means I have to finish work to look after the home and our bairns when they come along so that Harry can do his job, then that's fine by me.'

Lily shook her head. 'In truth I hadn't thought of men in that light.' But she still wasn't convinced. 'The thing is, if I hadn't met John, it wouldn't bother me that I wasn't married. And I certainly don't want to start a family yet.'

'Really?' Jean pulled a surprised face. 'I can't wait. Harry feels the same way.'

The idea of having a family in the first year of marriage horrified Lily. That's what had happened to Mam, with four pregnancies to follow, six if you counted the miscarriages, and she'd had no life to call her own. Though, to be fair, she seemed happy with her lot.

'Maybe it's because you've helped bring up the lads and mothered Jimmy you feel the way you do,' Jean said helpfully. 'After I left school, I went to college and learnt shorthand and typing and I've worked in an office. I feel ready to settle down.'

'I'm the opposite. I feel restless and I want to live a little.'

'Doing what?'

'I haven't figured that out yet, but there's more to life than housework and darning socks.'

Jean didn't verbally disagree but her expression said it all. 'Have you told John any of this?'

'I intended to have a serious chat when he came home but there was never the right moment with the wedding and all. I'm not worried, John's easy-going, and he'll want what's right for me.'

Jean raised her eyebrows as if to suggest Lily was being naïve. 'Then I hope he took precautions.' Her voice was sharp, most unlike Jean.

'Precautions?' Then what her sister-in-law meant dawned on Lily. 'Oh, that.'

Jean nodded. 'They're called condoms.'

It was such a relief to Lily to be talking about such things. Mam had never broached the subject of the birds and bees with Lily, as the older generation were tight-lipped about such matters. It had been Pamela Fellows, an older girl she walked to school with occasionally, who had told her and two others from the same neighbourhood the basics of how a baby got born. Pamela had been babysitting the night before and found a book with illustrations that she'd brought home with her. At their shocked faces, she'd told them, defensively, 'I wanted you all to see. I'll take the book back the next time I babysit, but I wanted to show you all.'

After the shock at what she'd seen, Lily found herself sneaking a sly look at Dad's Sunday newspaper. Seeing the words 'sexual intercourse' in print verified what Pamela had shown her and a guilty thrill had surged through Lily. She'd been thirteen at the time.

'To be honest, Jean,' Lily said shyly, 'I'm inexperienced and just presumed John would be more worldly-wise.'

'Aren't we all? All my mam ever told me – and it was my wedding day when she said this – was, "You'll be fine. It gets over with." Can you imagine?' She burst out laughing and Lily joined in. 'I didn't know what I was in for and was terrified. Harry thought he'd married a madwoman because I made all the excuses under the sun that first night rather than go to bed.' They both dissolved into fits of laughter and laughed until they cried.

Wiping her eyes on her apron, Jean reached for the string bag she'd placed on the floor.

'That reminds me, I've brought the album I promised you.'

Lily's spirit rose in anticipation. Dougie, the best man, had managed to get a roll of film for his camera and had taken pictures of the couple's wedding. As a wedding gift, Jean had offered to make an album.

She brought out the white book from her bag and handed it to Lily, who opened the cover excitedly.

'There aren't a great deal of photos but I thought you could use the rest of the pages for snapshots when you have a family.'

'That's so thoughtful. It'll be a lovely keepsake, thank you.'

Lily looked at the first page and there they were, a smiling bride and groom in black and white. She wore a flowing rayon dress, with tiara and long veil, while John, looking dashing in his uniform, towered over her. She studied his face: slanting eyes that crinkled as he smiled, a dimple in his chin, a face you could trust, which she had from the first moment she saw him when she sat in the Chi kiosk. Staring at him, an agreeable ache came into her groin, reminding her of making love with John in the seaside B&B.

Then for no reason at all, Lily's mind replayed the conversation with Jean.

Then I hope he took precautions.

Her mind raced on; it was over two and a half months since they'd got married. When was the last time she'd had the curse? The trouble was her monthlies weren't regular and she'd given up calculating when they should be. On reflection, though, she definitely hadn't had the curse since she got wed.

She remembered the saying about pregnant women. *They eat for two.*

As realisation hit her, the album dropped to the floor.

———

For days Lily moved around in a kind of stupor. Nothing in life seemed to register and she went about her work automatically. As each day passed and there was still no reassuring show of blood, blind panic took hold. Mam kept giving peculiar looks and, uncharacteristically, didn't enquire what was up with her daughter – a first for Mam, who normally wanted to know the far end of everything.

As the days turned into a couple of weeks, Lily began to realise her suspicions were true, especially when, cooking fried taties for Ian one morning before he started the early shift at the mine, the smell of food cooking in lard made her retch. Dashing downstairs to the outside lav in the yard, head over the bowl, she heaved, it seemed, from her toes.

Lily knew now for certain she was expecting.

After that, each morning, white-faced and nauseous, she avoided any contact with food, feigning a tummy upset. Nothing escaped Mam and, from her smug and knowing looks, Lily knew she suspected. But she couldn't bring herself to confirm Mam's suspicion – because saying the words out loud would make her being pregnant true, and then Lily would have to admit she was trapped.

———

Late one night, avoiding going to bed in order to put off lying awake thinking anxious thoughts, Lily sat in front of the dying embers reading *Murder on the Orient Express*, which she'd borrowed from the local lending library. At least, she was *attempting* to read, but her traitorous mind kept hopping about and wouldn't concentrate.

Her biggest worry was when she should write and tell John she was expecting. After all, it was his baby and he had a right to know. Instinctively, she knew he would be thrilled and the news would be such a boost, but Lily wasn't ready to put a brave face on and pretend she was happy, which she would have to do, like many a woman down the centuries.

Lily had thought deeply about the situation, wondering if she was at fault, especially after talking with Jean. No, she'd decided, she did eventually want a family with John but, at present, being a housewife and looking after a small child felt like jumping out of the frying pan into the fire. And what about her dream to escape domestic drudgery to be free to start a career? There was no way that was a possibility now. Lily gave a resigned sigh.

John would understand and be sympathetic about her doubts, because, as she'd told Jean, he put her happiness first, as she would if the situation was reversed and he was the one having doubts about starting a family. That's what she loved about him. He was a gentle giant of a man; he could be strong if needs be but was sensitive too, unlike her rowdy brothers, who suffered from rivalry and were continuously trying to outdo one another.

'Cheat.'

As if on cue, Sam's shout brought her back to the present.

It was a rare night when Dad and her two brothers were all home for supper. After the meal the three had started a game of pontoon.

'You hid that ace, our Ian, under the table.'

Ian's expression grew indignant. 'No, I did not.'

'Man, I saw it in your hand.'

Ian glared at his brother. 'Are you calling me a liar?'

'If the cap fits.' Sam gave a smug grin. 'You're a cheat.'

Lily shook her head in despair. This spelt trouble.

'Take that back.'

'You gonna make me?'

Ian's face turning dark, he leapt from the chair and made a dive for his brother. Sam, the bigger of the two, rose but Ian, sturdier, grabbed him by the shoulders and grappled him to the floor. Writhing and grunting, they wrestled with each other.

'You bloody well should be ashamed of yourselves.' Flinty-eyed, Dad stomped over to the lads and, taking them both by the shirt collar, hauled them apart.

'Ger off.' Ian tried to tug free. 'You're choking us.'

'It would serve you right,' Dad thundered, loosening his grip on them both.

'What's going on?'

Lily looked over to where Mam stood in the kitchen doorway, dressed in a long white winceyette nightdress, hairnet covering her hair.

Jimmy appeared by her side in striped pyjamas, his black curly hair falling over his brow as he rubbed the sleep from his eyes.

Dad fumed, 'These bloody fools are battling over a game of cards, when our boys over in France are giving their lives in a losing battle for king and country.'

Rage over, both lads had the grace to look shamefaced.

Dad moved to the table and, picking up the pack of cards, slung them onto the fire.

'Hey! They're mine—' Sam started to say but Dad's stony stare stopped him.

'Not another word,' Dad warned.

They all watched as the cards ignited and yellow flames leapt up the chimney.

Lily looked up at Mam, who had a protective arm around Jimmy's shoulders. 'What does Dad mean about our lads in France?' Her voice trembled.

Mam's brow riddled in a frown. 'I thought you knew, and that's why you've been so quiet recently...'

'What should I know?' She looked around them all.

'The allies are losing the battle in France, love.' Dad's anger dispelled as quickly as it had flared.

'Why, what's happened?'

'The Germans have pushed forward. They reached the Channel, and they've gone north along the coast, and the fear is they'll capture the ports and both the British and French forces will be trapped.'

Lily, struck dumb with fear, sat open-mouthed.

Mam looked Lily square in the eye. 'Don't you be worrying about that husband of yours. He's got a lot to live for.'

She gave an almost imperceptible nod towards Lily's belly.

———

The following night, when worrying about John reached fever pitch, it was as though a band of fear tightened in Lily's chest, crushing her to the point she couldn't breathe properly. And the discomfort in her lower back didn't help.

Unable to stand the tension any longer, Lily threw back the covers and, padding to the scullery, put the kettle on the gas to make tea. She carried her cup of tea to the bedroom, climbing back into bed and sipping the hot liquid. She wished for morning when there'd be distractions.

She must have dozed for, when she awoke, the empty cup was still in her hand, and also still there was the discomfort, which, in her befuddled, sleepy mind, Lily could only describe as cramping in her abdomen. Flinging back the bedcovers, Lily saw, where her nightdress had risen up, a red stain on the white sheet.

6

Lily didn't remember much about losing the baby, because she blotted the upsetting business out of her mind. Such was her absorption beforehand, her focus solely on how her life would be irrevocably changed, Lily had never given a thought to the fact that this wasn't an 'it' she was carrying, but a baby – her and John's baby. But the shock of losing their child unleashed emotions she'd never expected: emptiness, loss and, yes, she was riddled with insufferable guilt.

The heavy bleeding seemed to sap her of energy, and Mam coaxed Lily to eat to help keep her strength up. Mam also sent for Mrs Chambers, who lived at the bottom of their street, because, according to her, the woman knew about these things. Mrs Chambers didn't have any answers but asked the most bizarre questions. Did you ride a bicycle these past few weeks? Do you wear a corset? You haven't been reading any exciting books lately, have you? The result was that Lily was left with the idea losing the baby was all her fault and she vowed, as long as she lived, she'd never read another Agatha Christie novel again.

Two weeks later, the tumult of emotion still confounded Lily. Despite having been adamant she didn't want to start a family, now, mourning her loss, all she wanted was to have the baby back safely in the womb.

But as everyone else had apparently forgotten about the miscarriage, Lily felt isolated in her grief.

Mam was the only one who understood, and her final words on the subject were, in a fatalistic tone, 'Lily, I firmly believe these things were meant to be. The same thing happened to me twice. But as time passed and I thought about those little souls, it struck me that it was struggle enough to feed and clothe five bairns, let alone seven, and me and your dad would be in poverty street trying.' She heaved a great sigh. 'Maybe losing those two bairns was a blessing in disguise.' Though she spoke with conviction, Mam's anguished eyes told another story. 'But you know what, I still think of those little souls every single day and wonder what they'd be like now.' She let out another huge sorrowful sigh.

Lily knew what she meant because she suffered in the same way. Wondering about the baby's sex, imagining cradling the little body in her arms... Worse, haunted by the knowledge she'd let it be known that she was against starting a family, Lily was convinced this was her punishment.

She'd considered telling John in a letter but decided it would serve no purpose as he couldn't do anything and the knowledge would only distress him. Best to leave telling him about the miscarriage until he came back and could absorb the news in the comfort of home.

The news from the continent was a worrying distraction and Lily, scouring the newspapers and listening to wireless reports, grew concerned about the situation in France. But when it was announced that British troops were cut off and surrounded by German troops on the beaches at a place called Dunkirk, and exposed to machine-gun and air attacks, her anxiety knew no bounds.

Then came a report that British troops were being evacuated

from the beaches by ordinary men who'd braved the English Channel in little boats of all different shapes and sizes to save them. Lily prayed fervently to the Almighty that John would be one of them.

Time passed, and by the fourth of June, some 198,000 British troops had been evacuated from the beaches. But as the reports of this amazing feat came in – all the more astonishing when the total rose to over 338,000 with the numbers of allied troops (mainly French) included – Lily could barely react. She felt numb as she awaited news about John.

———

On Harry's birthday, Jean had arranged a gathering at tea time for the family at her downstairs flat. Lily, in no kind of mood to celebrate, wanted to stay at home, but Mam was having none of it.

'Our Lily, the trick is to keep busy. No good will come of moping. It won't bring news of John any sooner. Best foot forward and all that.'

Lily hadn't the list to argue and, besides, there was Jimmy bringing her shoes and giving her an apprehensive look. Poor kid, he didn't know what was going on except his big sister, who was like a mother to him, had had a big shock and now she was worried about her husband.

Lily thought it was time she tried to explain. 'Jimmy, you know John's a soldier away in another country—'

'France, fighting Germans,' Jimmy prompted.

'Yes, well, he's trying to escape the enemy from a beach in a place called Dunkirk and I'm hoping he's managed to get on a ship.'

'Can John not swim?'

Despite the anxious churning in her stomach, Lily smiled at his youthful logic.

'No, pet, the Channel's too far to swim.'

As the implication registered, Jimmy's eyes widened. 'What happens if he gets caught?'

'Jimmy, enough questions.' Lily was saved giving voice to her worst fears when Mam, bustling into the kitchen and hearing the end of the conversation, butted in. 'If we don't get a move on we'll miss Harry blowing out the candles on his cake.'

Jimmy didn't need a second telling.

———

'The birthday cake is made with real eggs, not the dried stuff,' Jean told the company when they'd arrived and were standing around the kitchen table. 'I've been saving coupons over the weeks for this very occasion.'

Jean's anxious glance at Lily suggested she was nervous about how Lily would be feeling, despite the happy occasion.

Standing next to her sister-in-law, Lily made a mental note to buck up, because everyone was treating her as if she was made of glass these days.

'Did you hear what the new prime minister said in his speech a couple of days ago?' Dad's voice boomed out from the other side of the table where he stood next to the birthday boy. 'That the last few weeks had been a "colossal military disaster". The bloke doesn't mince his words, does he?'

Harry nodded in agreement. 'Aye, and the papers say Churchill's proving himself a strong wartime leader by declaring Britain would stand against the Nazi menace. From what I hear, his "we shall fight on the beaches" speech did him the power of good with folk.'

'For heaven's sake,' Mam said, and Lily caught her making big eyes at her husband and nodding in her direction, 'can we forget the war for just this once.'

'Hear, hear,' Jean agreed.

'When are we eating the cake?' Jimmy wanted to know.

Later, the table demolished of corned beef sandwiches, homemade scones, half the Victoria sponge eaten, and the strains of 'Happy birthday to you' lingering in the air, Lily and Jean stood in the downstairs flat's diminutive scullery, washing dishes in the sink.

The silence between them was awkward, and Lily wondered what was up. It was the first time she'd been alone with her sister-in-law since the miscarriage and Lily wondered if it was something to do with that.

'You must be out of your mind with worry about John,' Jean finally said, but, as she dunked a china plate into the water, she didn't look up.

Lily didn't feel it necessary to answer.

As Jean handed her the dripping plate, she still avoided looking at Lily. 'I owe you an apology,' she surprised Lily by saying.

'Whatever for?'

'For being preachy that day when you confessed you didn't want to start a family. Then I found out you were pregnant.' Jean now met Lily's eyes, her own looking disconsolate. 'The ugly truth is I was jealous of you. When you lost the baby I... foolishly thought it wouldn't bother you. Unforgivable, I know, but I so wanted to be pregnant it coloured my judgement. I can see that now.'

Lily gaped at her sister-in-law. 'I didn't realise.'

'You see, Harry and me had decided to have a family straight away and every month when I started me period I despaired. It's over a year now since we got wed and I'm worried sick I can't have children.' She looked shamefaced at Lily. 'And there was you telling me you didn't want to start a family, who got pregnant straight away. I couldn't get over the unfairness.' She visibly slumped.

Lily, her emotions unstable, felt her throat tighten. She told Jean, 'I was cavalier about starting a family but things changed when I lost the baby. It was as though a maternal switch in my head clicked on and I wanted his baby so badly it hurt. But it was too late.' She gave a wobbly smile. 'What a fool I was.'

'Me too,' Jean admitted. 'I realise now being married isn't all about having a family and, if it doesn't happen, I'll be sad but not devastated. I'll have Harry, after all.' Jean wrapped her arm around Lily's shoulders and with a sob she said, 'Lily, I'm so sorry for your loss.'

Lily didn't know if Jean cried for her, or the baby she feared she might never have. Emotionally spent, Lily had no tears left to shed.

———

It was two days later that a letter with John's handwriting on the envelope arrived. Seeing it lying on the mat at the front door, utter joy surged through Lily. Then she froze.

John may have instructed someone to post this letter on if anything should happen to him.

Hands trembling, she tore the letter open.

Sweetheart,

I can't imagine what you've been going through when you heard the news, worrying about my whereabouts.

Lily paused, wilting with relief. Her prayers had been answered. John had survived.

It was hectic in France on the beaches (to say the least, she thought wryly) *but then I was fortunate to board a peacetime cross-Channel steamer. Luckily for me I was on a stretcher as it was standing-room only for the weary and soaked troops who'd waded through waves. With the fear of raiders in the air and hearing mines were in the sea, I was jolly pleased to see the white cliffs of Dover on the horizon, though it didn't register at first, I was that exhausted. When we arrived at Dover the WVS were waiting with sandwiches, buns, cigarettes and tea. God bless them. There's been no time since to put pen to paper but, darling girl, I've thought of you often.*

The thing is I was transported by ambulance train to a military hospital in Leeds – please don't panic, Lily, as I'm being well taken care of. The Luftwaffe's Stuka dive bombers gave me a present – shrapnel in the leg. The blasted thing isn't healing and I'm told I won't be discharged until it does. Lily, I don't want you to even think of travelling here what with crammed trains, not to mention the possibility of raids. I would be beside myself with worry. I heard tell of enemy aircraft dropping bombs in Yorkshire recently.

Stay home and keep safe and, sweetheart, write as soon as you can.

Would you please inform Mum and tell her I'll write soon?

Your loving husband,

John

Holding the letter against her heart, Lily gave a shaky laugh of relief. *Thank God John is safe after all.*

———

John's wound stubbornly wouldn't heal and it was almost a month before doctors thought him satisfactorily recovered to be discharged and make the journey home.

When John's train came into the station, billowing steam, and then chugged towards the platform, Lily, waiting for him, felt her knees go weak. Then she saw him through one of the windows and, as he opened the carriage door and stepped onto the platform into the throng, she gave a sharp intake of breath. A head taller than everyone else, John was a shadow of himself. His tall frame emaciated, his cheeks sunken, he was stooped, as if he wore the world's worries on his shoulders.

Lily ran, laughing and crying, towards him. His gaunt face lit up when he saw her. Placing his rucksack on the ground, he held out his arms and enveloped her in a bear hug she never wanted to escape. There, on the station, her undemonstrative husband gave her a tender kiss.

Her arms around him, Lily felt his bony figure beneath his khaki uniform. She told him, 'The first thing we're going to do is to fatten you up.'

His voice when he bent down and whispered in her ear was husky. 'I can think of better first things we can do.'

7

John's mum had offered for the couple to stay at her place while she visited with her sister who lived in the Borders. It made sense because, with all the comings and goings, Lily's home wasn't suitable. John was run-down and needed time to recuperate before going back into the thick of it.

'It won't be for long,' Mam said when Lily told her. Lily was unsure who Mam was trying to convince: herself or her daughter. 'I can perfectly well manage on me own.' She twisted her mouth. 'But it would do no harm if you looked in on wash day to lend a hand.'

It would be like a second honeymoon, Lily told herself. The idea she might get pregnant filled her with hope. Because, though she still grieved the baby she'd lost, Lily lived for the day when she would be carrying again.

She dreaded telling John about the miscarriage, but she would get it over with at the first opportunity.

———

Now, as John found the key under a large rock in the small forecourt garden, he opened the front door and the two of them entered the dim passageway. The house had a cold uninhabited feel but, passing through the passageway into the kitchen, Lily saw a plate of sandwiches and what looked homemade biscuits on a china plate on the table.

'Honey biscuits,' John declared, 'my favourite.' Dumping his haversack on the floor, he made a dive for the table and devoured a biscuit in two bites.

Lily picked up a note propped against the salt pot.

Make yourselves at home, I'm at a WI meeting all afternoon, then having tea with the chairwoman Mrs Bains to talk things over.

Can't wait to see you both,

Love Mum

Lily looked up at John. 'I thought you said your mum was going to her sister's place.' She didn't mean to sound so accusing.

John shrugged. 'She did. She's probably changed her mind or is going later.'

Placing the small suitcase she carried on the floor and sitting at the table, Lily hoped it was the latter.

John scratted in a drawer and, taking out matches, lit a gas ring and put the kettle on to boil. Sitting opposite Lily, eating a Spam sandwich, he looked around the room as though seeing things for the first time. Lily realised this homecoming wasn't easy for him, making her wonder what he'd endured on those beaches in France. Soldiers, she knew, wanted to protect their womenfolk and didn't talk about such matters.

One thing she knew, now was not the time to discuss her miscarriage.

As they sat around the scrubbed, wooden table, John miles away in thought, the silence was deafening.

His elbows on the table, chin in cupped hands, images played in John's mind's eye of the men left on the beaches.

'Was it very terrible, John?' Lily's voice broke into his thoughts.

Simply staring at her for a while, John was unsure how to reply. He didn't wish to spoil this moment by talking about the horrors of France. His division marching for days over fields with nothing in their bellies and watching their rear. They'd travelled mostly at night, and he couldn't remember anything about the villages except – he shuddered, remembering the grisly scene – snipers hanging from trees. The bombings and getting the wounded safely out of the towns before retreating to the port. The line of troops that snaked for miles, it seemed, in the waves and on the beaches waiting to board a ship to transport them home. Then had come the dive-bombing Stukas to wreak havoc on helpless men.

He told Lily, trancelike, 'I went down under the waves and Mikey caught me and dragged me back to the sands. I... never saw him again.' At her perturbed look he went on, 'Next thing I knew I was on a stretcher and being carried onto a steamer.' His eyes prickling, he blinked rapidly. 'We didn't know what we were in for. I was one of the lucky ones but I...' Scenes still vivid in his mind, he couldn't continue.

Lily pushed back her chair and, encircling his large frame in her arms, she buried her head in his chest. 'John, I don't know what to say except I'm eternally grateful that you were one of the lucky ones that came home.'

They sat like that for a while and then, sitting up, shoulders back and stroking her hair, John knew something had shifted in him, and the here and now called to him. Lifting her chin with a forefinger, he looked directly into Lily's mesmerising sky-blue eyes and saw the need in them.

Peppering her with her kisses on the temple, cheek, he then nuzzled her neck with his lips and Lily squealed with delight. He stood and, taking her hand, led her upstairs to his bedroom at the back of the house.

———

Lily took in the cluttered bedroom where a photograph of John in junior school, a head taller than the other boys, stood on top of a chest of drawers. He moved over to the double bed opposite the tall window.

She followed him and lay down on the faded candlewick bedspread.

He took off his battledress, boots, gaiters and breeches. Then, climbing onto the bed, he knelt and, on all fours over her, faces level, he looked down at his wife.

She stretched up and kissed him.

'Lily.'

'Yes.'

With one hand he began to unbutton the top button of her blouse. 'It is true we have to live every minute.'

'I know.'

John grinned. 'Can we live a little now?'

'Yes please.'

———

Next morning, when Lily awoke, John, elbow on the pillow and head resting on a hand, was staring down at her.

His face softened into a smile. 'I can't believe I'm home with you.'

'I can't believe we've slept the night through. It was light when we...' Lily suddenly remembered. 'Your mam. I didn't hear her come in last night. What she must think I don't know.'

'Knowing Mum, she'll think us two lovebirds are making up for lost time.'

'I don't know that I can face her.'

John laughed and pecked her nose, then he fell back against the pillows.

They lay in comfortable silence for a while.

Lily knew she couldn't put off telling John about the miscarriage any longer; it would only get harder as time went on.

She took a deep breath. 'John, there's something you must know.'

He must have heard the gravity in her voice because his eyes grew troubled. 'What is it?'

Lily sat up and, holding his gaze, she began to speak and didn't hold anything back. She confessed about not wanting to start a family, her dismay at finding out she was expecting, the grief she experienced after the miscarriage.

When she'd finished speaking, she could see the sorrow and pain in his eyes.

———

John didn't know what to say; he'd no experience of these things. That Lily had gone through this, without him by her side, hurt so badly.

'John, speak to me. D'you hate me because I didn't want to start a family?'

John remembered the unopened packets in his pocket on their honeymoon night. It had been his responsibility to shield her and he'd failed.

'I could never hate you, Lily.'

A heartfelt pang of sorrow overcame John for the loss of their baby.

He cuddled Lily and caressed the small of her back. 'We've plenty of time. We'll start a family when you're ready.'

John realised his biggest fear was that he wouldn't survive the war, and Lily would have a child to bring up on her own.

Lily's gaze sought his with that stubborn look. 'I don't want to wait. It's like having this baby, our child, awakened something in me. John, I want us to start a family now. Live for the day, remember?'

The memory of beaches, the dark outlines of figures that lay in

the sands, played in his mind. He owed it to them and the count-
less other soldiers who'd died so that he could live life to the full.

———

At breakfast time, Mum fussed making sure he and Lily had
enough food – porridge followed by homemade drop scones and
jam – and John answered his mother's questions about his
injury.

'Any ideas when you expect to return to the barracks?' Mum
wanted to know.

John didn't want to think about returning to duty yet as he
wanted to enjoy every minute with Lily, though his responsible
side, knowing that duty called, wouldn't allow him to relax fully.
But it was unlike Mum to probe like this.

'I wouldn't normally meddle, but something's come up.'

'What is it, Mum?'

Mum came to sit next to John and she smiled reassuringly at
Lily. 'My dear, I do know what it's like to have an interfering
mother-in-law.'

She addressed Lily, who, looking as though she felt out of
place, sat stiffly in a chair. 'Firstly, my apologies for being here
when you arrived. The intention was to make myself scarce but I
wanted to speak to you both before I left for Helen's.'

'Mum's sister, who lives in the Borders,' John told Lily.

'Helen's a widow,' Mum explained. 'There's only the two of us
and we're close.'

'Is everything all right with Helen?' John had long since
dropped the aunty title.

Mum frowned. 'That's the thing. Helen won't admit it but I
suspect she's lonely since she broke up with Terence.' She told
Lily, 'Helen went to tea dances and suchlike with Terence and
considered him a companion but he's decided he wants something
more serious. Helen decided that a dalliance is not for her and
Terence has... moved on to pastures new, so to speak.' She drew

herself up. 'I've come to a decision. I've talked it over with Helen and she agrees—'

'About what?' John looked up from smothering raspberry jam on a scone.

Mum shook her head and told Lily, 'Just like his father – always interrupting and making me forget what I want to say.'

John took umbrage because the idea of being anything like his impatient and bullying father was upsetting.

'I'm going to move in with Helen.'

'What! When?' John said, shocked.

'There's nothing to keep me here. So, I'm moving straight away.'

'How long for?'

As Mum sat back in her chair and straightened her spine, John knew she meant business.

'Permanently.'

Taken aback, John placed the scone back on his plate, while he considered what to say. He was about to lose his family home by the sound of things. But Mum was fair-minded and she would have thought this through.

She went on. 'Let's face it, son, why do I need to rattle around this big house?' So it was as John feared, but he had to admit Mum was right. 'And since you and Lily here will need a home it seems logical you have this one.' At Lily's sharp intake of breath, Mum turned towards her daughter-in-law. 'I realised the day you got married that my son was never coming home. And since Helen and I get along, and to save both of us from talking to the walls, it makes sense to team up. In fact, I'm rather looking forward to the company.' When he heard this John felt bad. It had never occurred to him how lonely she must have become. Fine son he was.

'What about rent? We can't live here for nothing,' Lily protested.

'Why not? I'm living at Helen's rent-free because her house is paid for. Besides, it means I won't have to sell up and these days it pays to hang on to property. One never knows what might happen.

And the furniture can stay intact.' She looked stricken. 'That is of course if you want it. My dear, as I said, I know enough of interfering mothers-in-law to know I never want to be one.'

'This is so kind, I'm staggered... I don't know what to say.' Lily did indeed look shocked, as was John but he could see the logic in what Mum was saying. He'd always sensed she didn't have strong feelings for her home.

'Then just say yes. You will be doing me a favour, and besides' – she turned to John – 'the house will be yours one day anyway.'

John met Lily's gaze and, grinning, she gave an imperceptible nod.

'Mum, Lily and I would love to make this our home and you can visit whenever you want.'

How John wished he could bring himself to give his mum a hug of gratitude, but theirs was not a demonstrative family and even the thought made him uncomfortable. When he was a young boy, John was caught giving his pet rabbit a hug and a kiss and Dad had called him a sissy. Thank God it was easier with Lily.

'What about when you go back to the barracks?' Lily asked, and he knew she was referring to the fact she couldn't just up and leave her mother in the lurch. 'It's pointless me living here all on my own when I can be of use to Mam at home. And what about you? It's your—'

'As I've said, Lily, this is *your* home now. I don't wish to live here any more. I have nothing to keep me here.'

She met John's eyes and he saw in the depth of hers the truth of the matter. It wasn't just he who had unhappy memories in this house, planted by his father. Mum's were unpleasant too and ones she would never share, nor would he want her to.

'That's settled then.' Mum, with a satisfied expression, started collecting the dirty porridge bowls.

———

Mum left two days later.

'It'll give you two young things a little time on your own.' She gave that wide grin John had seen few times in his lifetime.

'I can't remember the last time I had an adventure,' she declared, as John humped the heavy suitcase down the stairs.

'However will you manage?' John nodded at the suitcase.

'By taxi, then some kind porter will surely be there to help at the station. Helen will meet me with her car at the other end.'

There was no denying the glint of excitement in Mum's eyes. For the first time in years she had a carefree look about her.

When the taxi arrived and John had held the door open and Mum was seated in the back, he saw tears brimming in her eyes.

'It's a new start for us both, son. Take care of yourself and that lovely wife of yours. You know where I am if you need me.'

As the car pulled away from the kerb, Mum blew a kiss out of the window. John, an arm around Lily, a lump in his throat, gave a little wave.

Damn! he thought as the car disappeared around the street corner. *Why couldn't I let my guard down? Hugging Mum wouldn't hurt.*

———

The following days were the happiest John had known. Even the news that Hitler had returned to Berlin in triumph after conquering France, where huge crowds welcomed their Führer, didn't dampen his spirit.

Those precious summer days together were spent strolling hand in hand along the coastline where a vista of glittering sea met a blue horizon as far as the eye could see, or in parks where stretches of luscious greenery held a countryside feel. At night in their bedroom a soft sea breeze came through an open window, cooling their bodies as the couple made love.

With Lily providing wholesome home-cooked food – corned beef hash, mutton with vegetables, treacle steamed pudding that had all the kitchen windows streaming – John felt his strength returning. In mid-July, when he had been home for ten days, the doctor confirmed he was medically fit.

It was on a day when rain drizzled from a dour, grey sky and they had decided to go to the pictures and were just about to leave, that the door knocker banged. John answered the door, and returned with a telegram in his hand.

Tearing the envelope open, he read the couple of sentences, then looked up at Lily's stricken face.

'I'm to join my battalion.' He shrugged.

As she buttoned up her cardigan, he saw her hand tremble.

'Abroad?' she asked.

'No. The battalion will be under the command of Home Forces somewhere in Devon to defend the coast.'

Lily's lips bunched determinedly as if she were resolving to be stout-hearted about the matter of him leaving, but her gorgeous blue eyes couldn't mask the disappointment.

8

August 1940

'Our Lily, will you keep your mind on what you're doing?'

With a start, Lily, turning the wringer's handle, looked on as a tea towel, squeezing through the mangle's rollers, fell onto the concrete yard.

Mam, tutting disgustedly, plonked the bucket of water she was swilling the yard with on the ground, picked up the towel and exclaimed, 'Look, it's mucky now. I can't be hanging this in the lane for neighbours to scoff at.'

She held the offensive item at arm's length.

'Mam, I'll make it fine.' Lily took the tea towel from Mam's hand and headed for the scullery. There was no pleasing her mother these days, she thought, as she rinsed the dirt off the white cotton material into the sink with water from the tap. Then, turning the wringer's handle, she watched as the tea towel squeezed through the rollers yet again, and she made sure she caught the blessed thing this time.

'See. Good as new.'

Mam clicked her tongue. 'According to you, that is. Good job it wasn't your da's Sunday best shirt,' she grumbled.

Lily knew what the problem was. Ever since she'd heard Deidre Radley had given the couple the house to live in, Mam had acted like her nose was put out of joint.

Mam folded her arms. 'I've been thinking about yon woman giving you the house, our Lily.' Lily gaped; it was as though her thoughts were written on her head. 'Nobody's that generous to give a furnished house away. There must be a catch.'

Lily could never fathom Mam. She'd thought her mother would be pleased at her good fortune.

'Deidre's giving the house to her son, Mam, who will be inheriting it one day anyway.'

Mam stiffened. 'If you ask me the woman's after your affections.'

Then it dawned on Lily; Mam was jealous of Deidre and afraid she'd be ousted in the pecking order. 'Mark my words lass, yon woman will play on your sympathies and then you know what'll happen.' Dumbfounded, Lily shook her head. 'She'll end up living with you and you'll be looking after her in her dotage. As for me...' Her voice wobbled. 'I'll hardly ever see me daughter again.'

Lily mentally shook her head. Mam could be theatrical to get her own way but this was a bit much even for her.

'Don't be daft, Mam. Of course that won't happen. I'll always be there for you and Dad. Besides, Deidre prefers to live with her sister instead of in the house.'

Mollified, Mam's expression changed to that of incredulity. 'Is that what she said?' Lily nodded. 'Fancy, and her having such a posh house. You can never please some folk.'

Problem solved, the two women got on with their work, but Lily's thoughts ran on. It had made sense to return back home when John returned to his battalion because the thought of living on her own didn't appeal. But someday Lily would have to get to grips with being mistress of her own home. That day might fast be approaching. Lily dared to have the thought that lurked in the back of her mind as each week went by. *There's every chance I'm pregnant.* Seven weeks had passed since John was home, and there was still no sign of the curse. What if she were expecting? Would she carry on helping Mam? Should she move into John's family home? Lily didn't know, but she firmly believed everything happened for a reason and the matter would solve itself.

As she hung the washing out, a gust of wind howling down the narrow lane caused the sheets to billow and flap and the noise sounded as if they were clapping. The washing done, the pair of them made their way back into the yard, Lily eyeing the wringer and heavy washtub. She didn't want to do anything that would encourage another miscarriage. Leaving the heavy washing paraphernalia in the yard for her brothers to put away when they came home from work, she made for the backstairs.

Mam, following, told her, 'We'll have a cuppa and leave humping those' – she indicated to the wringer and washtub – 'for the lads to sort out.'

Lily marvelled again. She was convinced Mam was psychic.

———

A few days later Lily, on all fours, was washing the linoleum surround on the floor when she heard the back-door sneck rattle.

'Yoo-hoo. Anybody home?'

'Come up, Jean,' Lily called.

Jean, wearing the prettiest blue frock with ruched details on the bodice and puff sleeves, her face flushed a pretty pink, her eyes sparkling, flounced into the kitchen.

She stopped and stared down at Lily, who felt a perfect fright, with her hair pulled back into a turban-style headscarf, a pinny tied at the back and bare legs.

'I've just called in to see if you've got any chicory coffee to spare. Ours is all gone and the corner shop hasn't any left. Also, I don't suppose you have any rhubarb from your dad's allotment?'

Jean was always popping in these days and Mam and her were

as thick as thieves. It was Lily's turn to experience pangs of jealousy, because she felt left out.

Jean was the daughter Mam, if she were given the choice, would want. A homebird, Jean was happy with her lot and would never dream of leaving the area. Whereas Lily, although wanting to raise a family, desired more than the drudgery Mam, who she respected and loved dearly, had experienced as a housewife. Lily had always wanted to do something more with her life. She thought of her fanciful ideas in the past. She had this hankering to escape town life and live someplace new in the countryside and do a job that women could do as well as men. Where and what, she'd never figured out.

These dreams would now have to be shelved but one day Lily was determined she and John would make a better life for their family in the countryside. Didn't every generation strive to make life better? If they hadn't, mankind wouldn't have progressed from the Stone Age.

Mam had once told Lily with a wise expression, 'You remind me a lot of meself, Lily, when I was young. I had me future all worked out and I was determined I wasn't going to end up a skivvy like me mother with a handful of bairns, then life happened.' She laughed outright. 'But d'you know what? I wouldn't swap a single one of you for the good life.'

Lily was that touched she'd wrapped her arms around Mam's diminutive, skinny figure and given her the biggest hug.

'Soft lump,' Mam had said, disentangling herself, but Lily could tell she was pleased.

That was the reason, whenever Lily got fed up with her lot, she reminded herself of the sacrifices Mam had made and it made helping out at home all the more worthwhile.

It's peculiar, Lily thought, as she looked at Jean now waiting for an answer, *how you never think that your parents had hopes and dreams of their own, and selfishly you just take them for granted.*

'If you haven't much coffee to spare,' Jean was telling her, 'I can make do with a few spoonsful out of the jar. And even a stick of rhubarb would do.'

Lily stood up from her haunches and, moving to the alcove cupboard, took a jar of coffee from the shelf, handing it to Jean. 'There's a little bit left but we've got another jar.'

'Ooh, thanks. You've saved the day.' Jean smiled her gratitude.

'Why the sudden need for rhubarb?'

Jean's cheeks flushed pink. 'I just fancy eating rhubarb like we did when we were kids, remember, dipping it raw into sugar.'

An inkling of suspicion whizzed through Lily's mind. 'Hmm, that sounds like a craving...'

Jean hesitated. 'I... can't say.'

'Are you pregnant?' Lily guessed.

'I am,' Jean confessed. 'The last time I had me do-das was after we had that chat in my kitchen. Harry says it's his birthday present.' Her cheeks flushed. 'I had to tell somebody. I would've confided in you, to be honest, but seeing how you had—'

'I understand.'

'I told your mum and she promised not to say anything.'

So that was what the secret between Mam and Jean was, and as for favouritism, that was a figment of her insecure mind, Lily reproached herself.

Jean's face split into a broad grin. 'I can't believe my good fortune. I didn't think it was ever going to happen.' Then a shadow of guilt crossed her face.

It crossed Lily's mind to confide in Jean about her own secret but a little voice of warning in her head prevented her.

She forced a weak smile. 'Congratulations. Eee! I'm going to be an aunty.'

And hopefully your baby will have a cousin, flashed through Lily's mind.

———

But the fates weren't that kind.

In early September, when Lily thought she must be over two months pregnant, it started with cramps. She was at the stalls in the marketplace looking at a china vase when she overheard two women behind discussing the recent raid.

'They say the bombs were scattered countrywide,' one of them said.

'Aye,' the other woman replied, 'I heard High Heaton copped it. One poor bloke was blown through a bedroom window to the bottom of his garden and seriously injured.'

It was then, as another pain in her lower back started, knowing the signs, Lily placed the china vase back on the stall. Fear gripping her, she headed for home.

Please God don't let me lose this baby.

Hurrying along King Street and threading through the throng of shoppers, she made her way up Mile End Road and, turning into Fawcett Street, hurried for the front door.

Mam, polishing the brasses on the front door in the bright sunshine, saw her approach.

She called out, 'Lass, whatever's wrong?'

Lily, shaking her head, couldn't speak and headed up the dim staircase straight for her bedroom.

There, she hauled up the skirt of her summer frock and pulled down her knickers.

There it was: the evidence. The spotting of blood on the white cotton material.

Mam sent for Mrs Chambers as the bleeding and cramping continued and Lily, in a fog of distress, felt the blood seep from down below. Knowing she was miscarrying her precious baby, Lily dissolved into floods of tears when she arrived.

'Don't worry,' Mrs Chambers told her. 'You can try again.'

Lily didn't answer.

The same as last time, while others got on with their lives, Lily felt in limbo. Grief-stricken, she just sat staring at the walls, her mind switched off to everything but losing the baby. After that she felt wracked with infinite sadness. Her dreams were shattered.

And finally anger coursed through her; Lily wanted to howl like a banshee at the fates for being so cruel as to rob her of her baby a second time.

She wondered, should she tell John? What if she couldn't carry his child, would he still be interested in her? Her biggest worry was that she was still being punished for not wanting to start a family – and she feared for future pregnancies.

October 1940

Mam and Lily were sitting at the kitchen table, cups of tea in their hands, when they heard thumping footsteps from the backstairs and Harry appeared.

Lily was tired as the siren had wailed again last night and the family had scurried into the shelter. Though the raiders roared overhead, no bombs or explosions were to be heard in their vicinity. But muffled thuds could be heard in the distance. It had occurred to Lily what a strange world they were living in. Wars used to be about battlefields, horses and swords, and had now become a threat to civilians from the sky.

It was Sunday morning – baking day. With the meat in the oven, rather than let all those empty shelves go to waste Mam had filled them with what she fancied making – dictated by whatever she could find in the depleted cupboards in these days of rationing.

As he came into the kitchen, Harry closed his eyes and dreamily sniffed the air. 'That wouldn't be my favourite coconut cakes cooking, would it?'

Lily shook her head, amused; her brother could always sweet-talk Mam.

'Correct,' Mam told him, 'it wouldn't. It's rock buns and don't you go building your hopes up, our Harry, with the shortages there's not many and, knowing you, you'll scoff the lot.'

Opening his eyes, Harry came and sat down in a chair next to Lily. 'Mam, you wouldn't deny your favourite son just one teeny cake, would you?'

'I would. They'll all be gone if I give in and they're to last more than a day.'

'If they didn't get eaten then you'd be complaining.' When that remark didn't work, Harry tried another tack. 'You're the best cook in the world, our Ma, and no mistake.'

'Flattery won't get you anywhere. And don't let your wife hear you say that, or else there'll be ructions on.'

Harry lifted his head and took in a deep sniff of air. 'You realise, you're putting me through torture.'

Mam shook her head and laughed. 'Go on, then. There's jam tarts in the oven; you can have one when they're cooked.'

Lily had known her brother would win eventually.

Harry, grinning, rocked back on the hind legs of his chair. Thickset and handsome, he wore brown trousers with braces and a white shirt without a collar, a red cap sat at a jaunty angle over thick, dark brown curly hair. Lily knew many a local lass had been sorry when Harry Armstrong tied the knot.

'Pour us a cup of tea, will you, Lily?'

'You've got hands yourself,' she told her brother.

Mam reached for the teapot. 'Anyway, why isn't Jean baking today?'

Harry, shaking his head, gave a long-suffering sigh. 'She's always tired these days and last night's raid didn't help. She says making the Sunday dinner is enough for one day.'

'You should lend a hand more.' Mam poured tea through a strainer into a china cup.

In the silence that followed, kiddies could be heard playing in the lane. Jimmy was in his bedroom reading a comic as he wasn't allowed out to play, not on a Sunday. Dad was working overtime and Lily's two brothers were still in bed.

Mam handed the cup of tea over to Harry, clicking her tongue. 'Who'd have thought they'd put tea on the ration. I reckon if I make a cuppa any weaker, we'll be supping nothing but hot water.' She settled back into the chair. 'How's your Jean doing? She's been a stranger recently.'

'She's stopped coming too often because...' His tentative gaze swerved towards Lily. He gulped a mouthful of tea instead of going on.

Lily, feeling the atmosphere in the room tensing, plastered a smile on her face. She'd be damned if she'd allow her misery to show and, for the sake of harmony in the family, she'd fake her feelings.

'Jean's always welcome. Tell her not to feel awkward on my account. It would be grand seeing how she's getting on, wouldn't it, Mam?'

Liar, her mind screamed. The reality was that seeing Jean blooming and pregnant would be torment.

Mam visibly relaxed. 'Silly lass. Tell her to come over.'

Harry grinned idiotically. 'That's what I told her. But she didn't want Lily upset. I told her not to be daft, that you're bound to be over it by now.'

Feeling the heat rise from her neck into her cheeks, Lily felt like throttling her dumb brother. Nervous energy kicking in, she needed to be active. Businesslike, she stood and moved towards the cooker.

'Those buns smell cooked. I'll check and take them out for you, Mam.'

She moved into the scullery and, opening the oven door, a burst of hot air blasted her face. She decided the cakes could do with a few minutes more.

She heard Mam's voice coming through the closed kitchen door. Lily strained to hear.

'Before you say another word, our Harry, sit properly on the chair, else you'll break it. And where's your manners? Take off that cap.'

'Crikey, Ma, what's up now?'

'I'll give you what's up. You've got no tact, our Harry. When will you learn to think before you speak?'

'What have I said, like?'

'Of course your sister's still upset. She lost her baby.'

'I'm sorry, Mother, but how was I to know? Technically, it's not as if it was a real baby yet, was it?' Silence then, 'Ouch! Ma, that hurt.'

Kiddies were playing in the lane, their high-pitched voices coming through the small open window. One child cried out, 'Got you!' and Lily deduced they were playing a game of chase.

Her baby would never know the childish joy of running outside with abandonment.

Her vision blurring, Lily sniffed.

———

That night, after a day of pretence, and long after she put Jimmy to bed, Lily lay on top of the bedclothes fully clothed and feeling spent.

A rap came at her bedroom door.

'Can I come in?' Mam's wary voice.

Lily, head resting on the wooden headboard, wriggled to sit up.

'Yes.' She switched on the bedside lamp. Light spilled into the room that had space only for a chest of drawers with a top lid that opened to reveal a mirror, wooden chair – used for current clothes – and single bed. The cream paper dotted with pink rosebuds, put on by Dad, was peeling off in places around the walls.

Mam appeared and sat on the bottom of the bed.

Lily knew she looked a mess. She'd tried to hide the dark circles under her eyes with powder from the compact she'd received from John for her birthday, which she rarely used.

'Your brother's a thoughtless nitwit,' Mam commented.

'He doesn't understand. It'll be different when he's got a bairn of his own.'

There followed a silence during which the words Mam obviously wished to say hung in the air like unwanted interlopers.

Lily attempted to keep things general. 'Is Dad out on fire-watching duty?'

'Yes, poor soul, and after a full day's work. It's his turn to do a voluntary stint.'

'Where's the lads?'

Mam pulled an irritated face. 'At that place called "out" they always say they're at.' A pause but, silence being too unnerving for Mam, she continued, 'By, them Jerry raids are getting worse. Last week it was the turn of Newcastle and Sunderland.' Her eyes grew round with fear. For feisty Mam was terrified when raiders thundered overhead – what it could mean for her family.

Lily thought of John, still down in Devon where his battalion had joined Home Forces. She prayed each night he would stay safe and he wouldn't be sent abroad.

Mam nervously picked at the bedcovers. 'Then there was the raid here only the other night. Your dad says one of them bombs exploded in the river fifty yards short of a blockship called *Melba* that was lying at the Groyne Quay.'

Lily quickly put in, 'But no one was hurt.'

'Others aren't so lucky. There was a raid over Shotley Bridge way last week. And they say some poor old soul survived the raid but died from the shock.' Mam was determined to have the last word of doom on the subject. She chewed her lip.

Lily shuffled beside Mam and put her arm around her shoulders. 'Try not to think about the raids. It does no good.'

Hark at me, she chided herself, *when all I think about is the baby I lost.*

For a moment the two sat in silence, and then Lily asked in a small voice, 'Does it get any better? I can't get on with life for thinking about the baby. I keep going over in my mind if miscarrying was due to something I did or didn't do. Or if I'm ever going to be a mam.'

Mam regarded her with sorrowful eyes. 'You never forget – and neither should you. They're your bairns, after all. But it does get easier and you do learn to live with the loss. As far as being a mam, I've known women give up after years of trying and then lo and behold, when they least expect it, they're in the family way.'

Mam nudged heads with Lily. They sat companionably like that for a time then Mam removed Lily's arm from her shoulders and stood.

'I've got something to show you.' She made for the door and Lily, mystified but curious, followed. Mam led the way over the front landing to her bedroom.

The room, smelling of the liniment Dad used for his aching muscles, housed a walnut wardrobe, double bed and dressing table with a three-way mirror that stood in front of the window.

Mam opened the top drawer beneath the wardrobe doors. She rifled to the bottom of the clothes and brought out a parcel wrapped in brown paper.

Unwrapping the parcel, her misted grey eyes lifted to Lily's. 'I needed something to remember them by. Something tangible to prove they were here.' She laid the opened parcel on the bed. 'So, I made these.' Seeing two pairs of pink little bootees, mittens and hats made Lily gasp. 'The babies were both taken away before I saw them but I decided they were girls to make the numbers more equal.' Her voice wobbled. 'Four boys and three of you girls.' A lump grew in Lily's throat and she swallowed hard. 'I named them Rose and Maud.'

Lily contemplated the two sisters she'd never known. Would she have felt so left out being a girl if they'd lived? This feeling of wanting to be as good as any boy, would it have been so urgent, or would she have been content to play dolls and houses like the other girls at school?

'Could you make me the same keepsake?'

'Of course, lass. That is if me arthritic fingers can still abide knitting.'

Back in her bedroom, Lily thought things through. It was time to face facts and buck up. She might never have a family but she had John – and, like Jean once told her, her husband was enough. As for being worried he'd desert her, what rubbish that was. This was John, whose love was unreserved, and she trusted him like no other. Yes, he'd be disappointed but his main concern would be for her.

She would write and tell him and include her fears that she might never carry a child.

———

A few days later, there was a letter lying on the front doormat from John.

Sweetheart,

I'm devastated for you, if only I'd been there to give some comfort. I worry you're not taking care of yourself. As for making a baby Radley together – it would be wonderful but not essential to our future happiness. If it isn't in the fates that we're to have a kiddie then we have each other. We are a family.

My life started the day I met you and having you to spend the future with is enough...

Lily smiled through her tears. For a man who claimed he wasn't good with words, he outdid himself.

Despite his reassurances, the little ray of hope that one day she'd carry a baby full term didn't leave her.

March 1941

One spring morning, as the family were sitting around the breakfast table, the back landing door opened and Harry, face alight with excitement, came bursting through into the kitchen.

'Jean's had the baby. It's a boy and he's a whopper.'

Mam, sitting on the fender's horsehair seat, toasting bread with a toasting fork at the range's red embers, was the first to recover. 'Ee, I'm a grandma!'

Lily, buttering Jimmy's toast, felt her pulse race.

She'd decided when the baby arrived she'd act thrilled no matter how she felt. But it was one thing to wish to behave in a certain way and quite another to act it out.

'How big is he?' Sam wanted to know.

'Ten pounds two ounces.'

'Good gracious.' Mam's free hand flew to cover her mouth. 'How's Jean?'

'Happy it's over. So am I. I've smoked a packet of Woodbines while I've waited.'

'It must've been hard on you, son,' Mam teased. Taking the blackened toast off the fork, she stood up. Depositing the toast in the toast rack on the table, she exclaimed, 'I'm away over to see them.'

'The midwife's still there,' Harry told her.

'If it's Cissie Baines, she'll let me in. She knows I'm an old hand where babies are concerned.'

'I'm coming with you,' Lily surprised herself by saying.

Mam's face contorted in concern.

'I can't wait to see my nephew.' Lily started as she meant to go on; she didn't want to cause any awkwardness.

'Can I come to see the baby?' Jimmy asked, his young face eager.

'Not yet, Jimmy,' Mam told him. 'Jean won't be ready for too many visitors yet. You can see him maybe after school.'

Lily followed Mam from the room, conscious of Jimmy's disappointed expression and Ian and Sam plotting a night at the Criterion pub wetting the baby's head.

Moments like these, Lily wished John was by her side, not only to give her support but to simply see him, because she missed him so dreadfully.

———

'What's his name?' Mam couldn't take her eyes off her new grandson, swathed in a white shawl, who she cuddled in her arms.

Sitting up in the rumpled bed and wearing a pink nightie, looking tired and sweaty, Jean gazed adoringly at her infant son. 'Stanley Arthur, after his two grandads.'

Mam's face lit up. 'My Arthur will be over the moon.'

Lily had been prepared to feel envy but, staring at the red-faced, bald-headed baby, she didn't feel anything. 'Oh, my goodness, aren't you a cutie.' As their expectant eyes scrutinised her that was all Lily could think to say.

Mam laughed, relieved. 'D'you think so? He looks a right bruiser to me.'

Jean gave a sharp intake of breath.

'He looks just like Harry when he was born and look how handsome he turned out.' Mam attempted to wriggle out of her ill-received, tactless remark. 'Here – d'you want a hold?' She made to pass the bairn over to Lily.

'No thanks.' Lily didn't want to push her luck and feel the warm little body in her arms. 'I'll leave it to the expert.'

Cissie the midwife came bustling back into the room, a cup of tea in her hand. 'Time for baby to go back into his cot. Too much handling can be discomforting for his little body. And mum could do with a rest.'

They took the hint and, after congratulations were done and goodbyes said, they left Jean, eyes drooping, sipping her tea.

———

Lily couldn't sleep that night for thinking about Jean and her baby. The incredulity in her sister-in-law's eyes as she gazed lovingly at her son, and the pride in Harry's... Images that bored into her brain and kept Lily awake wondering – doubting – if she could endure the following months, watching young Stanley Arthur grow.

Loathing herself for being envious but unable to do anything about it, she sat up and, switching on the bedside lamp, started to read *Rebecca*, her current book. But she couldn't concentrate.

Lily's last thought before falling asleep was of John and when he might next be home. She gave a longing sigh. It shouldn't be long as he was due leave.

11

May 1941

The sky heavy with grey clouds, rain bounced like tennis balls on the pavement. John, opening the wooden gate, approached the front door and banged the knocker.

Two days before, he'd sent Lily a telegram.

Two days' leave starts Friday. Meet at Foley Avenue. Love, John

He heard footsteps from inside and then the door opened and, heart thumping, he saw his beloved Lily standing there as lovely as ever – but thinner, with dark tell-tale circles under her eyes. In a few strides he was in the lobby and, dropping the rucksack he carried on the floor and taking her into his arms, John never wanted to let her go.

'Welcome home,' she told him, nestling her head against his shoulder. 'I've missed you so.'

He heard the catch in her voice.

'You've had quite a year, Lily, since I last saw you. I wish I could've been here.'

'You couldn't have done anything.'

Sensing her mood, her feeling of failure, he gave her a tight squeeze.

She struggled free, and wrinkled her nose. 'You stink of cigarettes.' She gave a half-hearted laugh and John knew she wanted the serious moment to pass. 'Don't tell me being a soldier has driven you to take up smoking.'

'I thumbed a lift from an old dear driving a Morris. She chain-smoked for most of the way.' He pulled a face of mock horror. 'If it hadn't been for the fact I was desperate to see you, I'd have scarpered as soon as I opened the passenger door.' He laughed. 'I nearly suffocated.'

The sombre moment passed and, unable to resist those inviting red lips, he gave her a lingering kiss. When they broke free, he hugged her tight.

His voice husky, he whispered in her ear, 'I've missed you too.'

Lily insisted the first thing John must do was take off his wet things and have something to eat.

Though he grinned, John was deadly serious when he told her, 'I can think of better things to take my clothes off for.'

Her eyes danced. 'If it means it's the only way to stop you getting pneumonia then, I suppose, I should agree.'

Lacing her fingers with his, she led him up the stairs and over the landing to the master bedroom where his step faltered.

He shook his head. 'Not in there.' Taking the lead, he moved towards his bedroom.

Lily sat on the bed. Her mood had become one of sad reflection again, John knew, and he didn't want to rush her.

'How about we just cuddle for now?'

She smiled her appreciation. 'John, it's just I—'

'I know, sweetheart.' Sitting beside her, he put an arm around her shoulders.

'The thing is,' she told him, a wobble in her voice, 'now you're here I just want us to enjoy our time together. I don't want us to worry about making a baby. Or dwell on the war, or the future.'

She looked up at him. 'I want us to think only of ourselves for a time.'

John gave her a tender smile. 'I would agree with all that.'

———

Later, John lit the kitchen fire and they sat in companionable silence, bellies full of homemade mince pie and peas that Lily had brought from her mam's with the rest of the provisions to keep them going for a couple of days. Changed now out of his uniform into a white shirt and brown trousers held high by red braces, John felt that the house had taken on a new identity. He looked around. With its spruced appearance, a vase overflowing with colourful flowers placed on the table, the kitchen had lost its heavy forbidding atmosphere – which John attributed to his father's haunting presence.

Reminded of Lily's words – 'I want us to think only of ourselves for a time' – he shuttered his mind to thoughts of his intimidating father.

One thing he did understand was Mum wanting to uproot from the house, and begin a new life.

'Penny for them? You look downcast.' Lily, with a concerned expression, stared at him. 'Is it because we haven't... you know?'

'Not at all. I was just reflecting how good the place looks.'

A thoughtful expression crossed Lily's face. 'That's something I want to talk to you about. It's been nice spending time here getting the place ready for your homecoming – I realised I needed a bit of time away from the family and all the goings-on there. So I'm thinking of spending more time here.' She went on to tell him about her struggle seeing Jean with baby Stanley, and how ashamed she was at the envy she felt.

When she paused, thinking the matter over, John wasn't surprised. Lily had suffered two miscarriages in a short space of time and the timing of Jean's pregnancy couldn't have been worse.

'Lily, things have been difficult for you recently. You would be made of stone if you didn't feel envious.'

Her look of despair tore his heart. In a swift move, John bounded up from his seat and, taking her in his arms, held her tight.

'Don't be so hard on yourself, Lily.'

His words were inadequate, he knew, and John wished he could think of ones that would help mend her.

———

The next evening – after a pleasurable day strolling along the coast road, a fish and chip lunch eaten outside, seagulls swooping down to catch the chips the couple threw in the air – the couple sat by the fire in their nightclothes, a cup of cocoa now in their hands, savouring every precious moment of each other's company.

Out of nowhere came the depressingly loud sound of the air-raid siren.

'Blast Jerry. Of all nights,' John shouted against the noise of planes droning followed by distant explosions.

Pulling his pullover over his pyjama top, he grabbed blankets and pillows from the bedroom while Lily, donning her cardigan over her cotton nightdress, made a flask of tea. They headed into the dank and draughty shelter as, in the distance, terrifying whistling and explosions were heard. Lily snuggled in the comfort of John's embrace.

As the noise receded, turning her face up to his, John saw a smouldering look in Lily's eye.

———

Next morning, Lily walked a tired John to the railway station to catch his train. As he'd been awake most of the night, she'd talked him out of thumbing a lift back to his unit.

A whistle blew and the train – full to the gunwales with

service men – pulled out of the station, steam billowing in the air. She waved to John, hanging out of the carriage window and blowing kisses, until he disappeared into the distance.

His goodbye kiss fresh on her lips, a rather musty smell from his uniform jacket lingering in her nostrils, Lily kept a stiff upper lip as she returned to the sunny outside and made her way up the hill to her parents' home.

It would seem her mind had its own agenda for, despite what she'd told John, Lily found herself hoping that this weekend, and their lovemaking, would once again result in her being pregnant with a Radley baby.

12

August **1941**

Lily watched as Dad tapped the remnants of his pipe into the ashtray on the kitchen table.

'By gum,' he told her, 'Jerry made a right show of himself last night. Those planes we heard dropped bombs over Gateshead.' Dad clenched the empty pipe between his teeth.

Mam came bustling in from the scullery, a plate of bread and dripping in her hand.

She eyed Dad. 'Get that filthy ashtray off me clean tablecloth.'

Here we go, thought Lily.

'Woman.' Dad's voice tetchy, he gave an impatient grimace that accentuated the carved lines in his cheeks. 'This isn't the time to witter on about an ashtray.'

Mam, surprising Lily, didn't rise to the bait but gave Dad a measured look. 'What's wrong, Arthur?'

Dad gave a great sigh. 'I had a word with Bobby Fisher when I was at work yesterday.' He paused and shook his head in sorrow. 'The bloke went to pieces after his wife was killed. I reckon it's the first time he's mentioned Lottie's name since it happened.'

'Poor soul.' Her face distressed, Mam turned towards Lily.

'D'you remember about Bobby's wife? She was killed when that bomb dropped on Wilkinson's lemonade factory in North Shields. It was at the beginning of May.'

How could Lily forget? The public shelter beneath the factory was completely destroyed when over a hundred men, women and children lost their lives.

Lily's stomach went cold at the tragedy of it all. 'I've always meant to ask. What was she doing at that time of night in North Shields?'

'Lottie was visiting her widowed mother and staying over,' Dad intervened. 'The basement rooms below the factory were used as a shelter, apparently, because they were known to be heavily reinforced.'

'They were clean and comfortable, so they say,' Mam chipped in. 'And had a friendly atmosphere, with folk having a sing-song accompanied by an accordionist...'

Lily's mind drifting, she imagined the shelter. Wide-eyed youngsters in bunk beds, families sitting in groups, the hubbub of noise. Giving a small cry of anguish, and in an attempt to blot the heartbreaking scene out, she squeezed her eyes shut.

'What did Bobby have to say?' Mam was asking Dad.

'That today would have been their silver wedding anniversary.' Dad's voice was gruff. He ran his fingertips through his greying hair. 'Poor bloke's lost without his Mrs.'

'I bet he is.' Mam's eyes widened. 'Oh my God, Arthur, there was whole families in that shelter.' Her hand flew to cover her mouth. 'It's me nightmare, something should happen to all me family.'

They lapsed into silence as the horror of the catastrophe played in their minds. It occurred to Lily that it was best she didn't unnerve Mam by mentioning the idea of her going to John's house for a while.

'I could murder a cup of tea.' Dad broke the silence.

Mam nodded as it was her cure-all for such occasions. She took the tea caddy from the fireside alcove cupboard. 'Were you kept busy?' she asked, over her shoulder.

Looking relieved to be talking about something else, Dad shook his head. He had been out fire-watching with the means of dealing with small fires – a stirrup pump and scoop for picking up incendiaries – in his hands.

'Not especially in this area. Some small fires but the local street firefighting parties soon had them under control without much harm done.'

From January that year fire-watching had been made compulsory and Dad had his fair share of part-time duty.

At the thought of Dad doing his bit, stirrings of discontentment gripped Lily. The grain of hope had been quashed three weeks after John's leave when she'd started the curse, and yet another dream of starting a family was dashed.

Lily felt restless and down in the doldrums, and this time she knew something had to change in her life. The only way forward was to give up on her hope to start a family for now. She thought of her earlier dreams of working outdoors. She'd read an article in the newspaper about Land Girls out in the country working on farms to provide food for the nation. Something she would dearly love to do if only she could. But the thought of escaping town life to live in the countryside was so far out of her experience it scared her a little. Surely there must be something she could do for the war effort and still be on hand to assist Mam when she needed her?

The speech Ernest Bevin, the minister for labour, gave only unsettled Lily more when he'd declared that one million wives were wanted for war work. It was to become compulsory for single women between certain ages to register for war service. Lily was exempt because of domestic responsibilities, and being married to a serviceman she was only expected to do local war work – but she desperately wanted to be one of those women. The truth was, though she would never let it be known, Lily felt trapped helping Mam. Being married hadn't released her and with John away she felt uncomfortable in the Foley Avenue house, and frustrated that she wasn't able to call it home yet.

Jean, always popping in with baby Stanley, didn't help either. When Stanley was feeding and Jean was staring in adoration down at him, such was Lily's envy she almost hated her sister-in-law, God help her, then ended up loathing herself. Consumed with not only envy but bitterness too, Lily wanted to scream at the unfairness of it all. The worst was, she could see by Mam's pitying expression she knew what Lily was going through. Which left Lily hating herself even more.

Seeing Stanley in her mind's eye, with his wide and blue, transparent eyes, and cute gummy smile, made Lily realise that for sanity's sake she needed to do something about her present situation. She was tired of battling with her fragile emotions and so, determined to stop being weak-willed, she made a decision.

———

It was on a Sunday when Dad was sitting on the front step reading the newspaper, the bald patch on his head protected from the sun by a handkerchief tied in a knot at each corner, that Lily approached Mam. Ian was out with his mates and Sam was seeing his new girlfriend, while Jimmy played marbles in the gutter with his pals.

Sitting at the kitchen table peeling the potatoes that Dad had brought in earlier from his allotment, Lily rehearsed in her head what she was going to say.

Mam, washing breakfast dishes in the scullery, was prattling on. 'Our Lily, who'd have thought clothes would go on ration. I was talking to her next door and she said it was six coupons for her hubby's overalls and, would you believe, three for a pair of knickers. I mean that's just plain ridi—'

'Mam, I've come to a decision.'

Mam's puzzled face peered around the scullery door. 'What kind of decision?'

Rather than look at Mam, Lily dipped a potato, still clagged with a layer of soil, into the bowl of water on the table in front of her. 'I've decided it's time I did something about the house in Foley Avenue and made it more of a home.' She paused and, when Mam didn't comment, she continued, 'I thought I'd live there at the weekends.'

Mam's expression grew contemplative, then she gave a slow nod. 'I know what I said earlier but, if that's what you want, I won't stand in your way. In fact, our Lily, I think under the circumstances it's probably for the best. I've come to rely on you too much and I realise I have to let go someday, so I might as well start getting used to it now at weekends.'

'But how will you manage, Mam?'

Mam's thin face contorted into a determined grimace. 'There's always a way. Your dad and I will have to put our thinking caps on to find ours for the future.'

———

Lily closed the front door of the house in Foley Avenue. In the deafening silence, she moved around the ground-floor rooms, wondering, for an unnerving moment, if she'd done the right thing. Straightening her spine, she reminded herself this was her and John's future home.

She decided to make changes first in the master bedroom, which she knew John would never move into because who in their right mind would want to make love in their parents' bed? Then it would be the turn of the front room, with its stuffy and cluttered appearance – its dark and heavy furniture, gilt-framed pictures of hunting scenes around the walls, and dusty aspidistra that stood in the window. When her thoughts turned to making the small bedroom into a nursery, Lily made the bravest decision. Tired of endlessly moping for a baby, and having people feel sorry for her, she would go back to her former resolution and let it be known she no longer wanted to start a family. Even if it was pretence, it would make for an easier life all round and, who knew, one day she might believe it herself.

Lily made a to-do list: change bed, curtains, renew pieces of aged furniture, paint where necessary, gut the dining room of clutter. When she'd finished, her forehead crinkled in a frown. In these days of austerity and shortages, when there was a lack of timber for furniture and when some families, poor devils, had lost their homes and needed to start again from scratch, here she was having ideas of grandeur. But anything she didn't need or want Lily would give to a deserving home.

She told John of her intentions for the house in her next letter and confided her unease at changing so much at Foley Avenue without his mam's permission.

John must have written to his mam because a letter arrived for Lily from her mother-in-law the very next week.

Primrose Cottage
Selkirk
Scotland

Dearest Lily,

I hope this finds you well, my dear, and keeping safe from the bombing. I myself didn't use the shelter in the yard as I preferred the relative comfort of sitting under the stairs with the light on and a good book.

Deidre went on to tell of her life with her sister in the Borders and how she was settling, as at first she had found sharing space with someone again difficult.

Helen is easy to get along with and I'm pleased to say I've made the right decision. My dear, please feel free to change things to your advantage at Foley Avenue as the house now belongs to you and John. The furnishings were to my husband's taste and I have

*no wish to keep anything, except my mother's china dinner set and
the album of photographs you'll find on top of the wardrobe in
what was my bedroom.*

Lily wrote back to say how grateful she was.

Relieved she could now go ahead with her plans, Lily thought
things through. With the allowance she got from John's pay, and
after buying food and other essentials, there wasn't much money
left. So, with nothing else for it, weekends were spent scouring
market stalls, second-hand shops and *for sale* notices in the local
Gazette for bargains, which proved to be more fun than she'd
expected. She became an expert at haggling, much to the supposed
disgust of second-hand shop owners, who were as good at acting as
Lily.

Weekends became a haven of pleasure and Lily felt stronger
than she had in a long while. Her home life back at her parents'
became better too, and she even enjoyed seeing baby Stanley, who
was sitting up now and recognising Aunty Lily, his chubby face
lighting up when he saw her; he knew he was in for a treat as she'd
take him for a walk to the park in his pram.

Slowly, week by week, the Foley Avenue house became how
Lily had envisaged in her mind, a place where she could unwind,
somewhere she wasn't a sister, or daughter, but someone who was
beginning to find herself in the solitude of her own home. She
could be sad, angry, or dance around in abandon to music on the
wireless. The only downside was she was missing John to share
this luxurious existence.

13

'Our Lily, that terrible raid on the town two nights ago has made me jittery about you staying on your own tonight in Foley Avenue.'

Lily was helping Mam to change the beds in the lads' bedroom at home. It was second of October, and she had extended the time she spent at Foley Avenue to include sometimes as early as Thursday night, to make weekends longer. She knew, because of the recent raids in the area, Mam's nerves were getting the better of her. She thought it ill-advised to remind Mam that if a bomb did have Lily's name on it didn't matter where she was; here at home or in Foley Avenue, it would find her.

'Your dad says it's been reported that at present casualties from the recent bombing stand at eleven killed and fifty-five seriously injured and made over three hundred homeless.' Mam's eyes bulged. 'Furthermore, we got off lightly compared with North Shields where the death toll was at least forty-one killed.'

She folded her arms with a look that said if that didn't make Lily stay home at weekends with her family where she'd be safer, she didn't know what would. As for Lily, her thoughts were that Dad should mind his tongue and stop scaremongering, as Mam's nerves couldn't stand it. She was convinced Mam's asthma was getting worse with the stress.

As if to prove a point, Mam gasped a few labouring breaths. 'Your dad, like the rest of the workers are tired to the bone because they've had no time to rest.' She paused as she gulped air. 'God help us if there's another raid because essential services haven't been fully restored.' Her lips tightened. 'But I can feel it in me bones – those Jerry bombs are getting too close for comfort.'

Later, Lily was to wonder if the fates were listening in because Mam's prediction became a fact.

———

It was after seven that night when Lily drew the blackout curtains over the bay window at Foley Avenue and switched on the standard lamp. The subdued glow from the fringed shade enhanced the room, making it cosy, and Lily gave a satisfied sigh. She only wished John were here to see the transformation.

The old two-seater couch, with its plumped cushions covered with a colourful crocheted throw, looked renewed, while the two wing-backed chairs she'd bought from the second-hand shop looked grand with their sunny yellow covers washed. The skirting boards, doors and window frames and bookcase were painted cream from a pot of paint Dad had obtained from a painter at the shipyard.

Tapping the end of his nose with his forefinger, Dad had remarked, ''Tis best, Lily, if you don't ask questions.'

The floorboards scrubbed, a red rug lay in front of the hearth and Lily's pride and joy was the picture in a white frame of a vase of yellow sunflowers that hung above the fireplace.

She poked the fire and, taking the tongs from the black coal scuttle, placed two nuggets of coal on the red embers. Turning the knob on the wireless housed in a polished wooden box, she collapsed on the couch, head reclining back on a cushion, as she listened to the soothing music for a long while as it came from the fabric grille.

Then picking up the jotter and pen at her side, she began writing a letter to her husband.

Dearest John,

It was so good to receive your letter here at Foley Avenue where I don't have any interruptions especially by tiresome brothers who think they're funny and make smoochy noises as I read.

Don't be a chump – I don't consider your letters boring, they're the highlight of my day. I read them over and over and it's as though you're nearby.

Before I forget, I've got a surprise for you when I get around to having it made. It's the naming of the house. I only hope your mam doesn't think me presumptuous but she did say we could make changes and I do love the new name so. I can't wait for you to see it on the gate and no, I'm not going to tell you, I'm going to keep you guessing.

I worry about Mam as she's going through a bad spell of health and still insists...

Her hand poised to continue, a noise from outside made her freeze. The wailing sound of the public alert filled the air.

Putting her notepad and pen down on the couch, Lily hurried along the passageway to the kitchen. She struck a match, lit a gas ring and placed the filled kettle on it, then she collected the pack of cards (she played a solitary game of patience to pass the time), novel and knitting, along with the first aid kit she'd recently purchased. When the kettle's whistle shrilled, she made a flask of tea, then made a dash for the back door and into the yard.

The man in the moon, with a malevolent smile on his face, rode high in the sky, while sporadic clouds trailed by. The siren stopped now; distant guns blazed from the ground while up in the heavens twin searchlights criss-crossed, searching for raiders in the sky.

It was then that Lily heard the distant drone of aeroplanes.

Moving down the concrete yard to the back door and into the lane beyond, she stood transfixed as she saw planes coming over in waves, swooping across the sky like black birds of prey. Then came shuddering thuds of explosions and an orange hue on the horizon as buildings blazed. In horror, Lily realised the raid concentrated on the town centre and shipyards. A new terror gripped her as she thought of Dad working nights at Middle Docks. What about the rest of the family? Her two brothers were probably working the night shift at the mine but that left Harry and his family, Mam and her three brothers, who lived in the same area – where the raid was taking place.

As the raiders receded into the distance, a picture of baby Stanley, naïve and oblivious, sleeping peacefully in his cot, came into Lily's mind's eye. His life had just begun. A sickening dread took hold.

Please God let them all be safe, I'll never be envious again, I—

'What d'you think you're doing, standing there dumbstruck?' a voice yelled.

A man came out of the gloom in the cobbled lane, and Lily saw, by the light of the moon, he was of a similar age to Dad. His hands on his hips, the man wore a tin hat with the letter W on it and a black Charlie Chaplin moustache brushed his upper lip. An Air-Raid Protection warden.

'Mark my words, miss, we're in for a full-scale raid. Jerry, the bast— pardon, miss, will be back. Get yourself in the shelter. That's not a request but an order.'

The instinct to disobey, the result of wanting over the years to be like her unruly brothers, took hold.

She shrugged off his arm. 'I can't – my family might be in danger.'

'Miss, I haven't got time to argue. There's folk out there need my help.'

As Lily heard the ominous rumble of planes returning like bees attracted to honey, she told the warden, chin jutting, 'You're not safe either but I don't see you running to take cover.'

The warden wagged his head and made to move off. 'Miss, this is my job. It's been known for Jerry to sweep the streets with machine-gun fire and I don't want a lassie killed on my watch. Besides,' he called over his shoulder as he hurried off, 'what good will you be to your family if you're dead.'

His boots clattered down the lane and into the distance.

Common sense told Lily the warden was right but still she hesitated, then, as another wave of bombers came thundering overhead, blanking the sky above, Lily didn't have to think twice. Her legs shaky and heart pounding in her chest, she made a dive for the relative safety of the brick-built shelter-cum-washhouse in the yard.

The night air was filled with the terrifying sounds of bombs dropping and the incessant firing of the ack-ack guns. Sitting on the canvas bed placed against the shelter walls, she covered her ears with her hands. Still she heard them, the raiders and thuds sounding far away but now drawing closer. Then came a shrieking noise, when Lily held her breath and time stood still. A deafening explosion made the shelter walls shake, and dust and debris fell all around. As planes droned into the distance another wave could be heard, more shrieks, more explosions and the perpetual sound of guns.

Lily had nowhere to run and nowhere to hide. Arms crossed over her chest, she lay down on the camp bed and by the light of the lamp she looked up at the picture of John and her at the seaside, which she'd hung on a nail in the wall: his hair tousled by a sea breeze, his lips stretched in a smile, Lily beneath the crook of his arm, looking happy and carefree.

They came again, the planes, and as bombs shrieked down and the earth shook, Lily closed her eyes and detached herself from the sounds. If her time had come, she decided, her last thoughts on earth would be of her beloved John.

After what seemed an eternity, the all-clear alert sounded. Lily lay for a while savouring the moment. Opening her eyes, she realised the hurricane lamp had gone out and she was met with darkness – then came euphoria; the raiders had left and she was alive. Fumbling in the locker drawer next to the bed, she found the torch and, switching it on, she made for the doorway. By the light of the moon, she saw the house and windows were intact. Moving across the yard, she opened the back door and stood in the lane.

She stiffened as her eyes met the dark red glow in the sky over the town. Without thinking, Lily ran.

———

As Lily flew like the wind past gaps where houses once stood, she heard cries from people trapped beneath the debris and saw teams of folk clawing with their hands through the wreckage. By the light of the moon, she could see still bodies lying on the pavement in a silent row. She averted her eyes, but not before she glimpsed the body of a man who had a Charlie Chaplin moustache. Where the warden's tin hat was, Lily would never know.

Lily wavered for a moment then decided that with the number of people already at work her help wasn't needed. Besides, she had only one thought on her mind: to find her family.

As she ran down the hill to the bottom end of Fowler Street, the night air was filled with the sound of ambulance and fire engine bells. Looking along King Street to the sight that met her eyes – raging fires leaping into the darkened sky – Lily was sickened to the stomach at the extent of the alarming scene. The buildings surrounding the marketplace were burning down.

The scene of devastation was like something from a horror film. People were milling around with blank expressions, faces blackened, and they didn't look as if they knew where they were going. A child, hugging a rag doll, held on to her mammy's hand. Wardens barked orders and rescue teams were digging in the rubble and the air clogged with putrid smells from raging fires caught the back of Lily's throat. On she stumbled over the heaps of debris along the road and, turning into Fawcett Street, Lily sagged with relief as she realised some houses were still standing.

She looked along the row of houses to hers, and saw where the front façade should have been was an empty space. Moving closer, past the rescue and ambulance parties, Lily registered with shock the inside of her home had collapsed into a pile of debris on the ground.

Lily felt numb. Her first coherent thought was that her family would soon be on the receiving end at the WVS second-hand clothing depot. As a male voice shouted in her direction, Lily chased such an inane thought from her mind.

'Miss, none of these buildings are safe.' A warden, face taut with strain, dark smudges beneath his eyes, wiped his brow with a blistered and bleeding hand. 'Get yourself to the Rest Centre with everyone else.'

As two ambulance men carrying a stretcher made their way past, the warden stepped back out of their path, taking Lily's arm to encourage her to do the same.

Looking down at the stretcher, Lily stared into the deathly ashen and immobile face of Mam.

Before she could react, an arm came around her shoulder. She looked up and to her relief saw Harry. 'Do as the man says, Lily. You can't do anything here.'

'Is Mam alive?' Lily held her breath.

'Yes,' he told her. Breathing out, Lily sagged with relief. 'But she's in a bad way.'

'What happened?'

Harry ran his fingers through his hair. 'When the all-clear sounded, I went to check on Mam and Jimmy. Part of the shelter roof was down but Mam was outside, collapsed in the yard. Jimmy was by her side crying. She was unconscious but breathing.'

Lily found it difficult to take everything in. 'Where is Jimmy now?'

'I sent him down to our house to be with Jean. Our place got damaged so they've gone together to the Rest Centre.'

'And the lads?' In the semi-light she saw figures wandering around as if they were lost.

'Ian's doing the night shift. Sam as far as I know is out with his lass.' At that moment an ambulance bell pierced the night air. 'I'm off to the infirmary with Mam.'

'I'll come with you.'

Harry held up his hands as if barricading himself. 'No, Lily. Go to the Rest Centre at the school and find Jean. She'll need a hand.' His handsome face was strained as he sighed, 'I'll let you know about Mam as soon as I can.'

With that, Harry took off and was swallowed up in the dark.

Lily, walking in a dreamlike state, arrived at the local school. Inside the dimly lit hall, she was welcomed by a lady wearing WVS uniform. Lily's details were taken and she was told to find a seat and someone would bring her a cup of tea.

Folk lay on camp beds and mattresses on the floor, suitcases filled with garments and whatever they could salvage from their destroyed homes piled beside them. Clothes hung on pegs fixed to the surrounding the walls, babies cried and people talked in low voices. Her nerves fraught, Lily scoured the faces.

'Lily, over here.'

It was then she saw Jean, at the top end of the hall, sitting on the edge of a camp bed with Stanley on her knee. All the tension in her body releasing when she saw her family, Lily wilted with relief. Making her way over to her sister-in-law, she saw Jimmy lying in the next bed, a bandage on his forehead, sound asleep.

'I think it's nervous exhaustion, poor lamb,' Jean whispered.

Stanley's eyes were wide in wonder at his strange surroundings. When he saw Aunty Lily he smiled and jiggled with excitement.

'Have you seen Harry?' Jean asked. 'He went to check on your mam and the next thing I knew Jimmy came running down to our house bawling because he thought his mammy was dead. Before he left, Harry said I was to head here.'

'Harry's gone to the hospital to be with Mam. He told me I'd find you here.'

'How is she?' Jean's eyes were anxious as though afraid of the answer.

'She's alive but in a bad way.'

Jean nodded, then looked around the hall in shock. 'Can you believe any of this is happening?'

'Why don't we go and stay at my place? It'll be more comfortable.'

'Thanks, Lily, but no. I'd rather stay here where Harry knows where to find me. Then there's your dad and the lads.'

Lily made a decision. Looking around the room, she saw a bed that was empty. After her earlier terror at the thought of losing her family, the idea of being parted from them now was unbearable, so Lily claimed the bed as her own.

14

Next morning when Lily awoke it took time to collect her thoughts, to recall where she was and why. But soon last night's raid loomed large in her mind, Mam having been carted away to the infirmary, and fear clutched her throat.

People all around, looking as dazed and as overwhelmed as Lily felt, were in the throes of helping their kiddies get dressed, though they, like her, had slept in their clothes. Throwing off the thin grey blanket covering her, Lily made her way up the room to where Jean was changing Stanley's nappy on the bed.

Lily asked, 'Have you seen Harry?'

Picking the baby up and holding him on her hip, Jean nodded. She looked drawn and unkempt, Lily noticed, then decided she probably looked the same.

'He turned up here in the early hours and got a few hours' sleep. He told me that as soon as it was light, he was going back to your house to be there for when your dad and Ian arrived home from work. Sam turned up. He'd been at his girlfriend's house and spent the night in the shelter.'

Lily thought of the shock Dad and her brothers would get, and shook her head in sorrow.

She turned her attention to Jimmy, sitting up in the low bed, yawning and rubbing his eyes. 'Come on, son, I'll help you get dressed, then we'll find you some breakfast.'

——————

The school dining hall, with its high ceilings, was echoey and chilly and a babble of noise. Spoons clattered on dishes as young and old ate porridge daubed with treacle, and the smell, typical of these places, was as though years of cooking cabbage had seeped into the walls.

While Lily was eating, or attempting to eat, Harry and her other two brothers showed up. Moving up the bench, she made room for them all.

'How's Mam?' she asked Harry, as he sat down next to her.

'I haven't been to the hospital yet. I was there when Dad came home. Poor bloke got the shock of his life.'

'Me too,' Ian, next to Harry, bent forward and put in. 'Then Sam turned up, and Dad said we were to come and wait here so he'd know where to find us. Then he made off to the infirmary.'

The family spent an anxious morning waiting for Dad, who turned up at dinner time.

As they sat around the table eating indecipherable meat stew and mash, followed by prunes and custard, Lily spotted Dad, looking haggard, in the doorway. Cap in his hand, he looked around the hall and, when Lily waved, he came over.

Sitting on a wooden folding chair at the end of the table, he said without preamble, 'Your mam isn't injured, she's had a heart attack.' He gave them a moment for the words to sink in. 'The doctor reckons with her weak heart and having all you bairns it's a wonder she didn't have one before.'

Lily, straining to hear above the noisy chatter, asked, astonished, 'What weak heart?'

'Your mother had scarlet fever when she was little that affected her heart. She was advised to refrain from having children.'

'I was told she had asthma,' Harry put in.

'And me,' Lily verified.

'That's your mam for you. She doesn't like to worry folk.'

'Did you know, Dad?'

'Aye. She told me after yous lot were born.'

'How is she?' Jean asked.

Registering that Stanley was on her knee, Dad gave the bairn a faint smile. 'She's pulled through but needs complete rest, the doctor says.' He shook his head gloomily. 'The beds are full after the raid, so they've asked if I could bring her home where she'll be looked after by the panel doctor.' He shrugged. 'I told them I'd try and arrange something.'

Lily folded her arms. 'You're both to come to Foley Avenue and no arguing.'

Dad put on his determined face. 'I've been mulling things over. If I'm to keep Ida for a lot more years to come, things have to change. She needs an easier life.'

'Change in what way?' Sam looked around them all.

'Me and your mam have discussed this before but this time I'm going to make the decisions for what I think's right.' He looked at his youngest son, wolfing down mashed potatoes and gravy. 'Firstly, our Jimmy's to be evacuated.' There was a collective intake of breath around the table. 'It's for his own good. I'd never forgive meself if anything happened to him. Last night's raid was the worst we've known and proof it's not safe for him here any more.'

Lily's heart wrenched seeing Jimmy's opaque eyes widen with a startled look as he looked at Dad. Poor lamb, she thought; he knew enough to understand what being evacuated meant. Lily was about to protest but bit her lip because, in her heart of hearts, she knew what her dad said made perfect sense.

'I know a local billeting officer that finds homes for—' Jean started to say but Dad held up a hand of authority.

'No need. I've told you I've thought it through.' He looked around at them all. 'Your Aunty Prue in Jarrow has been in touch. She's renting a council house in a village in Lancashire with her two kiddies for the duration of the war.' He raised an eyebrow.

'Don't ask me how she managed such a thing but she was always one to wangle her own way, was our Prue. But she's a canny soul with a heart of gold and that's all that counts. She's family and will be happy to help out.' He looked around them all. 'I'd do the same if the shoe was on the other foot. Your Uncle Bobby's overseas and I reckon one more kiddie won't make much of a difference to Prue.' He heaved a sigh. 'Your mother's not going to approve but I'll tell her it's better than the alternative.'

There was silence as they all took in the seriousness of the situation.

Dad pulled himself up to his full height. 'Thanks, Lily, for your offer but I reckon it's time your mother and I have a place for just the two of us. As for you two' – he nodded at Ian and Sam – 'you're working lads and can fend for yourselves.' He addressed Lily again. 'You've got your own place and John to look after you.'

There it was again; her brothers could fend for themselves but she, being female, needed looking after. Lily knew Dad meant no offence because in his mind, like that of many a man before him, men were put on this earth to look after their womenfolk.

Dad looked around at their bemused faces. 'I've been talking to the WVS woman at the door and she says this here Rest Centre is only a stopgap for immediate care for families till they're moved on. But with all the recent bombings new accommodation is getting harder to find.'

Lily felt a shock wave strike her. It had just sunk in that their home, the place she was born and grew up in, was gone forever.

'You can stay with me until you're allocated another house,' she said, looking around the family. 'You all can.'

'Don't worry about us.' Jean gave a grateful smile. 'The rehousing officer reckons our place can be made habitable once the windows are replaced and the downstairs back wall's fixed.' She addressed Dad: 'If you don't want to move out of the area you can move in with us for a while. The council man said it won't be too long before the windows are put in.'

He looked at both Lily and Jean. 'Thanks, but I don't want Ida to be climbing stairs any more. Besides, there's no need.' His gaze extended to all the family. 'I'm going to see a fella about some accommodation to let before I visit your mam this afternoon.'

A wave of sadness washed over Lily as she realised the family unit as she knew it would be a thing of the past. And she was worried about Mam; the revelation her family was to be separated might be too much for her heart.

───────

Later, at tea time, when the family were all gathered around the table, a plate of cheese sandwiches and scones and jam in front of them, Dad explained, 'The fella I talked about at dinner time is Mr Briggs. He's me foreman at the docks and he let it be known that he has two downstairs rooms including a scullery to let. I went to see Briggsy and he showed me around. The accommodation looks champion for your mam and me.' He scratched his head. 'By, it must pay to be a foreman if you can afford a double-fronted house like that.' He gave a knowing expression. 'Or else, the conniving bugger married into money.'

Lily, rolling her eyes at his language, asked, 'What about a toilet and washing facilities?'

'Same as home. The lav's down the yard and you wash in the sink in the scullery. Briggsy's got a bathroom and flush toilet. Him and his wife prefer upstairs as they've got a lovely view over the sea and the twin piers.'

'Have you told Mam?'

'Aye, I did. But I don't know if she's in any fit state to take the news in. I haven't told her about Jimmy yet as that would be too much for her.' Dad's expression contorted into one of concern. 'She needs rest and building up.' He eyed Jean, then Lily. 'I'm grateful for both your offers but I think it's best me and Ida start as we mean to go on. It'll be grand for Ida living in the flat with no stairs to climb.'

Lily felt childishly upset that Dad was happy at the prospect of him and Mam being on their own without the family. She told herself to grow up and just be happy for them.

Sam spoke up. 'Ian and I have news.' All eyes swivelled to the two of them sitting next to each other. 'I've had a word with me girlfriend. Her mam says I can bunk up in the little front bedroom and she won't charge much rent.' He looked questioningly at Ian.

Ian appeared put on the spot. 'Me mate at work rents a two-bedroomed flat in Chichester Road. He's been looking for someone to share the rent. I went to see him this afternoon and said I was the man. It'll be swell having a room of me own.'

'You've been watching too many of those Yank films, lad,' Dad said gruffly, but as he looked around at them all Lily swore he had a tear in his eye. 'That's all settled then.'

Meanwhile in the dining hall an air of community spirit prevailed and families, glad to be alive and getting along, folk young and old, struck up a sing-song. The strains of 'Roll Out the Barrel' filled the room.

Lily smiled. Their homes might be wrecked and they had no place to live, but the British spirit overcame.

15

After Mam was discharged from the infirmary, she spent much of her time in her new bedroom in the house at Lawe Top. 'I feel listless all the time, our Lily, I think it's those pills I'm on.'

Lily looked after her while Dad was at work. It was a measure of how fragile Mam was that she didn't complain at being waited on.

When Lily first saw her parents' spacious and airy bedroom and living-cum-dining-room, she was pleasantly surprised. Both rooms had high ceilings, cornices, a picture rail and modern furnishings. The scullery was bigger than the one at home too, and Lily said so.

'I always managed with the scullery at home,' Mam retorted defensively. Sitting in a chair by the bed, her face clouded with misery at the thought of the home she'd lived in since the day she got wed.

'The place is champion, it'll do us fine, Ida.' Dad, just home from work, tried to chivvy her. He turned to Lily, handing Mam a cup of tea. 'Briggs said his wife would provide bed linen as he knew our situation, that we'd lost most of our possessions.' Dad's lips pursed into a thin line of disapproval. A proud man, it pained him to accept handouts from anyone, especially from the owner of the house who he could never call by his first name as the man was Dad's boss at work. 'I told him no. We were fixed up with such things.' Dad's face, set as solid as concrete, prevented any further discussion. 'Your mam and me will make do.'

'Good job, then, that I've brought bed linen from my spare bed at home.' Lily gave him a cheeky smile.

Handouts from family, she knew, were acceptable. The thought made her realise how resourceful Dad had been and how well he was looking after Mam in this hour of need.

Lily had the frustrating task of helping Dad replace the documents – identity cards and ration books – that had been ruined in the bombing. Very few of their clothes had survived and it was left to Lily to visit the WVS clothes depot and kit the family out. A lady in uniform gave Lily some bleached cotton flour bags.

'They've got many uses,' the woman told her, 'sheets, pillowcases, tablecloths, tea towels, even blouses and underclothing.'

Lily thanked her kindly, reflecting that the treadle sewing machine she'd found under the stairs in Foley Avenue would come in handy.

————

It was decided that Jimmy would live in with Lily until he evacuated. Apart from Mam not being fit enough to look after him, there was no second bedroom at the new flat – and Lily was glad of the company.

The day Jimmy left for Lancashire was as gloomy as Lily's mood. As they plodded along in the pouring rain to the train station – Jimmy wearing a jacket too big for him with sleeves that hung down past his knuckles and wellies that just fit, and Lily in a belted mackintosh – grey skies hung forlornly over rooftops.

Dad had to go to work that day and though Mam insisted she saw her son off, she was ready to see sense when Lily told her, 'Mam, you're in no fit state to be out on a cold rainy day. Besides, you're still weak and you'll get emotional.'

Mam had now come to terms with the idea that evacuation was the best and safest thing for her young son, but when the time came for him to leave, anything – be it certain music on the wireless, talking about the past, hearing about someone's misfortune – set her off weeping.

Her skinny neck flushing pink, Mam opened her mouth to argue, then she thought better of it.

'You're right, our Lily.' Mam's chin trembling, she tried to control her emotions. 'Me nervous constitution gets the better of us these days. I know I'll bawl when I see the bairn get on the train and, poor soul, he'll get upset and I don't want that.' As tears leaked from her eyes, she sniffed. 'I'll say me goodbyes here and keep a stiff upper lip.'

Lily took her young brother by the hand to meet the WVS woman who was going to escort him and two other evacuees to Lancashire. His eyes big as saucers in his ashen face, Jimmy watched on as Lily bent down to check the label that had his name and address on it, pinned to his woollen jacket.

'I don't want to leave home. Don't make me,' he implored.

'I know it's hard, Jimmy, and none of us want to see you go, but it's best you do. Those Jerry bombs will be back and we don't want you in the way of one of them, do we?'

His gaze lowered and he kicked the ground with the toe of his brown, lace-up shoes. 'I want to stay here with you and Mam,' he mumbled.

A lump rose in Lily's throat. 'I'd like nothing better.' In an over-bright voice, she told him, 'The war will be over soon and you'll be back in no time.'

Who was she kidding? Certainly not her young brother.

He gave a quivering breath. 'They don't want me.'

'Who don't?'

His shoulders slumped, he answered, 'Mammy and Daddy.'

'Whatever makes you think that?'

'There's no bedroom for me at their new place.' His chin trembled.

'Oh, pet, it's only till you come home again. I heard Daddy say that he's going to ask Mr Briggs if he can rent the spare downstairs room. You know, the one with all the books that looks like a lending library. He plans to make it your bedroom when you come back.'

'Honest to goodness?' Jimmy's expression was pitifully hopeful.

'They don't want to send you away any more than you want to go. It's because they both love you and want you to be safe.'

'We're ready when you are,' the WVS lady called rather impatiently as she stood by the open carriage doorway.

Lily stood upright. 'Aunty Prue will be there to meet you with her boys when you arrive at the station.' At his hesitation, she added, 'You'll have a great time. Aunty Prue says in her letter she has a big garden where the boys play footy and cricket and they can't wait for you to play with them.'

'Honest to goodness?'

Lily smiled. She didn't know where he'd picked up the phrase but it was Jimmy's favourite.

As they approached the train, the WVS lady held out her hand to Jimmy.

Lily told him, 'Honest to goodness.' She knelt and held him tight. 'Have a good time,' she said brightly as she wanted to keep the moment of parting as unemotional as possible. She kissed his smooth-skinned cheek. 'Make sure you let the other boys win at cricket sometimes,' she joked, as they both knew Jimmy, as the youngest lad in their street, was never in batting long.

Taking the WVS lady's hand, he boarded the train.

A whistle blew and the train, clanking to a start, picked up speed and chugged out of the station, snaking out of sight. The memory of Jimmy's solemn little face imprinted on her mind, haunting her, Lily departed the station.

Life's changing, she thought, as she made her way to Foley Avenue. Entering the house she'd finally begun to see as a haven of seclusion, now it appeared big and hollow. What she wouldn't give for her rumbustious former family life at Fawcett Street. *It is true you should be careful what you wish for.* John's face materialised in her mind's eye, and a sense of longing for him to be here overcame her. She couldn't wait for the day when he would be home for good, God willing, and the house would be filled with their love and laughter.

————

In November, Mam received a letter from Aunty Prue.

Mam, wearing spectacles, reported to Lily as she cleaned the inside of the living room windows, 'She says, after a shaky start, Jimmy's settling well.' Taking her spectacles off, she addressed Lily. 'D'you think Prue's just saying that to make me feel better?'

Lily had no idea but, seeing her mother's worried frown, she felt obliged to say not what she really thought, that Aunty Prue was possibly humouring her, but spoke words of comfort Mam wanted to hear.

Mam turned towards Dad. 'It isn't right, Arthur, you split the family like this. Families should stick together through thick and thin.' Her chin quivered. 'They're still me bairns and I miss them.'

Dad gruffly told her, 'They're all grown, Ida, and can look out for themselves. Besides, they know where we're at if they want anything.'

Lily told her now, 'I'm sure everything's fine. Jimmy's young and resilient. He'll be having a grand time in the country. Aunty Prue would tell you if she was concerned about Jimmy. Didn't she say when he didn't settle at first?'

Mam, wanting to be convinced, looked relieved. 'You're right.' A sheepish look crossed her face. 'Only, I want him to miss me a little bit.'

They both laughed.

————

The news of the war in December was that the Japanese had attacked Pearl Harbor, a US naval base near Honolulu, Hawaii. Lily, shocked at the invasion, had to confess geography was never her strong point and looked Hawaii up on the world map.

'Aye, Hitler's bitten off more than he can chew declaring war on the Americans and no mistake,' Dad gleefully retorted. 'Having the Yanks on the allies' side will do us a power of good.'

———

It was in January, when it was reported that the first influx of GIs had arrived in Britain to join the fight, that Lily was to think of Dad's words. And though the news America was joining the allies in the war was thrilling, it was the report on the home front Lily concentrated on. Parliament had passed a second National Service Act that decreed it was compulsory for unmarried women and childless widows aged between twenty and thirty to join the armed forces, work in a factory or work on the land.

More than ever, she wanted to do her bit to help the war effort. Lily thought long and hard. Her family home had gone, her parents were settled in a smaller place, Jimmy had been evacuated. It was time for Lily to take her life in her hands and do something towards the war effort.

So, on a cold wintry day, and before she changed her mind, Lily sought out the Red Cross at the local school, where she volunteered her services as an ambulance driver at night. She knew from the posters on billboards that women were wanted as ambulance drivers but she'd dismissed the idea because she couldn't drive. *Everyone has to learn sometime*, Lily reasoned, *so why can't I?*

An officer in charge – Mr Saunders – took her particulars, sitting at a table in the hall, and didn't baulk when she admitted she couldn't drive.

An older man with a friendly and easy manner, he had simply told her to follow him and led her to the school grounds, to a corrugated iron shelter where ambulances were kept.

'Madge, we've a new volunteer.' He called into the shelter, 'She can't drive. She'll be in your crew.' Without another word Mr Saunders made off.

Madge, middle-aged with short dark curly hair and a rosy complexion, in uniform with a Red Cross armband, watched him go.

When he was out of earshot, she turned to Lily. 'Poor soul, he hasn't got the gift of the gab but he's your man when there's a raid on.'

Lily, unsure whether she should reply or not, felt self-conscious. The only time she'd worked was at the Chi cinema and then she had been in the kiosk on her own.

She gave Madge a friendly smile. 'I'm Lily.'

Madge must have sensed her unease because her kindly face broke into a grin. 'Don't you worry, hinny, I'll keep you right. I'll have you driving in no time.'

Lily was on standby six at night until eight in the morning, reporting for duty if the siren wailed. Madge drove while Lily was her attendant. That first night, when Lily arrived, somewhat in trepidation, at the depot and with bombs dropping in the area, Madge hauled up to the driver's seat and indicated for Lily to climb in the ambulance.

'We go out now?' Lily asked.

Gunning the engine, Madge told her, 'When you're my attendant you do. Some drivers wait in the shelters until the raid's over but not me. I go out as soon as Jerry offloads his bombs.' Her eyes concentrated on the road, her expression steely. 'That's when we're needed to save folk, otherwise they die.'

As the ambulance rumbled over the cobbled roads, towards the red glow in the sky, Madge told her, 'Whatever happens, keep your nerve. There are people out there that need us.'

On Madge drove through the burning streets, while planes roared in the heavens and bombs screamed, followed by tremendous thuds as buildings toppled down. When the ambulance came to a halt, the strange thing was Lily, adrenalin surging through her veins, wasn't frightened, but more anxious to help those people who were in desperate need of transportation to medical attention.

Each shift had a first aid party of three who treated victims as they were pulled from the rubble. As instructed by Madge, Lily inspected the bodies lying beneath blankets on the pavement but thankfully there were no dead. Most of the early casualties were suffering from shrapnel wounds and, these being classed as minor injuries, they were transported back to the school where nurses waited.

The raiders now long gone, firefighters training their hoses on burning buildings, Lily climbed onto the ambulance ferrying the last of the injured to hospital. She walked down the centre of the ambulance, checking on the two casualties to make sure they would have a smooth ride.

As the ambulance crawled through the darkness, bell ringing, Madge's voice piped up. 'Well done, Lily. Except for one thing.' Lily heard a smile in the other woman's voice. 'Always remember to retrieve the blankets. They're like gold dust.'

Despite the slip-up, Lily's chest swelled with pride. She couldn't wait to get home and write to John, to tell him how her first shift had gone and how well she'd coped. Particularly, she thought, with the disagreeable task of cleaning the interior of the ambulance after they'd delivered the last of the causalities.

———

True to her word, Madge showed Lily the rudiments of driving and instructed her several times a week when they'd finished their shift, and hadn't been called out.

The first Monday before she set foot in the ambulance Madge told her, 'As the driver you'll have to check the tyres, radiator and battery each morning. But don't worry, you'll soon get the hang of it.'

Jumpy and nervous, Lily sat behind the wheel and the responsibility of driving such a heavy vehicle sent cold shivers down her spine. Remembering the thought that everyone has to learn, she bucked up and listened to Madge's instructions.

'We'll deal with stopping and starting first.' Madge spoke in a no-nonsense manner. 'That way you'll get used to working gears and pedals.'

After a shaky start, Lily, driving around the school yard, found stalling the engine the main problem. But after a week of practice, feeling more confident and encouraged by Madge, she was ready to take to the road.

Madge told her, 'Don't worry, this is a quiet area for traffic.'

Her brow wrinkled in concentration, Lily manoeuvred the lumbering vehicle – emblazoned with its identifiable red cross on the side – out of the school yard and into the narrow street. Surprisingly, she found the experience of driving along cobbled roads exhilarating. And when she drove the ambulance back into the yard, Lily was thrilled that she hadn't had a single driving hitch.

'You'll do.' Madge, climbing down from the ambulance, grinned. 'I only held my breath twice.'

So much for 'without a hitch', Lily thought.

———

Some weeks later, Lily was delighted when Madge declared, 'You're competent enough now to drive the ambulance yourself.'

With testing suspended now the war was on and examiners redeployed to traffic duties and supervision of fuel rationing, Lily was free to take to the road, and a feeling of accomplishment washed over her.

Lily's first attempt at the real thing, accompanied by Agnes, her attendant, was to drive the ambulance to the railway station one morning. After picking up injured soldiers, Lily drove the casualties to the town's Edgemoor General hospital. It was with a sense of accomplishment when her shift finished, she realised she was doing a man's job.

Her euphoria, however, was dashed when visiting her parents that morning after her shift finished to see if Mam needed anything from the corner shop. Mrs Briggs from upstairs met her at the doorway, informing Lily that Mam had been taken to hospital with another suspected heart attack.

16

DECEMBER 1942

As Christmas approached, Lily decided the festive season wouldn't, for her, be a time of great joy – as Christmas was the time when she missed John and Jimmy the most.

Dad insisted he and Mam have a quiet time as she'd never fully recovered her stamina after her heart attack. He told the family, 'Your mam won't be cooking and running after you lot this year.'

The heart attack had changed Mam. She now suffered from angina attacks, especially when she walked up the Lawe Top hill or if she got worried or upset. Though she would never admit it, the heart attack had shaken her and she was cautious where her health was concerned. Happy to stay in her home environment, she told Lily, 'I'm happy knitting socks and scarves for our boys on the front.'

Dad, too, was showing signs of his age and surprised everyone by giving up his allotment. The pair of them content in their world, they insisted Lily get on with her life and were immensely proud of the fact she drove ambulances. Lily realised she wasn't needed any more.

Jean kindly invited the family to her house for Christmas this year.

She told Lily, 'Ian and Sam and his lass are coming. It'll be grand to have you all at my house for a change.'

But Lily declined as, though she was usually delighted now to see her young nephew, she knew that seeing Stanley at Christmas would stir up painful 'if only's she would rather avoid. Besides, she didn't want to be there feeling alone, without John by her side.

So, Lily volunteered to be on duty over the festive period.

New Year, however, was spent at Harry and Jean's place with the family. Lily helped Jean lay the supper table, for when neighbours came first-footing.

'The food gets sparser every year with rationing.' Jean woefully eyed the spread on the table: sandwiches, cheese scones, jam tarts and currant buns. 'I've had to save coupons for this lot.'

Twelve o'clock sharp, Dad, being the eldest in the family, entered the front doorway, bringing in with him bread, coal and salt, representing prosperity for food, warmth and flavour in the new year.

Afterwards they gathered around Jean's piano for a sing-song. When she played 'There'll Always Be An England', Lily came over emotional and teary, probably caused by the sherry she'd drunk and the fact she was missing John terribly.

The celebrations were still going on at four o'clock in the morning when the menfolk, sitting around the fire in mellow mood, discussed war. They seemed to agree the new year looked brighter after the news report that the Second Battle of El Alamein marked a turning point in the North African front.

Dad raised his tot of whisky, quoting the prime minister's speech as he remembered it: 'This is not the end, not even the beginning of the end, but, possibly, the end of the beginning.'

Listening to these words made Lily even more determined to do her bit. In some way, she wanted to count in this war.

The day after New Year's Day, as Lily listened to the news on the wireless, her ears pricked up as the newscaster reported in his posh BBC voice that women could choose whether to enter the armed forces or work in farming or industry. Thousands of women, ninety per cent single and the remainder married, were, apparently, working in factories, on the land or in the armed forces. Prompted by the nation's need for more women in war work, and freed from caring for her mam now that Jean had agreed to help out more when Dad was at work, Lily planned to go to the labour exchange the very next morning and enlist, her preference being for working on the land.

It was now or never time and Lily, with no one at home needing her and John abroad, could at last follow her dream to do something with her life and do her bit for the country into the bargain. Driving an ambulance had given her a confidence boost, and she felt unafraid of the idea of leaving home and tackling new experiences. She couldn't wait to share all this with John in her next letter. She knew he'd encourage her because all the dear man wanted was for her to be fulfilled and happy.

That night, Lily was on duty when the ambulance service was called out. Dressed in her uniform and obligatory tin hat, she was relieved when, ambulance bell ringing out in the rainy night, she arrived at the scene, Agnes at her side, to find there was only one casualty. A poor old soul who'd been unlucky enough to trip in the dark when she went to the lav. A Mrs Binks from next door had called the ambulance out and had now returned home.

The old woman, Miss Purvis, was in great pain but didn't want to budge because she was worried about leaving her cat.

'Cats can take care of themselves,' Agnes told her, as she helped ready the stretcher to ferry the old woman to the ambulance.

'Mittens is all I have and she hates the rain – and who will feed her if I'm not here?'

Lily heard the despair in the old woman's tone.

'Where is Mittens's food?' she asked.

'In the scullery cupboard on the bottom shelf. Why?'

Lily didn't want the woman, who was ashen, further distressed and gave her a comforting smile. 'I'll ask Mrs Binks next door if she'll feed Mittens and take her in until you return home.'

'Why thank you, dear.'

Ten minutes later, Miss Purvis was placed on a stretcher and was taken to the infirmary with what Lily suspected was a broken hip.

———

The next day, Lily slept in. After a late breakfast of Weetabix, she dressed and made her way to the labour exchange.

Bundled up in a long grey woollen coat with lapels and square shoulders, headscarf tied firmly beneath her chin for warmth against the bitterly cold easterly wind (blowing straight from Siberia, as Dad would say), Lily hurried down Wawn Street and entered the building, making her way upstairs. As she passed the war recruitment posters on the wall, she studied them with a tense moment of indecision. She stared at a girl who stood in front of the British flag wearing a Woman's Auxiliary Corps uniform. Lily read the caption: 'Every Fit Woman Can Release a Fit Man'.

Lily frowned; she didn't want to be second best by releasing a man, she wanted to count in her own right.

Standing in the queue waiting to see the officious-looking recruiting officer behind the desk, Lily overheard the blonde-haired lass in front say to the overbearing woman, 'I've got me heart set on joining the Wrens.'

'You'll go where you're sent,' the stony-faced officer told her. 'You'll be drafted to the Women's Land Army.'

Visons of the poster Lily had just seen flashed in her mind's eye, of a smiling woman in the countryside, a pitchfork in her hand. The slogan read: 'For a happy, healthy job, join the Women's Land Army'.

The blonde-haired girl was saying, 'You mean, working with

cows and picking vegetables in the mud and catching rats?' The lass wrinkled her nose in disgust. 'Me mam's proud as Punch of us as I'm the only one in the family to have a grammar school education and she wants better things for me. She'll have a fit when I tell her.'

The official looked unmoved. 'You'll be joining the Women's Timber Corps.' Her stern tone suggested that there'd be no argument.

'I'll be working with trees?'

The officer nodded.

'I suppose that's better than being a Land Girl.'

Lily had heard of the WTC and the idea of working in forestry sounded both exciting and adventurous, but, more to the point, she'd be proving herself by doing a manual job.

When it was her turn to face the recruitment officer, Lily gave the woman a no-nonsense stare. 'I'd like to join the Women's Timber Corps, please.'

She was greeted with a grim nod of approval.

The woman opened a drawer of the desk she was sitting at and brought out a form. 'Fill this in and you will have to pass a physical test.' She handed over the form to Lily. 'Good luck being a Lumberjill.'

———

That night, the dishes, such as they were, done, Lily sat at the kitchen table, cup of tea in one hand, pen poised in the other as she composed a letter to John about what she'd accomplished today. A wistful sigh escaped her. There was no one to tell in person, to share her hopes and fears with about the future. It being Thursday, Mam would be at the WI meeting. Lily hardly saw her brothers as Sam, besotted with his girlfriend, spent the majority of the time with her and Ian was out with his mates whenever he got the time. Even Mam complained she hardly saw her sons these days.

The first flush of excitement at being accepted by the WTC

had been replaced by stomach-lurching terror, wondering if she'd made a rash decision and whether she would live to regret it. What did Lily know about the countryside or, for that matter, anything to do with tre— At that moment the front door knocker banged, echoing along the passageway.

Padding along to the lobby, Lily saw the outline of a tall, broad figure through the glass panel. A figure she recognised.

———

John banged the knocker again and, when Lily opened the front door, he saw her do a double take.

'John, is it really you?'

'No, my twin brother,' he joked.

'But I wasn't expecting you. It's such a wonderful surprise.'

A glow of happiness radiated through him.

Studying her, John thought she looked even thinner and she wore a careworn expression.

He came into the miniscule lobby and, closing the door, he bundled her in his arms. As she laid her head against his chest, John smelt the clean and familiar scent of the Lifebuoy soap she used.

Cuddling her close, he spoke over the top of her head. Euphoria that he was here, holding his beloved Lily in his arms, overcame him. 'I noticed the name plate on the gate.' His voice hoarse, he cleared his throat. 'But you've got me guessing. What does Olcote mean?'

Looking into her blue eyes he saw playfulness, and yet in their depths shone a need he understood as he too was aroused.

'It means "Our Little Corner of the Earth",' she told him.

'Perfect.' He made to kiss the crook of her neck, which always made her squeal because she maintained it tickled her, but Lily drew away.

'John, you should've sent a telegram. I'd have prepared a meal and—'

'There wasn't time. I only found out last night.' He tousled her hair. 'Tell me all about Christmas and your work driving ambulances.'

As she spoke, bringing him up to date since her last letter, Lily led him to the back of the house to the kitchen where a fire blazed in the warm and cosy room.

John sat on a chair, pulling her onto his knee, and Lily wrapped her arms around his neck.

'How long have we got?'

'Only a twenty-four-hour pass.' His expression became sombre and he felt her stiffen as if knowing what he was about to say would be difficult for them. 'I made the journey because I wanted to tell you in person. The rumour is, Lily, the battalion is being posted abroad.'

'Oh, John, I'd hoped you would stay on Home Forces in Devon, where it's relatively safe. Though deep down I knew this would come.' Her voice was shaky. 'But it's a shock.'

He saw the dread in her eyes but knew his wife was plucky and would never let fear for him show.

'So, we've only one night,' she said.

Hearing a tone of urgency in her voice, a warmth rushed through John as he anticipated what was to follow.

'How about you have something to eat?' The word 'first' hung in the air as she gave him that scandalous wanton look she kept for such an occasion.

He put his finger beneath her chin and lifted it so her eyes met his. 'Food is the last thing on my mind right now.'

She pulled away and stretched, a playfulness about her lips as she suggested, 'How about we have an early night?'

'I thought you'd never ask.'

'Then, how about we have a picnic?'

He grinned. 'You're a temptress, Lily Radley. What a splendid idea.'

Lily shuffled from his knee, and removing the folded woollen blanket from the back of a fireside chair, she placed it on the floor before the fire's dancing flames.

A shudder of delight rippled through him. Removing his great-coat, he flung it and his cap on the table. Taking her hand, John lowered himself down onto the rug, and Lily lay down beside him.

As they faced each other, John traced his little finger down her cheek. 'Is it permissible, Mrs Radley, for me to undress you?'

'Only if I can take your clothes off first.'

'Yes please.'

As she started to undo the buttons on his khaki trousers, she told him, 'You do realise this is only because I don't want you creasing your uniform.'

'I thought as much.'

He began to undo the top button of her blouse.

'John...'

'Yes?'

'Can we not prolong the agony any longer?'

He grinned. 'With pleasure.'

———

Later, Lily, wearing only a blouse, which, tantalisingly, showed off her knickers and long legs with muscled calves, appeared from the depths of the kitchen pantry and, moving like a gorgeous film star to where he still lounged on the blanket, she knelt beside him. In her hand she held a jar of homemade onion pickle (left probably by Mum) and a plate with slices of corned beef on it. Seeing the large crusty loaf Lily had brought from Pickering's the bakers, a precious ration of butter and homemade gooseberry jam (again Mum's contribution), John realised how starved he was.

Placing the pickle and plate on the blanket, her eyes held his. 'John, I was just about to write and tell you. I'd like to run something by you to see what you think.'

'I can't think. I'm still reminiscing and savouring the moment.'

He gave a cheeky grin but, seeing her serious expression and realising this was important, he quickly became sensible.

John found women complex and his wife was no exception, but delightfully so. He knew she had this inner struggle to prove herself, and that she tried not to allow her vulnerable side to show and in the main this worked, but not with John. For he too had learnt to hide frailties as it hadn't paid to let his father see. All John had ever wanted was for his father to be proud of him but, because of their different ideas of what success meant, that was never to be. John's natural instinct was to protect Lily but with her fiercely independent nature he had to tread carefully.

Lily handed him a plate. 'Here, make your own sandwiches. I would hate to think you'll end up like Dad. Mam made the mistake of catering to his every need, with the result he now has to ask how many sugars he takes in his tea.'

John knew she was stalling and, wondering what was afoot, his stomach clenched in an anxious knot. 'What is it you want my opinion on?'

She met his gaze. 'I should have talked this over or written to tell you first... I've joined the Women's Land Army... and I've been drafted to the timber section.'

'What!'

Lily's chin jutted defensively. 'I need to do something more towards the war effort than drive an ambulance. I'm fit and able and I can't... I'm not cut out to be content with domesticity, not while there's war on.'

Relief flooded through him that this was all her uneasiness was about. 'Lily, you don't have to ask my permission. You're old enough and wise enough to make your own decisions. I'm proud of you that you want to join the war effort. I've heard of women doing forestry work these days and if that's what you've decided I'm happy for you.' *Better than filling shells or enlisting in the forces where there's danger*, he thought, but had better sense than to voice it as he'd wound her stubborn pride.

Automatically she began buttering bread then, placing a slice of corned beef on it, smothered the sandwich with pickle.

'I know how Dad and Harry are about women working and they can't accept this war is changing things.'

'Lily, I'm not your dad or Harry.'

Absently handing him the sandwich, her eyes softened. 'I know that. It's one of the reasons I love you. You let me be me.'

'As if you'd allow anything else.' He shook his head in amusement. 'But Lily, I do think this will be good for you, to get away and do something new. I hate to think of you alone here without any company when I'm away so much of the time.'

She leant forward and, cupping his face with her hands, she gave him a long lingering kiss.

Placing the sandwich on the blanket, John forgot how starved he was.

17

FEBRUARY 1943

A whistle blew and the train, making a huffing noise, moved out of the station. Lily, watching through the window, waved vigorously at Mam's receding figure on the platform. Lily noticed how shrunken she looked these days.

Moments earlier they'd stood on the platform, and Lily could tell Mam was struggling to control her emotions.

As she hugged her mother close before boarding the train, Mam had whispered in her ear, a tremor in her voice, 'I think you're mad, our Lily, doing what you are. You can't run away and hide.' She'd pulled away, the whites of her eyes pink. 'Mind, you take care of yourself and come home safe and sound.'

Nothing could be further from the truth, Lily thought, as she stretched upwards to put the brown paper parcel and suitcase she carried on the luggage rack. She wasn't hiding herself in the depths of Scotland. She had come to terms with the two miscarriages she'd endured and the idea she might never have a family. See, she told herself, she could now think about her loss without becoming teary.

'Can you manage, miss?' asked a grey-haired gentleman in a

rather rumpled grey suit and trilby hat, as she struggled to shove the suitcase on the rack.

'Yes, thank you,' Lily answered. Giving the suitcase a final push, she then straightened the khaki wool overcoat she wore.

The compartment full, Lily stood in the doorway, cheeks burning, as she realised the other passengers were staring at her.

'Where you off to, hinny, wearing a uniform?' a scrawny woman asked. She had a toddler on her knee who was sucking orange juice from a banana-shaped bottle.

Beside the woman, a laddie, approximately Jimmy's age, and looking young and defenceless, cuddled into the side of his mam. The laddie wore round, wire spectacles, one of the lenses of which was white, obscuring the vision, and Lily knew it was to correct a lazy eye.

As she thought of her brother, too emotional to say much, Lily nodded and mumbled, 'I'm off to train.'

'What for, hinny?'

'I'm going to Scotland to join the Women's Timber Corps.'

The woman's brow creased in puzzlement. 'I've never heard of such a thing.'

The woman, looking Lily up and down, took in her uniform – three-quarter-length khaki coat, green beret, sturdy lace-up shoes and thick stockings reaching up to breeches below the knee.

Lily felt obliged to explain what the recruitment officer had told her. 'The timber section was once part of the Land Army then a new organisation was set up in April last year called the Women's Timber Corps.'

The trilby-hatted man, who'd clearly been listening in, looked over his newspaper and said with a smile, 'Nicknamed the Lumberjills.' He turned to the others. 'Due to ruddy Jerry sinking merchant ships that brought supplies, food and raw materials and suchlike, there's a shortage of timber.' He laid his paper on his knee and looked up as though he was just getting started. 'Plus, the fact foresters had left to join the forces, the workforce was depleted. The department for timber in the ministry of supply formed the

Women's Timber Corps to fell the trees and run forestry sites.' He raised his eyebrows, his stare travelling to each person in the compartment. 'Otherwise, where would we be without timber for pit props, telegraph poles, coffins' – he looked out of the window – 'yes, even railway sleepers.'

Everyone's gaze dropped in case they were expected to answer. Except Lily, who stood up straighter and puffed out her chest. After what she'd heard, she felt proud to be a Lumberjill.

The knowledge had dispelled the seed of doubt Dad had put in her mind when Lily told him that she'd enlisted in the WTC.

He'd rubbed his chin. 'I must admit, Lily, I find it difficult to accept, I mean, a woman doing hard manual labour. It just doesn't seem right.'

The woman next to Lily now finished giving the toddler a drink and pulled a derogatory face. 'I've never heard the like, lasses doing a man's job and working with trees.' She eyed Lily's breeches. 'Whatever's the world coming to when womenfolk wear trousers.'

The good thing about Geordies, Lily thought, was they were friendly and ready to chat at the drop of a hat; the bad was that some, like this woman, weren't shy of voicing their opinions. All Lily wanted was to pass the time of day with people and not have to tell her life story, but it was difficult staying detached without appearing rude. Though she did suspect the outspoken woman, besides being thick-skinned, had a big heart.

'You're homesick already, hinny, I can tell,' the woman said, confirming Lily's thinking. 'Here, take Henry's seat. I'll hitch up to make room.'

'Please don't bother,' Lily protested.

'Do as you're told, lassie.' The man with the trilby hat spoke with authority. 'It's never too soon for young lads to be taught manners.'

To save further rumpus, Lily sat down beside the woman. 'Thank you, Henry.' She smiled at the laddie, who clung to his mam's coattail.

Was this hollow feeling inside homesickness? Lily wondered. She thought of John, her family and home, and the mixture of longing and sadness inside intensified.

Then, Lily's natural instinct to persevere kicked in. She squared her shoulders and sat up straight. The days ahead, both terrifying and exciting, were what she wanted. To do something different with her life before she settled down.

———

Alighting from the train at Newcastle station, Lily stretched back her head and stared up at the wrought-iron ribs supporting the arched roof soaring overhead. The station, vast and airy, was a world of bustle and noise where throngs of people, including servicemen, milled around. Whistles pierced the air, while trains, billowing clouds of smoke and steam up to the rooftop, huffed and creaked into the station.

Asking a porter, who was pushing a trolley stacked high with suitcases, the way to her platform, Lily gave him a tip for his trouble (something Dad had informed her was the correct proce-dure). Weaving her way through the throng to platform three, Lily boarded the train bound for Edinburgh. Carriages packed, she looked for a seat. A soldier, broad and handsome, smoking a cigarette, who had a window seat, eyed her appraisingly.

'Here, miss, take my seat.'

He stood and, moving down the corridor, sat on his kitbag by the door.

Lily, sagging on the seat, put the suitcase and brown paper parcel containing the rest of her uniform on the floor by her feet – the luggage rack, she had noticed, was full. Taking off her shoulder bag, she rummaged inside and found the letter she'd received, along with the parcel containing her uniform, from the War Agri-cultural Committee in January.

Remember your ration book and identity card.

Lily checked that indeed they were in a pocket of her shoulder bag, then read yet again the letter.

I'm pleased to advise you've passed the physical test. It has been arranged for you to begin a month's training at Shandford Lodge camp in the district of Brechin in Angus arriving on Monday 1st February. Your nearest train station and travelling instructions are overleaf. Your starting wage will be forty-two shillings a week, board and lodging will be deducted. Ten pence deducted for Health and Pensions, one and a halfpenny for Unemployment Insurance contributions. Uniform will be sent to your home address.

On receipt of this notification, write without delay to the officer in charge at WTC, Shandford Lodge, Brechin, Scotland.

As the train snaked out of Newcastle station, a sense of nervous tension engulfed Lily. This was real.

———

The beginning of the journey took them through a dismal built-up area. Further up the track, the scene changed but, disappointingly, not to one of countryside views, which Lily had anticipated. Instead a grey sea fret now covered the landscape and nothing was visible. Laying her head back on the seat, she closed the curtain at the window and let the train's hypnotic chuffing sound wash over her.

She must have dozed because the next thing she knew she awoke to a male voice declaring, 'We're approaching Edinburgh.'

People started standing up and collecting their belongings and Lily did the same.

As the train approached the station, her neighbour, an elderly woman, spoke.

'Is this the first time you'll be visiting our bonny city?' She nodded to the suitcase Lily held in her hand.

Lily smiled. 'It is,' she told the woman, but didn't confess she'd be moving on.

'Then have a good time, hen, and I'm sure the visit won't be your last.'

Excitement mixed with trepidation choked Lily's throat. She was in Scotland.

The platform a heaving mass of folk, Lily was determined neither to be swept along by the crowd nor to panic. Her hands full of her belongings, she strained to listen to the woman announcer but couldn't make out a word she was saying.

Her heart beat a little faster as she glimpsed a lass with auburn hair wearing a Women's Timber Corps uniform walking further along the station. Hurrying through the crowds, Lily kept an eye on her, watching her pass through a gateway and walk onto a platform where a train waited. Lily ran the last few yards and caught up to the lass.

''Scuse me,' she called, and the girl turned and eyed Lily up and down. 'Are you off to—'

'Shandford Training WTC camp,' the girl finished. She hitched up the rucksack she carried on her back and grinned. Cocking her head to further along the platform, she remarked, 'We're not the only ones.'

Following her gaze, Lily saw groups of lasses all wearing WTC uniform, some ill-fitting.

'I'm Isabella Campbell.' The redhead heaved what appeared a long-suffering sigh, as they walked towards the other trainees. 'Go on, say it?'

'Say what?'

'You mean you don't know? "Isabella necessary on a bike."' She rolled her eyes. 'I get it all the time when people hear my name.'

'I've never heard that before.'

'Really? Then you're the first person I've met who hasn't. I go by Bella for short.'

'Lily Radley.' Lily introduced herself with a friendly smile.

Passengers started to board the train and automatically the pair of them did the same and, finding a compartment, they sat next to each other.

As the train started up and began to move, clouds of steam wafting past the window, Lily looked around the carriage where some WTC trainees were talking animatedly to one another, while others were sitting wooden and scared-looking. She knew just how they felt.

'And we're off to the unknown.' Bella spoke to no one in particular and Lily thought she spotted a look of doubt on her new friend's freckled face.

The train hurtled along the tracks like some spirited dragon puffing smoke out of a fiery mouth. Lily, looking out of the window, gasped as they crossed the stomach-dropping but impressive Firth of Forth bridge.

As the journey continued Bella, friendly and sociable, shared snippets of information.

'You're a Geordie? I can tell by the accent.'

'From South Shields,' Lily agreed.

'I live in Edinburgh.'

'You don't sound Scottish.'

'That's because I'm not. I was brought up in Lancashire and only moved here when I...' Bella swallowed hard, and, looking out of the window, she appeared downcast.

After a time, she seemed to collect herself and, turning towards Lily, the smile was back but a little forced.

Lily broke the awkward moment. 'You don't have a Lancashire accent either.'

'Not all of us say, "Hutch up, luv."'

They both laughed at the typical Lancashire saying.

'Seriously though, I worked in an upmarket hairdresser's and dropped the accent. How about you?'

What could Lily say but the truth? 'I've never had a proper job as Mam needed me at home. I've got four brothers,' Lily added so she didn't sound too much of a bore. 'Though, I did work as a cashier at the flicks for a time and recently I've been an ambulance driver.'

'I come from a big family too,' Bella chipped in, looking happier now they shared something in common. 'There's seven of us and I'm in the middle. My eldest sister brought us up. Mam worked in the mills as Dad was mostly out of work.' She shrugged as though that explained everything.

They were silent for a time and both of them gazed out of the window looking at the scenery hurtling past. Lily knew that the North Sea was over land to the right and she hoped that at the latter end of their journey she might get a glimpse.

'What service is your husband in?' Bella surprised her by asking. She nodded towards Lily's wedding ring.

After speaking to the recruitment officer at the labour exchange, Lily had decided she would wear the gold band. The officer had told her, 'There's only a certain percentage of married women in agriculture and forestry work.'

At first, Lily didn't want to appear different from the majority of lasses, then decided why the heck not. Besides, how awkward and improper it would be if she implied she wasn't married when she was.

'He's a soldier,' Lily said in answer to Bella.

'Did you meet him when you worked at the flicks?'

'Yes. How did you guess?'

'Because my eldest sister, the one I told you about who looked after us kids, she never got the chance to go anywhere or to meet anyone. So, I gathered things were the same for you.'

They lapsed into another silence. Lily's thoughts, straying to Mam fighting back the tears at the station when she left, caused her to say, 'It's difficult leaving home, isn't it? I bet your family misses you.'

Bella's face hardened. 'I suppose my brothers and sisters... but as far as Mam and Dad are concerned it's one less mouth to feed.'

Lily was shocked by the admission, but she also knew that being brutally honest was something else they had in common.

———

Lily emerged from Brechin station into freezing cold air. Glad of the uniform overcoat she wore, she stood by Bella's side, waiting for the rest of the trainees to join them.

A truck was parked at the kerbside and a short-statured but nevertheless robust man with greying hair, wearing an overcoat and sturdy black leather boots, emerged from the cab.

He made for the WTC trainees. 'I'm Mr Brodie, one of the instructors at Shandford Lodge.' And a man of few words, Lily sensed. 'Put your gear on the truck and make for the bus stop over the road. Morag the conductress will tell you when it's your stop.'

As the shivering trainees made for the truck, Mr Brodie added, 'Och, it'll take time for you townies to toughen up enough to deal with the raw Scottish weather.' He added, a twinkle in his eye, 'Folk around these parts go from blue to white before they get a tan.'

Bella told Lily as they made for the bus stop, 'At least he's got a sense of humour.'

'Yes, but my worry is the man's probably right.'

18

Arriving at Shandford Lodge, the trainees gathered around outside what Lily considered a palatial building.

'Shandford Lodge was originally a shooting lodge,' Mr Brodie told the trainees in a bored voice, as if he'd said this same speech many times before, 'but was requisitioned and now serves as a training camp for the duration of the war.'

'I didn't expect anything like this,' Lily told Bella, in a voice she thought was under her breath.

Mr Brodie must have overheard. 'Aye, lassie, and it's occupied by WTC staff. Trainees take their meals there and, apart from the odd talk in the dining room by staff, they never set foot in the place.' Again, a twinkle in his eye. 'No doubt you want to see your quarters. If you collect your gear, I'll take you.'

Leading the way, Mr Brodie took the trainees to a clearing in the spacious garden where they discovered army huts awaited them. Lily and Bella opted to stay together and found two vacant beds next to each other in hut number two. The hut consisted of two rows of army cots covered with coarse grey blankets, a cast-iron stove in the aisle, washing facilities and outdoor toilets.

As she dumped her suitcase on the bed, Bella declared, 'Why do I feel I'm in prison?'

The trainees all congregated at Shandford Lodge dining hall for a talk given by one of the WTC forewomen who introduced herself as Pat Finlayson. Looking around the earnest faces, Lily reckoned there were over sixty trainees. After the rules were explained they were told what was expected of a WTC trainee – chiefly that their behaviour should be exemplary so there'd be no cause for complaint from locals, and for good measure they'd be expected to attend church on Sundays.

After the talk a cup of Ovaltine was provided and Pat Finlayson told them, 'Training begins at first light in the morning and so I suggest you have a good night's kip.'

Making her way back to the hut, Lily discovered the stove had been lit.

'Fat lot of good that will do with all these icy blasts.' Bella collapsed on her bed.

After scurrying to get washed in cold water and bracing herself to get undressed in the freezing air, Lily opened the suitcase she'd placed on the bed. Rifling through the clothes for her nightdress and knee-length, thick woollen socks that she intended wearing at night, something pink caught her eye. Investigating, Lily gave a sharp intake of breath. Picking up the two tiny pairs of pink baby's bootees in her hand, she swallowed over a lump in her throat... Mam must have surreptitiously placed the keepsakes for Lily in her suitcase at the last minute.

———

As she lay in the bed in the dark later, Lily felt choked with emotions. A sudden longing for John overcame her and she fought the tears threatening to fall.

Bella's voice spoke out from the next bed. 'Huh! Lights out at ten o'clock and if the gates hadn't been taken away earlier in the war they'd be locked.'

'You mean to keep prowlers out,' a scared voice from further down the row of beds said.

Bella answered, 'No. To keep us lot in.'

Someone giggled – rather hysterically, Lily thought. For some reason, probably because it was better than giving in to crying, she joined in. Bella did too.

The cots, wooden frames with canvas tops, were as hard as nails and, staring into the darkness, Lily considered it was good to have made a friend to share a laugh with.

———

Then came the shock at six o'clock sharp the next morning when a whistle blew, startling Lily awake. 'What the—'

'Rise and shine,' came the cry outside from Pat Finlayson. 'It's time to toughen you townies up. You have to be physically fit to be working in the woods.'

Every morning before breakfast the trainees were subjected to a half-hour session of rigorous keep-fit. Then, after breakfast, they climbed aboard a lorry in the cold semi-light and were taken to the woods a mile and a half away, where Lily had another shock when Mr Brodie handed her a six-pound axe.

'Gather round,' he told the group of trainees. Mr Brodie, who had admitted he used to be a forester in his younger days, began to explain felling procedure. The trainees were shown felling and cross-cutting and the use of the bowman saw.

Around noon Lily, sitting with Bella and the others on logs, ate the grated carrot sandwich she'd been given in a bait tin in the dining room at breakfast time.

'You can boil water in the billycans on an open fire if you want to make tea,' Mr Brodie informed them.

The afternoon session proved much the same with a demonstration of loading logs onto tractors then trucks with the help of horses and chains.

At five o'clock a whistle blew and Mr Brodie's voice called out, 'Right, you lot. Home time. Follow the path and you won't get lost. Dinner will be served in an hour's time.'

'We're meant to walk home?' Sally, a young typist from York-shire, said incredulously.

'Apparently so,' Bella told her. 'And it'll be dark before we get there.'

Tired to the bone after such a long day, Lily couldn't feel her feet they were so cold. Crikey, this was just the first day and she was bushed, but there was no way she would admit any weakness on her part to the others.

She gave herself a shake and, as she headed for the uneven path in the woods, said, 'Let's get a move on. I don't want to be late. I'm starved.'

―――

Later, after a quick wash and brush-up, the trainees ready to make for the dining room, Sally piped up, 'I've got a blister on my ankle where my new boots rubbed and it's killing me.'

'You'll feel better once you've got some grub down you,' Audrey, a young brunette who looked as if she'd just left school, told her.

'No, I won't. Nobody cares about our wellbeing here and I wish I'd joined the forces now.' She looked around the others. 'We're treated like workhorses.'

'It's all to do with increasing our stamina and strength,' Audrey, combing her hair, said reasonably. 'We've taken on a man's job and I for one prefer to be treated and trained like one.' A spunky young lass after her own heart, Lily thought. 'By the way,' Audrey continued, 'I've heard it's best you don't mention where you live.'

'Why not?' Sally asked, round-eyed.

'Their reasoning is, the further away we are, the harder it is for us to hop off home if we get homesick.'

Lily knew this to be true as she had heard a lot of sniffing from beneath blankets last night after lights out.

―――

Lily was happy enough here, being outdoors in all weathers, riding around on a bicycle on her half day off, seeing the beautiful surrounding countryside, the soaring hills, the expectation each day of learning a new skill, and the empowering sense of being her own person. Most of all she enjoyed the camaraderie of the other trainees, especially Bella, who already felt like a firm friend.

Home seemed a lifetime away. Lily wondered if maybe Mam was right, she was running away from reality. Apart from John, who she pined for, she was content for the time being to be here at Shandford Lodge.

She had left her forwarding address with Mam, and on Monday after work a letter from John was delivered to her by the forewoman.

Sitting on her bed, Lily tore the envelope open. The slip of paper read:

> *Sweetheart, I'm sending this in a hurry. Don't worry if you don't hear from me in a while as the battalion being posted abroad is imminent. I'll write as soon as I can – in the meantime, take care of yourself, my darling. Your loving husband, John.*

Paralysed with fear whenever she thought of John in danger in a foreign land, Lily welcomed the hard physical work each day as it meant she was too tired at night to think.

As long as her family were safe and getting on with their lives, and John was safe and well, Lily was content with life as a Lumberjill. She told herself that when the day eventually arrived and the war was over, she would return home and settle down, and she would always have this great experience to think on.

The one thing Lily didn't join in with was the weekly dance, which was held eight miles away in Brechin on a Saturday night. Some lasses hopped off on bikes and spent the afternoon in Brechin before the dance.

'We had such a jolly time last week, you should join us,' Sally told Lily the next Saturday morning as she put iron curlers in her hair before going to work. 'A few of our gang went to the pictures in the afternoon, then out to tea, then to the dance.' She made a swoony face. 'There were heaps of dreamy servicemen there and we danced to the music of a Canadian forestry band – jitterbug, and ballroom dancing.'

Lily had no desire to mingle with dreamy servicemen, as she had one of her own, so she feigned being tired. Sally nodded in understanding, probably guessing the reason was because Lily was married.

The peculiar thing was that Bella, who appeared to be an otherwise outgoing lass, refrained from attending the dance too. On Saturday nights there were just the two of them sitting around the wood-burning stove, but Lily didn't enquire why Bella didn't go to the dance, because she assumed the subject might be too personal.

———

At the end of the second week the weather was cold and rainy. Lily and her gang were in a wood of Scots pine, and the trees' distinctive scaly orange-brown bark intrigued her. The gang were felling trees supervised by Mr Brodie's eagle eye.

Wearing an issued sou'wester and with the pitter-patter sound on the foliage all around, Lily swung the heavy axe, aiming for the bottom of the tree as no part could be wasted. She was partnered with Bella, and the pair of them started to saw the tree with a cross-cut saw on the thin trunk to finish the job. Her hands red and blistered, the bandage Lily was wearing for protection dislodged, but she refused to give in to the pain.

'Dinner time.' Bella, wiping her brow, made for the pile of logs and, picking up a rucksack, brought out her bait tin.

Lily, following, noticed how her friend was becoming muscular with all the manual labour. Sitting on the pile of logs, Lily breathed in the smell of damp foliage and fragrant pine needles, which always reminded her of Christmases at home when a real, albeit small, tree decorated with handmade wooden toys and candles at the end of each branch stood in front of the kitchen window.

She opened her bait tin and – always starved these days – she wolfed the cheese sandwich, then washed it down with cold tea from a lemonade bottle.

The rain had stopped now and the rest of the gang, sprawled on the logs, chattered amongst themselves.

Mr Brodie approached, wearing a sou'wester like the girls, and stood in front of Lily. 'A wee word, Radley.' Lily knew by his authoritative manner this was to be no light conversation. 'According to the form you filled in, lassie, you've driven ambulances.'

'Yes. Mostly at night for the Red Cross.'

Respect gleamed from Mr Brodie's hooded eyes. 'It's for that reason you're to be transferred to a camp on an estate down Hawick way.'

Lily's heart sank. 'I'd like to finish training here. Besides, I'm not qualified or officially enrolled in the WTC.'

'You've got two weeks' training left and next week would be spent in the sawmill, the final week learning driving a lorry and haulage. That's the thing why I've chosen you, lassie, because you can already drive.' He scratched his ear. 'As far as qualifying and enrolling's concerned, I'll sharp remedy that. It's my job.'

'Why do I have to go?'

He shrugged. 'A message arrived from head office informing us to send a driver to the Hawick neck of the woods because they're short. One of the drivers has developed appendicitis.' More ear pulling. 'I reckoned we should send you. If you can drive a wee ambulance, you can handle a lorry.'

'When do I have to leave?'

'Tomorrow morning.'

———

'I don't want us to be separated.' Bella pouted stubbornly.

The pair of them stood away from the gang who were now stripping pit props.

Lily knew she had to tread carefully. Even in the short time they'd become friends she'd learnt that Bella couldn't control her emotions when things got too much, and the way she dealt with things was to erupt, which she regretted later.

'It's because she's a redhead,' Mam would have said if she was here, but Lily had the feeling there was more to Bella's emotional flare-ups than that.

'I don't want that either, Bella, but we've no say in the matter.'

Bella put her hands on her hips. 'I'm going to have a word with Mr Brodie.'

'What about?'

'To see if we can stay together.'

'I'm disappointed too, but I don't want you to get in trouble because of it.'

A rebellious look crossed Bella's face, and Lily knew not to pursue the subject. She just hoped her friend would see sense and let the matter drop. She heaved a sigh; she was upset the pair of them were to be parted too.

———

That afternoon Mr Brodie gave them instruction on how to swing an axe with more force into hardwood.

'How you stand is vital,' he told the Lumberjills watching on, 'because if you miss-swing or the axe glances a blow off the wood you could end up with a nasty leg injury.'

He demonstrated the correct posture, his legs shoulder-width apart, knees bent, his feet firmly on the ground.

'See?' He glanced around at their observant faces.

The Lumberjills nodded and dispersed, some eager beavers to try it out for themselves. Lily, watching on, saw their faces growing red with the exertion, a grunt escaping their lips with each blow, and she became aware that in the otherwise eerie silence of the woods, the echoey chopping sound rang out.

She saw something out of the corner of her eye. Turning, she saw Bella approach Mr Brodie and begin talking.

Oh no!

Watching on, a knot of worry grew in Lily's stomach.

Mr Brodie was talking and Bella, her face appearing to darken, interrupted and she looked challenging.

Then Mr Brodie, with resolute shake of the head, turned on his heel and left her standing there.

Bella walked over to where Lily was standing, axe over her shoulder. 'Stupid man.'

'Why? What did he say?'

'"You'll go where you're sent, lassie."' Bella mimicked his deep, brisk tone. '"And only when you've completed your training and there'll be no arguing. And only if you qualify. It's me, remember, that decides."'

'That sounds threatening.'

'Exactly what I told him.'

'You didn't.' The knot grew bigger.

'I saw red. I mean, it's like we're at school. Worse. We're grown women for God's sake, with minds of our own. Some of us have... have...'

To Lily's horror Bella's face crumpled and, her chin quivering, she dropped the axe on the ground. Looking wildly around, Bella took off into the depths of the woods, paying no heed to the brambles and thorns surrounding the trees.

Lily retrieved her axe and stood up. She saw Mr Brodie leaning against a tree trunk, watching Bella as she disappeared into the distance.

Lily heaved a great sigh. She prayed Bella hadn't jeopardised her future in the WTC.

19

MARCH 1943

Next morning Lily's journey included a train ride back to Edinburgh, then onwards to St Boswells, which proved uneventful apart from the view of the country landscape covered in dazzling snow.

As she stepped from the train and onto the platform, Lily waved farewell to the young couple who she'd shared the journey with. The lad, his hair cropped to army regulation standard and wearing an army greatcoat, looked ridiculously young to be a soldier. The girl, equally as young, who wore a long brown swing coat and red beret complete with pom-pom that made Lily smile, carried a baby in her arms. For most of the journey the couple, wearing adoring smiles, only had eyes for their baby. Discreetly watching them, Lily's thoughts had strayed to John, imagining in her mind's eye his look of pride had this been their baby. As an ache of longing overcame her for the babies she'd lost, Lily dragged her eyes away and, for sanity's sake, concentrated on the snowy view speeding past outside the window.

The stationmaster checked the train and, waving to the driver, blew his whistle. As the train huffed its way out of the station and the steam lifted, Lily looked up and down the platform, noting in dismay that no one was waiting.

Feeling lost and forlorn standing there on her own, she wished Bella had been able to join her. The pair of them had said their goodbyes last night as Bella would be up and out early to work the next morning. They'd promised to keep in touch and Lily fervently hoped that would be the case. Though she'd only known Bella for a few weeks, she'd felt grateful for her friendship.

With nothing for it and, feeling unnerved in the isolated railway station, she passed the enticing waiting room with a fire burning merrily inside and made her way down the steps to the pavement. Standing in the biting cold wind, looking around, Lily observed the red sandstone buildings at the bottom of the hill. Then a horn hooted and she saw a truck advancing up the road.

As the truck slowed and pulled up beside Lily, she heaved a sigh of relief. A woman wearing a green jumper and enormous woollen muffler around her neck leant over and wound the window down.

'Throw your stuff in the back, Radley, and hop in.'

Before driving off, the woman turned to Lily. 'I'm Frances Patterson, by the way – Fran for short – forewoman at Teviot Hall estate.'

'Glad to make your acquaintance, I'm Lily.' Immediately the words were spoken Lily felt daft at being so formal.

Fran nodded. 'So, you've been sent to work driving lorries, Radley.' The lass, with cropped curly hair, apple-red cheeks and fresh complexion, didn't take her eyes off the road as she spoke.

'I've never driven one but Mr Brodie, an instructor at Shandford, assures me I'll manage.' Lily knew she was babbling, as the older woman's self-assured manner was unnerving.

In an attempt to overcome her nerves, especially about driving a lorry, Lily took comfort from Mr Brodie's words about her having driven an ambulance.

Then she sat upright. She didn't have to prove herself. She was a capable and proud Lumberjill eager to help her brothers in arms to win the war. She should act like one.

Fran gave Lily a sidelong glance as if she registered a difference in her demeanour. 'You'll do fine, Radley.' Lily, noticing the reassuring note in Fran's tone, reckoned her self-doubt had shown. 'Enid, the girl you're replacing, has had her appendix out and will be out of commission for some time.'

'Oh, dear, I hope she's better soon,' was all Lily could think to say.

Fran, still concentrating on the road, nodded. 'I expect you'll miss tree felling.'

Observing the forewoman's muscled arms and the cuts and blisters on her hands as she steered the wheel, Lily presumed the forewoman did a lot of felling trees herself. 'My aim was to have a go at heavier felling but unfortunately I didn't get the chance.'

'That's my favourite and I like to keep my hand in.' Fran's face split into a smile. 'I'm happiest out in the open air with a big oak tree. But' – she gave a rueful little smile – 'there's a mixture of sadness too. Poor old thing. Then I think of the trees we fell as railway sleepers or maybe sailing the seas in a ship and I don't feel so bad.'

Lily was taken aback; she would never have imagined Fran displaying such sentimentality. *It just goes to show*, she thought, *you should never judge a book by its cover.*

They continued the journey in amicable silence. Lily, gazing out of the window, saw more red stone-built houses shouldering against each other as if to keep upright, deadly-looking spiked icicles hanging from their guttering. Paths sparkled with icy diamonds; fields and distant hills were draped in a white blanket of snow.

As they sped through the frigid countryside, Lily's thoughts returned to Bella. It happened only occasionally in life, meeting someone and having a sense of connection, and belongingness. Beneath the tough exterior, Bella was vulnerable. Lily only hoped Bella hadn't vexed Mr Brodie and that he wouldn't send her

packing as, apart from loving being a Lumberjill and being mortified at failing the training, Bella would be returning to whatever it
was she was running away from.

———

Lily, sensing the truck slowing, gazed out of the windscreen and
saw they were approaching an impressively big stone-pillared
gateway that had been deprived of its gates.

'Teviot Hall estate,' Fran announced.

As the Bedford truck trundled along a long drive where tall
trees stood like sentinels either side of the path, making visibility of
the landscape impossible, excitement mingled with trepidation
enveloped Lily.

'Would you look at those trees.' Fran breathed a coming-home
kind of sigh as she gazed upon the trees. Lily wished she knew the
names of them but she was still learning and was too embarrassed
to ask.

Then the view opened out and Lily saw Teviot Hall, a huge,
spreading, grey-stone building, its roof covered by a layer of snow.
Two towers – one a clock tower – numerous chimney pots and two
rows of symmetrical windows could be seen each side of the main
structure. The arched, pillared entrance looked out over a terrace
of frozen grass onto lower-level grassy banks and, through the
distant trees, Lily spied a lake surrounded by snowy banks.

'Nearly there,' Fran said as she steered the vehicle along the
path at the back of the house. Looking past her out of the window,
Lily saw a vast snowy woodland covering the hillside.

Following the track into yet more woodland, the house now out
of sight apart from glimpses through the trees, they came to a
clearing where several army huts, made out of metal and shaped
into a half cylinder, stood.

Fran killed the engine and climbed out of the cab. Lily, following, felt the bite of cold air on her cheeks but the air smelt fresh and
wholesome.

Fran nodded to the huts. 'Your abode for the duration with washing facilities. The hut further up is the kitchen and for meals; further still is the recreational room. You're in hut one in Enid's bed. Get yourself settled in.' She checked her watch. 'The others won't be long.'

At that moment a woman in WTC uniform carrying a briefcase appeared from the far end of the nearest dormitory. Thin and willowy tall, with a harassed expression, she didn't acknowledge Lily, but made straight for the forewoman.

Lily noticed Fran stiffen.

'There's trouble in camp. *She*' – the woman nodded to Lily – 'won't be able to move into dormitory hut one.' She spoke with a refined voice but Lily picked up a trace of Scottish accent.

Casually, taking a packet of ten cigarettes from her breeches pocket, Fran put one in her mouth and lit it with a match. Exhaling a plume of smoke into the chilly late afternoon air, she asked, looking at the woman, 'What kind of trouble?'

The woman appeared to bristle. 'It's Nancy. She's moved herself out of dormitory two and into Enid's bed.'

'Because of—'

'I would have thought you would have picked up on what was going on.' The woman shook her head as though disgusted at Fran's neglect. 'Nancy says she doesn't want anything to do with Ethel and she won't suffer to be in the same dormitory with her, let alone the next-door bed.'

Fran took a long draw on her cigarette. 'You should've pulled rank.'

The woman's neck flushed pink. 'I've got better things to worry about. This lot for a start.' She held up the briefcase. 'I've told you before I won't take the matter any further. There's no evidence Ethel has broken any rules. She's a good worker and it stands to reason the pair of them talk when they both work in the stables.'

Lily, with no idea what they were talking about, wished they'd hurry up as her feet had turned to blocks of ice due to the frozen grass.

Fran sniffed as if in disagreement. 'You know fine well it's been said it's more than talk. The matter should be resolved so that Ethel can clear her name.'

'In my opinion it's waste of time.'

'Your opinion could be wrong.' Fran tossed the cigarette down on the grass and stubbed it out with the toe of her boot. Looking up, she told Lily, 'Sorry. It would seem you're in dormitory two now. I'll take you there.'

Lily wondered if the forewoman was sorry she'd witnessed this altercation or sorry she was now in hut two – but she wasn't about to ask.

As if realising her error in not introducing the pair of them, Fran went on, 'This is Muriel Fellows. WTC officer in charge.'

Miss Fellows gave a half-hearted smile. 'Welcome. We pride ourselves here at Teviot Hall estate at getting the work done. Our nation depends upon it. Follow the rules and you'll fit in fine.' With a cold look at Fran, she said briskly, 'Carry on, Patterson.'

With a nod of farewell to Lily, she started off towards Teviot Hall, careful of her footing on the icy path.

20

'Yours is the second last from the end.' Standing inside the entrance of the hut, Fran pointed to a bed. Seeing the window at the end, Lily was pleased she'd be close to daylight.

Fran folded her arms as though she meant business. 'Breakfast is at half six, then the lorry picks us up for work an hour later. We're collected at five and evening meal is at half six.' She spoke in the same bored tone Mr Brodie had used when the trainees arrived at Shandford Lodge. The thought made Lily a little homesick for the familiarity of the place, and especially for Bella.

'Curfew is at nine,' Fran went on, 'with tea and biscuits in the canteen, lights out at ten.'

'Does that include weekends too?' Lily wanted to know.

Fran frowned at the interruption. 'Late-night passes are provided for dances and suchlike on a Saturday night.' She unfolded her arms. 'Sandwiches and a drink for dinner are provided each morning by canteen staff. Mrs McGregor, otherwise known as Edie, is cook while Mr McGregor is head woodsman.' She took a deep breath, which ended up more of a beleaguered sigh. 'Any more questions, Radley?' Her penetrating glare said, *don't you dare.*

Lily had plenty, including: why had Nancy wanted to move

beds? And what rule was Ethel supposed to have broken and why would she want to clear her name? Though she longed to know the answers, Lily thought it wise to keep her counsel.

She shook her head.

Fran brightened in obvious relief. 'The thing is, Radley, since the WTC was formed, the women at Teviot Hall have worked hard to prove to villagers and menfolk alike we're capable of doing a physical job. There was much scepticism in the beginning and even now, so don't be surprised if you spot villagers taking a peek at us working when they're supposedly out for a walk in the woods. Some folks are still appalled at women doing a man's job, as they see it.' She raised her eyebrows. 'We must strive to keep on good terms with locals at all times.'

'I understand,' Lily said but in her head she baulked. She would treat folk as they treated her.

'Two other points: no fraternising with prisoners or conchies who work with us. And it would be wise to keep your distance from Canadian servicemen in the nearby camp, as some are just looking for a good time.' Fran glanced down at Lily's wedding ring. 'I suppose that won't apply to you, though.' As if relieved she had finally finished her introduction speech, Fran smiled. 'We're a friendly bunch in the main, Radley, and pleased to have you on board. If you want anything I'm over at Teviot Hall with the staff. Meanwhile, I suggest you go to the canteen and grab a cuppa.'

'I've forgotten the name of the cook, already.'

'Mrs McGregor, but everyone calls her Edie. Beware – she can be a tartar.' Fran opened the door. 'You'll get the hang of who does what once you've settled in.'

Then she was gone, leaving Lily to take in her new surroundings: the rows of cots, bedside locker tops filled with mementoes of home, photographs, trinkets. Lily's eyes travelled to the last bed, covered with a blanket made up of colourful squares. She wondered who her neighbour Ethel was and why she'd caused such a stir, but mostly Lily wanted to know why Nancy didn't want to have anything to do with her.

Weary with the early start and all the information buzzing around in her head, Lily placed her case on the floor and lay on the plank-like cot, closing her eyes but only for a minute or two, to rest them.

———

A door slammed, startling Lily. Rubbing her face to waken properly, she sat up. Three Lumberjills, talking amongst themselves, walked up the centre aisle. They made for their individual beds and began to strip out of their outer garments.

One of them made for a couple of beds along from Lily. Bundled in a three-quarter-length coat, baggy trousers, boots, scarf wrapped around both her neck and head, and woollen gloves, you could smell the cold air emanating from her.

As she unwound the scarf and glimpsed Lily, her eyes widened in surprise. 'Where's Nancy?'

'In hut one, according to Miss Fellows.'

The scarf unwound and Lily saw the girl's rosy-cheeked, open face and direct gaze.

'Ah! She's taken Enid's bed. I didn't believe she would.' Shrugging off her coat, she peeled off a green jumper, baggy work suit and woollen stockings and threw them on the floor. She looked up and the corners of her eyes crinkled as she smiled. 'And you are?'

'Lily Radley. I'm taking Enid's place.'

'Welcome aboard, Lily. I'm Vivian. The team's ganger.' This was said with a certain pride. 'Primarily, it's up to me to get the job done. I'm responsible for co-ordinating and supervising the work within my gang. If you've any queries, then just ask.' She wore an open and friendly expression. 'I'll introduce you to the others when everyone arrives. For now, though, I need to get out of these damp clothes.'

She undressed down to her undies and didn't seem the least embarrassed by the chin-high woolly vest and knee-length knickers she was wearing.

Seeing Lily's appalled gaze, she laughed. 'Special-issue undies. Don't ask. Suffice to say these undies come under "statutory requirement" and save us Lumberjills wasting precious coupons on everyday underwear.' A glint of jollity came into her eyes. 'Imagine the embarrassment at a dance when the skirt of your frock rides up. Talk about passion-killers.' Her giggle was infectious, and Lily couldn't help but join in. She liked this easy-going lass.

Dressed in a change of clothes, thick jumper and warm gaberdine trousers, Vivian padded over to where a gate-like clothes horse leant against the wall, and, placing it beside the stove, hung her damp clothes on it.

The other two women in the dormitory, now changed into dry clothes, sat on a bed, occasionally staring curiously at Lily, all the while carrying on their conversation.

Vivian came and sat on the edge of the bed facing Lily. 'It's been a long perishing cold day and I can't feel my feet yet.' She gave Lily that direct look. 'We miss Enid because she helps with the loading.'

Vivian stood and draped the blanket on the bed over her knees, then sat down again. 'Lucky you, being over twenty-one.'

Surprised at the statement, Lily was curious. 'Why?'

'Didn't you know? You've got to be over twenty-one in the WTC before you're taught how to drive lorries. That's what I intend to do next year. That is, if the war's still on.'

The thought of the war being over – when John would be home and they could get on with their lives – was a wonderful one.

'Where did you train?' Vivian wanted to know.

Lily told her about her time at Shandford Lodge. Questions, like bees searching for honey, buzzed in her mind and she felt comfortable enough to quiz the friendly Vivian – but she would start with the easiest one.

'Who owns Teviot Hall?'

'The laird, Sir Keith Henley. A kind old gent but don't let his age fool you, he's got all his marbles.' Vivian grinned. 'Sir Henley supports the WTC and does all he can to help the war effort.

Apparently like his family did in the Great War when Teviot Hall became a military hospital.' She smiled affectionately. 'He kindly allows us to take baths at the hall and we have a weekly rota going for the dormitories.'

'Is the laird's wife still alive?'

'No, Lady Jane died a few years back but there is a son, Fergus, who is posted abroad. Most of the employees, gardeners, woodsmen and household staff have been called up. The same with the estate workers – the farm is now run by Land Girls with the help of POWs.'

In the silence, Lily digested all this new information.

She then approached the next question. 'Who sleeps there?' She indicated with a nod to the end bed with the colourful knitted blanket on it. 'And why does Nancy refuse to be her neighbour?'

With a candid stare Vivian told her, 'It's Ethel Post's bed. Nancy is spreading a rumour that Ethel is fraternising with a German prisoner.'

The dormitory door burst open and a group of Lumberjills erupted in, in a hubbub of noise, bundled up in outdoor clothes.

'The tap's frozen again,' one of them called. 'Who'll volunteer to bring hot water from the kitchen to pour over the blasted thing?'

'Not me,' said a decisive voice. 'There's no way I'm getting washed in cold water tonight.'

'The sink's under a lean-to outside,' Vivian explained to Lily, 'and the cold-water tap's always freezing over in this weather. If it isn't your night for a bath at the hall you have to make do with a wash-down.'

Surely Vivian was kidding? 'Outside?' Lily asked. The firm nod of the head told Lily the lass was being serious.

'Some of us would rather smell,' a rather large Lumberjill removing a pair of wellies told Lily, her expression grim. 'By the way, I'm Joan.'

Vivian stood. 'Everyone, this is Lily.' She then went on to introduce each Lumberjill in turn to her.

'Where are you from?' Joan wanted to know.

'I'm a Geordie, from South Shields.'

'I thought I recognised the accent. Where did you work before joining up?'

A feeling of reserve came over Lily, as it had earlier on the train, and she felt reluctant to admit she'd lived a life of domesticity at home, helping her mam with a big family.

She told them, as it wasn't a lie, 'I worked in a cinema.'

'Oh, that sounds grand,' a brunette – Lily couldn't remember her name – declared. 'Going to the pictures is my favourite thing. I bet you got to see all the latest releases.' Lily refrained from correcting her. The brunette looked down at Lily's left hand. 'You're married. Has he been called up?'

'Yes. He's expecting to be post—'

'Inquisition over,' Vivian interrupted, holding up her hands.

The brunette looked peeved. 'I'm only being polite and showing interest.'

'It's usually me in trouble for asking too many questions.' Joan turned to Vivian. 'Which brings me to ask. Where's Nancy?'

'She's swapped into Enid's bed,' Vivian explained.

'Thank heavens. The atmosphere in here was getting more tense by the day. Nancy's likely to erupt at the least provocation.'

There was a united 'Hear, hear' as the Lumberjills stripped off wet clothes.

'To be fair, she's got good reason,' Joan told them. 'I mean, her twin brother is serving abroad and she's worried sick about him. Seeing Ethel Post consorting with the enemy doesn't help.'

'Is she sure there's something going on between Ethel and Karl, though?' the brunette piped up. 'We all know we're not supposed to speak to POWs but how can you not when you work in the same woods? Most of them manage a smattering of English.'

'There's talking and talking.' Joan's eyebrows shot up, suggestively.

'Personally, I find Jerry prisoners in the main polite and they have such good manners,' the brunette went on. Her eyes rolled provocatively. 'You can't deny some of them are smashing-looking.'

'Especially the tall blond I saw you giving a tab to yesterday.'

There was a communal intake of breath in horror.

'Don't tell me you haven't all done it,' the brunette, flushing pink, defended herself. 'They might get decent rations but some of them only have a crust of bread to eat at work. I've seen you sharing a sandwich with a POW, Joan.'

'The Jerry prisoner we're talking about,' Joan, neatly changing the subject, addressed Lily 'is called Karl Becker and is classed as a low-risk inmate, as are all the prisoners at the nearby camp.'

'Was he captured abroad?' Lily wanted to know. With John expecting to be posted abroad, the subject was close to her heart.

The brunette answered, 'Apparently he was captured when his Heinkel was shot down in a raid over Scotland and he bailed out.'

Joan took up the story. 'Mr Kinnaird, who runs the farm on the estate, vowed that "over his dead body" would he have a POW working on the farm. He's changed his tune since realising what hard workers most of them are. He requested permission from the War Agricultural Officer to employ prisoners on the farm.' She shrugged. 'Karl Becker proved to be familiar with working with horses and so Mr Kinnaird allowed him to bed down in the stables rather than trek back to the prison camp late at night.'

Lily was shocked. POWs free to spend the night on the estate. Whatever next? 'So, does Ethel work in the stables too?'

'Yes,' Joan told her. 'And there lies the problem. Muriel Fellows insists since Ethel and the POW both work with the horses it's only natural they communicate and are seen together. So, she won't take the matter any further.'

The brunette put in, her face scandalised, 'Nancy swears she saw Ethel with him after work at night. It makes you think, I mean what—'

'What I think' – Vivian stood up and looked around the dormitory – 'is we should stop speculating. As it says in this month's edition of *The Land Girl*: "The more trees we cut down in our woods, the more ships are freed to carry men and munitions of war."' She put her hands on her hips. 'Our job is to follow orders and leave the running of the camp to Muriel Fellows and Fran.'

Lily thought this a rather pompous statement, but she supposed it was Vivian's job to keep everyone focused.

'Nancy's eruptions have nothing on those two.' Joan shook her head. 'If one says "chalk" the other says "cheese".'

As everyone murmured in agreement, the mood of suspicion changed and Lily took what had just been said to be a common irritation.

'We all have our clashes, especially in these times of uncertainty when nervous dispositions can run out of control.' Vivian, apparently peacemaker too, spoke in a manner of tolerance. 'Prisoners are the enemy but they're someone's husband or brother too and serving abroad. Wouldn't we want our boys, if captured, to be treated decently? That's what the families of the POWs here would—'

At that moment the door opened. A young girl entered. She looked around and, with everyone staring at her, head down, she walked stealthily down the aisle to the end bed next to Lily's.

21

Swearing didn't come naturally to Lily, but in the cold weather the ancient haulage truck wouldn't start and she shrieked without thought, 'Bloody stupid engine, why now?'

Cold, exhausted and hungry, she still had one more run to the station to meet the quota of timber for the day.

She gave the truck's nearest wheel a kick and said, to no one in particular, 'I've checked and checked and can't find anything.'

Over the last two weeks it had been up to Lily to teach herself the basics of maintaining a truck as here, in the depth of the forest, there was no one else to fix the blasted thing if it broke down.

'Give it another go,' Joan, standing beside the pile of timber, shouted wearily.

Cross, Lily answered, 'Don't keep saying that.'

'What else can we do?' Joan replied shortly.

'Losing your temper won't help,' the brunette Lily now knew to be Violet said through gritted teeth.

Not trusting herself to speak, Lily climbed into the cabin and gunned the engine. Mercifully, it spluttered into life.

'Keep the engine running,' Joan yelled. 'Back up and we'll load the last of the timber.'

Taking hold of the stick, Lily changed gear and backed up to where the two women were standing. They started hauling timber by the one, two, three method onto the back of the truck.

Her foot on the pedal, ankles aching, she didn't dare move.

'We're fully loaded,' Joan called at last. 'I'll keep Violet company on top.'

Lily didn't envy the terrifying ride the pair of them would have in the open on top of the flatbed with timber beneath. It was forbidden of course but everyone did it. She would feel for the lasses every time she drove over a bump.

Her foot stiff, Lily moved the stick and changed gear, and for a heart-stopping moment the engine made a horrible grinding noise, then, revving up, moved forward. They were off. Travelling over the rutted and uneven forest track, she heard the two Lumberjills on top singing, 'Don't Dilly Dally on the Way'.

They're tired and keeping their spirits up, she thought. Regretting her earlier outburst, Lily would apologise to the two of them after they finished for the day. The truck being difficult to manoeuvre on such treacherous tracks, she gave her full concentration to the job in hand.

―――

Driving into the station yard, Lily steered the truck onto the weighing bridge. She told the railway clerk how heavy the truck was when empty, so he could compare with the weight now. The procedure done, the three of them lugged the heavy timber from the back of the truck and threw it onto the railway wagon.

'Blimey.' Joan mopped her brow with a hand. 'No wonder we've got muscles to match lumberjacks.' She climbed into the back of the empty truck, collapsing on the floor.

Violet, hauling up beside her, exclaimed, 'The worry is we might keep them forever.'

Tired to the bone, and as mucky as if she'd worked down a coal mine, Joan gave a satisfied grin. 'Another day over, girls, and a job well done.'

Climbing wearily into the cab, and taking her keys out of a trouser pocket, Lily held her breath as she gunned the engine. Thankfully, it behaved and started up first time.

As she drove back to Teviot Hall, Lily allowed her thoughts to drift and wondered if today would be the day she'd receive a longed-for letter from John.

———

Later, after the evening meal, when most of the Lumberjills had already made off to the recreational hall, Lily lay on the bed relaxing, talking to Joan, who was getting things ready to take a bath at the hall.

'It is Ethel who's in the bath now, isn't it?' Lily asked.

Joan nodded. 'Yes. I reminded her to leave the water in.' The Lumberjills conserved water by sharing the bathwater. 'And I've told her not to be too long. I don't want a bath in cold water.'

Lily had a motive for not joining the others yet in the recreational hut. She'd never had the time or chance – with Ethel always present in the next bed – to ask Joan any more about the discussion they'd had about POWs on that first night.

She seized the opportunity now. Placing the book she'd been reading on the bed, she sat up and faced Joan.

'You know that commotion about the POW from the camp...'

Joan, taking a towel from her locker, looked up, with a somewhat wary expression. 'Yes.'

'Are the locals aware he's bunking down in the stables and do they not object?'

An open book, Joan blabbed, 'I would think so. And not so much now. Most of the prisoners are Italian and Germans—'

'Have they been there long?' Lily knew nothing about POWs.

Joan continued. 'To start with most prisoners were shipped off to Canada and there were only a couple of camps with few Jerrys in Britain.' She plonked down on her bed. 'It wasn't until the

North African campaign when Italians were captured that Britain had a bigger influx of prisoners to encampments.'

'Gosh, Joan, you're a walking encyclopaedia.'

Joan shrugged. 'No. Just nosey and I ask lots of questions.' Her expression became serious. 'Originally the POWs in the camp here were taken everywhere by guard but, as folk got to know them individually, realising that prisoners are human beings too, and missing home life and family, the hostilities towards them eased off.' Moving closer, she told Lily in a low voice, 'Though Lumberjills aren't officially supposed to communicate' – she winked knowingly – 'human nature being what it is, you can imagine.'

'Are other Lumberjills fraternising too?'

Joan looked over her shoulder to check no one was listening. 'There's rumours.'

'How do they meet up?'

'Apparently, there's no regimental police patrolling the no-go inside perimeter of the compound, and it's been known for prisoners to escape through the barbed-wire fence at night.'

'This Karl doesn't need to do that?' Lily thought for a moment. 'Did Nancy say what time Ethel and the prisoner met up?'

Joan shrugged. 'Search me. All I know is she reported it to Fran, who was duty-bound to report the matter to Muriel Fellows.'

'And I gather they have different views.'

Joan heaved her shoulders. 'They always have. Don't get me wrong,' she quickly put in, 'they're both tops in their own way and great at their job but' – she rolled her eyes – 'they rub each other up the wrong way.'

'Why's that, d'you think?'

'I don't think. That's why I've never been promoted to ganger like Vivian. I'm content to keep my head down. But between you and me, Nancy's got it in for the POW, or any Jerry for that matter, because of her brother and all.' She shook her head. 'Who can blame her. We're at war with Jerry, after all.'

Lily, reminded of the ganger's speech, responded, 'As Vivian suggested, we're just the little people, with both sides following orders.'

A look of irritation crossed Joan's good-natured face. 'While I do think Vivian is smashing, she is sometimes too tolerant for her own good.'

So, that's the way of it, Lily thought. The conversation had given her an insight of what Lumberjills thought and, with feelings running high, presumably they'd take sides.

Lily made up her mind that until she knew the full facts of the matter, she'd stay neutral.

The hut door opened and Fran appeared, the mail basket in her hand. Lily, who had been in touch with John and Mam by letter informing them of her change of address, felt a rush of anticipation surge through her.

Fran handed Lily a letter. Lily's hopes were dashed, however, when she saw Mam's small and neat handwriting on the envelope.

Sitting on the edge of her bed, she read the letter, which mostly consisted of family news.

But Lily stiffened when she read:

You'll never guess!! Jean's expecting again. Your dad reckons it's all these boring blackout nights when the only thing for it is an early night. It'll be lovely for Stanley to be a big brother. It'll do him good because the lad's getting spoilt. He's just the right age for another kiddie to come along. Course we're all hoping for a girl this time.

I know this is difficult for you to read, our Lily, but your time will come, I'm sure of it. We're all fine though your dad's chest has been bad again. Jimmy's doing well at school and you should see the lovely picture he's drawn of where he lives.

Lily was surprised by the strength of her reaction to the news of Jean being pregnant, and must have been showing how she felt without realising as Joan's voice broke into her thoughts.

'Chin up, it might never happen.'

Lily sat up straighter and Joan, towel over her arm, looked at the letter in her hand. Her expression concerned, she asked, 'You look down. Anything wrong? Is that a letter from home?'

'Yes.'

'Ahh! A touch of homesickness. It happens.'

Lily didn't tell her the real reason for her downcast expression and was happy to let the matter pass.

'Look, how about we swap bath nights? A soak will cheer you up.' Joan laughed. 'Bearing in mind you're only allowed five inches of water, calling it a soak is pushing it, rather.'

Even so, a bath was the biggest luxury for the Lumberjills, and Lily was touched by the offer. 'That's very kind of you, Joan, but no thanks. I'll only laze in the bath and think.'

At this moment that was something she wanted to avoid.

Joan gave a puzzled shrug. 'If you're sure.'

Joan left and Lily picked up her book and attempted to distract herself by reading. Shortly afterwards, Ethel arrived in the hut, a towel wrapped around her head. Walking down the aisle, she kept her eyes averted from the few Lumberjills who were still there and headed for her bed. The women in their hut, though civil, avoided Ethel and she didn't help matters by appearing aloof. Lily had only spoken a few words to her and even then they'd been just formalities.

Lily peered over the top of the book. With her honey-blonde hair, arched eyebrows, pert nose and ridiculously high cheekbones, the lass seemed totally oblivious to her amazing figure and was wearing baggy trousers and a jumper that looked a size too big for her. She was just a kid, Lily thought, seventeen or so, she estimated. What on earth was she doing getting involved with a prisoner?

Knees bent and sitting up on the bed, Lily tried to concentrate on her book but to no avail because Jean being pregnant loomed large in her mind, bringing unwanted thoughts.

Lily could never understand how people could say they pushed a problem to the back of their minds, as she never could.

Determined to rise above her gloomy thinking, she babbled to the young girl drying her hair, 'Did you have a good bath?'

A daft thing to say and no wonder Ethel seemed startled. The girl appeared nervous like a skittish bird ready to take flight.

'Yes thanks. The room's perishing, though, with no heating.'

She spoke with a trace of a Geordie accent and Lily had kept meaning to ask which part of the north she came from, but with Ethel's reserve she feared rebuff.

Sitting on the bed, towel-drying her hair, Ethel appeared particularly lost and forlorn and Lily took pity on her and tried another tack. 'Friday night is usually practising for tomorrow's dance in the recreational room. Why don't you come along?'

'I don't go to no dances.' Her tone was flat.

'Neither do I, but watching the others practise is fun. There's always a game of something afterwards. Usually cards.'

'I can't play cards.'

You can learn, Lily's frustrated mind said. But, to be fair, meeting up with the rest of the Lumberjills might be an ordeal for the young lass.

'Some of us are content just to sit around the stove with needles clicking and have a natter.'

Ethel appeared to shrink. 'No thank you, I'm going to have an early night.' She picked up a book from her bedside cabinet and began to read.

Like always, Lily thought. Ethel, with head under the covers, was asleep (or pretending to be) most nights when Lily retired. *I've tried*, Lily told herself, *but I can't help her if she won't try to be sociable.*

The hut door opened and, seeing the figure who stood there, Lily gasped in surprise. For there stood her good friend, Bella Campbell.

22

'How did you manage to wind up here?' Lily couldn't believe that Bella was actually here at Teviot Hall.

The dormitory hut was almost empty as everyone, apart from Ethel, had made for the recreation room. Bella and Lily embraced then sat on two chairs around the stove.

Bella grinned. 'Mr Brodie has a heart after all. He kindly allocated me to be here with you.'

Lily's face must have looked surprised because Bella coloured. 'It was only a little white lie, honest. You must admit it was worthwhile if it meant we could be together.'

'Why? What did you say?'

'When Mr Brodie was doing the allocations, he asked if any of us had any background working with horses, as Teviot Hall camp were short of a stablehand.' Her expression changed to one of shame. 'You have to realise I was desperate and so I told him I had.'

Lily was taken aback. She wondered why the estate wanted a new stablehand. Had something been done about Karl?

She asked Bella, 'Have you really got any experience with horses?'

'I once sat on the milkman's cart when he was delivering milk in our street. I was allowed to stroke the horse afterwards; I count that as a bit of grooming. I've fed carrots to horses and I've had a ride on a donkey at the beach.' Bella, recounting her supposed equestrian skills, didn't bat an eyelid.

'What if you're found out?'

Bella shrugged. 'Looking after horses can't be that hard, can it?'

Lily shook her head; Bella was incorrigible.

'Besides,' Bella went on, 'I know a certain person, not a million miles away, who doesn't let anything stand in her way when she wants something.' As Lily pondered if this had any truth, Bella went on, 'Go on, admit you're tickled pink to see me.'

A smile tweaked the corners of Lily's lips. She nodded.

She glanced over at Ethel, who supposedly was reading *The Land Girl*, but her look of guilt as their eyes met proved the lass had been listening in to the conversation.

Bella followed Lily's gaze and common courtesy made Lily say, 'Bella, this is Ethel Post, who you'll be working with.' She saw Ethel blanch.

'Pleased to meet you.' Bella gave a friendly smile. 'Is there any chance of you swapping beds with me? I'm in hut one.'

'No,' Lily quickly put in to save Ethel embarrassment. 'We've... become friends,' she blurted. Then seeing the hurt look on Bella's face, she cursed herself for being so thoughtless.

As Bella made for the door, Lily realised how badly she'd handled the situation. She had refused Bella's request to swap huts because she knew Ethel would struggle to share a hut with Nancy. But by interfering, Lily had upset Bella.

———

Lily suggested they go up to the recreation hut before retiring to their different huts and Bella agreed, albeit half-heartedly. Lily hoped her friend didn't hold it against her that she appeared to want to stay next to Ethel. But Bella wasn't the sulky type and would soon come round, especially after Lily explained the tricky situation.

Leaving Ethel to her own devices, the pair of them, a torch in Lily's hand to guide them, made their way in the dark and silent night to the recreation hut where Lily intended to introduce Bella to the other Lumberjills.

On the way she said, 'You were awfully late arriving.'

'Mr Brodie insisted I do a morning shift before I left, then I missed my train connection.' All this was said in flat voice and Lily worried that Bella was miffed but, when her friend yawned, she realised it might be that she was tired after a long day.

'Ta-da.' Lily opened the door of the recreational hut and they both hurried in.

Bella's disbelieving eyes travelled the room, taking in the comfy but saggy chairs, green inlaid card tables, wooden table with a wind-up gramophone player and pile of 78 rpm records, table tennis table and a black stove where logs were burning merrily at the far end of the room.

'Who provided all this?'

'The laird, apparently. For the use of us Lumberjills.'

They found two vacant seats next to each other beside a gang of girls from dormitory two. Lily did the introductions and everyone was interested in Bella's history. Though she appeared happy enough to share parts of her life in Edinburgh and talked about working as a hairdresser, she kept mum about her home life, reinforcing Lily's belief that she was hiding something about her family.

The conversation changed to the locals' reactions to Lumber-jills. Sheila, an intelligent blonde, exclaimed, 'Honestly, we can't win. We're either treated by men with disdain for attempting to do a man's job, as they see it, or mistrusted by their wives who think us common because of what we do and the way we dress, and they imagine we're out to steal their menfolk.'

Lily laughed. 'It's a hard life,' she agreed, 'but I wouldn't swap it.'

As the night wore on the room became a hubbub of noise. Cigarette smoke fogged the air and, looking around at the lasses –

some sitting with a leg cocked over a chair arm in an unladylike fashion, one even sucking on a pipe – made Lily smile. No wonder the local wives were outraged.

Then came the dancing. Sheila was coaxed into demonstrating the jitterbug.

'I met up with a GI at my last billet and he taught me how. Come on, Bella, be my partner and I'll show you.'

Bella didn't make a move and, looking rather glum, shook her head.

Sheila went on, 'You must come to the dances. They're held every Saturday at the village hall. You'll have a jolly time, won't she, everyone?' She looked around the table for verification, then went on, 'These flings are on till late but there's a Canadian Forestry Unit nearby that give us WTC girls lifts on the back of their lorry. Some of those lumberjacks are real lookers, aren't they, girls?'

An uneasy look crossed Bella's face, and yet again Lily wondered at this sudden change in her friend.

'I'll sit here and watch and learn.' Though her smile was convivial, Bella's manner was oddly stand-offish.

'I'll keep you company,' Lily told her.

Sheila put a record on and, winding up the gramophone, soon Benny Goodman and His Orchestra's 'Peckin'' blared into the room.

As Lily watched couples dancing the rather hectic jitterbugging, she inwardly smiled, because, as an old married woman, the more dignified waltz and foxtrot were now more her style.

———

Later, the dancing finished and the mood convivial, folk were content to sit and natter around the warm and enticing heat blasting from the stove.

Gradually, one by one, they said their goodnights and retired to bed, until there were only six of them left, Bella and Lily amongst them. No one wanted to face a cold dormitory, especially the bed, as the last log would have burnt away by now and the temperature in the hut quickly dropped to a perishing cold.

'How about a go on the Ouija board? It's easy enough to make one,' Nancy said, looking around the group.

'No fear. Not me.' Jill looked horrified. 'Mum's family are spiritualists and she warned me never to go near a board; she's convinced they're dangerous.'

'Oh, why did you have to say that?' Violet's eyes gleamed with eagerness. 'Common sense tells me to leave it alone, but another part of me that wants a scary thrill is egging me on.' She shivered. 'Who's in?'

The gramophone and records were removed from the table and placed on the floor. Nancy wrote letters of the alphabet and 'yes' and 'no' in pencil on a jotter. Cutting them out, she placed the pieces of paper around the outer part of the table. Sheila produced a drinking glass and turned it upside down in the centre of the table.

'Put all the lamps out,' Nancy insisted, 'except the nearest one so we can see by. It'll be more atmospheric.'

As they sat around the table in the darkened room, their shadowy faces looking spooky, a cold shiver ran up Lily's spine. She had a premonition no good would come of this.

'What now?' someone in the shadows asked.

'Everyone put a finger on the glass, but lightly, mind,' Nancy instructed, 'and no pushing it.'

'As I said, count me out.' Jill's voice was hushed as though some being was listening in.

'Me too,' came Bella's voice. 'I'm pooped, but I'll stay and watch.'

'Everyone else ready?' Nancy said.

Four forefingers touched the base of the glass. For a few seconds nothing happened then, eerily, the glass started to move towards a piece of paper.

'B...' Nancy's lowered voice spoke. 'And E.'

Each time the glass moved Nancy spelt out a letter. W. A. R. E. Then the glass careered round and round the table.

'See, this is what happens when you press too hard,' Nancy complained.

'I'm not,' Violet protested.

Everyone insisted they weren't either.

The glass stopped suddenly.

Sheila's hushed voice spoke. 'Is this message for someone in this room?'

The glass began to move and glide over the table, making a scraping noise. It stopped at the piece of paper with 'yes' written on it.

Then moving again, the glass picked up speed.

'B,' Nancy spelt out and they all joined in chorusing the next letters, 'A. B. Y.'

'Beware baby,' Violet exclaimed.

A cold tingle started between Lily's shoulder blades and shivered over the top of her head.

She knew the message was for her.

———

The next day, Lily was tired and grumpy. All night long she'd lain awake and could think of nothing but the message on the Ouija board.

Fran collared her early morning before Lily left for work. 'You and the gang will be working on tractors in the forest today, Radley.'

Lumberjills at Teviot Hall were expected to work Saturdays but permission, according to Joan, was granted to those who lived nearby to go home for the weekend occasionally – not that Lily knew of anyone taking the offer up – or once in a while the women were given the afternoon off to go shopping.

'What about the horses?'

In Lily's opinion the horses were more reliable for hauling

timber out of the depths of the forest and didn't break down like the blasted tractors did.

'There's a new stablehand who needs to learn the ropes,' was the forewoman's clipped reply.

It was usually Karl, the Jerry POW, who worked in the forest with the Clydesdales, hauling trees over uneven terrain from the forest to the roadside. Lily wondered if this change of plan had something to do with him.

As she made her way to the ancient Fordson Major tractor, Lily sighed. She had more pressing things on her mind.

On one hand, some inner sense told her the message last night was intended for her; on the other, she scolded herself for believing such superstitious nonsense. She should've listened to Jill and let common sense prevail. Did she really think the spirit world had contacted her? Lily vehemently shook her head; the suggestion was ridiculous. You could make up anything to fit your purpose.

In a clearing in the forest, as Lily sat aboard the tractor, the sun shining in a faraway, blue sky shedding warmth on her back, the gang's muted voices audible as they worked deep in the forest, she tried to think about when John was last home. She recalled it was the day she went to the labour exchange – the thirteenth of January.

Before starting as a Lumberjill, Lily had religiously checked the calendar to see when her monthly caller (Mam's name for a period) was due. Now, too tired to think of anything but work, she didn't always know what day it was. Lily's period had never been any more than six weeks late, but she reckoned it was longer than that now.

She sat quite still, birds twittered, the wind whispered through swaying treetops, and the gang's voices receded further into the distance.

Could she really be pregnant? And could she go through all the anxiety, the torment of losing another baby again?

Of course she could, she decided. She was prepared to go

through the agony many times if it meant one day she would hold a baby in her arms.

Starting up the tractor and hearing the engine ticking noise getting faster, off Lily went deep into the forest to find the gang. She was glad of the hard day's labour ahead, when she wouldn't have time to think of spirits leaving messages or baby concerns.

But as the day progressed, Lily found herself regularly thinking of all those things.

———

It was late afternoon when, tired, hungry and longing for a break, the gang of four lasses Lily worked with hauled the fallen trees out of the forest. Singing as they worked – 'Show Me the Way to Go Home', quite apt for the occasion – their voices soared into the close forest atmosphere.

Vivian gave Lily the shout that she could start up the tractor, as the fallen trees were coupled and ready to be dragged to the road-side by chains. Lily's mind was not on the job as she drove along the uneven track, being thrown about in the seat, and it conjured up all kinds of 'what ifs' for the future.

Driving along the rocky and uneven ground, Lily felt the tractor shudder and suddenly come to an abrupt halt. She knew what was coming and braced herself as she pitched forward. Desperately trying to grab the seat to anchor her, Lily found herself hurtling through the air to land with a thud on the unforgiving, rutted ground. Winded, she lay feeling nothing but the thump of her heart. Then the pain started, ripping down the side she'd landed on. In the distance, through the trees, she heard the gang singing, 'Don't sit under the apple tree...'

It was pointless shouting for help as the gang wouldn't hear, but the agonising pain prevented her from moving from the spot. As she lay prone on the ground, the fear started.

What if I am pregnant and have damaged the baby?

23

Lying on her side, Lily viewed the stump that had stopped the tractor in its tracks. She decided she couldn't wait for help as that might take an age to come. She hadn't driven the tractor far, so the others couldn't be that far off.

Gingerly, she managed to get up off the ground to all fours then, despite the stabbing pain, to a standing position. She struggled to climb aboard the tractor. The discomfort in her chest hurting every time she breathed, Lily adapted by taking shorter breaths. Looking around the area, she calculated there was room to do a full swing with the tractor and timber. She started the tractor and, taking her time, reversed until it was free of the stump. Then, doing a full circle, she headed slowly back to the working site and the gang, watching out for stumps.

———

That night, as she lay on top of her bed in the dormitory, Lily remembered only snatches of the day that followed the accident. The shocked faces of the others when they saw her plight, the uncoupling of the timber, Vivian driving the tractor to Teviot Hall. Then Fran driving her in a painful journey to the hospital, where a doctor, with a grey beard and arms folded, told Lily she had a rib contusion and would need to rest up for a while.

The Lumberjills had fussed, bringing her rations of sweets and books to read, then most of them had set off for the Saturday night dance. Lily smiled, thinking of them all having a go at jitterbugging, the Canadian foresters watching on. Even the thought of the hectic dance made her side hurt.

In the dormitory, deathly quiet after they'd gone, Lily felt lonely and sorry for herself. She hated this feeling of being reliant on others, but in her present state there was nothing she could do about it.

Just be for a while, sweetheart. John's words sounded so real in her head that, looking around the empty dormitory, Lily almost expected to see him. It felt like a lifetime since she had last been with him. An aching longing washing over her, Lily's stubborn will wouldn't allow her to cry.

Fran had brought tea and a scone sent by Edie McGregor, the cook. Lily sensed that Fran felt responsible for all the Lumberjills, and she would blame herself that the accident had happened even though she couldn't have done anything to prevent it. The truth was that the 'accident', as everyone referred to it, was entirely Lily's fault. She should've noticed the stump that caught the timber being dragged and caused the tractor to stop so suddenly. Instead of her mind being miles away, which every Lumberjill knew was tantamount to asking for trouble when you were involved in working with trees, Lily should have been concentrating on driving.

Lily made up her mind that at this point she wouldn't tell anyone she thought she might be pregnant. Fran might send her packing when – provided she avoided any more stupid accidents – there was no need.

She'd pleaded to Fran, 'Please don't send me home on sick leave.' If Fran sent her home she'd just have time to think and drive herself up the wall, wondering if she really was pregnant and if this time, please God, she would stay so. 'Surely, there's something I can do here?'

'I'll think on it.' Then a gleam came into the forewoman's eyes that Lily couldn't define. 'When you're able, and if you can cope, Muriel Fellows will no doubt need a hand in the office. The woman finds it difficult to manage on her own.' With a satisfied smile that she'd had a go at her foe, Fran made to leave the dormitory.

She turned. 'You're sure you don't want any supper brought? I asked Edie to plate some up for you.'

'No. I'm not hungry. The scone will do me fine, thanks.'

The door closed as Fran left.

Minutes later, Lily, stretching to place her empty cup on the locker, yelped in pain. Mad at herself for her stupidity at causing the accident, she wished she could have the moment back; she would focus on her work this time.

As the dormitory door opened, Lily expected to see Fran returning and was surprised when Ethel appeared, still dressed in work clothes. No doubt the lass had waited till the others had left before returning to the dormitory after the evening meal. Lily couldn't help feeling sorry for Ethel as she led such a solitary life – *except for the POW*, Lily's mind reminded her – and the note of cynicism in her thoughts bothered Lily, who wanted to stay neutral.

Ethel sat on her bed facing Lily, with a concerned expression. 'I heard the others talking about what happened. Are you in much pain?'

Lily was taken aback; this was the longest speech she could remember since the two of them had become neighbours.

'Yes, but thankfully there's no bones broken.' Lily, sagging against the pillow, breathing lightly, gave a shamefaced grimace. 'Serves me right for not concentrating.'

Ethel gave a small smile of sympathy. 'Does talking hurt?'

Lily nodded.

Ethel stood as if that was the end of the conversation.

Though it was unwise, because of how painful talking was, Lily didn't want to miss the opportunity to ask a few burning questions.

'Where are you from?' Even to Lily's ears the abrupt inquiry sounded like an interrogation and she hoped Ethel understood her predicament.

The lass hesitated and then, seemingly making up her mind, she answered, 'South Shields.'

'Same as me.' Lily sat up. A sharp pain from her bruised rib made her crumple. 'Ohh!'

'Can I do anything?'

Lily shook her head. She eased back onto the raised pillow. 'Whereabouts?'

More hesitation.

'I'm being nosey.'

'No, it's just... I was brought up in an orphanage.' The lass looked uneasy.

'Oh! Sorry.' *Daft reply*, Lily's mind told her.

'Thanks,' Ethel surprised her by saying. She visibly relaxed and sat on her bed again. 'Most folk look horrified, as if I say I was brought up in the workhouse. Which, by the way, was what it felt like.'

'Sor— oh, how awful.'

It was Ethel's turn to look surprised. As if she wasn't used to such a considerate reaction.

'Blakely Hall, it was called. Mistress Knowles and her husband were in charge. He just did as he was told. All of us orphans were scared stiff of the mistress, even the staff.'

Her look of contempt told Lily how bad it had been.

'How old were you when—'

'I was orphaned?' Ethel finished for her.

Lily smiled appreciatively.

'Nine.'

'Ahh! You were so young.'

As Ethel stared into the distance, her face clouded in sadness and Lily almost wished she hadn't brought the subject up – but only almost. Because, as she spoke about her personal life, Lily saw a chink in Ethel's stand-offishness and she finally glimpsed the real lass, someone hurting and vulnerable.

'Do you have memories of your parents?' Lily pressed, not just because she was intrigued but more for Ethel's sake. She seemed to want to talk and Lily felt privileged she'd chosen her to open up to. But she instinctively knew she had to tread carefully, to take only as much as Ethel was ready to give.

'I was seven when Dad died.' Ethel's brown opaque eyes were unfocused, as though she was remembering. 'We lived in a tied cottage as Dad worked on a farm. He was driving a horse and cart to the mart, so the story goes.' She gave a bemused shrug. 'I can't remember being told so I must've overheard. A sudden loud noise from behind in the road gave the horse a fright and it went full gallop. The cart didn't take a corner and hit a kerb and overturned.' She sorrowfully shook her head. 'Dad didn't make it.'

There was a stillness in the dormitory as the two girls stared at one another and Lily knew they were both thinking the same. The same could have happened to her when the tractor came to a sudden halt. It wouldn't be the first time a tractor tipped over onto the driver and they were killed or seriously injured. Maybe this was why Ethel had opened up, because the accident had churned up the past for her.

'How did your mam manage? How did she overcome such a tragedy?'

'I don't think she did. She changed, got angry over nothing. I heard her tell Aunt Meg after we'd moved in with her, the farmer was more concerned about the horse having to be destroyed because its leg was broken, and who would pay for its loss, than he was about Dad.'

'Such a horrible time for you,' Lily commiserated.

'I don't think I fully understood the concept of death. I waited for Dad to return, like he'd just gone away for a while. He used to sit me on his knee and tell me about the camp and so I imagined him doing just that. It kept him alive for me.' That faraway glint came into her eyes again.

'What kind of camp?' Lily asked, puzzled.

'Stobs POW camp. It's near Hawick, not far from here.'

'Was your dad a guard there?'

Ethel looked unsure and eyed Lily strangely as if weighing her up, then, seemingly making up her mind, she took a deep breath and told Lily, staring her straight in the eyes:

'No. A prisoner.'

'Prisoner?' Lily repeated dumbly.

Chin jutting, Ethel appeared to retreat back into her aloof shell. Head held high, she went on, 'Dad was a German. He was captured on the Western Front in the Great War.'

Blimey! Lily wasn't expecting that. Still in shock, she found herself thinking, *It all makes sense; her being seen fraternising with a German. Ethel can probably speak the language.* Then it occurred to Lily that in these days of hysteria if anyone found out Ethel was half German, she'd be accused of being a spy.

Lily decided to be truthful. 'I wasn't expecting that. It came as a shock.'

Ethel, bunching her lips, stood up. 'Just forget it.'

Though talking caused Lily a lot of pain, she struggled to sit up and pressed on, 'I can understand now why you might... become friendly with a German POW. And understand why you can't say anything about your dad in today's climate.'

Ethel gave Lily a long, measured look. Then, to Lily's shock, she teared up. 'We're not friends. I love Karl but he's—'

At that moment, frustratingly, the dormitory door opened and Bella appeared.

Moving down the corridor towards Lily's bed, she blanked Ethel and spoke to Lily. 'How's the invalid? Sorry, I came as soon as I could.'

'Bearing up.'

'I would've been here earlier but, seeing how I wasn't going to the dance, I was elected to help clean the canteen tonight.' Bella put the enamel plate she carried on the bed. 'A present from Mrs McGregor.' Her eyes twinkled with mischief. 'She thought you might get hungry and fancy a cheese sandwich for a change.'

Because of the extra eight ounces a week ration for Lumber-jills, cheese had become their daily diet and Lily was sick of the sight of the stuff. Seeing the funny side, she laughed then, but a knife-like pain stabbed her, and she wished she hadn't. She wondered, if she were pregnant, if this could be a sign that she'd done damage to the baby she carried. Lily sobered at the very thought.

Bella gave Ethel a sideways glance as if vexed that the young girl was listening in. Lily, uncomfortable with the suspicious atmosphere, was surprised at Bella's reaction. Surely, her friend wasn't still cross about the swapping-bed saga? It was so unlike Bella to behave like this.

Turning to Lily, Bella continued, 'Mrs McGregor told me about the accident. She said everyone was talking about it at meal-time. You've been lucky.'

'I know.' Wanting to avoid any further conversation about accidents, Lily asked, 'How was your first day?'

'Miss Fellows collared me first thing to go over camp rules and fill in necessary forms and then this afternoon I hauled timber out of the woods for the rest of the day.'

'How come?'

'After the accident, someone from another gang took your place driving the tractor and I replaced her.'

'I thought your job was helping with the horses?'

Bella looked towards Ethel, who, by now, had moved over to her bed and was rummaging in her locker.

'Hopefully, that's all changed,' Bella said rather pointedly.

There was an awkward silence. Lily, mortified for Ethel, wished she'd had time to explain about the beds, and couldn't believe Bella was still being so silly about it.

'I'm choosy who I work with,' Bella continued, and there was no doubt who the statement was intended for.

Ethel stood up, a flush creeping up her neck and rising into her cheeks. Staring at Bella, she gave a despairing shake of the head, then stomped from the dormitory.

'That was uncalled for.' Lily couldn't believe Bella could be so mean. With Ethel gone, she needed to put the record straight. 'It's not what you think. Ethel couldn't change beds and I intervened to save her the embarrass—'

'I know why you didn't change beds. Nancy filled me in about Ethel, but I don't know why you're so defensive over her. She's consorting with the enemy, for goodness' sake, and I'm certainly not having anything to do with her.' Her eyes flashing, she jutted her chin. 'I'm surprised you are.'

Lily, at a disadvantage laid up in bed, considered Bella's outburst was out of order and she felt attacked. She had to speak up.

'I speak as I find and don't jump to conclusions,' Lily said, gasping with the pain. She really wasn't up to this but felt she had to make a stand. 'There's no proof that Ethel is—'

'Yes, there is,' Bella cut in and Lily wondered what had come over her to become so agitated over the matter. 'It was the middle of the night and Nancy couldn't sleep. She got up to have a smoke. It was while she stood in the shadows that she saw Ethel sneak out of the dormitory.'

'How did she know Ethel was meeting up with Karl?'

'Nancy said she was tired of not being believed the pair of them were fraternising. She's a bad sleeper and the next time she was up, which was recently, and she saw Ethel, Nancy followed her and guess where she ended up?' Bella looked jubilant as if it was her who'd made the discovery. 'At the stables.'

'But—'

'I know what you're going to say. Where's the proof the Jerry prisoner was there? According to Nancy, she snuck into the stables and heard them talking in the hayloft.'

Lily was rather taken aback at this.

'Nancy reported this to Miss Fellows, who agreed that now

something must be done... and only too right.' A vein pulsed in Bella's temple. 'He's been confined to the sin bin in camp till he's shipped out to somewhere more secure. And I hope she gets her comeuppance.'

So that's why another stablehand was needed here, Lily thought. And why Ethel had got so upset. Lily had a mind to divulge to Bella what she knew about Ethel, but under the circumstance of her friend's mounting anger, she thought better of it. Besides, the story wasn't Lily's to tell and had been related to her in confidence.

Overcome now by the happenings of the day, Lily attempted to defuse the situation. 'Bella, don't get worked up.' She took a few shallow breaths. 'It's not our problem. You've just arriv—'

'You think?' Bella's tone was hard. 'It mightn't be your problem but it's certainly mine. There's no way *I'm* going to consort with a... traitor.'

There followed a palpable silence during which the angry words hung in the air.

Lily didn't know what to make of what had just been said. Bella couldn't dictate who she saw or when. She thought of how the tolerant Vivian would handle the situation.

'Bella, arguing amongst ourselves... isn't going to help. There's enough hatred in this world without us squabbling.' She tried to keep her voice even, to not let the annoyance show. 'Can we leave this for now?'

Bella opened her mouth to retort, then, as if words failed her, she gaped in surprise. Inexplicably the whites of her eyes turned pink and, chin trembling, she appeared to crumple.

'Those Jerry bastards...' Her voice faltered. 'They killed my Ronnie.'

24

'Ronnie was my husband,' Bella explained.

Lily didn't let her surprise show, nor did she interrupt Bella's garbled account of her heartache.

Pacing between Ethel and Lily's beds, shoulders hunched, Bella said, 'In short, Ronnie and I had been sweethearts since our schooldays. When the news of the war broke and he was called up, he proposed. I moved up to Edinburgh after we were married.' A pause while she gulped, as though it was difficult to go on. 'Ronnie was killed on the beaches of Dunkirk. A bomb landed near him, and he was mortally wounded by shrapnel.'

At that moment the dormitory door opened and one of the Lumberjills walked in. She looked along the row of beds towards the pair of them and nodded. Moving towards her bed, she opened the locker door, took something out and without further acknowledgement left the dormitory.

Bella, who had stopped pacing, her face mirroring the pain she felt inside, slumped down on the edge of Lily's bed.

She continued, 'I was told about Ronnie's death by telegram from the War Office. *Deeply regret to inform you that your husband Sergeant Ronald Campbell has been killed on active service. Letter follows.*' She spoke as if reading the telegram.

Lily was speechless. She had never expected anything like this.

Bella shook her head. 'For a long time, I couldn't accept it. My boss at the hairdresser's insisted it would help if we held a church service for Ronnie. I played along but nothing changed.' Her hazel eyes sought Lily's. 'I felt guilty if I was having a happy moment. I still do. It was the doctor who recommended I had a complete change and suggested I joined the services to take my mind off things.' She shrugged. 'I was cross – I didn't want to take my mind off Ronnie. But everyone said a change was for the best.'

'Oh, Bella, I'm so sorry.'

'To be honest, I felt in the way. They all looked helpless about what to do with me. That's how I wound up here.'

'I understand now.' Lily nodded. She winced as sharp pain spliced in her side.

'No, you don't.' Bella's gaze was unwavering.

Lily thought for a moment. She did have heartbreak in her life but the idea of losing John was unthinkable. She'd been correct, though, in thinking there was a mystery to Bella – but she'd never imagined it was as tragic as this.

'Now you know why I'm so upset about Ethel. I mean, a Jerry prisoner...' Her lip curled. 'How could she?'

Lily recalled what Ethel had confided about her past. 'People have reasons for doing the things they do.'

'What's your reason for being here?'

Lily considered how to answer and decided that the truth was always best. She told Bella about how she wanted to prove she was as good as her brothers; how she wanted to do something with her life; about marrying her John and about the miscarriages.

She finished by saying, 'I thought now was a good time to get away.'

Bella's eyes were full of sorrow. 'How dreadful for you, Lily. I do understand, because if my Ronnie were alive I'd want a baby too.'

The tears came then, spilling from her eyes. Shoulders heaving, she gave shuddering gulps as if she were drowning. Lily –

stuck in the bed, every movement agony, unable to give her friend a hug – also started to well up.

When finally the tears stopped, Lily said, 'If anything happened to John I don't know what—'

'You don't need to explain.' Bella brushed the tears from her cheeks with her fingertips. 'If the situation were reversed, I'd probably feel the same as you. No one knows how they'll react when their world falls apart. Believe it or not' – a forced lightness came into her tone as if she wanted the subject changed – 'that's the first time I've cried since the telegram arrived. And boy, didn't the floodgates open.' She laughed, but Lily detected the lingering sadness. 'I've been a pain to live with since and I think everyone was glad to be rid of me.'

'I think not,' Lily replied levelly.

'Thank you.' Bella's voice held sincerity. She sat up straight. 'I can't promise to behave where Ethel is concerned but I'll try my best.'

Lily nodded; that's all she could ask. She decided to try and lighten the moment. 'There's something I've been dying to ask.'

Bella's brow corrugated. 'What?'

'What exactly is a sin bin?'

Bella laughed good-naturedly. 'Slang for jail.'

Lily, glad to have her friend back to her rational self, gave a sigh of relief.

————

Later, tucked up in bed with a stone hot-water bottle delivered by Bella, Lily felt exhausted.

She lay on her back by the light of the lamp's flickering flame and closed her eyes, but sleep wouldn't come. Her mind, a jumble of thoughts like unwelcome interlopers, flitted over the day's events. She didn't want to think of the accident, or Ethel confiding her German father had been a prisoner of war, or indeed, Bella's disclosure about her husband's death – what upset Lily most was her latest discovery.

After Bella had left, she'd struggled to the lav – basically a wooden seat over an opening whose contents would be put in a dug-out hole in the estate grounds. When she made the painful journey back to bed, and pulled back the blanket, the sight of the blood spots on the bottom sheet where she had lain was the last straw to a disastrous day. Her resolve to stay strong threatening to dissolve, Lily fought back the tears. She lay stiff as a post in the bed, afraid to move in case she started another miscarriage.

———

Next morning, Lily's injury hurting when she moved, she checked beneath the blanket and noted the black and blue patches covering her skin. Holding her breath, she looked further down the sheet and gave a deep sigh of relief (which hurt like blazes) when she saw there was no more blood. Not wanting to tempt fate by speculating about pregnancy, she banished the forbidden thoughts into a safety deposit box in her mind.

Deciding to skip breakfast – a rarity indeed, but she couldn't face the commotion of getting dressed and trekking to the canteen – she was surprised when Vivian showed up at her bedside, a tin plate and cup in her hands.

'Cook reckons bacon doesn't stretch to invalids.' Vivian handed over a plate of jam and bread.

Lily knew Edie wasn't being mean as the Lumberjills needed the fuel to cope with the hard day's labour ahead. There were often shortages of food, and when they did arrive, rations were of poor quality.

'I'm being treated like royalty.' Lily struggled to sit up.

'Don't get used to it,' Vivian called as she made for the door. 'I expect to see you in the canteen sometime soon.'

With all the Lumberjills gone for breakfast now, and then later off to church, the hut seeming big and echoey, Lily ate a solitary breakfast. When she'd finished and placed the dishes, with a yelp of pain, on the locker top, a wave of tiredness overcame her and she snuggled down beneath the blanket.

The door opening woke her. Rubbing her eyes, Lily was surprised when she saw Fran standing at the bottom of the bed.

'What time is it?' she croakily asked.

'Ten o'clock. I had paperwork to fill in and I found yesterday's post on my desk. I thought I'd drop this off.' She held out a letter. 'With all the commotion yesterday, I didn't get round to delivering post.'

Lily's spirits rose. 'Thanks, Fran. I appreciate it.'

'See you later.' Fran, walking the length of the dormitory, opened the door and left.

Recognising the handwriting on the envelope as Mam's, Lily winced in disappointment. She slit open the envelope and, as she removed the sheet of paper, out came a postcard with it.

The postcard was from John.

Sweetheart – I'm safe and in North Africa. Longing for a letter and please enclose your new address as you'll be finished your training now – John obviously hadn't received her last letter yet – *Don't worry, my darling, if you don't hear, as letters can take weeks.*

Your loving, John

She hugged the postcard to her heart; North Africa was so very far away. It was frustrating John couldn't tell her more but Lily knew it was because of censorship – the government's attempt at protecting secret information from falling into enemy hands.

Lily picked up Mam's letter and began to read. She smiled as Mam wrote the way she spoke.

Dear Lily,

Your dad's driving me crazy with his moaning. I've told him he should seek an audience with Churchill himself to put the man right on how to win this war. Apart from that, Dad's doing all right but working extra shifts is taking it out of him as he's not getting any younger. The main reason I'm writing is to make sure you get John's postcard; I couldn't help noticing he's in North Africa – Lily rolled her eyes at this – *It'll be a worry for you but keep your chin up, our Lily.*

All's well at home. Jean's having a time of it with morning sickness and young Stanley gets more gorgeous and troublesome by the day. I wish I could be more help but I tire easily these days.

The lads are fine – when I see them! One of them Bevin boys that's a mate of our Ian's at the mine was killed when a roof fell on him. I feel sorry for his poor mam. Fancy having your son avoid the fighting, only to get killed doing his job of work at home. God bless her, it doesn't bear thinking about. I'm only too pleased it's not me, but it just goes to show no one's safe in this war.

Take care of yourself, our Lily.

Love Mam

Lily shook her head; Mam would never change – but Lily wouldn't want her to as she liked her mother just the way she was. She did worry Mam was worse than she was letting on because admitting she was tired wasn't usually in her vocabulary. Jean was sensible, though, and wouldn't put on Mam.

She read John's postcard again then placed it under her pillow. Feeling tiredness creep over her once more, she sank back against the pillow and closed her eyes. Behind pink lids, she imagined John as if he was in one of those pictures on the Pathé news from North Africa she'd seen at the pictures. Wearing a khaki uniform, shorts – John had muscled legs – thick, knee-length socks, tin hat and—

At that moment Lily heard the dormitory door squeak open.

Her eyes blinked open, expecting to see Fran, but instead saw a dark figure she couldn't quite make out.

'Who's that?'

The figure made a dive for cover behind the nearest bed to the door.

A rush of ice-cold adrenalin surged through Lily. 'There's people around,' she fibbed. 'I'll scream if you don't show yourself.'

A man's head appeared above the bed. 'I do you no harm.'

The man stood and Lily recognised the worn and old-looking uniform with black patches sewn on the legs and backs – these, Lily knew, were to be used as targets if a prisoner tried to escape.

A German prisoner.

Lily struggled to sit up, terrified and ready to scream.

'*Nein, Fräulein.*' The man made a dash up the dormitory and stood by her bed. He was quite young, and had dark brown hair and matching eyes.

Lily knew screaming would be useless as there'd be no time for anyone to save her.

'I leave this and go.' He took a slip of paper from his uniform pocket.

Lily faltered.

'I work here in stables.'

Karl Becker.

Lily's mind raced as she wondered what she should do next. She was incapacitated, she realised; she couldn't do anything. Lily felt the hair on her arms stand up as fear gripped her; she was alone in the dormitory with a POW.

Her best course of action was to humour him. 'What is it?'

'I am told everyone at church. I bring for *Fräulein*.' His brown eyes pleaded with her.

'Ethel?'

A smile lit up his face. He nodded. Lily remembered Bella's words. *He's been confined to camp.*

'You've escaped.' She regretted her words as soon as they were out, as she might have unnerved him.

'I am permitted to walk around zee—'

Lily understood and nodded. 'Exercise.'

'Yes, in compound. I escape through... fence.'

'The barbed wire?'

His face turned solemn. 'You will give?' He held out the piece of paper. 'She is in last bed, she told me. I search for her in...' He nodded to the locker.

What else could she do? Lily nodded.

'*Danke.*' His eyes glowed with gratitude.

At that moment, the dormitory door flew open and Lily, jumping in fright, was shocked to see one of the military policemen burst into the room.

'He's here,' he called over his shoulder.

As Karl inched up the bedside, panic gripped Lily and her body shrank back.

A soldier – who Lily knew must be one of the camp guards – appeared, a rifle in his hands. He barked, 'Hands behind your head, Karl.'

Karl glanced her way and, seeing the desperation in his eyes, Lily froze, heart thumping. *What might Karl do to resist capture?*

Surprisingly, he did as he was told but, arms at his side, he first surreptitiously let go of the piece of paper in his hand and it dropped to the floor.

The soldier, moving up the aisle between the two rows of beds, stopped at Lily's and nodded for Karl to move forward.

He didn't seem surprised to see Lily. 'Are you all right, miss? Sorry to involve you in this. Not a word, miss.'

Lily, incapable of thinking straight, simply nodded.

The soldier's eyes searched the area and Lily held her breath.

'Did the prisoner approach any other area of the hut?'

She shook her head.

The soldier eyed Karl. 'Move.' He nodded to the door.

Just before they left Karl called, without turning, 'Tell Ethel, *Ich liebe sie.*'

25

The sequence of events had all happened so quickly Lily couldn't take them in. Sagging back against the pillow, she pored over the facts. Had Karl really been a danger? she wondered. He only wanted to deliver a letter to Ethel and he was defenceless. Karl had given her a turn but, to be fair, how was he to have known that she would be there?

She thought of the paper that had dropped to the floor. Favouring her non-injured side, Lily swung her legs over the edge of the bed and looked to the floor for the piece of paper. It wasn't there. It must have fluttered under the bed, Lily thought, and presumably that's why the soldier hadn't seen it. She thought of the baby she might be carrying and, rather than risk getting down on all fours, she swept her foot beneath the bed. When she touched the paper, for a moment she felt elated. She managed to retrieve the paper with her foot and bent down to pick it up.

What she held in her hand was a letter, she realised, though looking at it she didn't understand it, as it was written, she presumed, in German. She did, though, recognise Ethel's name and what looked like an address. She remembered that Ethel's dad was German, so Karl must have known she could read the language.

———

The rest of the morning was slow and, with only her thoughts to occupy her, Lily felt frustrated. She'd expected an inquisition, or at least to be told Karl was securely back at the prisoner camp, but nothing was forthcoming. *Not a word, miss.* Perhaps, no one in the WTC camp knew and the powers that be at the prison camp wanted it kept that way. To take her mind off things, Lily brought Karen Blixen's memoir, *Out of Africa*, from her locker. Normally she would have been delighted to have the time to read the book but now she found she couldn't concentrate.

Dinner time arrived, and Lily wondered what to do. She was starved, she decided. Sitting up slowly, the pain flaring with every movement, she reached for her clothes and, pulling her nightdress over her head, she got dressed in trousers and jumper. It was while she was resting before putting her boots on, that Lily heard the hut door open.

She turned. Fran stood there with a tray in her hands.

'Muriel's too busy and she's asked me to talk to you. The others are back and in the canteen.' Fran walked up the dormitory and, standing by Lily's bedside, she placed the tray – which had a plate with a sandwich and a cup of tea on it – on the locker top.

Lily met Fran's eye. 'It's about—'

'The prisoner escaping. Yes.' Fran, bringing a wooden chair from beside the stove and placing it next to Lily's bed, sat down and continued. 'It comes from top brass they want this kept hush-hush.' She made big eyes. 'Somebody's in trouble. The prisoner went missing when out in the compound for his daily exercise. The matter was reported to the sergeant of the day in charge.'

'How did they know where to look?'

'You'll probably have heard that Nancy has been agitating because she claimed Karl was fraternising with one of the Lumberjills.'

Lily nodded.

'It came to a head recently when Nancy claimed she'd heard

them together in the hayloft at night. Muriel was forced to take action, and reported the matter to the POW camp. Karl was detained in the sin bin. Apparently, he was being refused permission to send a letter, and then, when it was reported he'd escaped, the first place to look was obviously here.'

'Fran, I know the Lumberjill is Ethel.'

Fran nodded and went on, 'It sounds like the sergeant guessed that Karl had taken matters in his own hands and decided to deliver the letter himself. He sought out Muriel Fellows at the big house and asked whereabouts the girl worked.'

'Did they search the stables?'

'Yes. But no one was there. The sergeant and soldiers accompanying him then wanted to search where Ethel slept.'

'So, Muriel showed them here.'

'She did. Muriel was concerned as you were convalescing here and told the sergeant. She offered to accompany him but he was having none of it.'

'That was kind of her.'

'The woman has her uses at times.' Fran sniffed.

Lily was puzzled. 'How d'you think Karl knew where Ethel's bed was?'

'She must have told him.'

There was a pause as Lily wondered what had possessed Ethel to tell him where she slept. But perhaps the matter had come up naturally in conversation when they were comparing camps.

'What will happen to Karl?' she asked.

'According to the sergeant he'll be sent to a secure camp. Then possibly shipped to America.'

'Why America?'

'I know – I thought the same when I heard. Apparently, according to her ladyship' – Lily presumed she meant Muriel Fellows – 'Britain's POW camps are overstretched, and the US has agreed to take more prisoners as well as its own share.'

'Does Ethel know all this?' Lily felt it fair that she should.

Fran heaved a sigh. 'I thought it right to tell her. I met her as she came back from church.'

'What will happen to her?'

'Depends on what head office have to say, if they hear. If not, we'll deal with it ourselves.'

'How?'

'The laird himself is very fond of Ethel. I would think he might have something to say on the matter if she was told to resign.'

Fran's answer took Lily by surprise.

———

Later, at supper time, Lily managed to trail after the others to the canteen where she scoffed a plate of mince pie and mash followed by spotted dick and custard. She did fleetingly wonder if she was really eating for two. Because, though she'd been through a traumatic experience, it didn't seem to have affected her ravenous appetite. Still shaken by events, she worried about the baby that might be inside her and what effect all this would have on her body. After supper, emotionally drained, all Lily was capable of was lying on the bed, trying once again to get into *Out of Africa*. But her mind refused to concentrate.

All the Lumberjills, apart from the lass nearest the door, who currently was sound asleep, were over at the recreational room where a game of housey-housey was taking place.

Lily was longing to tell someone about her ordeal this morning; not because she wanted to blab, but to make it real. If she didn't have the letter to verify the whole sorry affair had happened, Lily would be forgiven for thinking she'd dreamt it.

Guilt nudged at her. Why had she kept the letter a secret from the soldier? She searched her mind. Despite everything she'd heard there was something about Ethel that drew Lily to her and made her want to protect her. It happened in life, this attraction to someone without knowing them properly, as if you'd been meant to meet. Lily wanted Ethel to receive that letter; after all, it was hers by right. She wondered whether it could be a farewell letter, as Lily doubted Ethel would ever see Karl again.

Her mind teeming, Lily gave up on reading and, as she closed the book, she heard the dormitory door squeak open. She tensed, then relief flooded through her as she saw, in the lamplight, Ethel appearing in the doorway. Head down, she walked along the dormitory and didn't look up as she passed but went straight to her own bed, where she sat still as a statue, her back towards Lily.

Placing her book on the locker top, Lily sat up. 'Ow!' she cried out as the pain ripped through her. She kept doing that, forgetting her injury.

Ethel turned. Her face red and puffy, it was her pink eyes with their despairing look that struck Lily.

'I saw Karl,' Lily blurted. 'He brought a letter.'

Ethel visibly flinched. 'Karl brought a letter?' she repeated. 'Did the soldiers take it?'

'No, it's here. I kept it.'

Ethel's hand flew to her heart. 'Where?'

'Under the mattress. It's the only safe place I could think to hide it.'

'But why?' she asked incredulously.

'Why didn't I hand it over?'

Ethel nodded.

Lily would have felt foolish if she'd simply said, 'Because I wanted you to have it.' So she improvised with, 'I thought it harsh Karl couldn't send a letter before he left.'

'Thank you.'

'I can't reach under the mattress and with the wretched pain as it takes me—'

'I'll get it.' Ethel sprang up.

Lily didn't argue. If, God willing, she was expecting and managed to get through the trauma of the accident and the encounter with the POW without miscarrying, she swore she wouldn't jeopardise the pregnancy in any way from now on.

They'd been speaking in low voices but now, in her eagerness,

Ethel raised hers. Lily, checking on the sleeping Lumberjill, put her forefinger to her lips.

Ethel gave a small nod.

Lily indicated to the top of the mattress where she'd stuffed the letter. Lifting the edge of the mattress and sliding her hand inside the space, Ethel brought out the slip of paper.

Sitting back on her bed, Ethel began to read. As Lily watched she saw her lips tremble, then a lone tear slid down her face. She sniffed and brushed the tear away with the sleeve of her work jumper. Lily instinctively knew this was no casual affair; the lass felt deeply about this Jerry prisoner.

It was seeing the hole in the elbow of Ethel's jumper that made Lily feel inexplicably sad for her and a lump came into her throat. Ethel looked up from reading and opened her mouth, but whatever she was about to say died on her tongue.

They sat like that for a while and, when Lily could stand the silence no longer, she remarked, avoiding the obvious subject, 'I've been admiring your colourful blanket on the bed.'

Ethel started, as if she'd been in a world of her own, and stared at Lily. Then she answered, 'Mam made it for me.'

Oh no! Lily thought. Trying to avoid one minefield of conversation, she'd stepped on another.

'Look,' she said, 'I think it's best if I leave you alone. You're upset and I—'

'That's the last thing I want. Can we just talk?' Her eyes pleading, Ethel went on, 'I've had the blanket with me ever since I entered the orphanage. I found it in the suitcase I was carrying.'

Taking the cue that the past was safe territory to talk about, Lily ventured to ask something she'd pondered about. 'How come you ended up in South Shields?'

Ethel took a deep breath. 'Me maternal grandma's sister, Great-Aunty Meg, met her fisherman husband when he was on the boats coming up to Berwick. They married and Aunty Meg moved into his house in South Shields. After Dad died leaving Mam destitute and we had to vacate the cottage, Aunty Meg took us in. A widow by then, with no family of her own, I suppose we were company for her.'

Lily digested this information, and waited for her to say more, instinctively knowing Ethel needed to talk about something else to avoid dwelling on the present.

Ethel continued. 'I was nine when Mam died. I seem to remember hearing people say the word "consumption" at the time but I'm not certain I didn't make that up. I do remember Mam coughing a lot and going thin as a rake. I once told her that I preferred her bigger because I loved cuddling into her big cosy tummy. Mam gave me a sad look and said, "Ethel, I'll never be that again."' Ethel turned to Lily. 'I regret saying that now.'

'You didn't know any better.'

'I know but it still doesn't help. Mam went into hospital and never came out. Aunty Meg was ancient by then and had all but lost her hearing.' Ethel shook her head. 'All I can remember of the journey to the orphanage was Aunty taking me through tall trees to a towering building with lots of windows and space outside and leaving me there. Before she left, Aunty Meg handed me a suitcase and said, "Ethel, your mother and me talked this over and we came to the conclusion it's best you came here. You need someone to take care of you and I'm too old and there's no one else. Be a good girl and say your prayers and remember how much your mother loved you."'

Ethel looked bemused, as if experiencing the same emotions she had on that fateful day in the past. At this point, Lily felt herself welling up.

'Then Aunty made for the doorway and disappeared, and I never saw her again.'

The story a sad one, Lily was mindful of her own rambunctious upbringing with her annoying brothers and loving parents. Even though she'd been treated differently because she was a girl, she'd never doubted she was loved and that her parents only had her wellbeing at heart. How lucky she was to have had such a secure childhood.

With nothing to say that could make Ethel feel better, Lily decided against saying anything at all.

Ethel sat transfixed, her thoughts a mystery to Lily. The silence between them was comfortable; they were like old friends for whom being in each other's company was enough. But there was so much more Lily wanted to know – especially what was in the letter – but that was Ethel's private affair. The rest would have to wait for another day, or maybe it never would be touched on again.

'Karl is a good person.' The statement took Lily by surprise. 'He hates Nazis.' Ethel had an intense look on her face.

'Ethel, you don't have to—'

'I do, Lily. I want you to know about Karl,' Ethel said, the expression on her face determined. 'His parents had a good life as they lived outside a small Pomeranian town in Germany, where his father grew crops and had cows, chickens, pigs and horses. Herbert, his father, was a principled man and let it be known he wasn't a Nazi supporter. He was especially disturbed after Kristallnacht.'

'Were Karl's family Jews?'

'No, sympathisers. After the war started, Herbert was arrested and taken to the local Nazi Party headquarters. He was deemed guilty of a political offence against the Nazi state, and imprisoned.'

'Oh my goodness.' Lily was horrified.

Ethel continued, 'Karl had the choice of either following Nazi Party orders or to face being tried and imprisoned. Still angry about his father's fate, he too opposed the Nazis but his mother, afraid she was going to lose her son, begged him not to let his political views be known. The Nazis sent Karl to train in the Luftwaffe.'

Lily didn't particularly want to feel sorry for a German who was, after all, the enemy, but compassion won. Karl sounded like just one of the little people, who had no say and ultimately worried for their family – only they were on a different side.

She voiced her thoughts.

'Yes, Karl worries about his mam and little sister. He's also afraid his family might be killed during one of the British raids.'

It occurred to Lily that British prisoners of war would live daily with the same fears. If only there was another way leaders could wage war instead of involving people, who mostly wanted a simple life without struggle and to not have to kill their fellow man.

Lily focused on Ethel, who was saying, 'In the last letter he received through the Red Cross, his mam informed Karl that she was moving away with his sister to live with his elderly grandfather.' Her young face lit up. 'Karl's put his grandfather's address in the letter so it's a way I can get in touch with him, even if we've to wait until after the war's finished.'

Lily couldn't help herself and said, 'He must think a lot of you to risk punishment getting that letter to you.'

'Karl is principled just like his father. The thing that upsets him most is, although he's a prisoner, he leads a relatively good life and he fears for his family living in Nazi Germany.' She looked down at the floor and shook her head. 'And now because of me it'll all be changed.'

Lily frowned and hurried to reassure her. 'Ethel, whether Karl is sent to a secure camp here or in America, believe me he won't suffer.' It was left unsaid: *Not like in Nazi Germany.*

Ethel visibly relaxed. 'Thank you, Lily. I know it's difficult for—'

At that moment the hut door opened and the two of them turned to see Bella appear in the doorway. She hovered awhile as if wondering what to do and, looking decidedly uncomfortable, she walked towards Lily's bed, stopping short of it.

Her gaze, fixed on Lily, didn't waver. 'I came to see how you are.'

Lily smiled brightly. 'Managing.'

'I would've come earlier but it was my turn for a bath at the big house and sorry but that was too much of a temptation.'

'Blimey. I should think so.'

Bella, appearing ill at ease, made to move away. 'You're busy. I'll come back another time.'

Determined to include Ethel and help Bella to get to know her, Lily told her friend, 'You're not interrupting anything. We were just chatting and you can—'

'No, that's fine. I promised Nancy I'd be caller for housey-housey tonight.'

She made her way back to the door. 'By the way, Fran insists I help out at the stables as there might be no one there in the future and she wants me to learn the ropes.'

'What about Ethel?' Lily asked, confused.

'Search me. It sounds as if the present stablehand might have to resign.'

She closed the door after her.

So much for Bella behaving, Lily thought.

26

APRIL 1943

Lily dared to believe it was true, she was three months pregnant. If she needed confirmation, apart from no sight of the curse, rushing to the office lavatory of a morning to be sick was evidence.

Though she now knew for sure she was expecting, Lily wanted to keep the fact secret for a little while longer from everyone. But she would write and tell John and her parents. How she wished John was here in person. She closed her eyes, imagining the masculine smell of him. A yearning akin to homesickness washing over her, she felt uncommonly teary. But she cheered herself by imagining him opening the letter, his face lighting up in surprise when he read the news. It would be such a boost for him, for he must have feelings of longing to see her too. She couldn't wait to hear his reply.

Wary, for the sake of the baby, of going back to driving trucks, she told Fran she didn't feel fully recovered and asked if she could do a lighter job for the time being. She duly was allocated to helping Muriel Fellows in the office at Teviot Hall dealing with mail, doing the Lumberjills' rota, typing letters with one finger. But

Lily, bored, hankered to be working outdoors again. Despite that, knowing the time was coming when Fran would deem it necessary for her to return to work, she was nervous. She harboured a fear that if she drove trucks, she mightn't be so lucky next time and she could lose the precious baby, and the thought overrode her normal devil-may-care attitude.

Then fate intervened.

———

'The news has spread like wildfire throughout the camp that a POW has been carrying on with a Lumberjill and he's been relocated to a secure camp,' Bella told Lily on a bright and sunny but chilly Sunday morning as the two of them walked home from church.

Lily remarked, 'Nancy started the rumour. She's made it known the Lumberjill in question is Ethel Post, who works in the stables.' She knew discussing Ethel with Bella wasn't the best of ideas given her views on the matter. But it was Bella who had brought the subject up, after all. 'It sounds as if you were right about Ethel. D'you really think she'll be made to resign?'

Bella made a knowing face. 'The whisper around the camp, again put about by Nancy, is that Ethel has friends in high places – namely the laird, Sir Keith Henley, himself.' Bella raised her eyes heavenward. 'Which I must say doesn't surprise me as anyone else found fraternising with a POW would have been fired on the spot.'

Lily knew Bella was vexed because, although Fran had told her that she might be working in the stables on her own, the situation hadn't materialised. She tried to understand her friend's position, though she didn't agree with her views herself.

As they walked along the path in the estate grounds towards the camp, Lily found pleasure in the April sunshine, admiring borders surrounding a building which was once, apparently, the estate's little theatre. Gazing at the nodding daffodils and eye-catching purple and white crocuses, it occurred to Lily that a row of spring cabbages in the borders would be more suitable. She chided herself; the war and rationing were never far from anyone's thoughts, but folk needed brightness too, things to cheer them, and those spring flowers fit the bill perfectly and lifted the spirit.

Passing the building that, on the laird's instruction, had been converted into an orphanage for evacuee orphans, Lily's thoughts turned automatically to Ethel, who kept very much to herself these days.

'It must be difficult working with Ethel, because of how you feel about her and all that's been going on,' she ventured as they approached the path passing the rear of Teviot House.

A belligerent expression crossed Bella's face. 'We both get on with our jobs and never speak unless it's to do with work.'

'Nobody speaks to her,' Lily remarked. 'Like you, everyone just suffers Ethel.'

Looking into the distance where trees rose up on the hillside, Bella had the grace to look uncomfortable.

Most Lumberjills, while being shocked at Ethel's behaviour, left her alone as they'd more pressing things on their minds: what their next meal would consist of, when was it their turn to bathe at the big house and what to wear they hadn't worn a 'million times' before at the weekly dance. Not so Nancy and her converted cronies, who were downright nasty to Ethel whenever she was in earshot.

As they walked, glancing sideways at Bella's discomfited expression, Lily decided to confide about Ethel's past – hoping it might help Bella to better understand Ethel and maybe she might condone the young girl's actions.

'I'm going to tell you something but in strictest confidence, mind.'

Bella must have heard the gravity in her tone as an anxious look came into her eyes.

Lily went on to tell what she knew about Ethel's woeful

previous life and her parentage. Bella might be hot-headed at times, but she was trustworthy to a fault and certainly not vindictive.

'Ethel's certainly had her fair share of bad luck,' Bella conceded, 'but I still find it difficult to overlook the fact she consorted with this Karl.'

That was progress at least, Lily thought – Bella referring to the German by name. She considered telling Bella what she knew about Karl, then thought that might be a step too far at this stage.

As they neared the clearing next to the camp, Bella stopped and turned to face Lily. 'I do feel rotten at times, as Ethel always appears on tenterhooks while we're working, as if she's expecting me to make some offensive comment.'

'You're too decent for that,' Lily confirmed. 'Though she obviously knows how you feel.'

'Lily, I can't ever ignore what Ethel's done but neither can I abide how Nancy and her cronies treat her.'

Lily knew Bella was having a difficult time wrestling with her feelings about Ethel and she decided to suggest the plan that had been whirling in her mind recently.

'Bella, I'm going to confide in you about something but first I want you to swear you'll keep it a secret.'

Bella nodded. 'I promise.'

Lily explained she was pregnant and Bella grinned. 'You're kidding me?' Her hands covered her mouth and formed a pyramid. 'You really are expecting?'

'I really am.' Lily was delighted with Bella's reaction. 'I'd like to keep the fact a secret for a while as I don't want to be sent packing quite yet but neither do I want to risk the dangers of driving a heavy truck and hauling timber.'

'I won't tell a soul, Lily, and I do understand.'

'So, I have a plan, and it involves you and your dilemma about working with Ethel.'

'I feel really rotten now after what you've told me but I can't help myself.'

'My replacement is doing a splendid job and so I'm going to ask Fran if I can work in the stables. I'll say I've lost my nerve driving a truck, which is kind of the truth. Then you'll be reassigned and work with the gang.'

Bella gave her a comical look. 'You don't know the first thing about horses.'

'Oh, yes I do. I once rode a donkey on Shields sands.'

Their eyes met and they both laughed.

'I'm so pleased for you.' Bella gave a little clap of the hands. 'It's something good to come out of this war.' Then sadness clouded her face. 'I also envy you. I'll never have kiddies... it would be disloyal to Ronnie to marry again.'

'Oh, I disagree.' Lily was surprised at how strongly she felt about this, considering she'd never consciously considered the matter before. 'I think it would be the biggest compliment if John should wish to marry again if anything happened to me. It would be a sort of testament to how happy he'd been and a sign he wanted to repeat the experience.'

Bella wrinkled her nose. 'D'you know I'd never thought of it like that.'

Lily so hoped she'd forged the way for her friend to find the happiness she deserved with someone in the future. Bella was too young and vital to spend the rest of her life single and without love.

Bella grinned. 'Be honest, wouldn't you be the teeniest bit jealous?'

'I'd be playing a harp up there' – Lily raised her eyes heavenward – 'and hopefully too saintly to have such negative thoughts.'

They both grinned at the image.

———

The next morning, the wistful feeling intensified when Fran appeared in the office with a letter for Lily in her hand. Seeing Mam's handwriting, a feeling of being isolated from all those she loved washed over Lily. She knew this was largely due to being pregnant, when her emotions were muddled.

'Fran, can you spare a moment? I'd like a word.'

Now was as good a time to put her proposal to the forewoman. As Fran listened to Lily's request her face gave nothing away.

'It was a nasty fall,' she agreed. 'If you two are fine with the plan it's fine by me. As long as the work gets done, I'm happy.'

For a moment it irked Lily that Fran would think she'd lost her nerve driving trucks but the desire to protect the baby was stronger.

But then the words, *Beware baby!* came to mind. Or, she wondered, could it have been, *Take care of baby?*

———

After Fran left, Lily sat on the bed to read Mam's letter.

Dear Lily,

First of all, we got your letter saying you're expecting and I had a tear in my eye and pray every night for a safe delivery. You take great care, our Lily, and don't go lifting anything heavy.

Now don't worry when I tell you this but Dad and I are off to live in the country to be with Jimmy. Your dad's chest got worse and then he started getting pains and he was an awful colour. I made him go to the doctor's and the upshot is it's his heart. That's two of us now with bad hearts and we've to look out for each other. The doctor's laid him off work because he says your dad's unfit to do his job at the shipyard. Can you imagine your dad not working!

Your Aunty Prue's over the moon we're going to Lancashire. She says she's bored stiff as there's nothing much going on there and she's hankering to go home and we can rent the council house. I've recently had a couple of funny turns and your dad reckons living in the country will do us both good.

It'll suit our Ian, as he's looking for rooms and he'll move in here – long story that I can't be bothered to tell you about now. Course I don't want to go but I will to please your dad.

Lily smiled at this; no one could make Mam move out of her home town if she didn't want to.

Your dad's reckoning on finding some light gardening work or helping on a farm which will do him good as he loves a garden and being outdoors. Between you and me, I've been worried sick about him, he's looking that gaunt and the change will be champion for him. We've got a bit of money put by so don't you worry about us.

Lily, you're not going to believe this, but when Harry heard of our plans, he insisted Jean moves to the safety of the country with us. I've told them now that Prue and her lads are hopping it back home there'll be plenty of room. Jean sees the sense as Harry's hardly ever at home as he does so much overtime these days. I must admit, although we'll have Jimmy, I'll miss having my family around and if Jean does come that would be the icing on the cake. Though I tire easily these days (which gets me down) and so I won't be able to give her as much of a hand as I'd like.

I hope all is well with you, our Lily, and you're still enjoying working in the woods.

I'll write when we're settled. It'll be lovely to see our Jimmy and I'll make sure to knit for that baby of yours.

Come and visit when you can because we miss seeing you.

Your loving Mam xx

Lily didn't know what to make of her parents diddling off to the country. It spoke volumes, though, that Mam hadn't argued with Dad and was willing to leave the town. Lily reckoned Mam was worried about the state of both of them more than she was letting on. Lily was glad her parents were being sensible and putting themselves first for a change. She was pleased Jean would be there to keep an eye on her parents and make sure they didn't overdo things.

Suddenly, the feeling that life was changing and the deflation her family wouldn't be there when she got home was overwhelming. But she was happy for them and it wasn't as if they were living a million miles away. She would write tonight and tell her parents how pleased she was for them and they were doing what was right for them.

27

The following week, Lily, wearing issued wellingtons a size too big, squelched in the pouring rain up the steep terrain, fearful she might slip.

Today's job was to help take the horses to the gang responsible for getting the felled trees from the forest, as it was impossible to drive a lorry on the slippery and rutted track up the hill. She was working with Ethel and the pair of them were leading the huge Clydesdales to the site where, with chains on their hindquarters, the horses would drag the timber from the dripping forest to the roadside where it would be collected by lorries and taken to the railway station.

Lily watched in amazement as Ethel, who appeared to have an affinity with horses, coaxed Champion, the mahogany-brown Clydesdale, to climb up the slippery slope. Whereas Lily, deficient in training, didn't understand Thunder, the horse she worked with, who was as stubborn as the proverbial mule and wouldn't budge from the spot, if he was so inclined. If Lily was truthful, she was scared of the huge animal that had a mind of its own and often found herself wondering if she'd made the right decision in choosing to work with horses.

At dinner time, as the gang sat around with bait tins open,

Vivian delved into her rucksack and surprisingly brought out a box camera.

'I want to take a snapshot for posterity,' she stood. 'Gather around, everyone, it'll only take a minute.'

'I look a fright,' Jill grumbled, but she did as she was told.

Vivian laughed. 'We all do, that's the point of taking the snapshot: so I'll remember what it was really like working in the forest.'

———

When the day's work was done, Lily and Ethel unhitched the horses and led them back to the stables. The fields weren't recovered from winter yet and Ethel deemed it necessary to keep the Clydesdales in the stable overnight as there wasn't enough for the horses to eat outside. Leaving plenty of feed and water in the troughs, bedding of straw, the stable door open for ventilation, the pair of them made their way back to the dormitory. A Thursday night, most of the Lumberjills, including Lily, would make for the recreation room after the evening meal.

'Why don't you come along?' Lily asked Ethel as she changed her top for a best poplin shirt. 'You could do that in the recreation room.' She pointed to the colourful squares of material Ethel was sewing together as she sat on the bed.

Ethel's startled expression said it all.

She said under her breath, in case anyone heard, 'People are afraid to be seen talking to me. I'm concerned you'll be ostracised too if you continue speaking to me outside of work.'

Lily moved closer and sat on the edge of Ethel's bed. 'The people who know and care about me won't judge me. I don't care what the rest think. Besides, folk are mostly involved with their own lives and have short memories.' Lily conceded, 'I will grant you Nancy will hold a grudge but, as the saying goes, "You can't please everyone."'

Ethel had a look on her face that said she wouldn't budge on the matter.

'You can't hide forever, Ethel. Avoiding people won't help. It looks like you're being... stand-offish.'

Ethel stopped sewing. 'Is that what people think about me?'

'That was my first impression until I got to know you.' Lily smiled to soften the brutal words.

Ethel paused for a moment. 'The truth is I do avoid people, I always have. At the orphanage it was everyone for themselves and people were wary of making friends as it was thought you wanted something.'

The statement reminded Lily of John, whose childhood experience had left him struggling to show his emotions with family and friends. Fortunately, it didn't extend to her.

Lily admitted she was glad Ethel had found love and a bit of happiness, even if it was with a Jerry prisoner. Lily believed in fate. You didn't choose who you fell in love with but it was what you decided to do about it that counted. They had chosen to be brave, even though they'd be condemned. Lily knew given the same circumstances, if it were John, she'd have no reservations about continuing a relationship with him.

Lily touched on that now. 'Now is the time to be your own person; you're free of the orphanage. Show people the real you and what a nice person you are. You'll make friends but there will be foes.'

Ethel stared at Lily for some time. Then, face resolute, she moved from the bed and began searching in her locker and pulled out a clean short-sleeved shirt that looked a size too big.

Ethel did what she always did when taking off her clothes or dressing: she got into bed and changed her clothes under the covers.

Lily imagined that must be another legacy passed down from the orphanage.

———

As Lily and Ethel entered the recreation room a blast of heat, music and voices met them and momentarily everyone appeared to stop what they were doing and stare. Appropriately, the calming strains of 'Let's Make Up' by Freddy Martin and His Orchestra blared from the gramophone.

Lily, leading, made her way to the area where Bella, Jill and Vivian were sitting. Vivian moved along a chair to allow the pair of them to sit together.

As the music came to a close, a loud voice was heard to say, 'It's lucky for some having friends in high places.'

Lily didn't need to look around the room to identify the source; she recognised the voice as Nancy's.

Ethel, cheeks colouring red, didn't falter as she smiled her thanks to Vivian.

Most of the Lumberjills chose to ignore the disruption, wanting only a fun night after a hard day's slog and, after all, the matter had been dealt with and the POW sent away.

Nancy stood, puce-faced and glared at Ethel, then flounced from the room, cronies following.

There appeared to be a collective sigh.

Later, the records finished, many Lumberjills had departed to have an early night. The few left sat in a group around the stove as the night was chilly and the room temperature had dropped.

In the half light of the flicking lamps, the room held a spooky atmosphere.

Sheila spoke. 'How about we have another Ouija board session?'

'I've told you before, it's dangerous,' Jill objected.

'Edith tells fortunes from tea leaves. Let's have a go at that,' Sheila persisted, checking her watch. 'It's time for our evening cuppa.' There were murmurs of approval as people rose to fetch tea from the canteen.

'I'll get ours,' Lily told Ethel.

Torch in hand, and making sure she pointed the beam down to the ground – a precaution in case enemy planes saw the light – she made her way beneath the moonlit sky to the canteen. One of the last in the queue, she took two cups from the tray on the counter and filled them with tea from the huge and heavy teapot. Taking both cup handles in one hand, she took two homemade biscuits from the plate and placed them in her trouser pocket and made her way back to the recreation room.

Inside, by the glow from the stove, Edith, a hefty lass whose broad shoulders could have matched those of any bloke, held a cup by its handle and swirled it in a clockwise direction three times.

'What's she doing?' Lily said as she handed a cup of tea to Ethel.

'It's my empty cup.' Sheila watched as though hypnotised.

'Edith always does this when she gives a reading as some of the tea leaves stick to the sides and others will stay on the bottom,' explained Vivian.

'Shh,' Sheila hissed. 'Edith's concentrating.'

A calm, absorbed expression on her face, Edith examined the scattered tea leaves in the cup.

'A large fish is near the top of the rim, which means the present. Good news is coming from another country.' Edith looked up at Sheila, who sat in wide-eyed concentration. 'The bird flying towards the handle means to expect an important letter. I see the letter M, which is the sender's initial.'

'Malcolm. He's been posted abroad,' Sheila blurted, with an expression of awe.

Lily wasn't impressed because Sheila had divulged this fact at mealtime and Edith could have heard. Others were eager to have their fortunes told and then it was the turn of Bella. She handed Edith her cup.

'I see dissatisfaction with a present situation.' Edith focused on the cup. 'The tea leaves form a long line so expect a journey in the not-too-distant future. Ahh! A big heart surrounded by dots. Marriage is on the cards.' Bella, looking upset, Lily could tell, squirmed and appeared as if she wanted the reading to stop. 'I see two apples,' Edith went on. 'You're going to have a long and successful life. Lucky you.'

'You next,' Lily told Ethel, when Bella's reading was completed.

'No, I—'

'Here.' Lily took hold of Ethel's cup and handed it over to Edith.

Edith checked her watch. 'I haven't time. It's quarter to ten.'

'It won't take long,' Vivian, looking on, encouraged.

With a disgruntled expression, Edith gave in to the ganger. Holding the cup by the rim, she rotated it then peered at the tea leaves. She studied them for a while and then meeting Ethel's gaze she told the lass, 'There's nothing here to read.'

Ethel, staring around at the watching faces, flushed. 'If you didn't want to tell my fortune, why didn't you just say?'

She stood up from the seat; shoulders back and head in the air, she made for the door.

———

'Edith was just tired and didn't want to continue,' Lily, hurrying to catch up with Ethel in the dark, cajoled, knowing she sounded unconvincing.

'Think what you like.' Ethel's voice was shaky.

'I'm sorry some people are treating you this way, Ethel, but they will forget and life will take a turn for the better.'

'I know you're trying to help, Lily, but it's not about just me. I get upset because they don't know the real Karl, how kind and caring he is. He's thought of as a cruel Nazi and it's not fair.' Her voice quavered. 'He says the best thing that happened was when he was captured and didn't have to be in the Luftwaffe any more. He has no quarrel with the allies and...' Gulping, she couldn't go on.

Feeling protective of the young girl, Lily was tempted to give her a big hug but, mindful of what Ethel had said about sentiment being frowned upon at the orphanage, she held back. Instead, she handed over a handkerchief she took from her trouser pocket.

The pair of them walked in silence for a while. The clouds, now a thin veil, passed the moon and it could be seen riding high in the sky. The silence, a tangible thing, felt companionable, and a big-sisterly kind of caring for Ethel washed over Lily.

She broke the silence as she didn't want Ethel going to bed with recent events on her mind.

'I've never met the laird; he seems nice.'

'He is,' Ethel, watching the moon, said. 'After the war started, us orphans at Blakely orphanage were told we were to be evacuated into the country but none of us knew quite what to expect.' She looked at Lily. 'I was a senior girl by then and was sent ahead with Miss Balfour, the kindest teacher, to help get the theatre here on the estate ready for when the little ones arrived. Sir Keith turned up every day and supervised the work.' Lily heard the smile in her voice. 'I was astonished one day when the laird spoke to me and was interested in my background. When I told him my father was German, he told me it would be best to keep quiet about such matters.'

Sound advice, Lily thought, as now Germans were being arrested by the police and interned and held in camps.

'When I turned fifteen and it was time to leave the orphanage, I was apprehensive about the future, what I would do next. Sir Keith, when he heard, offered me a job here at Teviot Hall as a domestic. When I turned seventeen, the Women's Timber Corps had begun and the laird had a word with head office and I was recruited as a Lumberjill here in the woods. Sir Keith told me that it was time I set foot out in the world and it was best I started here on the estate.'

Lily told her, in a jokey way, 'So you really have got friends in high places.'

'I do.' Ethel smiled cheekily. 'You should be grateful to me because, when Sir Keith asked how I was getting on as a Lumberjill and I explained how cold it was at night in the dormitory, not only did he supply me with a stone hot-water bottle, but all the other Lumberjills too.' Her expression turned serious. 'Sir Keith's been very kind and taken me under his wing.'

By now they had come to the footpath leading to the huts. Ethel, hesitating, stared at the dark clouds gliding across the skies, obscuring the moon again and plunging the two Lumberjills into darkness. The silence deepened and a cold shiver ran down Lily's spine as, intuitively, she knew something momentous was about to happen.

Ethel's voice came out of the darkness. 'I used to sneak from the dormitory to meet Karl when I thought everyone was asleep.' Her voice was low and urgent, as though she needed to talk, tell Lily what had happened. 'I knew I shouldn't but I couldn't help myself. I never counted on Nancy being outside smoking.'

'You met in the hayloft?'

'Yes.' A pause, then, 'I miss him so much, Lily.'

So much grief in her voice, Lily felt compelled to comfort her. 'Ethel, you're young. One day you'll meet someone and you'll forget Karl and get on with your life.'

Ethel turned towards Lily, her expression resolute. 'I don't want to forget Karl; he's the father of the bairn I'm carrying.'

Lily gawped. 'You're kidding me.' A stupid thing to say – as if Ethel would joke about something like that.

Lily was flabbergasted.

———

It took a while but Lily managed to control her shocked thoughts and asked, 'Did Karl know about the baby?'

Ethel's expression was stricken with guilt. 'I meant to tell him.' She looked down at the floor. 'I guess I felt ashamed.'

'It takes two to make a baby,' Lily reminded her.

'It's all my fault.' Ethel's eyes glazed as she looked down the months, remembering. 'It was winter and cold outside and we were cuddling to keep warm in the hayloft. Karl was worrying about his family and missing them and I just wished I had a family to care about. I'd never felt so close to anyone before and I couldn't believe it when Karl announced he loved me.'

Lily's heart went out to Ethel as her young face lit up pitifully at the memory.

'He'd made me a present of a brush from horsehair and he was sad because that's all he had to give. I had nothing.' She bit her lip before going on. 'I told Karl I wanted us to make love so that whatever happened we'd have this one time to remember.' Her opaque brown eyes met Lily's. 'Now I'll always have something to remember him by.'

8

Next day, Lily, finished work for the day, was sitting cross-legged on the bed reading two letters from John. The letters had arrived in this morning's post and Fran had just delivered them, much to Lily's delight.

Reading the letters, it was as though John was at her side speaking the words, and a warm glow suffused Lily.

The first letter was written with more detail about his arrival in North Africa.

Sweetheart,

Sorry I've taken so long to write, here in North Africa we're – the next bit was censored by an ugly black smudge – *for the allied campaign to free the area from the clutches of German and Italian troops. The journey was uneventful, as our troop ship survived the torpedoes in the Med, thank God.*

He went on to describe his camp and the weather.

We don't get much kip and we're kept busy so there's never time to write but you're in my thoughts constantly. Censorship makes it difficult to tell you what's going on but be assured there's plenty of action. Let me know how you're getting on as a Lumberjill. I think of you in a smart figure-hugging uniform but seeing you would be better. Big hint!

Time to go and hoping to receive a letter soon,

All my love,

Your John

As Lily laid the letter on the bed, she grinned. Figure-hugging uniform indeed! Most of the time she wore a bib and brace overall that would better fit someone a size bigger than her.

The next letter was full of John's excitement at receiving her letter informing him she was expecting again. His response was:

After all the whooping, yelling and telling the men what it was all about, that I'm going to be a dad, I finally got down to writing a letter.

I'm so happy even the damned flies don't bother me. I have this soppy grin on my face as I write, but my main concern is you. I want to wrap you up in a big bear hug and not let you near any heavy timber. But knowing you, you won't be mollycoddled.

Take care of yourself. Third time lucky, my darling. I love you so very much.

Your John

Lily lay back on the bed and luxuriated in thoughts of John and thanked God he was safe. *Please watch over him*, she prayed.

She turned and looked at Ethel's empty bed. The poor lass had no one.

Lily's thoughts turned to last night, and the shock of Ethel's revelation. She'd insisted she wanted her pregnancy to be kept a secret from the others for as long as she could. Then, without another word, she'd made for the dormitory.

This morning, Ethel had carried on as if nothing had happened. Lily was loath to bring the subject up because it was none of her business, after all. But she did worry – how far gone was she? Did she have a future plan? Lily's chief concern was that Ethel was in denial. This afternoon the lass had even spoken about the summer and that she'd have to get one of the estate labourers to check all the fences where the horses grazed.

Lily, climbing off the bed, placed John's letters in her locker. Making for the door because it was evening mealtime, she made a decision. Just because Ethel had clammed up about the subject of the baby it didn't mean Lily should. Even if she did get told to mind her own business, Lily felt obliged to get her to at least face facts.

———

Later in the canteen, Lily, sitting at the end of one of the long trestle tables, strained to hear the news report on the wireless over the hubbub of high-pitched voices.

'The British have taken Longstop Hill in Tunisia after bitter fighting,' the newscaster's urgent monotone voice could just be heard saying, 'a key position on the—'

'Pass the plates down.' Sheila, who was on mealtime duty, stood at the table end, a tray in her hands. Plates of indistinguishable meat stew (it was a case of spot the cube of meat), taties, carrots and limp cabbage were passed along the table. As cutlery clattered on plates, Lily gave up trying to listen to the wireless.

When the news finished, Edie, turning the wireless's knob, changed channels to *Music Club*, a programme in which a panel answered questions about music put by members of the forces. As she ate, Lily's mind speculated on the news she'd just heard and if it would affect John.

'Penny for them?' Bella, opposite, asked in a raised voice, then popped a forkful of mashed potatoes in her mouth, which seemed these days the Lumberjills' staple diet.

Lily shook her head. She wasn't keen to discuss her husband over the table. 'Just this and that,' she answered evasively.

Bella nodded in understanding.

The main meal finished, empty plates were passed along the table to be replaced by a dish with a portion of bread-and-butter pudding and custard in it. Devouring a spoonful, Lily saw Ethel at the counter filling a tray with white dessert bowls. Lily hadn't noticed she was on dinner duty before.

Lily studied Ethel as she pressed against the counter. She was wearing a rather large dress shirt and trousers, and she noticed a small mound at her abdomen was visible – but that was probably because Lily knew to look for it.

It was at that moment she saw Dulcie Sinclair, one of Nancy's cronies, who was also on dinner duty, sidle up alongside Ethel at the counter. She said something and Ethel, face blanching, retorted.

Dulcie gave her a shove and the dishes almost slid from the tray as Ethel overbalanced.

Edie, standing behind the counter dressed in wrap-over pinny covering her clothes, turned the sound down on the wireless and pointed with a spoon in her hand at the two Lumberjills. 'Now, ladies, behave.'

'Aren't our lads good enough for you?' a lass from Nancy's table shouted.

Oh God, Lily prayed, *please don't let this be about the baby.*

Dulcie's eyes travelled around the room. 'The slag's trying to hide she's pregnant by a Nazi prisoner.'

Everyone stopped what they were doing and in the shocked silence all that could be heard was, incongruously, a muted burst of laughter from the wireless sitting on the counter.

'Go on – admit it,' Dulcie jeered.

Lily glanced over at Nancy sitting at the table wearing a smug smile. Her cronies were doing the dirty work for her.

Hands trembling, Ethel put the laden tray down on the counter. Her skin complexion ashen, she faced Dulcie. 'I'm expecting a bairn by someone I love and who loves me.'

'Is he the POW from the camp?' Dulcie, pursing her lips in distaste, wanted to know.

Ethel, looking rather nervous, didn't answer.

'Go on, admit it.'

Lily, seeing the intrigued faces in the room turning hostile and the atmosphere going tense, knew this altercation was headed for trouble.

'Yes.' The word tore from Ethel.

'Slut,' someone yelled.

Dulcie visibly bristled with rage. 'You... Kraut whore.' Pitching her head forward, she spat in Ethel's face.

Globs of spittle could be seen on Ethel's cheek. Stunned, she brushed them with the back of a hand.

Lily leapt from her seat but Bella, opposite, beat her to it.

'That's enough,' Bella cried as she raced toward Ethel, shoving Dulcie out of the way.

Taking a shocked Ethel by an arm, she turned to face the Lumberjills. 'You should be ashamed of yourselves, all of you.'

No one stirred but the atmosphere in the canteen was fragile and as ready to flare as a lit match next to tinder. As Bella led the stunned Ethel out of the canteen, Lily hurried to follow, proud her friend had been the one to step in and protect Ethel despite how she'd previously felt about her.

All that could be heard was another burst of laughter from the wireless.

———

'Why didn't you take precautions?' Bella asked and Lily cringed at her forthrightness.

The three of them were sitting around the dormitory stove. None of the other Lumberjills had returned to the dormitory after the meal and Lily assumed they'd made their way to the recreation room to mull over tonight's events.

While Ethel was still in shock, her face had regained its natural colour.

She told Bella, 'The time it happened I decided I couldn't bear it if something happened to Karl and we never, you know, did it. Karl was worried because he didn't have one of those things... but I wouldn't listen. It was only the once, and I told myself nothing would happen.' Her chin jutted. 'I'll never regret it. As I've told Lily, at least I've got something to remember Karl by.'

Lily averted her gaze from Bella, who she knew would find this particular conversation difficult.

Ethel told them, 'Afterwards Karl said he couldn't help but worry that we might get parted and he wouldn't be able to find me. I imagine when he found out he was being sent away, that's why he escaped to deliver the letter.'

Bella's brow creased into a frown. 'Hang on, what letter?'

Lily, throwing caution to the wind, explained how Karl had escaped and found his way to the dormitory and left the letter.

'You didn't think to tell me?' Bella's tone displayed the hurt she felt.

'Fran swore me to secrecy because the whole affair was to be kept hush-hush.'

She refrained from admitting that at the time she was wary of mentioning anything about Ethel because of Bella's hostility towards the lass.

Ethel told them, 'I expect Karl was desperate to send me the information and took matters in his own hands.'

'What information?' Bella wanted to know.

'An address to help find Karl after the war if needs be,' Ethel told them.

That would be the address Lily had seen. She thought about Fran's disclosure about Karl being shipped to America but decided it wasn't a good idea to bring this up just now as it would only distress Ethel more.

'You can count on us to help all we can.' Bella's voice held the ring of sincerity.

Lily's estimation for her friend soared a hundredfold. She'd laid to rest her grievances, and stood up for Ethel when it counted.

Bella caught her eye. 'I can't abide injustice or bullying.' It was as though she was trying to justify her change of heart.

'And what's your plan for the future?' Lily asked Ethel, taking a leaf out of Bella's forthright book.

'I've no idea. I've been putting it to the back of my mind.' The pallid look had returned. 'But now people know, it's scary.' Fear lurked deep in Ethel's shocked brown eyes.

'And you've got no one?' Bella's expression held concern.

Cupping her chin in her hands, Ethel shook her head.

———

Next morning at breakfast, Lily, feeling judgemental eyes staring at her, picked at the bowl of porridge in front of her. Ethel had chosen to go without breakfast and who could blame her, but there was no way Lily would hide.

Later, meeting up with Ethel at the stables, the familiar horsey smell of sweat, manure and hay assaulting her nostrils, she handed over the bait tin containing cheese sandwiches she'd picked up from the canteen counter.

'Thank you for thinking of me.' Ethel placed the tin on the ground.

Lily stroked the elegant Clydesdale's forehead as the horse poked his head out of the stable door, her hand trailing down his white flat nose to his muzzle.

'Morning, Thunder, are we a team yet?'

In answer, Thunder shied backward, hooves clattering on the concrete floor.

'Woah, boy,' Ethel reassured the horse as she approached carrying a harness. At that moment Fran appeared at the main stable doorway. She didn't smile but looked edgy. Lily tensed, sensing this wasn't a social call.

'Morning, both.' Fran addressed Ethel. 'It's best you don't work today,' she said, without preamble.

Ethel's brow corrugated in bemusement. Then a look of enlightenment crossed her face.

'This is about me being pregnant, isn't it?'

'Yes,' Fran, never one to be afraid to voice the truth, answered. 'Someone reported the incident in the canteen to Muriel this morning.' She gave a significant sigh. 'Feelings are running high and Muriel thinks it's best you lie low until she finds out what to do next. I must say I'm in agreement.'

A first, Lily found herself thinking.

'Does this mean I might get finished?' By the look of dismay on Ethel's face, the full implication of her actions were dawning on her.

'I can't guarantee that you won't be.' Fran's tone held a note of regret.

————

At dinner time, Lily headed from the work site in the nearby woods. Thunder had been dragging timber all morning from the depths of the woods to the roadside and Lily was leading him by the reins back to the stables. The intention had been that she would eat her sandwich with the rest before making the journey back. But, feeling like a leper as none of the gang looked her way, Lily abandoned the plan.

The gang were burning brushwood (left behind from felled trees), which was a highlight and everyone sat around the fire on tree trunks laughing and chatting as they ate their cheese sandwiches. Tall, thin trees surrounded the area, while smoke – infused with the aroma of pine needles, a refreshing citrusy smell – billowed high in the air.

Observing the scene, nostalgia for how things used to be when

Lily could be part of the happy group washed over her. She knew now what it was like to have a difference of opinion from everyone that made you an outcast. But, even if she could go back in time knowing the outcome, she would still have befriended Ethel.

Vivian got up and, stretching, sauntered from the group, then quickening her pace, she caught up with Lily.

She gave an overbright smile. 'Where's Ethel?'

'She's been told not to come to work today.'

The ganger nodded in understanding.

They lapsed into silence for a while as they walked. Then Vivian spoke. 'The gang will get over it, you know, in time. Things will get back to normal.'

'Not one of them stood up for Ethel except Bella,' Lily accused.

A small blotch of pink tinged both Vivian's cheeks. 'I'm guilty too, but I must say I was shocked.' She nodded backwards towards the group. 'They're a good bunch at heart.' She turned to face Lily again, with an abashed look. 'Thing is, it makes life easier if you follow the herd. I admire you for standing up for what you think's right.'

It was Lily's turn to blush as she knew she'd been quick to criticise. She admitted, 'I confess I was shocked too when I first heard.'

With nothing more to say on the matter, the pair of them chatted for a while, then Vivian returned to the group.

Lily stopped walking and, resting her head on Thunder's neck, she stroked his mane. The horse seemed to recognise her need for companionship because for once he didn't make any objection by shying away.

As horse and human stood together, a deep silence shrouded the woods when not a bird tweeted or tree rustled, and all Lily could hear was her breathing. A sensation of being hemmed in by the high trees that blotted out the sky overcame her.

Vivian's words played in her head. *Things will get back to normal.*

What was normal? Being here, in the woods, or at home at Olcote?

But the question was, Lily realised, what was important? The answer was simple. The fear of losing her baby. That thought led to another: that she now felt vulnerable doing such a manual job.

A breeze started up and, as it blew through the tops of the trees, they rustled an answer.

As she picked up Thunder's reins and they walked together side by side, Lily knew what she must do.

Her mind made up, she took Thunder back to the stables where she slipped the feed bag over his head.

————

Later, she went to seek Fran, who she knew was out in the woods driving a Caterpillar tractor.

Fran was just about to drag heavier timber to the roadside to be taken to the nearby sawmill when Lily spotted her.

Looking up, Lily shaded her eyes from the dappled sunlight. 'Can I have a word please, Fran?'

'Can't it wait?'

'I'd rather get the matter over with now.'

Looking none too pleased, Fran climbed down from the tractor. However, her expression changed to concern when Lily made her request that she wanted to resign from the WTC.

'Is it because of what's happened with Eth—'

'It's nothing to do with Ethel.'

'Good. I thought you were made of sterner stuff. What's brought this on, then?'

'I'm three months pregnant and I've decided to play safe and go home earlier than I intended.'

Fran looked rather taken aback. Then, appearing to think about the news, she nodded. 'I understand. The work here's tough. Not the place for someone pregnant. If I'd known I would have sent you packing.' She gave a friendly smile.

Lily felt oddly emotional. It was then she realised something else. Gone was the obsession with competing with her brothers, or the will to be as strong as the male foresters. She'd proved herself already, and now what she wanted was to deliver this baby safely, for John and her to love.

'You'll be missed, more than you know.' As Lily raised her eyebrows, the forewoman went on, 'I know you think everyone's against you because of your stance about the Ethel Post situation, but that isn't true. There are those who admire you. You stuck to your convictions, and it hasn't gone unnoticed how loyal you are.'

'What about Ethel? What d'you think will happen to her? She has no one.'

'We're aware of that. The only option for Ethel is a hospital for unwed mothers, then to have the baby adopted.'

Shocked at the answer, Lily couldn't bear such a thing to happen to Ethel. She might be young and unmarried but it was patently obvious that she loved and desired to keep the baby she carried.

'What about the laird? Would he have a say in this?'

Fran looked uncomfortable. 'It would be inappropriate to involve Sir Keith in such a delicate matter.' She gave a glum sigh. 'Thing is, some of the locals see Lumberjills as a threat, by the way they dress and do a man's job. Unlike their daughters, they're free of parental restrictions and so it follows, in people's minds, that morals are relaxed. We wouldn't want the doubters to be proved right and so we're keeping the lid on this situation as best we can.'

It was then that Lily made her next spur-of-the-moment decision. 'That won't be necessary. Ethel can come and stay with me until she's decided what she's going to do about the baby.'

29

Three days later, Lily was on the train, hurtling through open countryside, steam wafting past the window, when she felt it begin to slow.

As she looked out of the window at the lambs gambolling in the fields, Lily thought about the final moments when they'd left Teviot Hall. What Fran had said proved to be true as the Lumberjills (excluding Nancy and her cronies) turned out to wish Lily farewell and good luck in the future for her and the baby, their voices ringing with sincerity. But for Ethel only Jill, Vivian and Bella had been brave enough to say goodbye.

'Hexham.' Ethel, next to the window, was first to see the sign. 'What a cute station,' she remarked as the train stopped at the platform.

Lily, sitting beside her, bent forward to peer out.

The station had two platforms, a bridge that crossed the track and tubs filled with pink tulips.

The journey so far had been tiring, with changes of trains because the main Edinburgh to Newcastle line was busy transporting troops – but the picture-postcard scene of the countryside was worth the longer journey.

As passengers boarded the train and found seats, a whistle

blew. They pulled out of the station and Ethel, sitting back in the seat, grew pensive.

'Is everything all right?' Lily asked.

Ethel gave a wistful smile. 'I was thinking of the journey all those years ago when the orphans set out from the orphanage. The prospect of living in the countryside was scary but life seemed full of promise, especially since we'd escaped that harridan, Mistress Knowles.' Her face fell. 'I never thought it would end like this.'

Lily couldn't help but feel sad for Ethel when she thought of her own optimistic future.

Third time lucky.

As she gazed out of the train window, at a River Tyne that meandered along and would eventually, she knew, flow into the North Sea, Lily wondered about the thoughtful Ethel sitting beside her.

When Lily had explained that she too was pregnant and returning home, and invited Ethel to live with her until she'd worked out a plan, she hadn't expected Ethel to be thrilled – but she had anticipated something more than a simple nod. It was only later that it occurred to Lily that Ethel had no other option but to agree.

The country scene outside the train's window, fields and undulating hills on the horizon, changed to a conglomerate of dreary buildings as far as the eye could see. A shadow of doubt that she was doing the right thing crept over Lily, which was quickly dispelled at the thought of home.

Alighting from the train at busy Newcastle station, Lily led the way through the throng, Ethel trailing behind. As she found the platform and boarded the train bound for South Shields, Lily felt excitement grow within her.

The pair of them didn't speak for the journey, which took over half an hour. Lily, gazing out of the window, enjoyed the familiar scene, while Ethel, sitting opposite, stared into space looking glum.

'We're here,' Lily announced unnecessarily when the train huffed into South Shields station. Ethel nodded.

It wasn't until they were on the trolleybus and on their way to Lily's home in Foley Avenue that Lily, seeing Ethel's woeful face, asked, 'Tell me what's wrong, Ethel?'

Ethel turned and her eyes, displaying misery, alarmed Lily.

'I really am grateful for what you're doing, Lily, inviting me to live in your home and all.' She spoke in a low tone so as not to attract attention from other passengers. 'I was at me wits' end what I could do and the thought of ending up in the workhouse was terrifying, but coming back here is difficult because it's a reminder how bad it's all turned out.' She groaned. 'I had such high hopes when I left and vowed I'd never set foot in the place again.' Ethel, turning, her face despairing, looked out of the window. 'Here I am back where I started from at the orphanage.'

Lily, upset for the lass, tried to think of how to avert her thoughts from the bad times to perhaps happier memories of the town.

'Whereabouts did you live with your Aunty Meg?'

Ethel's gaze softened. 'Aunt Meg rented an upstairs flat in a street off the marketplace. Me and Mam shared a bedroom. Aunty liked to be thought of as posh and so the third bedroom was a front room, that nobody ever used.' She smiled fondly. 'Aunty Meg was houseproud and spent her day polishing and cleaning. Mam helped but she always made time to take me to the stalls where we'd listen to the merchants selling their wares.'

She paused and looked as if there was something else on her mind. Lily knew times like this it was better to wait until the lass had formulated what she wanted to say.

Ethel gazed out of the window to the passing scenery, the magnificent town hall where a statue of Queen Victoria stared regally out, the shops with striped canopies, an anti-invasion blockade at Westoe bridges, then Ethel turned to Lily again.

'At the orphanage' – she spoke as though carrying on from the previous conversation – 'we were never allowed to forget we were charity cases. When we lived at Aunty Meg's, Mam couldn't accept charity and worked at first to pay board but then she got sick. The thing is, Lily, I've saved me pay from work but I doubt it'll cover board and lodgings for very long. I don't want to be a char—'

'Stop.' Lily thought fast how best to handle this. 'First of all, it was my idea to invite you to stay at my place. And this arrangement benefits me too.' Ethel arched a curious eyebrow. 'You'll be doing me a favour by keeping me company. If it makes you feel any better, you can pay me back by helping around the house – that is' – she grinned – 'until we're both so big we can't see our feet.'

Their eyes met and, both imagining the scene, they grinned.

The mood lightened, and Lily went on, 'Enough talk of charity cases. Just remember you'll be a godsend for my sanity.'

Their stop now, Lily rose and, as the pair of them alighted from the trolley's platform and stood on the pavement, Lily thought she saw a hint of enthusiasm in the young girl's expression.

———

When Lily opened the door and entered the lobby, the house had a cold and echoey, unlived-in feel. Dumping her belongings on the strip of worn red carpet running along the passageway, she moved into each room and opened the blackout curtains. Yellow, welcoming sunlight streamed into each room.

'Go and investigate upstairs and open the curtains while you're at it,' she told Ethel, who was still hovering in the passageway. 'I'll investigate the coal situation and we'll have to think of getting some rations in. I was registered with Thornton's corner shop in the next street before I went away,' she informed her, unnecessarily.

Hearing Ethel's footsteps on the stairs, Lily called up, 'Choose the bedroom you'd like. Ours is the one with the floral bedspread and dressing table at the window.'

Ours, Lily thought, *what a comforting word*. She opened the back door and crossed the backyard. Unlocking the coalhouse, she peered in and was pleased to see lumps of black coal.

She thought of John and it made her smile. She promised herself to tell him the latest development that she was back home.

As Lily came back into the silent and echoey house, she considered it really was true, Ethel was doing her a favour by moving in.

————

Later, after a supper of fried Spam sandwiches made from a grey, unappetising National Loaf, the only bread left at the corner shop, the blackout curtains drawn, the two of them sat in comfortable chairs in front of the flickering flames, toasting their feet.

Ethel's voice broke into her thoughts. 'Fancy you owning a house as big as this.' Marvelling, she gazed around the airy, high-ceilinged kitchen. She'd unpacked by now and was concentrating on sewing colourful squares together. Her young face did appear to have a healthy glow, often attributed to women that were expecting. Lily wondered if the same was true of her.

'The house isn't ours,' she told Ethel. 'But one day, according to John's mam, it will be.' Ethel's expression dropped and Lily realised she'd put her foot in it. Ethel had no such good fortune.

Realising this prompted Lily to say, 'Tell me if it's none of my business, but d'you have any ideas what you're going to do?'

'I've been wracking me brains. I've thought of two but neither seems feasible.'

'Let's hear them, then.'

Ethel laid her sewing on her knee. 'I could ask Sir Keith if I could go back into domestic service at Teviot Hall after the bairn's born.'

'Who'll look after the baby?'

'That's the problem, there's no one and I'd have to give the baby up for adoption.'

Lily saw by her upset expression the heartache that would cause.

'And idea two?'

'To write to Karl's mam at the address in the letter. Tell her about the baby. The trouble with that is, even if I could, I wouldn't want to go to Germany. Besides, his mam might think I'm a hussy getting pregnant by her son.'

'Ethel, he's responsible too.'

'Yes, but will he want to take on responsibility? We never discussed marriage or family.'

'You said yourself what a good person he is.' Lily remembered the anguished call from Karl as he was marched from the dormitory that day. She'd guessed at the time what the words might mean.

'Remember what Karl told me to tell you, "*Ich lieve see.*"'

'*Ich liebe sie*,' Ethel corrected and gave a wobbly smile. 'I love her.'

'You see. He does love you.' Even to Lily she sounded as if she was trying too hard to convince her.

'I don't know any more.' Ethel, in obvious torment, clapped her hands on her cheeks. 'I genuinely believe Karl is a good person but war changes people. Dad, for instance, didn't want to return to his homeland, as he called it. And would have nothing to do with his parents.' She shook her head. 'So there lies a tale. They said Karl would probably be shipped to America. What if he can't get home after the war? What if he decides to return to his family in Germany— What if he meets—'

Lily interrupted. 'Ethel, we could "what if" all night. What do you wish to happen?'

'For Karl to return to England,' Ethel replied without hesitation, 'and we bring this bairn up as a family. The thing I definitely don't want to happen' – her expression became fierce – 'is for the baby to be brought up in an orphanage. I'd sooner it was adopted.'

'When is the baby due?'

'Sometime around August.' She picked up the sewing again.

'What exactly is it you're making?'

'It's a memory quilt for the—' Ethel froze as an unaccustomed noise outside the window sounded.

The warning wail of the air-raid siren. An adrenalin rush of fear made Lily momentarily question her decision to return to the town, with its dangers of full-scale raids due to the close vicinity to shipyards. Though planes had thundered overhead while she lived at the WTC camp, no bombs had dropped in the area of Teviot Hall. Galvanised into action, Lily concentrated on remembering the air-raid drill.

'Ethel, go in the living room and bring the blankets from the backs of the chairs and anything else you might need. Hurry.'

Lily, lighting the gas ring, boiled the whistling kettle and made a flask of tea. Hurrying under the stairs, she brought out a string bag, packed for such an occasion, including necessities such as candles, spare batteries and the torch. She paused to think, then, racing back into the kitchen, placed the fireguard around the fire.

Lily met Ethel in the passageway, carrying the blankets over an arm, a carpet bag in her hand, and the pair of them hurried to the back door. Outside, guns muttered in the distance and twin spotlights searched the darkened sky. Hearing the drone of raiders moving closer, dread, like a stone, weighed in her stomach.

Leading the way into the shelter, Lily cursed herself for not checking the lamp oil earlier.

She fumbled in the string bag and brought out the torch. By its beam she saw the lamp was half full of oil. Lighting and adjusting the wick, the lamp's flame cast eerie, shadowy shapes on the red-brick wall.

'There's deckchairs against the back wall,' she told Ethel, 'or a canvas bed if you want to lie down.'

As planes thundered nearer, Lily inwardly ridiculed her remark. *As if that is likely.*

'Here they come,' Ethel's shaky voice said as the throbbing of planes came terrifyingly close. Putting up the deckchairs side by side, she plonked down on one, then covered her ears with her hands.

Ghastly shrieking noises, like screaming firecrackers, were followed by muffled explosions. *The raiders are after the docks,* Lily thought. What a relief it was to know Dad didn't work there any more.

The planes roared overhead and into the distance, and there came a lull when the quiet was deafening. Ethel took her hands from her ears and, her eyes big and round, said in a small voice, 'What I find terrifying is it's a case of here one minute and gone the next.'

———

As time passed, and the raiders didn't return, Lily, still trembly after Ethel's last remark, sighed with relief. 'Thank the Lord that's over.'

'Until the next one.'

'Ethel, we can't think like that. Stiff upper lip and all that.'

Looking at Ethel's downcast expression, Lily decided a cup of tea was in order to calm their jittery nerves. Bringing out two enamel mugs from the string bag, she poured tea in each of them from the flask, then handed one to Ethel.

Placing the sewing she was doing on her knee, Ethel looked up and Lily saw the seriousness in her eyes.

She bit her lip. 'When I heard those bombs screaming down, it made me think. For some folk it'll be the last thing they'll hear.'

'Blimey, what a ghastly thought. One I'd rather not think about, thank you very much.'

Ethel continued, 'It set me thinking. What would happen to the bairn I'm carrying if anything should happen to me? It would be an orphan. And you know what I think of orphanages.'

'You've set me thinking now. What if John didn't make it through the war and a bomb had my name on it?' An adrenalin rush of anxiety surged through Lily.

Mam couldn't cope with a bairn, she thought, *though she'd want to, bless her*. Then there was Harry and Jean, but they would have two kiddies of their own. She liked Jean but she was old-fashioned and set in her ways.

The atmosphere in the shelter changed.

Ethel looked at Lily, her expression deadly serious. 'Lily, I want you to promise me something. If anything should happen to me, you'll look out for my baby, and see that it finds a decent home.'

Lily nodded. 'I will if you promise to do the same if anything should happen to me and John.'

'But you have a family.'

'Ethel, whole families have been wiped out due to the bombing. Anything could happen in this war.'

30

Late July 1943

As Lily picked up the two letters from the doormat and recognised John's writing, her heart lifted. Still in her cotton dressing gown, she padded along the passageway to the kitchen and, sitting at the pine table, she opened the envelope.

Looking at the date, she groaned. As usual John's letter had taken forever to arrive.

Sweetheart,

You've probably heard by the time you've received this letter that the campaign to free North Africa from German and Italian troops has ended in victory. We've moved to a new camp and some of us boys celebrated in town with a few beers.

I bought a round and told them it was because I'm still celebrating that I'm going to be dad – I felt so proud saying the word out loud.

I'm glad you've made the decision to resign from the WTC. I know how much you enjoyed being a Lumberjill and know what a wrench it must be for you to leave.

Not long to go now, my darling, and you'll be busier than ever. I'm devastated I won't be there to greet our little one. The word is...

The rest of the sentence was, frustratingly, censored but Lily surmised that John would be aware of this and that this was his way of telling her he expected to be posted elsewhere.

As she folded the letter and put it in her dressing gown pocket, Lily felt a pang of sorrow that John wouldn't be there for the birth of their baby. She remembered telling Ethel to keep a stiff upper lip and, scolding herself, she decided to practise what she preached and be strong through the hard times.

It struck Lily that she hadn't told John about Ethel yet. She tried to remember if she'd told him about her parents' move to the country either. Blimey, she told herself, being pregnant was affecting her brain as well as her figure.

She'd rectify the omission in the next letter, as he liked to keep up with the news on the home front.

As though the baby knew her thoughts and approved, Lily felt it kick. Pressing her hands either side of her inflated abdomen, she mentally told the bairn, *Only three months to go, little one.* A surge of excitement welling within her, Lily grinned. Sometimes she still couldn't believe it was really happening.

'You look like the Cheshire cat.' Ethel, wearing fur-lined slippers and extra-big pyjamas, waddled into the kitchen. 'I take it you've had a letter from John.' Moving over to the cooker, she put the kettle on the gas ring.

'I have, but only the one.' Noticing Ethel's massive bump, she giggled. 'We're starting to look like bookends.'

Ethel giggled too.

It was good to see the young girl looking merry as a change from the world-weary expression she mostly wore, as though trying to figure out how life had come to this. Ethel rarely went out and try as she might Lily couldn't convince her to get a green ration book issued to pregnant women which would entitle her to receive extra rationing and vitamins.

Ethel's face had stayed mutinous when Lily had brought it up. 'You know how it is, folk are disgusted because unmarried mothers are included in the extra rationing scheme.'

Exasperated, Lily had expounded, 'Take no notice of them. It's for the good of your baby.'

Lily had also suggested that Ethel at least go for a medical check-up at the clinic.

'There's nothing to be afraid of,' she'd coaxed. 'The midwife only checks down below and your baby's heart and takes a urine sample. The hardest part of the procedure is finding a bottle to wee in.' By joking, she'd been trying to take the seriousness out of the occasion.

It hadn't worked. 'Don't you see,' Ethel told her with a woebe-gone expression. 'If I do attend a clinic or register with a doctor then it'll be on record I'm expecting. I don't want it officially known that I am.'

It was then Lily had understood.

Deciding not to interfere any more, she'd made a mental note to share her extra rations with Ethel.

Lily now picked the second letter up from the table and exclaimed, 'I can tell by the writing, this is from Bella.'

Dear Lily,

It was great hearing from you and though I'm glad you and Ethel are making a great team I'm also jealous and missing you.

Blimey, I don't miss the bombing, though, it must have been scary. I can imagine what you mean about missing the peace of the countryside. I'll miss it too when I've to go back to normal life.

I'm on Nancy and co's blacklist as they never speak to me and you can imagine how heartbroken I am (ha ha!). The thing is, other Lumberjills are wary of befriending me, as they're worried that they'll be targeted by Nancy. To keep the peace, they ignore me as much as possible. Of course, Jill and Vivian aren't in that group. See what you get for having standards.

There's nothing much to tell, we've got a couple of new faces which meant there wasn't enough beds so Fran's had to move into the hall with Muriel. We'll see how that turns out!!

Anyway, that's all for now. Give my regards to Ethel.

Your loving friend,

Bella

Lily related Bella's news to Ethel but she could tell by the lass's blank expression she was miles away.

'Spill the beans,' Lily told her.

Ethel's young face intent, she said, 'The baby was awake last night and kicking and I couldn't get to sleep.' She laughed, a happy tinkling sound. 'As I lay there, I tried to think how I could bring the bairn up on my own.' She pushed a lock of blonde hair behind her ear. 'Can you remember, Lily, when women were encouraged to contribute to the war effort in their roles as mothers? To do their bit for the war effort by being foster mothers to evacuees, or childminders for working mothers by staffing war nurseries.'

'Yes, I can. Why?'

'Thing is, why don't I apply to be staff at one of these war nurseries? I could take the baby with me, and with me pay I could find a one-room bedsit off a house to live in.' Her excitement faltered when she saw Lily's face. 'What?'

'I'm only saying this to help, honest.'

Ethel looked wary. 'Go on then.'

'If you do go looking for employment, I suggest you wear a curtain ring on your third finger. Unmarried mothers don't get employed as a rule.'

Ethel nodded. 'I'd thought of that. It was while you were reading Bella's letter the idea came to me.'

'You're going to pretend you're a war widow,' Lily guessed.

Bella had opened up about her husband being killed and it wasn't a secret any more.

'I don't want to tell a lie but I'll do anything to keep the baby.'

Lily, seeing her point, told Ethel, 'Most folk are decent but there are some mean-minded folks who—'

'—will class the bairn as a bastard.' Ethel gulped back her tears.

'I know,' Lily commiserated. 'In my book any bairn being called a bastard is a hard pill to swallow. The other thing is...' She hated to put a dampener on things but it was best Ethel was fully aware of the facts. 'There'll be forms and birth certificate and—'

'Who am I kidding,' Ethel exploded, expression despairing. 'Folk will find out one way or another and the bairn will carry the stigma of being a bastard throughout their life. And it's my fault.'

Lily wished she hadn't asked Ethel what the matter was because, with only a few weeks to go, Ethel's emotions were all over the place.

As Ethel's eyes filled with unshed tears, and her pretty young face went red and blotchy, Lily's mind fixated on the comment the lass had made about a one-room bedsit.

'I have a better idea than yours.'

Ethel's expression changed pathetically to one of hope and Lily felt her heart tug. 'What?'

Lily outlined the plan. 'You could have a one-room bedsit here in the front room. We hardly ever use it.'

Ethel was open-mouthed with astonishment. 'But think of the problems that would cause.'

'Like what?'

'What if I can't afford to pay the rent?'

'That's the whole point. There wouldn't be any. The money you earn could then be saved so that you'd have enough to start out on your own one day.'

'But I'd be in the way.'

Lily made big eyes. 'There were six of us at home and we survived. I'm used to having a lot of people around, in fact, I realise now, I prefer it.'

'What will John have to—'

'Ethel, we could go on like this all day. You can't plan the future these days, you just take things as they come. If you're worried about John, believe me, there'll be no objections from him.' She didn't add that that was one of the things she loved about her husband: he was kind and generous to a fault and would go out of his way to help anyone in trouble. 'The bottom line is, if you want to keep this baby then this is the only way. I know I speak for John as well when I say we're happy to help out.'

Ethel's eyes shone and she looked overwhelmed, as if this wasn't really happening.

'Lily, before you change your mind, I accept your kind offer.' She meant the comment to be humorous, Lily knew, but, a sob escaping Ethel, she welled up. 'It's a godsend.'

———

After a breakfast of bread and dripping, Lily decided to get the rations. She wanted to be out in the cool of the morning as the past few days had been hot and humid by midday. Wearing a navy maternity skirt, light green cotton smock, white sandals with ankle strap, and taking her shopping bag from the pantry, she set off.

Outside, Lily got a surprise because, even at this time of day, the sun on her skin was blazing hot.

There was a stillness about the day. Lily could hear blackbirds singing and the occasional rush of a vehicle in the distance and, as she stood breathing in the flower-scented air, it felt good to be alive.

The morning, however, deteriorated after that. All the housewives in the area must have had the same idea to shop early because already the queues were ridiculously long. The silly thing was, sometimes people didn't know what they were queuing for and hoped for a lovely surprise, which rarely was the case. Though Lily was happy with the couple of oranges she managed to obtain.

'Came all the way from Spain, those oranges did,' the weary-looking lady greengrocer told her.

For the next hour, Lily waited patiently in queues. The butcher's, chemist's, Co-operative society shop, but she decided to call it a day when she saw her ankles were beginning to swell.

It was on her way home, when she met June (who used to work at the Chi pictures) with her two young daughters, that Lily, while chatting, the sun beating down on her head, began to feel dizzy.

'I feel all peculiar,' she told June.

'I'm not surprised, in this heat. Get yourself home and put your feet up,' was June's advice. 'D'you want me to give you a hand with the shopping?'

'No thanks, I'll be fine.'

Walking home, Lily felt dreadful and the shopping bag she carried felt like a ton of bricks. How she made it home, Lily never knew. When she arrived at Olcote and found the front door open, she could have cried with relief. Making her way along the dim and cool passageway and collapsing in the chair in the kitchen, she put her head in her hands on the table, and that's how Ethel found her.

'What's the matter, Lily?'

'I think the heat must've got me. I feel rotten.'

'Go and lie down.'

'I think I might.'

She stood and with both hands Lily massaged the bottom of her aching back.

Making her way up to the bedroom without taking her sandals off, Lily collapsed on the bed.

———

She must have gone straight to sleep as the next thing she knew, Ethel – a glass of water in one hand and sewing draped over an arm – was standing by her bedside.

Placing the water on the bedside locker, she moved to the chair by the window and sat. 'I thought I'd keep you company for a while.'

'You should be the one with her feet up.' Lily sat up.

Ethel gave a look of reproach. 'I wasn't the one overdoing it in the heat.'

'What time is it?' Lily wanted to know.

'It's late afternoon.'

'Blimey, have I been asleep all that time?'

'You must have needed it.'

They lapsed into a contented silence. Lily lay staring into space and Ethel began sewing.

Noticing what Ethel was doing, Lily sat up. 'You never did finish telling me about the memory quilt.'

'It was Mam's knitted blanket that gave me the idea. It's for the baby when it's older.' Ethel stood and shook the quilt out on the bed. It was now almost as big as a full-sized blanket. 'Each square holds a memory from the past. See.' She smoothed the material so the patchwork colourful squares were clearly shown. 'On this square I've embroidered my parents' names.'

'How clever, one pink and one blue. Is the German flag to signify your dad?'

'Yes, and that the baby is half German.'

It was then Lily saw the name Karl Becker embroidered in a blue material square.

'This one signifies my time at the orphanage,' Ethel was telling her.

Lily looked at the cream square with purple and white pansies painstakingly embroidered on it. 'Why pansies?'

'I wanted only good memories on the quilt. The pansies grew in the borders that lined the orphanage's front path and I always thought they looked like they had faces.' She smiled at the memory.

Lily pointed to a topmost square, which had a fir tree mounted on a royal crown. 'The Women's Timber Corps badge,' she exclaimed.

Ethel nodded. 'To represent my time as a Lumberjill at Teviot Hall.'

'Crikey, you're amazing at needlework.' Lily's eyes travelled to all the squares beautifully sewn together by the neatest running backstitch.

'As an orphan I was prepared for a life of domestic service.' Ethel shrugged. 'That was the expectation of us orphans.'

'Until you broke the mould.'

Ethel shook her head. 'Not just me. The mistress either broke you or toughened you up.'

Lily was saddened that such people were allowed to be in charge of children. She changed the conversation to a lighter subject. 'Is this for the work you did in the stables?' She pointed to a horse's head.

'No, that's to represent when I first met the bairn's father there.'

So much for a lighter topic, Lily thought.

'I'm busy with a square that represents the time spent here with you, then I think I'm done.'

'Can I see? I can't wait.'

'No, not till it's sewn on.'

———

Lily, feeling lethargic, took it easy for the rest of the day. Later, at night time, changing into a cotton nightdress, she climbed into bed and flung off the bedspread. There was no air in the room and she wished she could open the sash window but it was stuck down with old paint. Weary, she lay back against the pillows and her last vision before succumbing to sleep was of the memory quilt Ethel had made.

———

Lily awoke with a start and stared into the claustrophobic blackness. Then she remembered the drawn blackout curtains that barred any light entering the room.

She listened, wondering what had woken her, dreading that

she might hear the drone of aeroplanes – but, the air still, the night was silent. As she moved to turn on the bedside light, she felt a huge gush of liquid down below.

Please God no, don't let me be haemorrhaging. Switching on the light, she saw a trickle of fluid running down her legs. Lily realised, in dismay, her waters had broken.

31

Lying in bed, Lily felt a tightening in her lower back and her stomach hardening. This was it; she'd started labour. Fear gripped her – it was too early for the baby. Lying still as a post, she willed the contraction to stop. As time passed and nothing happened, she dared to think that the few contractions were a false alarm.

Starting to relax, she sank back against the pillow. Lily didn't know how long she dozed but another contraction, stronger this time, woke her up. She cried out in both frustration and pain.

Minutes passed, then the bedroom door opened and the light clicked on. Ethel stood there.

Another contraction started and, in a haze of pain, Lily cried out in desperation. 'It's too early.'

Taking in the scene, Ethel told her, 'Try and stay calm. I'm off to the telephone box to phone the midwife. I'll be as quick as I can.'

Lying in the bed, Lily had never known such loneliness, and not having a clue what to expect didn't help. She was terrified, not for herself but for the baby. When another contraction started, the thought that the pains might go away if she relaxed entered Lily's brain. So, she transported herself away from the scene to the woods. Smelling the fragrant pine trees, the squelching mud below her feet, somewhere in her being Lily was aware of the pain but refused, for the baby's sake, to tune in.

Time passed, Lily didn't know how much, then the door opened and old Doctor Porter appeared, dressed in a shabby tweed jacket, with what looked like his pyjama top underneath and carrying a black bag, followed by Ethel.

'The midwife was out on a call so I phoned the doctor,' Ethel told her.

'Stay,' he said to her as she made to leave the room. 'You might come in useful.'

An urge to push overwhelmed Lily and, in a haze of pain and incomprehension at what was happening, she found herself wishing the tale Mam told her when she was little was true, that babies really did arrive in a doctor's black bag.

The doctor and Ethel started talking but Lily, imagining, with difficulty, she was floating between the tops of trees, didn't hear a word spoken.

She moaned as she gave another mighty push.

'Now then, Mrs Radley.' The doctor came to stand by the bedside. 'What have we here?'

As he bent down to examine her, the smell of pine trees disappeared to be replaced by that of a whiff of tobacco.

'Mrs Radley, are you listening?'

'Yes.'

'The head has been delivered. I don't want you to push until I tell you, is that clear?'

'Yes.' Lily held her breath to stop the overpowering urge to push.

'Right, Mrs Radley, now, one final push.'

Lily did as she was told and pushed, with all her might, and she felt something between her legs.

A long silence followed – too long – and something inside Lily collapsed. She just knew... Lily just knew.

She struggled to sit up, resting her elbows on the bed and looking into the aged doctor's lined face.

He shook his head. 'Your baby didn't make it.' He told her, 'It's just one of those things. It came too early.'

He then turned to Ethel. 'Find some newspaper and fetch it here.'

Lily transported her mind to the oblivion of a deep and dark forest. She didn't want to face reality; it was too painful.

———

'I've made some chicken broth, Lily. Try and eat some.'

Ethel's voice penetrated Lily's blurry mind. She'd hardly eaten or done anything that meant getting up from the chair and getting involved. She felt numb, and staring at the wall ahead was all she could manage. Two days had passed since she'd delivered Jennifer – Lily had confided in Ethel that that was the name she and John had chosen if they had a baby girl.

Coming to terms with the strength of grief felt like climbing a mountain covered in ice. One treacherous thought and she was back to the bottom of the steep path.

Lily wanted Jennifer back, to see the colour of her hair, touch her little feet, dress her in the matinee coat she'd knitted. Last night, when she awoke in the middle of the night, she'd been convinced she heard a baby crying. It was then she decided she couldn't stand the pain of losing her beloved baby and her instinct was to howl like a banshee at a universe that allowed such a thing to happen.

'Lily, are you listening? I've put the soup in a cup so that it's easier to manage.'

As Ethel stood in front of her, arm outstretched as she held a china cup, all Lily could concentrate on was the huge mound of her abdomen where her baby lay safe and secure.

'You've got to eat, Lily.'

There was something about Ethel's voice, a timidity that made Lily search her face. There it was in Ethel's eyes: the look of fear – though fear of what, Lily had no idea.

'Not now, I'm not hungry.'

Looking down at the spots of damp each side of her nightdress, Lily thought, *Even my body's letting me down.* Tight and tender, her breasts ached to feed her baby.

Devastated, she covered her face with her hands and collapsed back. The longing for the baby she'd lost overwhelming, anger erupted within her at the fates that had allowed such a cruel thing to happen.

Ethel placed the cup on the locker top. 'Lily, I don't know what you're going through but to lose your bairn is hard enough, then having to see me with me bump must be a nightmare. D'you want me to go?'

Her anger bursting like a balloon pricked with a pin, Lily's hands dragged down her face and she blurted, 'I'm not angry at you...' Her voice high-pitched and squeaky, she welled up and couldn't continue for a minute. She swallowed hard. 'I can't stand the thought I've to write to John to tell him I've lost our baby.'

The lump in her throat hurt, her eyes brimmed over and then the tears rolling down her cheeks dripped off her chin.

Ethel hurried over to her. 'Lily, if only there was something I could say to make you feel better.'

'There's nothing anybody can say.' Lily lifted up her tearstained face. 'But please don't go. Having you here keeps me sane.'

———

Two nights later as Lily sat in a comfy chair in the front room, the wireless on for background noise, she couldn't concentrate for the relentless tight and painful engorgement of her breasts. She knew her milk was coming in and she was resentful that Mother Nature allowed such a cruel thing to happen when there was no baby to benefit.

'Cabbage leaves.'

'Pardon me?' Ethel, sitting opposite, engrossed in sewing, looked up at her.

Surprised she'd uttered the words out loud, Lily remarked, 'Jean, my sister-in-law, applied cold cabbage leaves to get some relief for her tender breasts after Stanley was born.'

'What a good idea.'

'But I never found out how she got them so cold.'

Ethel put her sewing down. She gave Lily a ponderous look. 'You should go and see Jean. She might be able to suggest something to help.'

'I can't. She's moved to the safety of the country to be with Mam and Dad.'

'Lily' – Ethel's voice was tentative – 'I don't like to interfere but why don't you get in touch with your mam? I know how close you are, and she'll want to come and—'

'I'm not telling anyone yet about Jennifer.' As she spoke the baby's name a deep sadness engulfed Lily. *I didn't get to see her. I don't know what my baby looked like.*

'You've got to tell those close to you,' Ethel pressed. 'They have to know sometime and, from what I've heard, you've got such a lovely family.'

Lily knew why she couldn't write to her family yet – couldn't even tell John – but she didn't want to say the reason out loud. She couldn't bear their reactions – having to hear her family's condolences, and having to cause John grief – because then it would mean losing Jennifer was real.

'I will when I'm ready,' she said evasively.

Surprisingly, Ethel didn't offer up any resistance. She simply laid down the quilt she was embroidering and, standing, arched and massaged her back.

'If you don't mind locking up, I'm off to bed. I'm whacked. Have a good night, Lily. See you in the morning.'

———

Hours passed, during which Lily couldn't settle and dreaded going to bed where she knew she'd toss and turn like she had for the past two nights. In her present anxious state, she worried about John and missed him. She avoided the thought that she must write to him.

After reading the *Gazette* from cover to cover, she played a few games of patience. Her eyelids heavy, Lily decided to go to bed. Passing the bay window, she peeked out of the blackout curtains up to the night sky where banks of clouds, high above the dark rooftops, drifted slowly over a brightly shining moon.

As she gazed, Lily realised, there were people out there grieving a son, or husband killed in the war. If they were strong enough to get over their tragedy then so could she. She still had John, after all. She would take it day by day. Then Lily stiffened as, staring into the heavens, two twin circular lights beamed into the night sky. Before she could gather her thoughts, the siren wailed, followed by the sound of guns blazing from the ground. She froze as shapes, likened to big black birds of prey, were caught in the criss-crossing beams in the sky.

She tried to make her sluggish mind think what to do. They came then, the raiders, droning at first in the distance, then roaring overhead, causing Lily to put her hands over her ears. The sound of the engines seemed to go on forever, then followed the squealing of bombs and deep thuds of explosions.

Lily closed the curtains and, looking around the room, her eye caught the quilt discarded on the chair.

She and Ethel must make for the shelter.

She moved to the bottom of the stairs.

'Ethel,' she shouted up the staircase, 'hurry, we've to get in the shelter.'

No answer.

Ethel couldn't have slept through the raid.

Making her way up the stairs, Lily called, 'Ethel, can you hear?'

At the top of the stairs, Lily moved over the landing and

opened Ethel's bedroom door. The room in darkness, she switched on the light. Ethel lay on the bed, knees up, feet planted flat on the bedspread, a long deep moan coming from her.

Lily was at a loss at first then, seeing Ethel's pink and sweaty face scrunched up in pain, it dawned on her: Ethel was in labour.

———

They were in the dark shelter, shadows on the walls, the air hot and stuffy, when Ethel, lying on the camp bed, let out another low moan as another contraction gripped her. Lily could hear planes droning in the distance and it sounded like some poor souls further up the coast were copping it.

'The pains are coming closer.' Lily disentangled her hand from Ethel's. 'I'm going to phone for the midwife.'

Lily had managed to guide Ethel, cloaked in a blanket, down the stairs and into the shelter for safety. There hadn't been time to grab luxuries like a pillow or a damp cloth for Ethel's sweaty brow – or even gas masks – but Lily couldn't worry about that now.

'No,' was Ethel's decisive reply.

How Lily wished they'd had this conversation before now.

Ethel fell back on the bed and Lily had to wait for more of an answer till the contraction Ethel was having passed.

She finally looked up at Lily. 'I don't want anyone to know,' she gasped and there was a look of steel in her eyes. 'If it hadn't been for the bombing, you wouldn't have known either, like I intended.'

'You were going to have the baby on your own?' Lily was horrified.

'I wanted to keep this bairn a secret. You'd insist on calling the midwife.' The words came in short bursts.

'And you'd be right.' The unsaid words *what if there are complications with the birth?* buzzed in Lily's mind. 'When did your labour start?'

Ethel raised her head from the bed. 'Last night, backache and cramps. Had them all day. Worse tonight. They started coming closer.'

Lily couldn't believe Ethel had managed to carry on, covering the early stages of her labour without Lily suspecting. At this point Ethel gave a sharp intake of breath and her face screwed up with the pain. Lily realised in dismay that only a couple of minutes had passed since the last contraction.

Collapsing back on the bed, Ethel grasped Lily's hand. 'Please don't leave me.' Her eyes wide showed how afraid she was.

'I'm not going anywhere,' Lily reassured her, but in truth she felt equally as scared.

She had no experience, and not a clue what was needed. She tried to think back to her own delivery but that was all a blur. This was not the time to reflect on what could or could not be done, she rebuked herself; the truth was there was only her here now, and she must cope.

As a distant droning noise drew closer, a new terror presented itself.

———

The raiders came in full force from the coast, thundering overhead.

Ethel, biting her lip till it bled, wouldn't give in to the pain and yell. The lass was gripping her hand that tight, it felt like the bones could break, but Lily was prepared to suffer the discomfort if it helped her friend get through.

The planes, mercifully, roared into the distance, presumably making for Vickers armaments works in Newcastle.

When Ethel started to push, Lily had never felt so helpless.

Then she saw the baby's head and remembered Doctor Porter's instructions, and called out, 'Don't push.' The problem was she didn't know what she was supposed to do.

Then Ethel gave a final push, and Lily caught the baby's little body and cuddled the bundle to her, checking as best she could whether the baby was breathing and seeing whether it was a boy or a girl.

She told Ethel, a catch in her voice, 'You've got a beautiful daughter.'

'She's early. Is she all right?' Ethel's voice was panicky.

Lily held her breath. They couldn't both be that unlucky. Then a cry came from the scrap of humanity in her arms, and she gasped with relief.

'Her name's Joy.' Ethel's face radiating elation, she held out her arms. 'Let me see her.'

Knowing the cord had to be cut – something Jean had told her, insisting it didn't hurt – Lily remembered the scissors in the first aid kit. Opening the bedside locker drawer and taking the scissors out of the kit, hand poised, Lily took a deep, steadying breath, then cut the cord.

After cuddling the warm little body in her arms, it was with a pang of regret that she handed the baby over.

———

Later, Ethel, her face sagging with exhaustion, fell asleep. Fearing she might drop the precious bundle, Lily gently lifted the bairn, now wrapped in the blanket, from her arms. Lily was reminded what Mam had told Jean after her son, Stanley, was born, that 'too much handling a newborn hurts its little body'.

Gazing down at Joy (Lily thought the name perfect) and seeing her darling little fingers and innocent unfocused navy-blue eyes, a sense of peace washed over her, something Lily hadn't experienced since she lost her own baby. Though she would rather hold on to Joy awhile longer, Lily wanted what was best for the little one. She looked around for somewhere to place the baby but there was nowhere suitable.

She recalled seeing a baby asleep in a drawer when she was in a public shelter. Thinking the idea a good one, she thought of using one of the deep drawers in her bedroom. While she was on the subject, Joy could do with wearing something more fitting than a stained blanket and Ethel could do with a clean nightdress.

It was an age since the last plane had flown by, and Lily decided the raid was done for the night. It would only take a few minutes to pop over to the house and fetch the few things she needed. Pre-empting the all-clear siren going off, Lily checked on Ethel, who was sleeping soundly, and, blowing the lamp's flame out, she crept out of the shelter, cuddling Joy in her arms, into the moonlit and starry night.

Entering the kitchen, she closed the door and switched on the passageway light. She made her way up the stairs and into her bedroom where she placed the now sleeping Joy on the bed. Pulling out the top drawer from the tallboy, she emptied its contents, a collection of John's underwear, onto the floor. Opening the bottom drawer, she rummaged through the layette she'd prepared for her baby, taking out a white knitted shawl, long cotton nightdress, knitted matinee coat and put them on the bed. It was while she was lining the drawer with the shawl that she heard it, the noise that sent a cold shiver of fear down to her buttocks – the sound of the raiders coming back.

Heart racing, Lily placed the sleeping Joy on top of the shawl and, putting the rest of the layette at the bairn's feet, she picked up the drawer and made a dash for the kitchen. She was halfway down the stairs when a sound outside made her stand stock-still – the mutter from anti-aircraft guns on the ground.

Jerries after the docks again.

The raiders came roaring over from the sea, bombs rained down and thudded on the ground followed by distant explosions. Dropping their load, the bombers made off.

Hugging the drawer next to her chest, Lily, trembling and undecided, stood rooted to the spot. Should she make a run for the relative safety of the shelter or stay and take cover? Hearing guns start up again, Lily's mind was made up.

As the drone, like a mighty swarm of bees, came over, Lily made for the cupboard under the stairs. Placing the drawer on the floor she walked in and closed the door. She waited with bated breath. As raiders thundered over the rooftops, bombs shrieked down, dangerously close this time; Lily fell to her knees and curled her upper body over the drawer. She heard an almighty thud as a building toppled down and glass fragmented in a long crescendo. Then there was an ear-splitting shriek, and for a time the world stood still and then— blackness.

'You're a lucky lass,' Lily heard a male voice say as if through a long tunnel.

Lily didn't feel lucky, only bruised and disorientated. She looked around and realised she was lying down on a back door in the lane, an ARP warden standing over her. An acrid smell of burning pervaded and the air, filled with dust, made her cough.

'You were out for the count there for a time.'

'Out for the count...' Lily repeated stupidly.

'Aye, the blast blew the top wall of the stairs out and the staircase fell down, giving you a nasty blow on the head. The bairn crying alerted the team someone was beneath all the rubble.' By the light of the moon, she saw him wipe his grime-stained, sweaty face with his hand.

Lily let his words settle on her befuddled brain. It all came back now. A memory of awakening to claustrophobic darkness, dust clogging her nostrils and throat, she'd come to and found herself lying on her back.

A small cry had alerted her.

The baby.

Feeling all around in the darkness, her hand had touched the drawer and for a heart-stopping moment all she could feel was rubble and crumbled brick. Turning on her side, Lily's hand had sifted through the debris and, feeling a warm little body, she'd pulled the precious bundle from the wreckage. Then blackness had overtaken her again.

Lily asked the warden, 'Joy, the baby, is she—'

'As far as we can tell, the bairn's come to no harm. You're both off to the infirmary to be checked out.'

'Thank the Lord the baby's safe,' Lily breathed. 'What about Ethel?'

Struggling to sit up, which made her dizzy, Lily looked wildly around. The backyard door was gone and looking through the space she tried to discern what she saw. Palm over her mouth, Lily let out a gasp. The shelter had gone, reduced to a pile of rubble on the ground.

'My friend, Ethel... you must... she's in...'

'Steady on, lass.' The warden's hand on her shoulder, Lily realised she'd attempted to stand. 'I was about to get to that.'

Lily didn't like the cautionary note in his voice. 'Where's Ethel?' she cried.

'I'm sorry, lass,' he said, audibly sighing, and he nodded over to where a row of bodies lay on the ground covered by blankets. 'Your friend didn't make it.'

It took Lily some time before she realised the low, agonised moan she heard came from her.

———

Staff Nurse Cooper, a brunette with an efficient, bustling countenance, shook the glass thermometer she held and placed it under Lily's tongue.

'Doctor Moor has examined your baby and it appears she's none the worse for her ordeal. That's comforting news, isn't it?' She smoothed the counterpane on the bed and plumped the pillows either side of Lily then stood at the bedside. 'Has she got a name yet?'

Lily, hauling herself up to a sitting position beneath the starched sheets, heard the words but they didn't properly sink in. She felt disorientated and everything around her, the tall windows in the ward, women sitting by their beds knitting, the nurse wheeling the trolley giving out medicine, the staff nurse in front of her talking non-stop, didn't seem quite real. As the scene of bodies on the ground covered by blankets flashed yet again through her mind, Lily's stomach turned to jelly.

It couldn't be true; Ethel couldn't be dead.

The staff nurse looked at her watch, then retrieving the thermometer she checked the reading, and, making a note on a clipboard, placed it back on the bed rail.

She smiled encouragingly then bustled away. She stopped and spoke to the young nurse who was giving out the medicine.

The nurse, wearing a navy and white striped uniform and starched cap, looked at Lily then nodded.

Next thing Lily knew she had come over and was putting a screen around her bed.

'I want to go home, Nurse.'

The young nurse gave a sympathetic shake of the head. 'You've had a shock, Mrs Radley, and a nasty bump to your head. Remember what the doctor said. He wants you and the baby to stay for a night or two for observation. It's just a precaution.'

Lily frowned as she tried to concentrate. A vison of a doctor in a white coat examining her came to mind.

'You said your baby was born during the raid, Mrs Radley. Have you had her on the breast yet?'

Lily, confused, tried to think, but her brain had turned to treacle. 'My baby didn't survive.'

Talking of breasts made Lily aware of the discomfort in hers. She looked down at the white gown she was wearing, and didn't recognise it as hers.

When she looked up the nurse had disappeared.

Fear crawled over her, like a black spindly-legged spider, and

Lily, numb, was incapable of speaking, or moving. All she was capable of was lying still in the bed staring at the wall opposite.

A voice remonstrated, *Pull yourself together, Lily Radley.*

She didn't know if the voice was Mam's or hers but Lily took a deep steadying breath and sought to gain control of herself. Minutes passed and the young nurse returned with a bundle in her hands. Lily recognised it as a baby that was crying.

The nurse grinned good-naturedly. 'I reckon this will remind you.' She came over and, placing the baby in Lily's arms, undid the tie at the back of her hospital gown.

Lily stared down at the bairn: the anguished pink face, with the wide-open mouth as she hollered. It seemed most natural to take the warm head in her hand and steer the little pink lips towards her engorged breast.

'You're a natural.' The nurse beamed.

As she felt the tug on her nipple, exhilaration washed over Lily.

'Her name is Joy,' she said.

———

'You've got to eat something, Mrs Radley.'

The words reverberated in Lily's brain. She'd heard them before. Ethel coaxing her to eat. Something inside Lily collapsed, and fear, shame and guilt swirled inside her.

Her heart thumped. Ethel was too young to die. It was all Lily's fault for leaving her friend alone in the shelter. If only Lily had stayed, she could have woken Ethel – got her out of the shelter – and she would be here to feed her baby. Lily shivered; the feeling persisted that Ethel's shadowy presence was near. She wondered if she blamed her, if she was outraged that Lily had fed her baby.

'Mrs Radley.' The young nurse removed the plate of mutton stew from the over-bed table. 'How about I get you a drink of Bovril and some crackers, something light. You've got to keep your strength up to feed that baby of yours.'

The nurse bustled along the ward. As Lily sank back against the pillows, she felt that the essence of Ethel, her spirit, was all around, warm and friendly; she wasn't accusing, she wanted what was best for her daughter. If Lily had stayed with Joy in the shelter then all of them would have been killed. The truth wouldn't bring Ethel back but it helped allay Lily's feelings of guilt.

'You must eat.' Was that Ethel's voice?

As Lily nibbled one of the crackers from the plate, the ache of sorrow for her friend increased and, as tears spilled from her eyes, Ethel's whisper was all around.

Remember the promise. Look out for my baby.

———

When Lily alighted from the ambulance, the baby in her arms, wrapped in a shawl, the first thing she saw was that next door's front wall was now a pile of rubble on the pavement. Looking up, she noticed all the windows were boarded up. Along the rest of the street, workmen, wearing dungarees and tin hats, stood on tall ladders that leant against the façades of buildings, or they sat precariously on rooftops, while others were generally milling around carrying building materials. Rubble was piled everywhere and the stench of acrid burning hung in the air. A WVS mobile canteen with a queue in front stood at the far end of the street, while behind the canteen stood a national emergency free washing service for the families who now had no facilities to wash their clothes.

Olcote had survived, albeit minus a staircase, but Lily could live downstairs for the time being. She'd refused the offer to stay at the Rest Centre but not the clothes offered for her and the baby. The two days' stay in hospital had helped regain her mental state but Lily was still emotionally fragile.

'Get yourself inside, lass,' the robust, no-nonsense woman ambulance driver told her. 'Apart from a top window missing, your house looks intact.'

Words failed Lily and, feeling wobbly, she thanked the woman and made her way down the short path to the house – her home.

Inside the house there was a film of dust on all the surfaces. Investigating the front room, Lily discovered lumps of plaster on the floor and wooden laths bare on the ceiling.

Her eyes wandered to the chair where Ethel had been sitting the night of the raid and there, abandoned on the arm, was the colourful quilt she'd been stitching.

33

August 1943

The weather warm and humid outside, Lily expected the day to end in a thunderstorm. Joy was asleep in her pram in the lobby with the door open. The young midwife at the clinic had advocated that the baby should breathe as much fresh air as possible as it would help her to thrive.

Lily had been nervous to go to the clinic but what was best for Joy being uppermost in her mind, she tried to quell her anxiety. Surely someone would put two and two together and realise this couldn't be Lily's baby? So far, she hadn't seen her regular midwife from before and, on enquiring about Doctor Porter's whereabouts, she was told he was showing a new doctor the ropes because he was due to retire.

A team of builders from the council worked tirelessly in the street to make buildings safe and though the front upstairs window at Olcote hadn't yet been replaced, a new staircase had recently been put in. Lily didn't know if she'd receive a bill or not as it was a privately owned house, but that was a matter for another day.

Lily, stretched on the couch in the front room, heard the clattering of workmen's boots outside on the cobbled road. She wondered if she should close the front door as the noise might awaken Joy. She smiled tenderly. A brass band wouldn't disturb the two-week-old little minx. It was at night time, when Lily craved sleep, that Joy would stir at the drop of a feather. Lily, happy to accommodate, had changed her sleeping habits to during the day when the bairn slept.

But there were times like now when she couldn't close her eyes for fear her anxious mind would relive the screaming aeroplanes, the baby slipping from Ethel's body, the shock of seeing her friend's still form lying on the ground amongst the dead. Her heart pounding, Lily felt she couldn't breathe enough air into her lungs.

Thankfully, the thin wail coming from the passageway distracted her. Hurrying through to the pram and pulling back the covers, Lily picked the warm bundle up and, breathing in the heady newborn baby smell, a rush of love enveloped her.

As she moved into the kitchen, removing the shawl Joy was wrapped in, Lily acknowledged that what she hadn't worked out was how to live with the deceit of not telling John or her parents that her pregnancy had ended.

A stab of guilt ran through her. What about Karl? Should she try and contact him? He loved Ethel and would want to have been informed of her death, and that she'd had his baby before she died. By not contacting him Lily was denying him the chance to be a father. But she had no way of knowing where he was; he could be in America for all she knew. Even if she did contact the POW camp they'd never disclose where he was.

She picked a nappy from the pile on the table and, sitting on a chair, she changed Joy on her knee. Those times she'd helped Mam with Jimmy when he was a baby had come in useful, as seeing to Joy's needs didn't faze her.

Since the raid, having Joy to love and concentrate on had helped Lily through the worst of her grief at Ethel's death, but there was always the guilt that she'd survived while her friend hadn't. The sorrow was raw that Ethel had only had a short life and wouldn't see her baby grow.

Preparing to feed Joy, Lily tried to put these distressing thoughts to the back of her mind. Loosening the buttons on her blouse, Lily, in a dreamlike world of fulfilment, felt pain mingled with guilt consume her as the bairn latched on to her nipple, wide eyes searching her face as she sucked. Pain at losing her own precious baby, and guilt because she had confessed to no one that the baby wasn't hers. But, as the darling little fingers of one hand kneaded her breast, and the baby concentrated on feeding, a maternal feeling overwhelmed Lily.

Joy would remain Lily's secret for now.

———

The only person Lily knew to contact about Ethel's death was Bella and she did this in a clipped note before the funeral. Bella's reply by return of post was how shocked and sorrowful she was but, regretfully, it was too short notice for her to attend. However, both Ethel and Lily would be in her thoughts on the day.

Ethel's funeral was a heart-rending affair, as only Mr Newman, the funeral director, and the clergyman from the local church, who said a few words over the grave, were present. If Mr Newman was surprised when Lily requested only one car as there'd only be her and a baby attending, his face didn't lose its professionally grave expression, but his eyes gleamed with compassion.

At the graveside, Lily had picked up a clod of earth and, hugging the baby close, she'd whispered into the grave's dark depths, 'I promise I'll do my best to look after our baby.'

As she sprinkled the earth over the lid of the coffin, the reality hit Lily that Ethel was gone forever. The enormity of death, how inevitable, how final it was, disturbed her.

———

As time slipped by, Lily's world revolved around Joy. She lived for the bairn and John's letters to arrive. She hadn't heard from him for the past few weeks, which was normal but she still couldn't help being concerned. She would be relieved when the next letter came.

A deep-rooted notion that the baby would be taken from her was ever-present, and Lily was still troubled by thoughts of the night Ethel had lost her life.

Apart from going to the clinic, Lily rarely ventured out and then only for essentials. The reason she'd become reclusive was because she was nervous of meeting people and what to say when they assumed Joy was hers.

Neighbours, shopkeepers and folk who knew her would stop her in the street as she pushed the pram. They'd make such comments as, 'Congratulations, you've had your bairn. Let's have a look, then. What's her name?'

Lily, at a loss how to answer, would reply, 'She's called Joy.'

It was so much easier to treat Joy as her own; besides, while caring for her, Lily felt like the baby really was hers.

Her anxieties were fuelled one day when she met June Lloyd outside the corner shop.

Pressing the pram's brake with a foot, Lily heard a voice from behind call, 'Why, Lily, you've had the baby. Congratulations. A boy or girl?' She turned to see a beaming June hurrying towards her with her two girls in tow.

After a moment of anxious indecision, Lily realised it had become perfectly normal for people to treat her like a new mam. In too deep now, she had this sense that from now on she had no other option than to go along with it.

'Hello, June. I've got a girl.'

———

Today was wash day and, picking up the bucket filled with clean nappies, Lily made her way down the yard to the cobbled back lane. Passing the new shelter, her gaze lingered as it so often did on the place where Ethel had been sleeping the night of the raid. Lily forced herself not to think about what had happened – the horror of the bomb screaming down and Ethel waking – but remembered instead the hand fate had dealt her in sparing Joy's life and giving her this chance to honour her promise to her friend. Her guilt at surviving was relieved by the rational thought that if Lily hadn't sought a place for Joy to sleep that night, the baby wouldn't have survived and that was what helped her live with her conscience.

The nappies billowing in the warm breeze, contentment with her lot washed over Lily. At that moment, the kettle's shrill whistle pierced the air and, hurrying up the yard to the kitchen, Lily switched off the gas.

Keeping an ear out for Joy sound asleep at the front door, Lily reached for the tea caddy on the mantlepiece.

A sound coming from the lobby made her cock an ear.

'Yoo-hoo,' a voice called softly.

Lily, tea caddy still in her hand, moved to the kitchen door and peered along the dim passageway.

Her palm moved over her mouth in surprise when she saw a figure, dressed in gaberdine breeches, shirt and tie, and a bottle-green beret, standing beyond the pram.

'You're a dark horse!' Bella exclaimed in an excited whisper, nodding at the pram. 'Fancy not writing to tell me you'd had the baby.'

Lily was taken aback that Bella assumed the bairn was hers. Then she realised, apart from telling Bella when she was three months pregnant that she was expecting, she'd never mentioned to anyone else when the baby was due.

Joy, startled at being disturbed, started to cry. Picking the baby up, Lily led the way into the kitchen. She couldn't speak, and though she knew she should've corrected Bella, holding the baby in her arms felt so natural Lily knew why she hadn't. Joy felt like hers and she wanted the sensational feeling to continue for a while longer at least.

Joy wouldn't be pacified and, her little face scrunched up, she bawled. Knowing the only way to calm her was to give her a feed, Lily sat on a chair in front of the fire and, lifting up her loose blouse, she opened her nursing bra. As Joy latched on to her breast, the sensation of pleasure washed over Lily and she gave a sigh of contentment.

'I've caught you in a bad moment.' Bella's cheery, suntanned face looked uncomfortable as she hovered in the doorway.

Lily shook her head. 'Don't worry on my account. But if me breastfeeding makes you—'

'You're kidding me. I was thinking of you. I can't think of a time years ago when a baby wasn't attached to Mam's breast.'

This was what Lily had liked about Bella from the first; she was always forthright and you knew where you stood with her. The feeling of closeness they'd always shared enveloped Lily and she was pleased to see her friend, but it was difficult to believe Bella was actually here.

She nodded towards a wooden armchair. 'Come and sit down and spill the beans about what's happening at Teviot Hall and why you're here. And if you're on holiday, why don't you spend the night?'

Bella threw the green pullover she was carrying over the back of the chair and sat down opposite Lily.

'I've only got the afternoon off and I wanted to come and see you. Guess what, Lily? I've been transferred to the sawmill in Gateshead.'

'Oh, that's the best news! But how come?'

'I complained to Muriel Fellows that I was fed up with the treatment I was getting from Nancy and her cronies.' She tutted. 'Of course, that wasn't true because I really don't give a hoot about those ninnies but it did the trick, especially when Gateshead was looking for someone to work in the sawmill.'

Lily rolled her eyes. 'Since when did you know anything about sawmills?'

'Lily, how hard can it be?' Bella gave Lily a knowing look and they both grinned. 'Besides, we covered sawmills in our initial training at Shandford.'

'I'd left before then, remember?'

Bella nodded, then pulled a conniving expression. 'All it took to gain Muriel's consent was to tell her that Fran wasn't in favour of the transfer.'

Lily shifted Joy's head from the crook of her arm because her skin was getting sweaty.

Watching on, Bella's expression turned to one of concern. 'To be truthful, I was missing you and knew you were going through a tough time, being pregnant and all. But I never expected to find you'd had the baby.' Her face broke into a beaming smile. 'Congratulations. I'm so happy for you. What's she called?'

Lily knew this was the moment she should confess that the baby wasn't hers. But for reasons she couldn't understand – perhaps because she felt embarrassment at feeding another woman's child, or because she couldn't, as yet, give up the notion Joy was rightfully hers – Lily didn't.

She simply answered, 'She's called Joy.'

'Is John thrilled, does he—'

'You know how it is, feast of or famine where his letters from abroad are concerned. His unit was patrolling the desert on trucks but the last I heard John was expected to be posted elsewhere.' She chewed her lip. 'I should've heard from him by now, though.'

'I remember, it's the waiting that gets you.' A faraway glint came into Bella's eyes and Lily knew she was thinking about her own husband.

'This little tinker,' she said, trying to distract Bella's mind from painful thoughts, 'never seems to be full.'

The ploy did the trick and Bella's attention was diverted. They chatted about Teviot Hall and the people they knew for a while.

'D'you have far to go to work?' Lily asked as she checked Joy's nappy.

'Two miles or so, but Mr Roberts, the stationmaster, has lent me a bike.' Bella looked at her watch.

'How about you stay for tea?' Lily asked. 'I've got a tin of apri-
cots and tinned milk we could celebrate with.'

'I'd like that, but the billet I'm staying at is Mr Roberts' house.
His wife is the prim and proper type and she pointedly told me tea
would be at half five.' Bella picked her jumper up from where she'd
slung it on the chair. 'I don't want to fall foul of her because billets
are hard to come by, at least half decent ones.' She raised her eyes
heavenward. 'Believe me, some of the other lasses' accounts suggest
their billets are no better than pigsties.' She made a move to the
door with a grin. 'Today's just a short visit but I promise I'll be
back.'

A few moments later, hearing the front door slam, Lily smiled
at Joy, who now lay in the folds of her skirt, which acted like a
hammock. 'Did you hear that? Aunty Bella says she's coming back
to see us. Won't that be lovely.'

As Lily removed the safety pin, then the sodden nappy, Joy,
kicking her chubby legs with the dimples in the knees, gurgled
with pleasure.

Lily continued to tell Joy in the baby voice she reserved when
speaking to her, 'I didn't tell my best friend a lie, I just omitted to
tell the truth, didn't I?'

———

Bella kept her promise and returned to Olcote on her time off from
the sawmill, which was a half day on Saturdays and all day Sundays.
The weather recently rather humid, with occasional rain, they spent
their time outdoors as much as possible. Lily wasn't worried she
would be seen out with a pram as she knew her family in Lancashire
didn't correspond with anyone from home, and she never saw sight
of her brothers, who were wrapped up in their own lives – though if
Lily was to need them, they'd come running, of that she was certain.

'It's warm rain,' Bella told Lily on a Saturday afternoon as they
wandered through the leafy grounds of South Marine Park and a

shower of rain had just finished. 'I don't know about you but since becoming a Lumberjill I can't abide being indoors. Being inside at the sawmill is killing me. I'm going to ask if I can work in the woods.'

'You can only ask.'

'Hang on, I won't bother. Unlike the sawmill, Lumberjills don't have Saturday afternoons off and I'd only be able to visit on Sundays. And I'd miss seeing you and Joy rather.'

Lily was glad as she enjoyed Bella's company too and was grateful to have someone to talk to, especially about Ethel as it kept her memory alive.

The start of September now, Joy was five weeks old and getting cuter by the day. Life was easier for Lily as she was settled in a routine and, getting better sleep, she didn't feel exhausted all the time.

Bella remarked now as they strolled past the boating lake, 'The tragic thing is there's only us to remember Ethel. It's so awful that she and her unborn baby died in the bombing.'

Grimacing, Lily bit her lip. Of course, Bella would assume the baby hadn't been born. It was then that she realised when you evaded the truth the lies kept piling up.

Bella looked pensive as she gazed into the distance where people were choosing their seats at the bandstand in readiness for the brass band to start. 'D'you ever think of Karl? What became of him? With ships being torpedoed did he survive the journey to America, I wonder?' She shook her head sorrowfully.

'Bella, it was never a certainty he was shipped off to America. For all we know, Karl could be in a secure camp anywhere in Britain.'

Bella nodded. 'That's true. But if Karl does make it through the war, he will never know about the child he almost had.'

Lily's stomach plummeted like a brick, leaving her feeling sick. She closed her eyes. She couldn't keep up this deception. But if she confessed Bella would lose all respect for her and their friendship would be over. But the truth would out anyway when she told John.

As though the unreal world she'd been living in since Ethel's death was stripped from her mind, clarity struck and Lily suddenly knew the truth of the matter. Her befuddled mind had deluded itself into thinking the baby in the pram really was hers and she wanted to keep Joy as her daughter forever.

Bella looked at her with a frown. 'Are you all right, Lily? You've gone as white as a sheet. Stupid me, going on like that after all you've been through. Blimey, I came to help not to make things worse.'

'Bella, stop.' Lily needed to say the words that burnt in her brain. 'I've got something to tell you. Promise you won't hate me.'

Bella's expression became concerned. 'Don't be so dramatic, Lily. You're scaring me. I could never hate you.'

Lily, pressing the pram's brake with a foot, sank down on a park bench by the lake. She watched on as ducks, gliding through the water, headed for the morsels of bread a toddler had thrown.

As the brass band started up, and strains of 'Nimrod' from *Enigma Variations* – Lily's favourite, which always made her cry – began to play, she stated matter-of-factly, 'Joy isn't mine.'

Bella's brow furrowed in puzzlement. She came to sit beside Lily. 'What! How d'you mean, she isn't yours...'

Lily, in a low voice and staring straight ahead, told Bella how she'd lost her baby and what had happened the night of the raid, when Ethel died.

The silence after she finished unnerved her.

Finally, Bella turned towards her, a dumbfounded expression on her face. 'I need time to grasp what you've told me, Lily.' She rose and, wandering up the grassy hill, appeared to stop and listen to the band.

Lily watched her. She realised she might have lost her best friend, but the terrible thing was she didn't regret what she'd done. It was the right thing to have told her – to have admitted the truth at last.

Bella turned and, sauntering back, sat next to Lily on the bench. 'I'm in shock and can't quite take it in. Ethel's baby didn't die and you delivered it and pretended it was yours...'

Lily answered simply, 'Yes.'

Bella's expression was scarily serious. 'What made you do it?'

'I don't know... it just seemed natural at the time. The nurse put Joy in my arms and... it just felt so right.'

Bella gave her a long piercing look. 'Lily, I can't condone what you've done but I understand what drove you to do it. It was a heartbreaking time, losing your own baby, then having to help deliver Ethel's during a raid. Then the shock of her being killed...' She gave a sharp intake of breath. 'It's difficult even to absorb the enormity of events, never mind having to experience them.'

'It's wrong, I know, but having Joy felt heaven-sent.'

Bella gave her a curious stare, her brows knitting together. 'I'm not an expert but, Lily, I do think what you've been through has affected your mind.'

Lily sat for a moment absorbing the words. 'You might be right, but my love for Joy is real.'

'She isn't yours, Lily.'

'I know that and I feel guilty that I'm betraying Ethel. Oh, Bella, Ethel didn't have much of a life. It's so unfair she died so young. And I promised her I'd take care of Joy, no matter what.' Her chin quivered.

Bella said, shamefaced, 'I feel bad because of the way I treated Ethel at first.'

'You stuck up for her in the end.'

They sat for a while lost in thought.

Lily spoke first. 'You're right. I've acted—'

'It's normal to act strangely when you're faced with strange circumstances,' Bella interrupted.

'So now you're saying I'm normal?' Lily said, tentatively.

They looked at each and laughed.

Bella sobered first. 'Seriously, when Ronnie died I went to pieces.' She gave a laboured sigh. 'I didn't tell you the whole story.

After I received the telegram, it was like a black cloud settled over my mind and I couldn't think clearly. I wouldn't go out or meet people and it felt like I was losing my mind.' Her eyes dark, it was as though she relived that terrible time. 'It got to the stage when I couldn't see the point of living.'

Lily's hand flew to her chest. 'Oh, my goodness. What got you through?'

'My boss at the hairdresser's.'

'Really?'

Bella nodded. 'She was older and took me under her wing. She asked if I thought this was what Ronnie would want. Me giving up and having no life. I was angry at first but it got me thinking. I asked myself what I would want for Ronnie if it was me who didn't make it.'

Lily, curious, asked, 'And what was the answer?'

'Ronnie was one of those people who lived life to the full.' Bella smiled, remembering. 'He was the most easy-going person and I couldn't bear the thought of him changing, being miserable on my account.' She looked deep into Lily's eyes. 'So, you see, I do know what it's like to go off the rails, but the thing is, in the end, you've got to be able to live with yourself. I understand why you went along with caring for Joy as if she was your own, but Lily, it's the deceit of what you're doing that's wrong.'

Lily said in a small voice, 'I can't give Joy up now.'

Bella gave her a long, measured look. 'Only you can decide what to do about this now, Lily. If you carry on with this deception, as I said, I won't condone it but neither will I say anything... and you can count on me as a friend.'

Lily didn't know what else to say, and the sound of music from the band drifting on the salt sea air was enough to tear her heart out as the two of them hugged.

34

'Does anyone else know?' Bella asked.

Walking out of the park, they made their way along Pier Parade, past the decorative canopy which housed the 'Tyne' Lifeboat, a reminder of the bravery of the men who risked their lives rescuing those in peril in stormy seas.

Realising she was avoiding Bella's question, Lily replied, 'I've only told you.'

'What about your folks? Aren't they nearby?'

'Not any more. Mam wrote to me a while ago to say Dad had been laid off from the shipyard due to ill health. They decided to join my youngest brother where he's been evacuated and my sister-in-law and her young son have joined them.' Lily sighed. 'I do miss them but being out in the country is the best thing for them.'

'D'you keep in touch with the family?'

Lily tensed as she knew where these questions were going. 'Yes. Mam and I write often.' She pre-empted Bella's next question. 'I told her I was pregnant though I've never given her an exact due date.' She reddened, aware she sounded as though she'd planned keeping them in the dark so she could make up a date to tally with Joy being born. 'John was home in January and so she'll assume the baby isn't due till October.'

'So, she doesn't know you've lost the baby?'

Staring down at her feet, Lily shook her head.

'What d'you say if she asks about the baby?'

Lily decided to come clean and tell Bella the truth. 'I don't want to tell lies so I evade answering.' She rubbed a temple with her fingertips. 'Mam must think I'm avoiding talking about the pregnancy because I'm worried about the outcome. So she's simply stopped asking. But she always ends her letter by saying, "Always remember, I'm here if you need me for anything, Lily."'

Bella groaned and gave a small headshake, as if disbelieving what she was hearing. 'What about John? Have you written to tell him you've miscarried the baby?'

Lily didn't admit that in the strange, unreal world she lived in now she didn't feel she had miscarried their baby.

Bella frowned. 'You haven't, have you? What about Joy?'

'I intend telling him when the time is right. It's too complicated to explain in a letter.' Her tone sounded defensive, even to Lily. 'We'll work out what to do then.'

Bella tipped her head, a confused look on her face. 'Did Ethel say anything about what she intended to do about the baby in the future?'

Lily explained the conversation she and Ethel had, and the suggestion Lily had made.

'You offered her a home after the baby was born?' A look of esteem for Lily crossed Bella's face.

'As I said, Ethel was adamant she didn't want the baby put in an orphanage and I don't blame her. Offering Ethel and the baby a home seemed the right thing to do.' Lily went on, 'We made a pact and promised, if anything should happen to either of us, the other would find our baby a decent home.'

Saying this caught Lily off guard and tearily she remembered Ethel at the time, so young and vibrant. The idea of anything happening to her had seemed such a remote one.

Bella took a minute while she digested this new piece of information, then smiled. 'You realise that's exactly what you're doing, giving Joy a decent home.'

Then her expression became concerned.

'What?' Lily asked anxiously.

'Lily, you can't keep this a secret from John.'

'I won't. I intend telling him as soon as I feel the time is right.'

———

Arriving back at Olcote, as Lily opened the front door, she saw an airmail letter lying on the doormat.

Bumping the pram backwards over the front step, Lily pulled it along the passageway and put the brake on. Checking Joy was still asleep, she moved to the kitchen and tore open John's letter.

Somewhere in Sicily

Sweetheart,

Sorry about the long delay. As I explained in my last letter we've been on the move. A lot has happened and I wish I could tell you more but it's not allowed, as you know. I've received your letter which has uplifted me enormously, especially the snapshot of yourself which I look at often.

After a long patrol when I was feeling rough, I was told to see the medical officer in charge. Don't worry, sweetheart, I'm on the mend now but I've had a bout of dysentery and ended up in the field hospital but I expect to be back in action soon. I'm sorry this letter is short and to the point but there's not much else to say.

I love you more than I can say and think of you constantly. Wish the snapshot of you was with your bump so I could see with my own eyes our baby growing.

Missing you more than ever.

All my love,

John xx

Lily felt wretched. Why hadn't she written and told John that she'd lost their baby? Bella was helping her to think clearly again, and she tried to process the events and her actions. All Lily knew was it had been all-consuming, losing her baby and then having Joy in her arms. She could honestly say she'd acted in the only way her dazed mind that craved her baby could at the time.

John sounded down. Lily couldn't tell him that she'd lost their baby till she was confident he was strong enough to receive the news by letter. But the longer she put off telling him, the harder it would be to confess her actions, she realised.

A new terror seized her. What if the authorities found out about her deceit – her claiming the baby was hers? Lily would be classed as an unfit person and Joy would be taken from her. Her mind reeling, another thought struck her. When Jean had given birth to Stanley, she'd wanted Harry to register the baby's name.

'What's the rush?' Harry had replied at the time. 'We've six weeks to register the baby's name. Anyway, why me? You know I hate form-filling. I always muck it up.'

'Harry Armstrong,' Jean told him with pursed lips, 'the one job I ask you to do and you're opting out. For your information either parent can register their baby and I thought you'd be proud as Punch to do such a simple job.'

'What if the baby has no parents?' Harry asked, obviously trying to defuse the matter by changing the subject. 'I would imagine that happening these days.'

Jean, easily upset after just delivering Stanley, had become tearful. 'It doesn't bear thinking about.' She sniffed. 'We should say now, Harry, who we'd want to bring Stanley up if anything happens to us. As it's the person who is responsible for the baby that has to register the name.'

The person Ethel had made promise to be responsible for Joy was Lily. Remembering this now, Lily struggled to know whose names she should put on the register as Joy's parents.

35

The highlight these days for Lily, apart from the delight of having Joy to care for, was the weekends when Bella stayed over at Olcote on her day off.

Apart from being impatient for the mail to arrive with a letter from John, Lily's world revolved around Joy. Despite all the worries plaguing Lily – the fear of how to tell John and her family what had happened, and the terror of what the authorities might do when they knew, because Lily would have to inform them once her family knew the truth – she was happy. The baby's name was apt because joyous was how Lily felt since she'd lost her own baby and she felt she'd been given a replacement.

———

It was following a restless night, after being disturbed by Joy and spending a couple of hours feeding and willing the baby to go back to sleep, that Lily awoke in an anxious state. She just knew something bad was about to happen.

In the early morning, bleary-eyed and feeling as though she'd not slept at all, Lily padded down the stairs, and she automatically went along the passageway to check for post. Opening the lobby door, ears cocked listening for sounds from upstairs where she'd left Joy sound asleep in a cot she'd discovered at the WVS second-hand depot, Lily picked up a letter from the mat. Staring at the airmail letter, she had a déjà vu moment and the hairs on the back of her neck stood up.

Lily didn't recognise the writing on the envelope. Her hands trembly, she ripped the letter open and read:

Dear Mrs Radley,

I'm sorry to inform you that your husband Corporal John Radley has been wounded. He has been operated on by a specialist surgeon who cleaned the wounds to try and save his leg below the knee. Unfortunately, the wound haemorrhaged and Corporal Radley's state weakened.

Lily tensed, afraid to read on.

After a blood transfusion your husband's condition stabilised and the surgeon specialist thought it best his leg was amputated below the knee. Corporal Radley has since been transported to the UK by hospital ship to Queen Mary's (Roehampton) hospital.

Sincerest best wishes for your husband,

Sister Riley

Lily felt light-headed. This couldn't be happening. She reread the letter to make sure she hadn't missed anything.

She pictured the disabled men she saw in the streets, limbs missing, their trousers or sleeves pinned up, and realised that her husband was now one of them.

A nervous energy took hold and, for want of something better to do, Lily made her way into the kitchen where she boiled the kettle on the gas. Pouring the boiled water in a dish, she began to wash the kitchen cupboard doors and bench tops, listening all the while for sounds from upstairs.

While she worked, the memory of a recent newspaper article she'd read surfaced in her mind and Lily stopped what she was doing and clapped a hand over her mouth. The article had reported transport by sea carried the threat of a ship being attacked by the enemy; even one marked by a red cross wasn't safe any more – which breached the international convention rules.

John would be travelling on a hospital ship.

———

It was a Saturday afternoon and Bella arrived, a rucksack slung over a shoulder. Opening the front door, Joy in her arms, Lily had never been so pleased to see her friend.

'What's up?' Bella asked, her face contorted in concern. 'You look dreadful. Is it news about John?'

Too overwrought, Lily felt incapable of answering. She led the way into the kitchen and picked up the letter she'd received from the hospital, handing it to Bella.

When she'd finished reading the letter, Bella looked up, her face shocked. 'Lily, I'm so sorry. Have you heard anything more?'

'No and I'm worried sick because of ships being attacked by the enemy.'

Bella touched her arm, in a gesture of concern. 'As far as I know, there's been no reports recently about ships being attacked.'

Chewing her lip, Lily picked up a banana-shaped bottle from the table and gave Joy a drink of boiled water. 'I can't get *Centaur* out of my mind.'

She involuntarily shivered. *Centaur* was a hospital ship that had been torpedoed and sunk off the coast of Queensland, Australia, in May when over three hundred souls met a watery grave.

Bella held up her hands. 'Blimey, you can't think like that.

We'd all go insane if we thought about every eventuality that could happen in this war.'

'I suppose so, but I'm a nervous wreck.'

'Lily, you're the most capable and strong-minded person I know. This news is bound to floor you.' She gave a gentle, encouraging smile. 'The letter was posted ages ago. John's possibly safely on British shores by now and you'll receive notice from the hospital soon.'

Lily had tried to hold herself together, but it wasn't working; she blurted, 'I need to know now.'

'Then why don't you ring Queen Mary's Hospital and see if they know anything?'

Lily's mind in a whirl of emotions, she couldn't make a decision. 'It's a Saturday.'

'Hospitals don't close, Lily.'

'What if—'

'I'll look after Joy while you ring the hospital.'

———

As she closed the telephone box door behind her, Lily, deep in thought, walked down King George Road. Turning into Foley Avenue, she headed for the front door, which stood ajar.

Entering the lobby, she made her way into the kitchen where Bella was sitting on a chair, with Joy asleep on her lap.

'Did you get through to Queen Mary's?'

'Yes. John's been admitted. They put me through to the ward. I spoke to the sister, who told me his wound has become septic.' Her face crumpled. 'Oh Bella, Sister says his condition is serious.'

———

Lily felt Bella's eyes on her as she folded the dry nappies and put them in a pile on a chair. This was how she handled upsetting news, by keeping her hands busy.

Bella stood up from the chair. 'I'll put Joy in the pram and make us a cup of tea.'

Returning from the passage and putting the kettle on the gas, Bella turned towards Lily. 'I've been thinking. Why don't you go down to London and see John?'

Lily stopped folding the nappies. 'I can't. What about Joy? The bombing, it's worse down there...'

'I've thought it all out. I'll ask for a few days' holiday, I'm due some. I'll move in here to look after Joy while you're gone. I've had enough practice looking after kids when my brothers were little.'

Lily opened her mouth to speak but nothing came out.

'Feeding Joy shouldn't be a problem. Not if I use National Dried Milk. I could put it in the bottle you use for giving her a drink of boiled water.'

Lily listened carefully, slowly warming to the idea.

'As far as the bombing goes, they say there's a lull just now. Besides, nowhere's safe these days. You could stay in your own bed and cop it.'

Lily's brain was ticking over. She was desperate to see John and Bella's plan sounded feasible.

Bella added, 'You'd never forgive yourself, Lily, if you—'

Lily's mind was made up, and she interrupted, 'Ask if you can have a couple of days off next week, please Bella, would you? And thank you – from the bottom of my heart.'

36

John looked across the ward at the high ceiling above the tall windows. He heard voices around him and wondered what he and his unit were doing in this echoey room. Then, his eyes heavy, he gave in and let blessed sleep overcome him.

———

The next time John awoke, a nurse was peering down at him.

'Medicine time, Mr Radley.'

She looked so clean and fresh in her striped navy and white uniform and starched cap, but he wondered why her young face looked so concerned.

Somewhere deep in his memory John knew where he was and struggled to bring the knowledge to the surface.

Failing, he asked in a thin voice that he didn't recognise as his own, 'Where am I?'

The nurse smiled a pleasant smile, as though something had been achieved. 'In hospital in London, you were brought here after a journey in a ship, remember?'

Suddenly John did. Not the journey, but being carried on a stretcher off a ship and left with others on the quayside. Then being lifted onto an ambulance and the agonisingly painful journey that followed. Pain? A cold sensation came into the base of his spine as realisation hit him. The pain couldn't come from his leg because...

John struggled to sit up and, resting on his elbows, looked down to where a dome under the covers proved what he was beginning to recall. He had... he'd lost part of his leg.

'The wound became septic,' the nurse told him in a no-nonsense voice. 'Your condition's more stable now, Corporal, but you must rest. You're not out of the woods yet.'

She gave him his pills and he swallowed them with water she provided in a small cup. Then John sank back on his pillow and, closing his eyes, descended into oblivion.

———

A female voice woke John. 'He's in bed B7. It's clipped on the bed rail.'

Swimming up from the black void, he opened his eyes. Yellow sunlight beamed through the tall windows opposite, hurting his eyes, and he squinted.

'John, I'm here.' A different female voice spoke, this time one he recognised, but who it was he couldn't yet fathom.

A warm hand reached down and held his where it rested on the cover.

In a moment of clarity John realised he knew who the person was.

'Lily.' He shaded his eyes with his free hand.

There she was, the love of his life, paler, thinner, but her face as beautiful as ever.

Tears burnt the backs of his eyes.

'It's not manly to cry.' His father's stern voice spoke in his mind.

'John, love, you can't imagine how good it is to see you.' The strict presence vanished and John focused on the words of his lovely wife. 'Listen, John, you've got to concentrate on getting better. You must fight.'

Her voice sounded apprehensive and John wanted to convey that he didn't want to cause her worry, but the effort to form a sentence was too great. Lily continued to speak, and though John didn't catch the words, it was enough just to hear her soothing voice. Listening, he dozed off.

———

Thinner?

The word, large in his mind, awoke him. Darkness wrapped around him and if someone hadn't coughed, he would have thought he was dead. He closed his eyes and began to sleep again.

But then he woke again with a start.

Thinner?

John wondered again why the word was so important. It occurred to him it was something to do with his wife, something imperative he had to ask her... but what it was, John had no idea.

He opened his eyes and was surprised it wasn't dark any more and sunlight was streaming through the windows.

Lily sat by his bedside and was telling him, 'I'm staying in a relatives' room here at the hospital, but tonight will be the last time.'

John felt refreshed after his sleep and it was such a good feeling. Lily smiled at him, her eyes showing the tenderness he felt in his heart.

'That's more like my John.' She beamed and he noticed she was wearing lipstick on her Cupid's bow lips. He wondered at the catch in her voice.

The pain in his lower leg came then like an electric shock, but in a moment of clarity he recalled that was nonsense because he didn't have a leg.

'My leg, it's—'

She touched his lips with her fingertips. 'I know, love, but let's not worry about that now. All you have to do is to get well. I need you at home.'

She went on to talk about someone called Bella, who was good company, and his mum, who sent all her love, then, exhausted trying to keep up, John closed his eyes just for a minute.

———

He awoke at night time. Something niggled in John's brain that he'd omitted to ask Lily but he still didn't know what. What he did recall was she needed him at home.

He became aware of her voice speaking to him. 'John, this is my last night.' He opened his eyes and there she was, his Lily. 'I'll write, John, often. Sister assures me that the way you're improving, you'll soon be writing back.'

He didn't feel so tired and was content to just lie there looking at her.

Then, in a moment, of clarity, John knew.

'You're thinner. You've had the baby,' he said excitedly. He remembered the heartache and third time lucky.

For a heart-stopping moment when she didn't reply, he asked, 'Is it all...'

Lily hesitated. Then she said, 'It's a girl, John.'

Tears pricking his eyes, a smile on his face, John fell into a deep and restful sleep.

37

Mid-September now, the weather warm, and Sunday dinner over, Lily and Bella were out for a walk with the bairn in the pram. Passing St Michael's church, Lily said a silent prayer for John.

What made her mind up that Saturday afternoon, when Bella had offered to look after Joy so that Lily could travel to London, was she knew in her bones that if she could see John and hold his hand he'd know she was there and her presence would help to give him the strength to fight and pull through. Lily had been right. Since her trip to London last week, John had gradually improved enough to correspond by letter.

Now, walking up Mortimer Road with Bella, inevitably the talk turned to the state of the war.

'I never asked you before. Did you hear the news that Italy had surrendered earlier this month?' Bella wanted to know.

'Yes, but not the details.'

'The lasses in the sawmill reckon the fighting will be over soon.' Bella pulled a sceptical face.

Lily chipped in, 'A woman in Thornton's corner shop yesterday said she was heartsick of the war and blackouts and she'd turn grey overnight if she thought the war would go on for another winter.'

Bella's eyebrows arched. 'Can you imagine the shock of waking up with a head of grey hair?'

They both saw the funny side and laughed.

As they walked over the brow of the hill below, the vast sparkling blue sea spread before them in the distance. They drew nearer and looked past the golden dunes and rolls of barbed wire to waves, which tumbled in one after the other to the shore – and Lily imagined the swishing noise as they receded. Her gaze wandered way out to sea, to the horizon, where a miniature ship heaved up and down as it travelled through the choppy waters.

'I feel sick just watching that ship,' Bella commented.

Lily's thoughts turned to John and how dreadful the journey must have been when he was on the hospital ship headed for home, and him being so desperately ill.

'I phoned the ward yesterday,' she remarked.

'I meant to ask if you did. Is John still improving?'

'Sister said they're pleased with his progress and he's now able to sit up in a wheelchair.'

'Eee! That's smashing news, Lily.'

Lily was still getting over the shock of John's disability, but she'd vowed that – whatever it took – she'd do all she could to ensure he led as normal a life as possible. Losing him was never an option. Here he was, now able to get around the ward in a wheelchair, and there was talk of him coming home one day.

As they walked on for a while, Lily was conscious of Bella's sidelong glance.

'What?' She prepared herself, knowing there would be no beating about the bush with Bella.

'Did John ask about the baby when you saw him?'

'Yes,' was her clipped reply. This was a subject she'd rather not discuss. 'He realised I was thinner and asked if I'd had the baby.'

'What did you say?'

'That it was a girl.' Bella gave a sharp disbelieving breath. 'John's still weak and cries at the drop of a hat. There's no way I'm going to jeopardise him getting well by telling him that I lost our baby.'

Bella held out her hands in a gesture of disbelief. 'D'you not think it'll be harder for him when he finds out the truth?'

'What I think is' – Lily's tone was defensive – 'I'll know when the time's right to tell him.'

'By gum, Lily, you've really got nerve. But what I think is, it's none of my business.'

Like a bolt of lightning zipping through her brain, the thought struck Lily that she wondered if she might not tell John at all.

As time went by, John's letters were increasingly about the hospital and his treatment and care regime, and Lily wondered if he was becoming institutionalised, as there was never any mention of him coming home. Queen Mary's did all they could to make the amputees stay comfortable with homely surroundings, and they were encouraged to take part in sports. But everything was done to aid rehabilitation and the ultimate aim was for them to be part of society again.

Then a letter arrived with the news that Lily had long been waiting for.

Queen Mary's Hospital
Roehampton Lane
London

Sweetheart,

I've seen the specialist today. He says my stump has healed and I'm to be fitted with a prosthetic limb and, would you believe, Queen Mary's is a centre for making them.

The end is in sight and I'll be coming home, sweetheart, to both of you.

He went on to tell her what the travel arrangements would be when the time eventually arrived, but Lily barely took these in.

The time of reckoning had come, and she had to make a decision. She'd thought long and hard and decided she couldn't be deceitful, not with her husband, and the only choice she had was to tell him the truth. John was stronger; he could take hearing that she'd lost their baby. But Lily still couldn't bear to see the devastation on his face.

Her stomach quaked. John loved her and would understand that she hadn't been thinking straight after losing their baby. The strange thing was, Lily realised, it still didn't feel like she'd lost the baby, because Joy *was* her baby. Lily felt she was being disloyal to Ethel but her heart seemed to have a mind of its own on the matter.

38

The day of John's arrival, Lily was up early. Looking out of the window at the darkened, thundery sky, Lily was disappointed as she wanted John's homecoming to be perfect.

Dressing Joy in a white, smocked frock and knitted matinee coat, with cute pink socks, Lily told her, 'My, what a bobby-dazzler you look. Wait till Daddy sees you.'

Lily started, surprised at the slip.

Her nerves on edge, she filled the day by getting rations in from the corner shop. She made a pan of vegetable soup then tidied the house, cleaning windows and washing the kitchen floor. Anything and everything to keep busy.

It had been decided that Lily would wait at home for John to arrive rather than greet him at the railway station. He had written that a nurse from the hospital would be travelling with him and they'd be met by an ambulance that would bring him home.

Late afternoon, as the time drew near for him to arrive, Joy, who seemed to know something was up, was fractious. Lily didn't want John to meet the baby when her face was scrunched up and she was bawling. Lily had fed her, brought her wind up, changed her nappy so, with nothing else for it, she put her in the pram. Wheeling the pram back and forth in the passageway, Lily was rewarded when the bairn finally stopped crying and, eyelids drooping, she fell asleep.

As Lily covered Joy with a pink blanket, a noise in the distance made her stiffen. The drone of planes came closer. Fear knifed through her. *Please God, not on John's homecoming.*

It then occurred to Lily: she hadn't heard the siren's warning. Moving into the lobby, she opened the door. Peering up into the powder-blue sky, she saw two low-flying aeroplanes approaching. As they roared overhead Lily let out a sigh of relief as she recognised two Halifax bombers. Relief flooding through her, Lily made to close the door when a vehicle rumbling along the road caught her attention.

An ambulance.

Heart thumping, Lily moved to the kerbside and waved to let the ambulance driver know they'd arrived at the correct address. The ambulance drew over and came to a halt. A rather stout woman got out.

'Afternoon.'

Before Lily could reply she heard noises from the back of the ambulance. She turned and saw a nurse wearing a uniform and navy cloak appear.

'Mrs Radley?' The nurse was quite young and had frizzy hair, which looked permed, beneath the cap she wore.

'Yes, but please call me Lily.'

'I've got a very tired John waiting to see you.'

Lily swallowed the biggest lump in her throat.

The nurse helped John from the ambulance but he insisted he'd make the journey to the door with the aid of a crutch himself. Lily, feeling redundant, stood aside. John, wearing a now too-big uniform, looked up and gave Lily a wink. He managed to make his way slowly to the door, over the small step and into the lobby.

As she watched him struggling to manoeuvre the crutch in the confined space, Lily felt herself blanch. The fact her husband had lost part of his leg had never really sunk in but, seeing him struggle for real, his plight was distressing. Hand on her heart, she watched him make his way into the front room where, drained and gaunt-looking, he sank down on the couch. This was her beloved John and she found the notion that he'd have to contend with this disability for the rest of his life unbearably heartbreaking. Remembering her promise to make his life as normal as possible, Lily squared her shoulders.

The nurse brought John's things in, which didn't appear to be much. After a few pleasantries, during which the nurse confided she was from the north and had trained at Newcastle Royal Victoria hospital, Lily offered her tea.

'You'll be gasping,' she said, 'and how about a sandwich?'

'That's very kind, but no, thanks. It's been arranged for me to stay overnight at South Shields general hospital and I'd better get a move on or it'll be time for them to change shifts.' She nodded to the driver, who made for the door.

'Good luck for the future, John.' The nurse nodded and smiled. 'Remember, don't push yourself too hard.'

Lily saw them off, and as she closed the door and returned to the front room, she let out a cry of surprise to see John, standing, supported by a crutch, holding out his free arm.

His face broke into a smile and Lily noticed the deep lines carved into his skin. 'Sweetheart.' His voice was hoarse and there was an air of insecurity about him. 'I've waited for this moment so long.'

She moved towards him and when she wrapped her arms around his thin torso he appeared to stiffen. She looked up and, as he bent down, the kiss he gave her was perfunctory and not the deep and sensual one she'd imagined.

He pulled away and nodded to the pram. 'I can't wait to see our baby.'

Something moved deep within Lily and she stood rooted to the spot.

'Joy's asleep.'

He smiled. 'I liked the name Jennifer that we'd chosen, but Joy is so much better.' His eyes misted. 'The idea of our baby kept me going through the dark days.' He gave a contented smile. 'Lift her out so I can see properly.'

Dread, like an anchor, weighed her down. She forced herself over to the pram, collapsed the hood and, removing the blanket covering the tiny form, she lifted the baby out.

Joy squirmed, as though impatient she'd been disturbed, then settled again in Lily's arms. John gazed for a long time at Joy's peaceful, sleeping face: the shining skin, the tiny lashes, button nose.

'We made a baby at last,' he told Lily gruffly.

It was his eyes, filled with love and pride, that convinced Lily. How could she possibly tell him the baby wasn't theirs?

Lily was stricken with a pang of guilt. Had she always intended to keep Joy as theirs? And what would Bella think about Lily not telling John? But hadn't she admitted that while she didn't condone Lily's actions, she wouldn't tell anyone?

———

It was the next morning, when Lily awoke, that she realised the time had come when she needed to write and tell Mam about the supposedly newborn baby. It was conceivable that Lily had delivered her baby by now. She agonised what to say as she couldn't tell an outright lie. This world of deceit was of her own making, Lily realised. Ethel came to mind, her young face intent and serious. What would she want? All Ethel had wanted was for her baby to have a secure and loving home, and that's what Joy would receive in the Radley household.

Secure in the knowledge she was doing the right thing, Lily found a pen and writing pad and, sitting at the kitchen table, she composed a letter telling Mam about the baby. She didn't tell a lie by saying the baby was hers, but just informed Mam the baby had been born and that it was a girl. She then went on to tell Mam about John returning from hospital and his having to adjust to living at home with his disability.

She finished by saying:

I know you'll want to see your new grandchild and I can't wait to see you both but it would be best if you left visiting for a while as John isn't up to visitors yet. (Which was true, Lily comforted herself, John definitely wasn't himself and until the couple were on a more even footing she couldn't risk dealing with others getting involved, however well-meaning they might be.) *Besides, the journey here would be too much for you in one day and I'd love for you to stay longer when you do come. I want our time together to be a happy one.*

Don't worry about me, I'm doing fine as the baby is as good as gold.

Take care of yourselves,

Much love, Lily

As she licked and sealed the envelope, she experienced a longing for Mam like she did when she was little and in trouble, when her mam could make Lily's world right again. A tender smile touched Lily's lips as she inwardly promised Ethel she would be Joy's protector against all evils.

———

John's homecoming wasn't what he'd expected. Whereas in the hospital he'd felt able to cope, here he was literally out on a limb (he grimaced at the pun), negotiating furniture, feeling a sense of unsteadiness as he climbed the stairs – for all they'd shown him how to cope with stairs at the hospital. With Lily's help and clinging on to the banister rail he eventually managed. He'd become used to the hospital routine and the fellows who were all in the same boat, nurses who he could speak plainly to and could handle any situation, be it mental or physical.

The peculiar thing about coming home was his self-conscious-ness around Lily. It had been so long since they'd seen each other the familiarity of living together had gone.

That first night he opted to sleep in the spare room. 'I don't sleep well at nights,' he told Lily. 'I'm worried I'll wake you. You need your rest with the baby and all.'

That wasn't the real reason. After the operation John's mind had gone numb for a long while and he hadn't been able to accept the situation. As the time neared for him to come home, though he welcomed the prospect, a feeling of being overwhelmed and help-less set in. What played like a broken record in his mind most was the idea Lily wouldn't love him any more – she hadn't bargained on marrying a cripple. He couldn't face her reaction when she saw his stump, and tried to fathom out how to do his aftercare without her seeing it, the aftercare which was vital if he didn't want to get a sore from wearing his prosthetic limb and end up with an infec-tion. He was aware he was avoiding kissing her and shrank from her touch when she tried to hold his hand or embrace him. He saw the way she looked at him when he moved away, the hurt in her eyes, but he was at a loss to know what to do about it.

One night, while he lay in the dark listening, he heard the familiar sounds of his wife putting the baby in her cot, then his bedroom door creaked open.

The light switched on, blinding him. Struggling to sit up, he saw Lily in her nightie looking down at him, hands on hips.

'John Radley, what's going on?' Her chin trembled. 'Don't you love me any more?'

John was aghast. 'How d'you mean? How could you ask such a thing?'

'Because since you came home you've been avoiding me, and not once have we had a proper kiss, and I can only think—'

'It's me,' he interrupted, shocked at her outburst. Deciding only the truth would do, John continued to tell her his true feelings, about feeling inadequate at home, worrying about her seeing his stump, and him not being the man she married.

Open-mouthed, Lily sank down on the bed. 'Silly man, I had no idea.'

She started to pull back his covers.

He grappled to retrieve them.

'John, I want to see this stump you think I'm too feeble to handle.'

She tugged at the sheet and, staring down at the upper part of his leg, she gave a sharp intake of breath as though shocked at the sight.

John had known this might be her reaction. He himself couldn't stomach looking at where his leg was cut off just below the knee. As Lily's eyes sought his, her features softened.

She stood up. 'John Radley, get a move on out of this bed. Help me take your things to our bedroom.' She commenced to take his clothes from the chair, while John, with the aid of crutches, followed her to the master bedroom.

Lily pulled back the sheet on his side of the bed. 'This is where you'll remain from now on.'

'You never did explain how it happened,' Bella said to John.

A Sunday morning and breakfast over, each of their precious eggs for the week boiled (or, in John's case, fried and made into a sandwich from the loaf of homemade bread), the two of them sat at the table finishing their tea. Lily was at the sink making up a bottle in readiness for Joy waking up. She'd carried on bottle-feeding Joy ever since her visit to London when Bella had looked after the bairn.

Lily was delighted that since the first weekend Bella had come to visit and been introduced to John, the pair of them had got on, though they did tend to rib each other occasionally. Initially, Lily had been fearful of them meeting as Bella, knowing the truth about Joy, might have felt uneasy when she met John.

And there'd been a moment when, introductions over, John had remarked, 'I'd like to thank you, Bella, for looking after my daughter while Lily visited me in hospital.'

A pause had followed as Bella looked helplessly at Lily, a dash of red burning on both of her cheeks.

John must have taken her reaction as embarrassment, as he'd quickly put in, 'I wanted you to know because the visit made such a difference to aiding my recovery.'

The tense moment passed, but Lily had felt a pang of guilt at putting her friend in such an awkward position.

John asked now, a twinkle in his eye, 'What have I not told you?'

Bella pulled a 'you know fine well' face at him.

'Oh, the leg, you mean? I had a fight with a ruddy mine while driving a vehicle.' Typically, John didn't say anything more as the memory, Lily knew, was both mentally and physically painful.

His convalescence so far was proving successful; he didn't go grey any more when he got tired and the dark swathes under his eyes had disappeared, but he still had an air of frailty about him.

'So, what happened next?'

John looked blank.

'How did they get you to hospital?' Bella, her quizzical eyes on him, took a slurp of tea waiting for an answer.

Lily, placing the made-up bottle of milk on the wooden drainer to cool for later, wondered if she should intervene to stop Bella's inquisition, then decided John was big enough to look after himself.

John sighed, tolerantly. 'If you must know, nosey parker, I was assessed at the regimental aid post where it was decided I couldn't be patched up and sent back to the fighting,' he said dryly, 'then shuttled by stretcher and eventually transferred to a hospital at base area before boarding this ship for the journey home.'

Taking a swig of tea, he drained the cup and stood as if that was the end of that particular conversation. 'What's the agenda for today?' he asked Lily.

Lily came over to stand beside him. 'I forgot to tell you I bumped into Madge at the corner shop and—'

'Who's Madge?'

'I thought I wrote and told you about her when I did ambulance service for the Red Cross? She taught me how to drive.'

John, leaning against the table for support, shook his head. 'I can't remember. Never mind, go on.'

'We got chatting and she told me that she's a widow now, and at a loose end on her morning off, so she helps out at the local Rest Centre. She didn't know the family had been bombed out. I told her I'd like to show my appreciation one day for the help the centre provided for the family, and Madge suggested I join her. She's doing a first aid training session this week when local kiddies volunteer to be pretend casualties.' She turned to Bella. 'You can come if you like, I can take Joy, she's fed and will be no bother.'

'What does it involve?' Bella, looking up at Lily, didn't sound too keen on the idea of spending her day off indoors in a Rest Centre, and who could blame her.

'Apparently, kiddies are given a ticket at the door which says what kind of injury they're supposedly suffering from. Hopefully my pretend casualty won't have anything I can't handle.'

Bella's face was the picture of indifference.

Lily added a temptation she knew her friend couldn't resist. 'Madge says the catering department make soup, and usually homemade bread and tea and biscuits are served mid-morning.'

'Now you're talking.' Bella grinned. 'I'll look after Joy for you. Then afterwards we can take her for a walk in the pram.'

Lily saw John's face drop, as he'd have liked nothing better than to join them, but he was still going through the learning process of walking distances with a prosthetic leg.

Lily was pleased she'd made the decision to bottle-feed Joy because it meant John could help out on occasion, which both satisfied his independent temperament and his craving to bond with Joy. As for Lily, though she'd never admit it to John, she did get bushed, what with Joy's needs and her husband having reduced mobility and being unstable – she was afraid of him falling, especially on the stairs. He easily tired and Lily did as much for him as he'd allow. Though she wouldn't change a moment of her life there were times when she wanted peace and quiet to recharge her batteries.

She told John, 'I've left everything ready on the bench for your dinner. It's only a fish-paste sandwich, I'm afraid.'

'Don't worry about me. I'll be glued to the wireless listening to

Albert Sandler's Palm Orchestra. And I'll have a read of this.' He picked up yesterday's newspaper off the table. 'Though, if newspapers get any thinner there'll be nothing left to read,' he grumbled. 'I'll be through this in a jiffy.'

'With all the shortages, you're lucky to have a newspaper,' Bella scolded.

John heaved a mock sigh. 'I'm off. A fella has no chance against two women.' He grabbed the crutch that leant against the table. 'And don't keep my girl out all day. I want my share of her before she goes off to sleep for the night.'

Using the crutch to aid him, he made a slow journey for the door and, after a series of clumps along the passageway floor, Lily heard the front room door slam.

Lily started to pack a bag with Joy's requirements for the morning: bottle, spare nappy, cream, baby talcum powder; the list was ever-growing.

Bella came to stand beside her with a questioning arched eyebrow.

'What?' Lily asked.

'You know what! When are you going to tell him?'

Lily continued packing Joy's bag.

'Come on, Lily. When are you going to tell John that Joy is not his?'

Lily checked the kitchen door was firmly shut. She looked Bella straight in the eye. 'I'm not and before you say anything to make me feel worse than I already do about Ethel, I know I'm being evil.' She shook her head. 'When he arrived home, I just couldn't tell him. Bella, you should have seen John's—'

'I can imagine,' Bella said, po-faced.

'Bella, I'm in too deep now. I know you can't condone what I've done and I don't ask this for my sake.' She thought for a moment, then said, 'That's a lie; since I first held her in my arms after Ethel died, Joy became mine, it was like the baby I lost had come to life. I'm convinced now after three tries I'll never carry a bairn of my own and I so desperately want John to father a child.'

In the silence that followed Lily went on, 'Is it so bad I keep her and fulfil the promise I made to Ethel by giving her a loving home?'

Bella, biting her lip, appeared to be weighing up what to say. 'Lily, there were other options. For instance, you could have adopted her yourself—'

'But I might have been denied and Joy taken awa—'

'I can understand why you wanted to keep her,' Bella cut in. 'As I've said before, you'd just lost your own baby, and were going through a very difficult time. Then with the bombing and the shock of Ethel being killed and finding a baby in your arms... I just can't imagine what it was like for you. I've considered what I would have done but I honestly don't know. Though I would hope I'd tell Ronnie.'

Lily found herself wondering if Bella would. Probably, but who could say for sure.

'I did think of the people that adopt and never tell the children they're adopted,' Bella went on. 'If that happened to Joy, she would never know Ethel was her mother.'

Lily had never thought of that, and she felt absolved a little.

'I'm not accusing you, honest,' Bella, closing her eyes, groaned, 'but it feels wrong not to tell John. I promise I won't say anything. It's not my place.'

It hung in the air, *on your head be it.*

———

Later in bed, Lily couldn't get to sleep for a voice in her head wouldn't be stilled. The voice of conscience.

The decision that had been so difficult and she'd wrestled with, like a weighty opponent, for weeks, surfaced yet again. Whose name should she put on the birth certificate? She couldn't leave it any longer. Lily calculated. Joy had been born the end of July and it was the beginning of October, three weeks over the official grace period for registering a birth. Though Lily could fudge when she was born – who would know any different?

Lily's conscience, ever-present, pricked; the deceit was growing. If she put her own name that would be the ultimate betrayal to Ethel. And if the truth came out, she couldn't bear to see the disappointment, the recrimination in John's eyes.

Lily couldn't go that far. One day Joy might want to know her origins, her true parents. Lily would never deny Joy that right; she loved her too much for that. Lily's mind made up, she would go on Monday morning and register Joy's birth.

May 1945

John plonked into the easy chair in the front room, *Gazette* in his hands, the wireless on a table in the alcove playing music from Glenn Miller's band in the background.

It was a Monday night, and Lily and her new-found friend Madge were out gallivanting at the pictures. John, though physically tired after work, was happy to look after Joy and let Lily have time for herself.

The front room door was ajar so he could hear Joy upstairs if she wakened. The little minx, out of her cot and in a bed now, took advantage and most nights could be heard trotting around upstairs. For safety's sake, John had had to fit a gate at the top of the stairs. Most nights, his daughter found her way into her parents' bedroom and, thumb in mouth, she stood, a small, dark form at the side of the bed, until John, aware of her presence, woke and pulled back the sheet and allowed her to climb in the bed and snuggle between him and his wife. Lily made a show of disapproval about this but John knew that, like him, she was weak-willed where their adorable toddler was concerned.

These days John was glued to listening to the wireless as it had been quite a time recently with all the news. He still couldn't take it in that Hitler was dead.

As doubting Tom (who got his name because of his mistrustful outlook) at work had said, 'Bloody man's taken the easy way out by committing suicide.'

John's thoughts turned to those men left on the beaches at Dunkirk and his blood boiled. He wasn't a vengeful man but in the case of Hitler, dying by gunshot was too good for the man and John, like other folk, wanted to see the sod have the nasty end he deserved. Then there was the fall of Berlin, but the big news that was splashed over the newspapers nigh on every day was that the war would soon be at an end. The strain of when the event would actually happen was getting to everyone, and John's place of work was no exception.

The lads could talk about nothing else and bets were made.

Doubting Tom reckoned last week, 'Aye, I bet VE Day's on a Saturday.' His beady eyes searched the workmen sitting on a plank of wood supported by two pails at either end, eating their bait. 'Cos then they won't have to pay us for a day off work.'

It had taken John over a year to learn to walk properly without the aid of a crutch or cane and his mobility meant he no longer felt like a cripple that folk stared at with pity. A proud man, John didn't want handouts and, determined to provide for his family, he approached Sloan's builders, where he'd worked before the war. The boss had heard about his injury and, overloaded with work with all the bombed buildings, he was only too glad to give John a try and set him on as a plumber's mate.

'The thing is, lad, there's a lot of fetching and carrying and tidying up after Ted the plumber, who you'll be working with. D'you think you can manage?'

All John had known was he'd do his darndest. So, wearing navy overalls and cap and with a coarse material bag slung over his shoulder, John had started work the following week. When the lads good-naturedly started calling him 'peg leg' he knew he'd proved himself and become one of them.

He must have dozed because the next thing John knew he woke with a jump to find the newspaper covering his face. He wondered where Lily was, then remembered she'd gone to the pictures. A jolt of guilt seizing him, he scrambled up and made for the door and, though no noise came from upstairs, John wouldn't be content until he'd checked. Climbing the stairs with the aid of the banister rail, he moved to Joy's bedroom and, bending over his sleeping daughter, by the light from the landing he noted her darling chubby cheeks and tangled, blonde curls spread on the pillow.

Smiling fondly, he returned to the front room where Glenn Miller played no more, having been replaced by a male voice that John recognised as the newsreader. Listening to the news, John heard that the war in Europe was over and that the eighth of this month would be Victory in Europe Day when the prime minister, Winston Churchill, would speak at three p.m.

Although John, like everyone, had been expecting this news for days, it still came as a shock and, an adrenalin rush of anticipation surging through him, he felt his heart racing.

———

Lily, walking from the Savoy picture house in Ocean Road in the late evening sunshine, was only half listening to Madge prattling on about how restrictions on shop display lights and houses had ended. She concentrated on thinking about *National Velvet*, the picture they'd just seen about a fourteen-year-old girl called Velvet who had disguised herself as a boy and entered the Grand National steeplechase. Clearly a girl of true grit, it made Lily think of family traits. Joy was of German descent and Lily felt sure that Ethel's contribution to her personality was her determination to win through. Joy was entitled to know these things and how could Lily deny her. Neither could she deceive John any longer.

It had taken a long time, and she knew John would be shocked at how long she'd kept her secret, but Lily was growing more and more certain what she must do.

———

John switched off the wireless and checked the time on the wall clock. Nine o'clock. Concerned about the womenfolk getting home in the dark, he only hoped they'd remembered to take a torch.

At that moment he heard the front door rattle, and Lily's voice calling out, 'John, have you heard the news?'

Footsteps in the passageway were followed by his wife bursting into the room – her face flushed and eyes shining – and he saw a very pregnant Lily wearing her black and white checked swagger coat.

When the couple had found out Lily was pregnant again, they were over the moon as they'd given up hope of having another child. Though John had said that having his beautiful daughter in his life was enough for him, and he'd be content with that.

'The war's over, John.' Lily laughed now. 'I know it was expected but I can't believe it.'

'How did you find out?' he wanted to know.

'As we came out of the pictures in Ocean Road, we saw folks coming out of the Criterion pub. They yelled to us, '"It's official, it's over." They gave us the Victory V sign.'

Lily, placing her handbag on the floor, shrugged out of her coat and, slinging it over the back of the couch, looked fixedly at him, urgency in her eyes. 'John, we need to get the flags and bunting out. They're in the top cupboard in the dining room alcove. We'll need stepladders, they're in the tall cupboard in the kitchen.' John grinned. Lily, at thirty-five weeks pregnant, had developed a mania for being organised. Once she got something in her head it was as though there was no tomorrow and whatever it was had to be done instantly.

'Lily, it's late, we can do it in the morning. Besides, look at your ankles – they've swollen. You should put your feet up.'

Lily looked down as best she could to regard her ankles, and said, 'Madge noticed that too and said I should go and see the midwife, but it's to be expected when I'm this far on.' She lumbered along the passage. 'It's VE Day tomorrow, John, let's make a start.'

John gave it another go. 'It's dark outside. We can't see to put anything up.'

'We can be prepared for the morning,' came the resolute reply.

John was overprotective, he knew, but he worried about Lily doing too much in her condition and felt it his responsibility to protect her. His wife was capable, though, his logical mind told him; hadn't she been through this before, and on her own, when she'd delivered their Joy?

John had never been told the details of his daughter's birth. Even had he been around at the time it would have made no difference, as childbirth, in all its mystery, was something men were strictly excluded from.

His mind replayed the time he'd received the letter to say Lily was pregnant – the pure joy that had surged through him – and he knew fate couldn't be so cruel as to snatch their happiness away a third time. Far from being upset that Lily had changed the name they'd chosen he was thrilled, as Joy suited his beautiful girl. With the exception of Lily, she was the best thing that had ever happened to him.

The only thing that rankled was that Joy wasn't christened, and though he wasn't particularly a church-going man, John did have faith and would have preferred to have his daughter baptised in case (God forbid!) anything should happen. Her mum had let it be known on one of her visits that she wasn't pleased either, saying, 'Our Lily, I reckon if a bairn isn't christened by the time it's six months, you're tempting fate. I thought you, of all people, would heed that after what you've been through.'

John would normally side with his wife but in this matter he kept quiet as he was in agreement with Ida, which was surprising as her notions were usually too outlandish for him.

Lily was adamant, saying that the war would be over soon and everyone would be in a better frame of mind to have a christening. Which made no sense to John but he knew his wife was under a lot of strain at the time, and much of her fatigue was his fault, which distressed him. So, he left the matter alone, telling himself organising a christening would only be added pressure for Lily.

It was Lily's sister-in-law, Jean, who broached the subject next. Jean had returned from Lancashire with Stanley and Edward – the newest addition to their family – to an overjoyed husband, Harry.

'How about we have Joy's christening now?' she suggested to Lily. 'Then the family could celebrate the war ending and the christening all at the same time.'

Lily's smile was polite but resolute. 'Good idea. I'll think about it when I have time.'

John noted his wife's guarded look. He worried, not for the first time, what the dickens had she to hide? For someone so organised, there were times when she behaved irrationally, like form-filling, when names and birth dates and suchlike had to be filled in for the family. She worked herself up into a panic and then it was left to John to complete the form. And he'd noticed that, during an ordinary conversation about family life, or when he enquired about their lives at the WTC camp, Lily and Bella would exchange glances, giving John the uncomfortable feeling there was something they weren't telling him.

But he didn't question or pry, as he trusted his wife implicitly and knew if there was something he should know Lily would tell him when the time was right.

———

It was ten o'clock and still light outside. As she lay on her back in the double bed, Lily wondered if the coastal area dimout would still be in effect now the war was over. She decided to play safe and draw the blackout curtains. The idea of not having the rigmarole of war was an amazing one but Lily doubted normality would come back to the country soon.

Thoughts churned in her mind. The trawler that was missing and thought to be sunk by a U-boat on Thursday off Iceland. The families grieving for the folk killed in an explosion at the Royal Ordnance Factory at Aycliffe. Poor souls, survived six years of war only to be killed at the final curtain. *But when your time's up*, Lily thought fatalistically, *there's nothing you can do about it*.

She turned her mind to brighter thoughts. The world as she'd known it in these recent years appeared to be waking up. The light restriction from shops and houses and traffic had been lifted, apart from around the coast. Even fire-watch duties had ended.

Her own world was about to change too, Lily marvelled. She'd gone full term and was soon to deliver a baby. She felt relaxed and hadn't been alarmed over the past day when she hadn't felt a movement from the baby. Mam had told her that babies often didn't move before birth and it was as though they were readying for the arduous task of being born. Lily smiled at the thought.

She had a notion the baby was coming soon as she had backache and her belly was lower, which was supposed to be a sign.

Did Ethel, that night in the shelter when her baby was due to be born, have the same fear mingled with excited anticipation, the maternal instinct kicking in even before Ethel had clapped eyes on the baby and wanting only what was best for her child? Lily, too, experienced these feelings and couldn't suffer the thought that her child would never know that she was its mother or, indeed, that John was its father.

When it grew up she wanted the bairn she carried to know its heritage. She couldn't bear the thought of their baby being denied this. The thought cropped up yet again in her mind, so why was she denying Joy? Seeing Joy with John made her think of Karl, who had seemed a good man the day she met him seeking out Ethel in the WTC hut. Lily never dreamt their lives would be entwined in this way. A wave of culpability surged over her when she allowed herself to face the fact she was denying Joy the chance of knowing her biological father.

She loved Joy with all her heart and not only did she know what she must do – more importantly she knew now was the right time to do it. She owed it to Ethel and Joy and, yes, to Karl too. Perhaps then peace would reign within Lily and she would learn to live with herself.

———

John, hauling himself up the stairs, walked with a steady gait across the landing to his bedroom door, surprised to see the blackout curtains drawn, the light on and his wife sitting up in bed.

'Is everything all right?' he asked, concerned. Lily was usually sound asleep by now and his unconscious mind was alert to any sort of difference to suggest the baby was coming.

'Not really.' It was difficult to define Lily's expression but something about her stiffened manner suggested there was something going on.

'Is it the baby?'

Lily shook her head. Then, picking up a colourful quilt large enough to cover the bed, she told him, 'This was made by a Lumberjill called Ethel but she never got to finish it.'

John came to sit on the side of the bed next to his wife and took a good look at the quilt. He knew by Lily's tense expression and the fact she didn't meet his eyes that this was difficult for her.

'John, I have something to tell you and there's no easy way than to say it straight out.'

He looked at her, feeling a wave of panic rise up in him. 'You're scaring me, Lily. What is this?'

'It's called a memory quilt. Ethel from the WTC made it for her baby.'

Confused, he asked, 'Why've you got it then?'

Lily's chin dropped to her chest, hair falling like a curtain over her face so he couldn't see to gauge her expression. He noticed her hands holding the quilt were trembling.

'Ethel gave birth the night of the raids; she was killed when our shelter was demolished.'

'Our shelter? I don't understand.'

'She lived here with me, John. She had no family and nowhere to go and I offered her a home here for the time being.'

'What about her family?'

'She had none.' Lily told him how she and Ethel were friends at Teviot Hall and Ethel had become pregnant by a German prisoner of war. How Karl had scared the living daylights out of Lily when he escaped to give Ethel a letter.

She ended, 'Ethel made this quilt for the baby she carried.'

'What happened to the baby?' John wanted to know.

Lily swallowed hard. 'John, this is so hard but I must tell you. Days – I can't remember how many as my mind from that time is hazy – before Ethel was killed in the raid, I miscarried our baby.'

'What!' John leant back, his expression incredulous.

'It's true, John.' Tears spilled from her eyes, rolled down her cheeks. 'You asked what happened to Ethel's baby.' Watching the tears drip off her cheek, John automatically brought out a handkerchief and passed it to his wife.

Lily wiped away the tears. 'Ethel delivered a girl, and she named the baby Joy.'

'The same as our Joy.' John was more confused. Then, like a dart stabbing him, the truth pierced his heart. 'You mean, Joy is... this Ethel's?'

Lily's gaze dropped, cheeks burning with shame. 'Yes.'

Confusion turned into outrage within John. 'You pretended the baby was ours.'

She crumpled under his stare. Haltingly she told him about Ethel's fear of the orphanage and their pact.

He didn't know how to feel. Betrayed, deceived, angry. *Lily of all people*, his mind cried. 'I can't believe you've kept this from me all this time.' His voice was hoarse. 'Why didn't you trust me and tell the truth?'

Lily looked at him with a strange, vacant expression as if she was as dumbfounded as him.

'I can't answer that, John, because I've no recollection what I was thinking in those first months. All I do know is I so desperately wanted Joy to be mine.'

41

John could see by Lily's distraught expression what confessing the truth had cost her. He was no physician but even he could tell the trauma of losing another child had unbalanced Lily's mind for a time, and she had believed Joy was hers. But to continue the deceit over the months, years, beggared belief.

Thoughts and emotions teeming through his mind, John needed time to take it all in. But even as he began to think it through, he realised that what hurt most was Lily hadn't had the faith to tell him she'd lost another baby, and share the grief.

Joy isn't mine – the words hitting him like a sledgehammer, John covered his face with his hands.

'John, I'm sorry I deceived you.' Lily spoke in a small voice. 'Please forgive me? I really did think not telling you about Joy was the best thing at the time because you were so unwell at first, and then it was too late. Now, I just don't know what I was thinking. I only know I so wanted Joy to be mine.'

John pictured Joy, her brown eyes, her adorable pout when she asked him, 'Daddy, aren't I a big girl now?'

Damn it. Joy would always be a part of him. She was his little girl. He asked, 'Why tell me now?'

Lily was rubbing her shoulder in a concentrated manner. Her brow creased as she considered the question.

'Because of the baby I'm carrying.' Her blue eyes met his and he saw sincerity in them. 'My conscience pricked me, John, and I couldn't go along with the pretence any longer. If anything happened to us, I would want our baby to know its true identity.'

John felt concern rising in him. He didn't like the way her train of thought was going. 'Never knowing their true parents sometimes happens with adopted children,' he found himself saying to put her off track.

She looked up and the stubborn expression of old was back. 'That's what Bella said. But it's not going to happen to Joy. I owe it to Ethel to be truthful.'

'Bella knows?' Shocked, John's mouth fell open in disbelief.

'We were talking about Ethel one day and the truth just came out. I think I needed to tell someone and I trusted Bella.' Lily coloured as she realised what she'd said. 'John, you weren't here. Without question, I'd have told you if you were. When you came home you weren't strong enough. As time passed and I realised what I'd done it got harder to say, even if I wanted to.'

John ran his fingers through his hair, bemused. He had to concede Lily was right. He'd been in no fit state to hear such news when he came home from hospital back then in '43.

'What did she say?' As the enormity of what Lily was telling him sank in, John's heart rate increased and with it came an anger threatening to erupt. He wondered if he even knew the woman before him at all. He wanted to rage obscenities at her for her devious behaviour. He opened his mouth, but, ordinarily a temperate man, he found he couldn't allow angry words to escape, especially to Lily, and taking deep breaths he attempted to get his fiery emotions under control.

'Bella insisted I should tell you but she promised not to say anything.'

John felt that at least that was something; he couldn't fault

Bella's loyalty to Lily and he was glad she'd tried to talk sense into his wife.

Lily rubbed her forehead with her finger. Then, climbing from the bed, she moved to her wardrobe and opened the doors, taking out a small brown suitcase from the back of the bottom shelf.

She brought the suitcase over to the bed and sat on the edge. 'Ethel's belongings.' She opened the suitcase and drew out a slip of paper. 'This is the letter I told you about when Karl escaped.' She handed him the piece of paper.

Looking at it, John couldn't understand a word.

'It's in German,' Lily, stating the obvious, continued, massaging her forehead. 'See, there's an address. Apparently, the address is where his grandfather lives, so Ethel told me. She said Karl was relieved his mam and sister escaped to the house when his father had been taken away by the Nazis. Karl, apparently, wanted a place where he and Ethel could make contact after the war finished.'

At that moment, no matter that Karl was a German, he became a real person to John and, like him, his main concern was for family. Cold fury took hold of John on Karl's behalf, mingled with devastation that Joy had another father somewhere out there. Then realisation hit John – he wasn't, after all, Joy's real dad.

'What d'you intend us do about Joy?' he asked, his tone clipped.

'When she's old enough to understand Joy should be told who her parents are.'

In the dimness of the room, John looked at the quilt in Lily's hands made by a young girl who'd only wanted the best for the baby she carried. Perhaps a girl little more than a child herself, who hadn't known her days were numbered and that she'd never see the child within her grow.

His mind's eye picturing the bombed-out shelter, the still body, John's shoulders slumped. He touched the quilt, smoothing the material.

His throat tight, he said, 'Did Ethel ever tell you the meaning of the squares on the quilt?'

Lily nodded. She wore a wary expression, knowing it was her fault she'd taken him to the brink and perhaps wondering if he was his rational self again.

A half-hearted smile was all John could manage.

'It was the afternoon before I lost the baby. I was lying in bed and Ethel was keeping me company.' Then reality struck John of what Lily had endured during that terrible time, when all her hopes and dreams had died with the baby.

Lily pointed to a square. 'See, each square has meaning, a memory of someone or someplace. This one here, as you can see, is the German flag and—'

'To represent the father,' John cut in. He peered down and there it was in the neatest stitches. Karl Becker – Joy's real father.

Lily didn't answer, probably thinking it wise. 'This square has a piece of lace on it from the handkerchief her Aunty Meg gave her when she left Ethel at an orphanage.'

'Who was Aunty Meg?'

Lily, looking up, told him, 'She was the person who took Ethel and her mother in after the father died. The next square that has a primrose on it represents Primrose Cottage, the tied cottage where Ethel spent her formative years... a time when she was happiest. And this one here was the last square she...' Lily choked. '... stitched.'

'Olcote,' he read, noticing the embroidered red heart by the house name.

'It's to represent her time spent here.' Her voice had gone quivery again. 'Oh, John, she didn't have a very good time of it in her short life.' He saw his wife was welling up again, not surprising in her condition.

His anger dispelled as though doused by a fireman's watery hose, John felt only sorrow for all the players in this extraordinary scenario and yes, even for his wife.

'That's enough for now, Lily. You're getting upset.'

Lily sat up straight in the bed, sniffing hard. 'No, John, I want you to know the meaning of the squares. I owe it to Ethel that one day Joy knows about every single square on this quilt.'

As he remembered the young girl dying alone in the shelter, John conceded Lily was right.

She proceeded to tell him the meaning of the remaining squares.

Afterwards in the hush of the bedroom, both of them deep in thought, a new fear came to grip John. 'What if, after Joy is told, she wants to find Karl?'

'Then we'll write to the address in the letter.'

A new fear gripped John. 'What if we do find him and he wants to bring Joy up as his own?'

Lily's agonised expression told him she felt the same way as him. 'It would kill me but it's his right, John. I made the decision and it's on her birth certificate that Karl is her father.'

John, exhausted by the range of emotions he'd experienced, did realise Lily's honest nature would baulk at doing anything else but put the truth on an official document.

Lily's face crumpled. 'All I know is Joy deserves to know who her parents are. And I owe it to Ethel to tell her. Promise me that we'll tell Joy who her mother was and try and find her father.'

John procrastinated. 'The promise you made to Ethel,' he found himself arguing, 'was only to find Joy a decent home.'

Those clear blue eyes challenged his. 'Answer me this, John, wouldn't you want this baby I'm carrying to know you are its dad? Besides, you're too noble a man to let your love for Joy stand in the way of what is right.'

'Lily, I won't deny your revelations have put me through the mill tonight. But in this' – he sighed heavily – 'you're right. I promise I'll do what is right.'

John noticed Lily distractedly massaging her forehead again. Concern for his wife overruled any other emotion.

'Lily, you're bushed. Let's leave this for tonight.'

She gave him an appreciative smile. 'If you don't mind, John, I would like to call it a night. I've got such a bad headache.' She squinted. 'And the light's hurting my eyes.'

Unease gripped John. He pecked Lily's nose to reassure her. 'Sweetheart, you've to take care of the two of you, remember.'

She patted her bump. 'Nearly there.' Her eyes shone. 'John, I'm hoping for a boy.'

John cocked his head and thought about it. 'I'm happy with either. By choice I'd rather like two daughters.'

———

John couldn't get to sleep, but he didn't switch on the light and read because he'd disturb Lily and she needed the rest. He counted frisky lambs, then relaxed each part of his body in turn – but nothing worked and chilling thoughts continued to invade his mind.

How could he switch off from being Joy's dad, give her up to a stranger? The fear that one day this might happen grew in him like some threatening monster until he was struggling to breathe.

'John, are you awake?'

'Is it the baby?' John readied to leap out of the bed.

'No, my headache's worse and I can't sleep.'

The bedside lamp switched on. As John blinked in the stark light, he saw Lily massaging her forehead.

He sat up in the bed. 'Lily, your hands look swollen.'

She struggled to sit up. 'They are so swelled my ring hurts, and I can't take it off.' She showed him.

'D'you feel all right otherwise?' John asked, concerned.

Her eyes closed, Lily put her head in her hands. 'I've got what I can only describe as a clouded head.'

'Right. First thing in the morning you've to see the midwife.'

'D'you think she'll be working on VE Day?'

42

Next morning, John was taking no chances. Firstly, he dressed Joy and gave her porridge for breakfast.

He told Lily, who he insisted stayed in bed, 'I'm going to take Joy by trolleybus up to Jean's house and ask if she can stay there for today. Then I'm off to phone the hospital before going to work.'

'But Jean will be busy with the boys—'

'She'll be happy to oblige,' John told her. 'She's a walking textbook where babies are concerned.' He gave a broad smile though inside he worried. 'You just lie there and rest until I get back.'

When he arrived at his sister-in-law's house, it was to find Jean pinning a Union Jack on the front door, young Stanley watching from the front step. Her face lit up when she turned and saw John standing there, Joy in his arms.

She pushed back a lock of hair which had escaped from her turban-style headscarf. 'Is it the baby?'

John explained Lily's symptoms and Jean's face clouded with concern. 'Don't you worry about Joy, she'll be fine here for as long as it takes. I'll have her overnight, if you like. We'll manage somehow. Edward's asleep. He's still in his cot and he'll be happy to have a playmate when he wakes.'

She took Joy out of his arms. 'Get yourself off to the telephone box.'

———

'What are your wife's symptoms?' one of the midwives on maternity asked.

John told her about the swelling and headaches.

'I think it's best if I call an ambulance to bring your wife in so she can be checked out,' the midwife told him.

Returning home, John told Lily that an ambulance would be arriving shortly.

'A lot of fuss over nothing,' Lily remarked, but her eyes looked anxious. 'I suppose it's best to be checked out. Look at my legs, John, they remind me of tree trunks.'

Indeed, Lily had no ankles any more.

———

Later, as Lily climbed into the back of the ambulance, John handed her suitcase to a woman dressed in a St John Ambulance uniform and stood back to allow the doors to close.

'Wait!' He climbed aboard the ambulance and, passing the startled woman in uniform at the door, he made his way to Lily sitting on the bed.

Bending down, he kissed her. 'Love you, Lily Radley.'

She smiled but John saw the shadow of fear of the unknown in her eyes.

'Move along,' a female voice came from the driver's seat. 'We haven't got all day.'

'When can I visit?' John wanted to know as he made his way back to the pavement.

'Visiting's at two, but your wife might be in the labour room and it won't be worth coming. Best to ring first and ask.'

John clambered down and the ambulance doors closed, the engine starting. Standing at the kerbside, he watched as the vehicle, trundling down the road, turned the corner and disappeared out of sight.

'But Lily's not having the baby yet...' he muttered, confused.

With nothing else to do, he made his way back into the house. The truth was, he felt inadequate and out of sorts.

Meanwhile, in the early morning pink light, John became aware of front doors opening and neighbours venturing out. Some carrying ladders, others with bunting in their hands.

John thought, *Of course*. He'd quite forgotten, today was Victory in Europe Day and he had the day off work.

———

John couldn't settle as his mind was distracted with all kinds of thoughts. Lily's revelations last night... What the outcome might be if they did contact Karl... The fear of what was wrong with Lily. Were these symptoms of hers normal? Was their baby about to be born? These thoughts clamoured for priority in his mind, like runners trying to edge to the front of a race.

All that morning John suffered from nervous anxiety and kept checking his watch as time crawled past. He couldn't eat any breakfast and, his fingers all thumbs, he dropped a best china cup and it smashed to smithereens on the slate kitchen floor.

Attracted by noises coming from outside, John opened the front door. Standing at the front gate, he watched the neighbours' activity taking place.

A woman wearing a blue flowered frock with short puffed sleeves and slippers stood on a stepladder, poking a rather large Union Jack through the top of an open sash window. Two other women, one wearing a headscarf with curlers peeping out of the front, were studying red, white and blue bunting that stretched from one top window to the next.

Toddlers holding hands ran along the pavement while two men dressed in trousers held up by braces and shirts with sleeves rolled up struggled to negotiate a piano out of a front doorway.

'I see Mrs Radley was taken to hospital earlier.' Mrs Ainsley from next door stood on one side of a flowering cherry tree in her garden.

John's lips twitched as he recalled Lily calling her 'Mrs Busybody'.

'Yes, she was.'

The two women neighbours over the road stopped their chattering and listened in.

'Is she off to the General to have the baby?' Mrs Ainsley asked.

'Something like that.' John shrugged. He wasn't good at chitchat.

'It's best you ring before you go.'

'Aye, they won't let you in if she's in labour,' the woman wearing curlers called. 'Seeing a bairn being born is no place for a man. I should know, I've had three. Though, it would do my old man good to see the purgatory I go through. Cos if the bugger did, I guarantee there'd be no number four.'

'Really!' Mrs Ainsley, obviously affronted by such common language, looked as though a bad smell was lurking beneath her nose.

'It's true. I'm only speaking what us women think.'

Ignoring her, Mrs Ainsley gave John a beatific smile. 'I'll be thinking of Mrs Radley. Do let me know when the little one arrives.' Before John could reply, she bustled back into the house.

'That one's a right toffee-nose.' The woman in curlers sniffed. 'She thinks I'm not good enough for the street.'

'If you have an inclination to decorate your house,' the other woman told John, obviously wanting to change the subject, 'me hubby has a pair of stepladders if you want to borrow them.'

'That's very kind but not with my gammy leg.' He smiled goodnaturedly. 'Besides, I'm a bit jittery and all thumbs today.'

'That's natural.' The curlers woman spoke up. 'My old man diddled off to the pub and got sozzled all three times when I had the bairns. You can give us a hand with the bunting if you like. It'll fill in the time.'

———

For the rest of the morning John helped with decorating the street and bringing out equipment – table, chairs, tablecloths – required for the street tea party later on.

At one o'clock sharp he made his way to the phone box. Posting his coppers in the box, he dialled the number. The operator connected him to the hospital.

After John asked to be connected to maternity, a voice said, 'Sister Jones speaking.'

'I'm enquiring about my wife, Mrs Radley.'

A pause. 'Mr Radley. It's best you come in to see us.'

A tingle in the base of his spine. 'Is anything wrong?'

'It's difficult to speak over the telephone. We'll expect to see you soon. Goodbye, Mr Radley.'

His stomach clenched, John put the receiver in the holder.

———

Walking up the long driveway, John entered the main building and there was the usual hospital smell of antiseptic mingled with undertones of cleaning liquids. Arriving at maternity reception, John was told to wait while the receptionist made a telephone call. Soon, a nurse wearing a blue and white striped uniform greeted him and showed him to the waiting room.

By now John, his nerves jangling, couldn't tolerate to wait. A woman with greying hair under her nurse's cap and wearing a navy uniform bustled in.

Though smiling, her eyes had a forbidding look. 'Hello, Mr Radley. I'm Sister Jones. I'm pleased you're able to—'

'Is something wrong with Lily – my wife?' John blurted.

'Let me explain,' Sister told him. 'When Mrs Radley was admitted her blood pressure was checked. It was very high and she had all the symptoms of pre-eclampsia.'

'Isn't that toxaemia?' John remembered his mum worrying

because his cousin, Fiona, had the condition when she was expecting twins. Fortunately, mother and babies had been fine and the twins were now rowdy toddlers.

'It is, Mr Radley. Your wife was put in a side ward where a nurse monitored her all morning.' John's mouth went dry and he wasn't able to ask any questions. 'Unfortunately, Mrs Radley's BP continued to rise very high and Mr Bishop, the consultant, thinks it best to perform an emergency caesarean.'

'Is it dangerous?'

Her eyes met his. 'It would be worse if we didn't operate.'

John nodded.

'Mr Radley, I must tell you, if Mr Bishop has to make a choice between the baby or your wife surviving, he will choose Mrs Radley.'

John felt the blood drain from his face. 'Can I see my wife before—'

'I'm sorry, she's already gone down to theatre.' A pause. 'Sit down, Mr Radley, and we'll bring you a cup of tea.'

'Can I wait while my wife has the caesarean?'

'Yes, if you must.'

————

The next hours were the worst in John's life, surpassing any emotion he'd had during the war. The fear was paralysing. He read every magazine on the table and knew all tonight's wireless programmes. As time dragged on, he couldn't stand the tension any more. He popped his head through the doorway and, looking up and down the corridor, he heard distant cries of babies but saw no one.

Finally, when John thought his nerves couldn't take it any more, the waiting room door opened.

An older man, with slate-grey hair, manicured beard, and wearing a crisp long white coat, a stethoscope sticking out of the pocket, appeared in the doorway. The young nurse in the blue and white uniform accompanied him.

'Hello, Mr Radley. I'm Mr Bishop. I performed your wife's caesarean—'

'How are they? Did the baby survive?' John couldn't contain himself any longer.

There was something about Mr Bishop's hooded eyes behind the dark-rimmed spectacles he wore – nice eyes with a sympathetic look – that caused fear to clutch John's throat.

'You have a beautiful son.' He nodded in confirmation. 'I'm told seven pounds one ounce.' Mr Bishop's compassionate eyes grew serious. 'Mr Radley, prepare yourself for a shock.' Automatically, John held on to the back of one of the high-back chairs. 'Your wife came round, though in a drowsy state, and met her baby.' His eyes turned grave.

A cold shiver ran down from John's spine to his knees; he just knew the news was bad.

'Mrs Radley took a turn for the worse, her blood pressure rising to a dangerous degree. We did everything we could to control it but I'm afraid your wife suffered a fatal stroke.'

The words didn't sink in at first and John found himself wondering if medical staff were trained to tell someone news like this. No one could make John do such a thing and he felt sorry for the man.

'Mr Radley,' the nurse said, her voice soft. 'Is there anything you'd like to ask Mr Bishop? Or would you prefer to see your son?'

Mr Bishop waited as if to let the words sink in. John, staring at him, his mind reeling, tried to understand his words. *Fatal... that means dead. That can't be.*

'Lily's robust, she always has been.'

Mr Bishop nodded. 'Nothing could be done. I'm so deeply sorry, Mr Radley.'

———

Later that afternoon, sitting in the front room, cup of tea now gone cold in his hand, the celebrations taking place outside felt like a mockery to John.

He'd asked to see Lily, because John couldn't believe there hadn't been a mistake. The body he saw in the coffin in the chapel of rest was indeed hers, but it was now just a shell.

When asked if he wanted to see his baby son, the irony was not lost on John that their desperation to have a baby had cost Lily her life and his heart felt heavy as a stone with grief.

Seeing his son asleep in the cot, wearing a little white bonnet John recognised as one Lily had knitted, he felt nothing.

Now, a piano struck up outside in the street and a rendition of 'For He's a Jolly Good Fellow' by the neighbours rang out.

Part of his mind, the part that didn't accept any of this was happening, remembered that the prime minister was giving a speech from Downing Street at three o'clock. John checked his watch: five minutes to go.

The singing outside now finished, only a few excited voices could be heard. Rising from the couch, John moved over to the wireless and turned the knob. Within moments Churchill's voice with its powerful delivery boomed through the grille.

Yesterday morning at 2.41 a.m. at General Eisenhower's head-quarters, General Jodl, the representative of the German high command...

As he listened John imagined Lily beside him, that small smile of concentration he so loved on her face.

It was when Churchill said, *we may allow ourselves a brief period of rejoicing, but let us not forget for a moment the toils and efforts that lie ahead*, that John thought of his future spent without Lily by his side.

Unshed tears prickled behind his eyes and, switching the wireless off, John moved to the couch. Sinking down in its soft cushions, he covered his face with his hands and wept unconsolably like a child.

43

The next day, John, numb with shock, went through the motions of living. Getting dressed, drinking a cup of chicory coffee for breakfast (he couldn't face food), looking at the clock to see if it was time for work. His body shuddered; the very thought of having to face people brought out goosebumps and he had the good sense to realise work was something to be avoided.

Slouched in a wooden chair at the kitchen table, the clock ticking in the background, John found it difficult to believe Lily had gone.

Is there a relative you can contact to keep you company, Mr Radley? The voice of the nurse at the hospital spoke in his head.

John didn't want company; he only wished for it to be two days earlier when life was normal, and he and Lily had been excited for the new arrival. Life, John realised, would never be normal for him again.

With a jolt, he thought of Joy, innocent of what had happened. She'd be missing her mummy. Tears burnt his eyes; he couldn't bear to think of his daughter without a mother. The realisation hitting him that he alone was responsible for Joy now, he stood and roughly brushed his eyes with the backs of his hands. Joy needed him. He was desperate to hold her warm, sweet-smelling body in his arms.

———

Jean's eyes wide in shock, she stood in her kitchen, silent, Joy clutched in her arms. The atmosphere inside was grim, while from outside in the backyard came the boys' excited voices.

'John, it's unbelievable. I'm so very sorry.' Nervously, Jean ran her fingers through her brunette curls. 'I can't imagine what you're going through.'

'No, Jean, I'm afraid you can't,' was the only thing John's paralysed mind could think to say.

'I don't know what I can say to help.'

'There's nothing.'

'But I can do something.' Her face contorted into a relieved small smile. 'Leave Joy here with us. You'll need time to think straight as you've got...' She choked up. '... a funeral to arrange.'

Joy, now twenty-two months, appeared to know what was being said because, stretching out her arms towards John, she said, 'Joy go home, Daddy.'

John knew then he needed Joy as much as she needed him.

'Thank you, Jean.' He took the toddler out of his sister-in-law's arms, snuggled Joy against his chest. 'But she's coming home with me.'

Dismay crossed Jean's face. 'How will you cope?'

A flash of irrational anger zipped through John at Lily for leaving him to cope on his own, but it quickly dispelled as reality took hold and he realised this was the last thing his beloved wife would want.

'I'll manage somehow.'

As he moved to leave, Jean laid a hand on his arm. 'If you need anything at all, we're here for you. Don't worry about letting Lily's parents know; I'll get Harry to tell them.'

John nodded. It was then he noticed Joy's clothing. She was

wearing a pair of Edward's short pants and a blue open-necked shirt. If he couldn't think to provide Joy with clothes for one night, how on earth did he think he could manage in the future? Lily was the one who did everything for Joy.

––––––

Later that night, Joy, after a supper of Weetabix and stories read to her, was tucked up and asleep in her bed.

Having her to care for during the day had helped as John had focused on her needs. Now he sat in the living room feeling lonely and isolated, and the cold light of reality hit him. How could he make this work?

Taking a deep breath, he forced his mind to focus. He needed to make a list. Firstly, he must tell his mum. They corresponded often as she doted on Joy and wanted to know what her grand-daughter got up to. He could write and ask if she'd be willing to help out for a few days until John had a better idea how to cope. Mum visited whenever she could and especially liked to be at Olcote over Christmas when she and Lily had managed to provide all the trimmings for a festive dinner, even when rationing was on.

It dawned on him that future Christmases would be spent without Lily. A lump threatening to lodge in his throat, John concentrated again on the list.

Bella. He would have to tell her.

––––––

Next morning at breakfast (Weetabix again for Joy), Joy chattered constantly throughout the meal, asking for Mummy and telling him what a naughty boy Edward was.

'He told me, Daddy, "You're not my friend."' Upset, her mouth turned down at the corners. 'Where is Mummy?'

At a loss how to answer about Lily as the truth would distress

Joy, something John couldn't abide, he answered inadequately, 'Mummy has gone away for a while.'

As Joy's bottom lip trembled and her eyes became awash with tears, he quicky put in, 'Hurry, sweetheart, and finish your Weetabix. We've to phone Aunty Bella this morning and you can say hello.'

Her childish mind switching to this new piece of information, Joy's solemn expression changed to one of heightened excitement. 'Let's go now.'

————

The pair of them stood in the claustrophobic telephone box, John holding on to Joy's harness with one hand, the telephone in the other.

'It's me, John,' he said, and the croaky voice didn't sound like his.

'Is something the matter, John?'

He opened his mouth but couldn't form the words.

'Speak to me, John.' Bella's voice sounded uncharacteristically panicked. 'I can tell by your voice something's wrong.'

Hearing her familiar friendly voice made him well up and he could only manage to say, 'It's Lily.'

'What about Lily? Has she had the baby?'

'Yes.'

Joy started to whinge as there was no air in the telephone box. He put the telephone on the shelf and managed to scoop her up and hold her in one arm in the confined space. He picked up the telephone again.

Bella was saying, 'Goodness' sake, John, put me out of my misery. Just tell me.'

Joy's face inches from his, she gazed at him with a wide-eyed trusting stare that made him take deep breaths, otherwise he'd break down. He hoped she wouldn't understand what he was about to tell Bella.

'She's gone.'

'Gone!'

Remembering Mr Bishop's words at the hospital, John repeated them. 'Bella, prepare yourself for a shock. Lily died after the birth.' A slap of guilt made him add, 'I'm sorry for telling you like this.'

A long silence followed, during which all he could think was if they didn't hurry, he'd run out of telephone time and he had no more coppers to put in the box.

'Lily died,' Bella repeated. 'I can't take it in, John.' Her voice was barely a whisper.

He squeezed his eyes shut. 'Me neither.'

Joy began to squirm in his arms. 'Me want Aunty Ella.'

'John.' A few shaky breaths. 'I'll be with you this afternoon.'

'There's no need. I'm writing to Mum asking if she'll come and stay for a few days. She's family, after all.'

'Lily's my family too, John. See you later.'

The telephone clicked, and the conversation was over.

John hung up the receiver and held Joy tightly as he gathered himself. Glad Bella was so obstinate, relief flooded through him.

———

Early afternoon, the front door knocker banged.

John, leaving Joy to watch the colourful top spin round on the kitchen floor, hurried along the passageway.

Bella stood there, holding a small suitcase, her freckled face white as a ghost.

She pushed past him into the lobby. 'I'm here until your mum arrives.' Her voice businesslike, Bella made off down the passageway.

As John followed her familiar figure into the kitchen, it occurred to him how comfortable he felt with her. She was family.

Her hazel eyes as she faced him had a steely glint, as though she was determined to stay strong. 'Don't argue. I've told them at work there's been a death in the family and I needed to return home.' She bent down beside Joy. 'Where's my favourite girl?'

'Joy's here,' the toddler said, as always.

Bella gave her a cuddle and John detected her chin trembling. Then, to the little girl's delight, Bella pumped up the top and they watched together as, making a rattling noise, it whirled around.

John knew there was no use pointing out this wasn't Bella's home as she'd retort in that forthright manner of hers, 'It feels like home.' Like she'd told Lily many times beforehand. Not that John minded; Bella was always welcome in their home. The reality suddenly hitting him there was no 'their' and only him and Joy, the lump came back, threatening to take over his throat.

'There'll be no argument from me, I'm only thankful you're here. I need all the help I can get. Lily usually...' Damn it, caught off guard saying her name, he welled up.

'John, don't fight the grief, just let it come. You're allowed.' Her voice, gentle, made trying to pull himself together somehow more difficult.

He nodded and, covering his face with his hands, rubbed his eyes. The moment of aching sadness passing, he looked up and saw tears in Bella's warm eyes.

Joy ran over to her, the spinning top in dimpled hands.

'What have you told her?' Bella asked as she took the top from Joy and made it whirl.

Feeling inept, John shrugged. 'That Lily has gone away for a time.'

'I'd tell the truth from the start. She has to know sometime...' For a moment Bella's façade of coping slipped, and her face crumpled as she struggled to compose herself. 'What are we going to do without her, John?'

Incapable of speaking, he shook his head.

44

Lily's funeral was a blur. Friends and relatives came together, including John's mum, Lily's family – all distraught at their loss.

Bella had opted to stay behind at Olcote to look after Joy.

'A funeral is no place for Joy,' she'd told him, 'and I'd prefer to remember my best friend as she was, and not being lowered into the ground in a coffin.'

John couldn't have coped without Bella those first few days; she'd helped with Joy, the meals, the funeral arrangements. But now his mum was here, Bella had moved back to her billet.

The baby was still in hospital, not because there was anything amiss – on the contrary, it was reported on John's daily visits that his son was thriving. John couldn't look after a toddler and a small baby while still dealing with the shock of Lily's death. So, it was agreed with Sister Jones that the baby be left in the maternity nursery until after the funeral when arrangements could be made for him to come home. What those arrangements would be, John had no idea.

At the funeral, John surprised himself by managing to keep a stiff upper lip until he got home and held Joy in his arms. She was in her playpen in the kitchen, and seeing her stocky little body, innocent brown eyes gazing inquisitively up at him, tears welled in his eyes. Picking her up and noticing Joy's chin tremble at the sight of her daddy upset, he struggled to regain control.

The funeral party was invited back to Harry and Jean's place for refreshments but John made his excuses, saying that Joy needed him at home. Mingling with people, even if they were family and friends, was the last thing he wanted to do. At the church doorway he thanked everyone for attending his wife's funeral and after the burial headed for home.

Mum returned to Olcote with him after the funeral. As John stood with his daughter in his arms, Mum – a determined look in her eye that suggested to John she'd come to a decision and wouldn't budge – told him, 'Ida and I have had a chat. I won't bother you with the rigmarole of what was discussed but only tell you the outcome.' She folded her arms, in a businesslike manner. 'I've decided that I'll move into Olcote so that the baby can come home and you can get yourself back to work. I'll stay as long as you need me. Bella says she'll come at weekends as usual as she insists she wants to help out. Ida says she's prepared to travel from Lancashire once in a while if I need a respite.' Flint-eyed and resolute, Mum continued, 'There'll be no arguing, John.'

John knew he wasn't in a position to argue. Even if he did leave work and cope with two small children on his own, it would be a stretch to manage on his pension.

Choked, he heaved a big sigh of relief that his problem was solved. 'Thank you from the bottom of my heart, Mum.'

Her features softened. 'You'll be doing me a favour as your Aunty Helen and Terence have become close again and I feel a positive gooseberry.'

The arrangement worked perfectly. John hired a domestic and a young girl to help with the children for a few hours a week to relieve Mum as the baby needed feeding in the night. Bella helped out at weekends, giving Mum a break. His sister-in-law, Jean, did her bit by having Joy around to the house to play with her two sons during the week.

As weeks went by, John felt as though he was only going

through the motions of living. Since Lily died there seemed no point any more. There were times when he would swear he felt his wife's presence and heard her voice whispering in his ear. He was going mad, he told himself. He found solace burying himself in work and did overtime – or at least as much as his conscience would allow, because he didn't like to leave Mum alone at night in the house. Apart from idle chatter with Mum in the evenings, when she did the talking and John grunted an answer, he didn't do much else and was happiest when he took himself off to bed to the merciful oblivion of sleep.

Things came to a head one morning as Mum was putting a bowl on the table of Joy's high chair.

'John, this won't do,' Mum, with a frown on her face, surprised him by saying.

Sitting at the table, John gulped his toast. 'What won't do?'

He'd been deep in thought about his working day with Ted, the plumber, and the bathroom fixtures they were installing in one of the bombed buildings. He and Ted had discussed the job last night at the pub. It was payday and the two men had taken to celebrating Friday nights at the pub.

Mum went on, 'Your baby boy needs a name and... you could be more interested in both your children, don't you think?'

John stared at her disbelievingly. Didn't Mum know he was doing his best? He avoided the children, especially the baby, because they were a reminder of his wife's death and all she was missing. The situation of him being here to enjoy his children when Lily wasn't was unbearable and John was riddled with guilt that sometimes tipped over to anger.

Leaving the rest of his toast, John, scraping back his chair, stood. 'I'm doing what I can. I provide for them both, don't I?'

Registering his mum's open-mouthed shock, John, picking up his bait tin and haversack, left the room.

As he closed the front door after him, John felt bad. The vision of Mum's face still in his mind, he knew she was hurt. What was wrong with him? He didn't know himself any more.

But for the life of him, John was incapable of changing his ways.

———

One Saturday, John had worked the morning helping Ted finish the bathroom he was working on and then headed home. As he closed the front door and walked along the passageway, he smelt a meaty aroma drifting from the kitchen.

Voices came from the kitchen and John recognised one as Bella's, the other as Mum's. Bella had changed towards him lately, she wasn't her usual friendly self, and John got the impression he irked her for some reason. He was surprised how much that niggled him, then realised he'd come to rely on her as a sounding board and valued her opinion.

As he walked into the kitchen, she stood, baby in her arms, while Mum stacked dishes in the sink.

'There you are, John,' Mum said over-brightly. She turned to Bella and the two women exchanged conspiratorial looks as though they'd been talking about him.

'Dinner's in the oven; it's leftover mince again. Joy's at Jean's house playing with the boys.' She wiped crumbs from the bread-board. 'Bella and I were just discussing how things are just as bad as before, weren't we, Bella?'

Bella, appearing stand-offish, didn't look at him, instead speaking to Mum. 'We were. The long queues at shops, and demobbed soldiers needing housing and jobs, and d'you know it's been reported homeless families are being put up in army camps?'

Smelling the meaty aroma made John's stomach growl. 'I'm starving.'

He moved over to the cooker. Bending over, he opened the cooker door and, spying a plate of mince and golden dumplings and taties heating on the top shelf, John gave a sigh of satisfaction.

'Before you start eating, John,' Bella spoke up, 'put the kettle on for the baby's bottle.'

The two women gave each other a significant look.

'I'll be off then.' Mum took her coat off the hook behind the door.

John straightened. 'Where are you off to, Mum?'

'Didn't I tell you?' Mum wore that guarded look she used when she addressed him these days. 'It was arranged last Sunday just before Bella left. I'd been saying how I was a fan of Judy Garland and her latest picture, *Meet Me in St. Louis*, is on at the pictures. Bella has kindly suggested I go and see the afternoon showing today while she babysits.'

'By yourself?'

'No, with Mrs Ainsley from next door.' When John raised his eyebrows, Mum prattled on and John noticed for the first time increased lines etching her face. 'I've known her for years and she's got a lot on her plate with that husband of hers.'

While the two women discussed times for the baby's feeding for the afternoon, John switched off from the conversation and put the kettle on.

'Off you go, Deidre, I'll manage,' he heard Bella say as Mum shrugged into her coat. 'If not there's always the possibility of a message for you to come home on the big screen.'

'As if you would.' Mum laughed.

'It's been done many times before.'

'You're perfectly capable,' Mum stated firmly. 'Ta-ta for now.' Kissing the baby in Bella's arms on the forehead, she picked up her handbag from the table and left.

Bella walked over to John. 'Here, you hold him while I make his bottle.'

Startled, John stepped back a pace. He avoided touching his son whenever possible.

'Can't a man have a bit of peace? I've been at work all morning.'

Bella's eyebrows came down together and she glared at him. 'John, I've never stopped. Neither has your mum. She hasn't had a chance to wash the dinner dishes yet or to hang the nappies out. I want everything shipshape before she returns. She's worn out, if you hadn't noticed, and needs help at times.' Her tone terse, he wondered what the dickens had got into her. 'So, why not give your son a bottle for a change.'

'What d'you mean, if I hadn't noticed?' John asked, aggrieved. 'Many a time I've offered help but Mum maintains washing and cooking is women's work. And don't forget the domestic I've hired to help with the load.' He paused, collecting words to justify himself. 'I make sure I bring the coal in and I wash the pots when she's busy with the kids.'

'That's not the kind of help I mean, John. You could do more for the children and relieve your mam.' Bella bit the inside of her cheek as if considering what to say next. 'You could bath them, help put them to bed and read Joy stories like you used to do. They're your children, John.'

Stung, he replied, indignantly, 'I don't need reminding. I can't help it if I have to work overtime – there are a lot of wrecked houses out there. Anyway, Mum understands.'

Bella shook a despairing head. 'John, believe me, I'm trying to help when I say this, your mum is as good as gold but she allows you to wallow in grief.'

Bella's gaze was unwavering as she looked at him. Nevertheless, her body tensed as if she braced herself waiting for his answer.

Damn the woman. Narrowing his eyes, John pointed a finger at her. 'What gives you the right to judge? Anyway, what business is this of yours?'

'None at all. But I care, John.'

Her expression showing genuine concern floored him. All through this exchange, Bella had been rocking the baby and, his little pink lids now drooping, she placed him on the couch and surrounded him with cushions.

She came to stand directly in front of John and looked at him, her pretty features softening.

'You're right, I shouldn't judge but I do know something about bereavement and all its upsetting emotions. You can be so heartbroken, so consumed by grief that you have no life and only go through the motions. That's what had happened to me when my husband, Ronnie, died, but becoming a Lumberjill and meeting Lily was my salvation. I realised that Ronnie, like your Lily, had a generous soul and he wouldn't want me to spend my life grieving. He'd want me to go out into the world and find happiness. Lily would want this for you too, when the time is right.'

Listening to her, John heard the sincerity in her voice. He knew Bella was speaking from the heart and trying to help but inside he felt lost, lonely and, yes, his emotions were frozen.

'I could never find anyone to replace Lily.'

Bella moved closer towards him. 'Me neither. Ronnie was the love of my life, but there are other ways in life to find fulfilment.'

'I know you're only trying to help, Bella, but nobody can. I accept I've been a bugger to live with of late but the truth is, I've lost the way without Lily.' His fists bunched as though he wanted to punch something.

As Bella looked up at him, her hazel eyes mirroring the pity and heartfelt sorrow she felt inside, something splintered in John. 'I feel so angry at times that she was taken from me. God help me, I sometimes wish it was the baby that died and Lily spared. I can't look at him without thinking Lily would be here but for him.' His voice choked with emotion, he couldn't continue.

They stood silent for a few minutes. There was relief in John that he'd expressed his true feelings, even though they were deplorable.

Bella's hand reached out and touched his arm lightly. 'John, it's hard, isn't it? Lily's death was unfair, and you have every right to be angry, bitter even, and despairing. But her memory deserves more. She loved you and wouldn't want you to mourn forever; she would tell you to find your own way.' John's heart thumped in his chest as he listened. 'You have two children who've lost their mother. They need their father. Lily's dream was to bear you a child; she would want you to care for the children in her absence, for you to make time for them and have fun together. Living your life, you wouldn't be disloyal, John.' His eyes misted at that. 'You know I'm right. It's what Lily would want.'

They stood looking at one another in silence while the words hung in the air. John knew with certainty if Lily were here she'd tell him the exact same thing as Bella.

At that moment the baby stirred on the couch and both their gazes strayed over to where he lay.

John, giving a long shuddering breath, felt his body sag. Without thinking he moved over to the couch and picked the baby up. Cradling his son in his arms, the warmth of his small body melted him to the core.

'He's called Freddie,' he said, looking up at Bella.

She blinked hard, smiled at him and remarked, 'Freddie's a lovely choice of name.'

'That's what Lily said when she first thought of the name. Only, his full title was Frederick, then.' His eyes glazed as he remembered. 'Lily thought Frederick Radley sounded as if he could be a solicitor or doctor.' John smiled tenderly. 'But then she added that if we did have a boy she would be just as pleased if he ended up as a plumber's mate just like his dad.'

He looked down at his son, took in every feature. 'I wasn't keen on Frederick though I guess I would've given in. I would have insisted we called him Freddie, though.'

The pair of them smiled at one another.

———

As Bella prepared Freddie's bottle, John continued to observe his son – his cute button nose, pink lips forming an O as though searching for the teat – and all the love for his boy John had denied himself came rushing in like a tidal wave.

Lily's words came back to him. *Answer me this, John, wouldn't you want this baby I'm carrying to know you are its dad?*

There was no question about it now; of course John would.

'Penny for them.' Bella, busy dunking the bottle of milk in a jug of cold water to cool it down, gazed at him, a small frown of concern on her forehead.

The desire to share his worry overcame John. 'The night before Lily went into hospital, she confessed about Joy being—'

'Ethel's...' A cautious look crossed Bella's face. 'Did she tell you that I knew?'

He nodded. 'I was vexed you knew before me.'

Bella gave a thoughtful shake of the head. 'I'm convinced Lily's mind was deranged at that time, John, losing your baby and all. She deluded herself into thinking Joy was hers.'

'She told you the truth.' His voice was more accusing than he intended.

Bella came to stand in front of him, hands on her hips. 'John, believe me, Lily had to tell someone and I was only a substitute. If you'd been here or hadn't been ill, you would have been the first to know. But she left it too long, and by then you were besotted with Joy and confessing the truth became too difficult. I'm glad she told you in the end.'

'Lily said after she became pregnant with Freddie her conscience bothered her. She wanted Joy to know who her parents were and that she owed it to Ethel to tell her,' John continued, shamefaced. 'I panicked at first when I found out that she intended to confess what she'd done – like her, I wanted Joy to be ours.' He traced a finger down his son's silky-skinned cheek. 'But again, like Lily, having Freddie I now know it's the right thing to do.'

Bella gave a deep gratifying sigh. 'I agree.'

'Lily suggested we tell Joy about Ethel when she's old enough to understand.'

'That sounds sensible,' Bella agreed.

His conscience prodded him. 'I don't know what to do about Karl.' *The man deserves to know he has a child*, John thought. All the 'what ifs' ran through his mind – until John, usually a decisive man, couldn't make one at all.

Bella looked at him squarely. 'What's your inclination?'

A step too far at this point for John consider, he backtracked. 'That's something to think about in the future.'

'John, just enjoy having your two children to love and care for and let the future take care of itself.'

Exactly John's thoughts. *Hopefully the far-off future.*

In the stillness of the room, John, looking at Bella, realised how lucky he was to have someone so understanding in his life.

Her gaze met his and there was something unreadable in her eyes. She gave him what appeared to be an unstoppable smile then, extraordinarily, she blushed.

45

November **1953**

Still shaken that Joy had found the memory quilt while she and Freddie were playing hide and seek in the house, with nothing else for it, John decided to tell his daughter the details of her birth, like he'd promised Lily.

Joy, ten now, was old enough to understand, but he doubted if she could absorb all the information he was about to tell her. But it was time.

'Joy, I've got a story to tell you.'

She giggled. 'You know I'm old enough to read my own story-books now, Daddy.'

'This is a true story about how you were born.'

'Really?' Her face grew eager.

'And who your mother is.'

She rolled her eyes. 'Stop kidding me. I know that.'

John hitched up the bed to sit closer to her. 'Listen carefully and I'll begin.' This was something he'd said every night before he told a story when she was younger. It did the trick and Joy settled back against her pillow.

John then had a brainwave about how to tell the story in hopefully the simplest terms. 'Once upon a time there was a lady called Lily—'

'Is she Mam?' Joy's childish voice held a tinge of excitement.

John went on, 'Who joined the Women's Timber Corps when the war was on.'

'It is Mammy because you've told me that before.'

John nodded. 'Lily befriended a lady called Ethel who slept in the next bed. The pair of them did everything together. One day Ethel told her friend Lily she was going to have a baby.'

'That would be in her tummy,' Joy said, proud of her knowledge.

'How do you know that?'

'Bella told me when we saw a lady with a big tummy in the corner shop.'

John smiled. *Thank heavens for Bella.*

'Ethel had no family—'

'Not anyone?' Joy looked rather upset.

'Nope.' John quickly went on, 'So, Ethel was worried if anything should happen to her there'd be no mother to look after her baby.'

John held his breath expecting the obvious question: 'Where was the daddy?' He had a sinking feeling he'd handle this badly as he wasn't mentally prepared to answer.

'What happened?' Joy asked.

John gave a sigh of relief. 'Lily promised if anything should happen to Ethel, she'd love and look after the baby as her own. Happy that was settled, Ethel began making a memory quilt for her baby.'

'That was in her tummy,' Joy prompted.

'Yes. Then one terrible night the two friends heard enemy planes coming over and they had to run to a shelter for safety. And that's where Ethel's baby was born.'

'Out of her tummy.' Joy sat up.

Before she could ask further questions, John hurriedly continued, 'Lily decided to find the little baby girl some pretty clothes and leaving Ethel in the shelter she ran with the baby into the house.'

A sense of tension grew in the bedroom as if Joy knew what to expect. Maybe somewhere in her being, his daughter already knew the outcome.

'Then the enemy planes came over and a bomb dropped on the shelter and—'

'Lily's friend Ethel died,' Joy finished for him.

John looked into the knowing brown eyes of his daughter and a shiver ran up his spine.

He swiftly moved on. 'Before Lily left Ethel told her what her baby was called. Can you guess?'

The smooth skin on Joy's brow wrinkled. She shook her head.

'The baby's name was Joy.'

'Same as me.' Joy's eyes were wide in surprise.

'It is you, darling. You were the baby born to Ethel. And Mammy Lily kept her promise and loved and looked after you.'

Joy stared ahead and John could see the wheels ticking in her brain.

Eventually, she spoke, a puzzled frown on her face. 'So, Daddy, I have another mam and she's the lady in the story called Ethel.'

'Yes, sweetheart.'

Joy lay down and turned on her side away from him. For a moment she was unusually quiet and it appeared she'd fallen asleep. Though he seriously doubted his inquisitive daughter could sleep without a further questioning after what she'd just been told.

'Daddy.' Joy, fully awake as he suspected, turned and lay on her back. Her opaque brown eyes engaging with his were unflinching. 'Why didn't the other mam called Ethel run out of that place when she heard the bomb coming?'

Crikey, of all that he'd told her that was the part Joy fixated on. John had promised himself to tell his daughter only true facts and he wasn't going to start fantasising them now.

'Ethel was tired after you were born and so she fell asleep.' Seeing the doubt on her face, he quickly amended, 'So, she wouldn't have felt anything.' He told himself he could stretch the truth in certain circumstances. 'There is no doubt, Ethel would have wanted to stay with you and protect you forever.'

'And my real mammy promised she would take care of me.'

'Yes.'

Joy smiled and moved as though to turn over again. Then, 'Daddy...'

'Yes, darling.'

'Will you show me what the squares mean on the memory quilt the other mam, Ethel, made?'

'Sweetheart, it's late and—'

'Pleease.'

His daughter could wrap him around his little finger when she wanted. A ridiculous saying, John thought as he stretched down and grabbed hold of the folded quilt on the bottom of the bed.

'If you promise you'll go straight to sleep afterwards.'

Joy duly said, 'I promise, Daddy.'

John shook the quilt out, telling Joy, 'Each square has a meaning for someplace or someone.' Remembering those were almost the exact words Lily had used the night before she died, John faltered. Then, swallowing the lump in his throat, he carried on explaining the meaning to Joy of each square.

When he came to embroidered names, he didn't disclose Karl as her father as he decided he'd reveal further information in small snatches later, so as not to overload Joy now.

Much later, when he'd stopped talking, Joy covered the bed with the quilt. John noticed by her concentrated expression that her mind was still at work.

He stood up from the bed and was just about to give her a kiss when she spoke.

'Daddy.'

'Yes?'

'Where was the other mam, Ethel, when she died?'

Good grief, was Joy going to be traumatised over Ethel's death? John agonised that any minute Joy would ask about her real dad –

where and who he was. He wasn't ready for such a question nor would he ever be.

'I told you, pet, in the shelter.'

'No. Where was the place she lived? Which house did she live in?'

John's lips twitched into a smile; he could never fathom his children's way of thinking. 'She lived here at Olcote with Mammy.'

Joy nodded as though pleased. 'I've got two mammies now to pray for in heaven.'

'They both loved you very much and didn't want to leave you.' John could never stress that point too much.

The revelations exhausting for them both, John decided to call it a day. He said firmly, 'It's time to go to sleep.'

His daughter turned on her side and snuggled under the bedclothes. 'Night night, Daddy.'

'Night night, Joy.' He bent and gave her a kiss on the forehead.

His eyes misting, John switched off the lamp and left the room.

———

The next day after tea, when Freddie was playing outside in the street on his homemade soapbox cart with his mates, Joy sidled up to John while he read the *Gazette* at the table.

Curling a strand of brown hair around her forefinger, she was wearing a puzzled expression.

'What is it?' John leant back in his chair.

'I told Freddie about me being born to the other mam, Ethel.'

Holy Moses, John should have known this would happen. The pair of them were as thick as thieves and told each other everything.

John asked evenly, 'What did Freddie say?'

'He wanted to know if he was born to the other mam, Ethel, as well. I said I'd ask.'

Joy, being the eldest, was the spokesperson for the two and the trier-out of new experiences, like jumping from the diving board at the swimming baths.

John rubbed his eyes with his hands; this was getting more complicated by the minute.

'I'll speak to him, but his mammy is the same as always, Mammy Lily.'

Joy continued curling her hair before she spoke again. 'We want to know if you are our only daddy?'

John would swear his heart missed a beat. He'd known this moment would come but he also knew he could never be prepared for it. Telling Joy he wasn't her real dad would break his heart, but it was paramount he never let on, as he couldn't bear to see her distressed on his account. He plastered an encouraging smile on his face. What to say?

'You have different daddies,' he told her. 'I'm Freddie's and you have someone called Karl.' John thought it wise to let this new piece of information sink in and not to elaborate.

'I don't want him. I want you as a daddy,' Joy said, getting upset. 'I don't know this man, Karl. I've never seen him before, he's a stranger.'

John wished Bella was here just now; she knew how to handle the two children. Bella had continued to be his constant after Lily died, and he relied on her.

A year after the war ended, when the Women's Timber Corps disbanded, Bella had refused to return home and found employment at a riding stable, where she lived in.

Their hearts guarded and fragile, neither of them wanted to love again, but they had grown close and felt lucky to have one another's friendship.

John groaned. He needed to think of something to calm Joy. 'You know Mary who you play with along the street and she goes to your school?' As was Joy's wont, her face quickly changed to interest.

She nodded.

John went on to explain how Mary was adopted but the people

who brought her up were now her mam and dad.

'So, you see, I'm still your daddy.'

She gave a thoughtful little nod. Thankfully, she didn't ask if she was adopted.

That was the moment when John knew he had to keep his promise to Lily. He'd kept the first part by revealing to Joy that Ethel was her mother; now it was time to do something about finding Karl.

The very idea struck fear in his heart.

———

Reaching for the small suitcase on top of the tall, mahogany wardrobe in his bedroom, John opened it and found the letter written by Karl. As he held the piece of paper in his hand, John was transported back to the war, men lying on the beaches at Dunkirk, North Africa, the flies, and eventually the landmine that had cost him half of his leg. But the world had moved on and it was time that John did the same. Getting in touch with Karl was the first step. He was no longer the enemy.

That night, John wrote a letter.

Olcote
6, Foley Avenue
South Shields
County Durham
England

To whom it may concern,

This is to enquire if the whereabouts of Karl Becker are known at this address. I have information that is of some great importance to him. Please get in touch at the above address.

Yours sincerely,

John Radley

John put the letter in an envelope and, sealing it, put the address from the letter on the front.

He realised whoever received it might possibly be unable to read English but he would leave that side of things to fate; he'd fulfilled a promise and couldn't do any more.

He tried to put the matter at the back of his mind and get on with daily life but the anticipation of hearing back was too great to bear, and over the next few days John grew tense and irritable. As the days turned into a couple of weeks and nothing came of his correspondence, John began to relax. He'd done his best, he conceded; now was the time to let the matter drop.

————

Then came the shock one morning the next week, when John came downstairs to find a letter with a foreign stamp lying on the front doormat.

John, with a sense of dread, moved along the passageway and picked up the letter. He put it on the table, staring at it for a long while; he realised this letter could irrevocably change his life.

Reaching forward, he opened it and read:

Dear Mr Radley,

I am sorry for the wait. I had your letter translated by the schoolmaster, Herr Kaufmann, who speaks English. He writes this for me. I am the sister of Karl Becker and his only living family.

Karl now lives in England. I write and send your letter to Karl.

Ingrid Becker

John let out a somewhat fraught sigh. So, Karl was alive and in this country. John knew that many Germans hadn't returned to their homeland after the war and, presumably, this was what happened to Karl Becker. He also knew that once the ban preventing 'romantic liaisons' with local women had been lifted in '47, many POWs were reported to have married British women.

Karl's sister didn't say much, for instance, whether he was married or not. But what did it matter? The man mightn't even be interested in replying. Though John knew in his bones that this was only wishful thinking.

———

More days passed, during which John's first duty was to check behind the door for post. If an envelope did lie there, he could barely breathe until he'd opened it and been assured it wasn't from Karl Becker.

One Wednesday morning, a letter in a white envelope lay on the doormat and, picking it up, John didn't recognise the neat handwriting. His heart rate quickened as he opened the envelope.

The letter was from Karl, and it was short and to the point.

Dear Mr Radley,

I have received notification that you wish to be in touch with me about some matter of importance. You can reach me at the address below.

The address was at a place called Ringwood in Hampshire.

John looked up on the map where Ringwood was and experienced mixed emotions when he saw how far down south it was. He didn't know if it was good news or bad that Ringwood was so far away.

He told himself there was no immediate need to reply and got on with everyday life. But as the days passed, being a fair and honest man, his conscience wouldn't allow him to stall any longer.

On a day when everyone was out, John sat at the kitchen table, pen in hand. He concentrated. What the heck could he say?

Deciding there was no other way but to tell the bare bones of the matter, he proceeded to write:

Dear Mr Becker,

I write to you with news that might startle you. I believe you were a prisoner of war at a camp near Teviot Hall estate where my late wife Lily worked as a Lumberjill. Lily befriended Ethel Post, who was, I believe, your girlfriend at that time.

Ethel confided in my wife and said she was pregnant and that you were the father. I was able to contact you as I have in my possession the letter you left Ethel if she needed to contact you.

John went on to say that Ethel had been killed during a raid but the baby – a girl named Joy – had survived and about the promise Lily had made. He finished up by saying:

My wife passed away several weeks before Joy was two and I recently decided she was old enough to be told the truth of her

*birth. Joy has made no mention of wanting to meet with you and I
leave the matter up to your own discretion.*

John thought this a bit harsh but justified it by thinking that he
spoke the truth and he couldn't think of a better way to put it.

———

The following week was purgatory waiting. If John was truthful,
the little he knew about Karl Becker made him think the man was
genuine. Which was good news if he was to meet with Joy – but
not for John. He wanted him to be a selfish scoundrel, who wanted
to get on with his life unhindered by a child he'd fathered.

But it would seem his real opinion was correct, as a few days
later a letter arrived from Karl. That evening, John visited his
daughter when she was in bed reading. He chose that time because
he didn't want to speak about Karl in front of his son, who was
confused enough about the matter of Joy's birthright. Amazingly,
Freddie didn't tease Joy any more and did all her bidding – which
John knew proved how fragile he felt about his relationship with
his sister.

'Joy, I've got something to tell you.'

She laid the book she was reading on the floral bedspread and
in the lamplight looked up, wide-eyed with expectation.

John sat beside her on the bed and putting an arm around her
shoulders he gave her a cuddle. He had Lily to thank for his ability
to physically show affection – and Bella for reminding him how
much his children needed his love when he'd lost his way in the
aftermath of Lily's death – and John was never happier than when
demonstrating his affection.

Trying to recall the words he'd rehearsed, he heaved a regretful
sigh. At times like this he missed Lily as she always knew how to
broach a delicate subject.

'I've been in touch with Karl, your daddy.' Joy's expression
dumbfounded, he ploughed on. 'I've received a letter from him

today. Would you like to hear what he said?' John had decided that it was best to be upfront with Joy.

Her face unreadable, she nodded.

John took the letter from a trouser pocket. He'd decided not to read it as it was full of detail that might confuse her. Scanning Karl's correspondence, he picked out the bits his daughter would want to hear.

'Your daddy wrote to say—'

'Other daddy,' she corrected.

'That he lives down south in a place called Ringwood and he works on a farm.'

Joy, intent on listening, bit a thumbnail, a habit he'd thought he'd persuaded her to give up.

He carried on, 'That sounds fun, doesn't it? He's married with children—'

'Are they babies?'

Joy, though at an age where she'd stopped mothering dolls, loved babies.

'He didn't say, sweetheart. What he does say is he's happy to hear he has a daughter and he's asked if you would visit him so the pair of you can meet and get to know one another.'

Joy didn't say anything but sank back against the pillows. That closed expression he knew so well on her face, she was making sense of what she'd just heard.

Before folding the letter and putting it away, John reread it to himself for the third time. Karl started off by saying the letter had come as a great shock and at first he couldn't take the content in. He went on to say:

> I left the north under guard, and was taken to a camp down south near the New Forest. Not a secure camp as expected as I am considered not to be a threat. It was the need for farmhands (especially with my working knowledge with horses in forests) that saved me from being shipped off to America.
>
> After the war ended, I am discharged and given alien

certificate which helped get me paid work. I get a job as labourer on a farm where I settled. I'm married and have a family and live in a house on the farm and have a good life. I never forget Ethel and tried to reach her by letter at Teviot Hall estate but they never write back. I thought Ethel had got on with her life and it was best to forget her. I'm sad she died.

A poignant moment. He finished by saying:

I am amazed I have a daughter but happy too and my wish is to meet her so we get to know each other. Would it be possible for her to visit and I meet with her?

For Joy's sake John hoped the man was as sincere as he sounded. Although the thought unnerved him that Joy might think Karl wonderful, the bigger part of him didn't want her to be hurt. He loved her too much for that.

He decided she needed time on her own.

'If you haven't any questions, sweetheart, lights out in ten minutes.' He struggled to stand.

'Daddy,' she said tentatively.

'Yes?'

'I don't want to go and see him.'

John felt a releasing of tension in his chest. 'Then you don't have to, sweetheart.'

A hint of eagerness gleamed in her eye. 'But he could come here and visit.'

As he folded the letter, a thought made a cold shiver run down John's spine. *What if Karl wants Joy to live with him?*

———

As they walked along the Leas, a vast landscape of towering clifftops of grass stretching for two miles along the coastline, John held Joy's little hand tightly in his own. A November day, while the sun shone, a freezing cold north-easterly wind blew. John smiled at his daughter, bundled up in winter clothing – warm coat, knitted hat, scarf and gloves – who had roses in her cheeks.

Earlier he'd decided on a walk with Joy to give her the chance to speak about tomorrow's visit with Karl if she so desired, but he wouldn't press the matter.

Bella had taken the day off from the stables where she still worked, and was looking after Freddie. Mum, who now lived in a downstairs flat in Whale Street to be close to her grandchildren, would have helped out, but she had a previous engagement with a friend that she couldn't cancel.

'Daddy.' His daughter squinted in the weak morning sun as she looked up at him. 'You wouldn't give me away to this other dad, would you?' The worried little frown she wore looked incongruous on the smooth skin of her forehead.

Gazing thoughtfully out to sea, where a white ship appeared to glide along the horizon in sparkling waters, John searched his mind. It was imperative he said the right thing so Joy wouldn't misunderstand or be disturbed. Though the subject of her other dad was painful, John had promised himself not to show any emotion or fabricate the truth whenever Joy inquired about the past.

'Why would I give my gorgeous girl away?'

'The other dad did.'

Over time, since his daughter had discovered the quilt, John found that he'd been right in that Joy, too young to absorb all the information, kept asking questions about her past. In turn, he patiently repeated the details, in the hope that one day she'd grasp all he told her.

Relieved to have a rest, as walking any distance was sometimes telling on his stump, he stopped and regarded the anxious face staring up at him.

'Remember, I told you, the other dad' (this was how they referred to Karl for clarity's sake) 'went away before he knew anything about you.'

'Why did he go away?'

'Because he was sent. That's what happened to soldiers in wartime. They don't have a choice.' He wanted to leave the issue of Karl being a prisoner of war for later as Joy's young mind had enough information to deal with.

Joy pondered this. 'Like I have to do as I'm told.'

John smirked and ruffled her curls. 'Like coming for a walk with your daddy on a freezing cold day, you mean?'

Joy giggled. 'I like it here.' Disentangling her hand, she began to walk on. 'Can we go right up to the lighthouse? Will the horn blow while we're there?'

Known as Souter Point, the hooped red and white coloured lighthouse was a beacon perched on the clifftop, and a sight to behold.

'Yes, we can. And no, the foghorn won't go today, as it only sounds when there's a thick fog to warn ships to stay away from the rocks.'

Joy turned, waiting for him. 'I can hear it in bed sometimes. It's a scary wailing sound.'

'People hear the foghorn for miles around.'

'And he never knew I was in my other mam Ethel's tummy?'

It took a few seconds for John to catch up with his daughter's flitting mind.

It grieved him that she had no memory of Lily even though Joy was adamant she did. He reckoned it was because of the reams of photos of Lily he'd shown Freddie and her so they wouldn't forget their mother. He'd wanted to keep her alive in their minds, for them to know everything about Lily, the colour of her hair, favourite music, that she was a tomboy when she was young and wanted to outdo her brothers.

'Nope.' He told Joy jokily, 'And if the other dad had known, he would have skedaddled straight back home to see you.'

For Joy's sake he wanted to show Karl in a good light, as John didn't know what tomorrow would bring when Karl visited.

December 1953

Karl was expected at the railway station at one o'clock on the train from Newcastle and John was taking Joy to meet him. He could tell while she waited that she was nervous, pushing her hair behind her ear, biting her thumbnail all morning. Her continuous questions had broken his heart.

Do I look pretty in this dress? What if the other dad doesn't like me? Daddy, will you be there all the time when I'm with him?

He'd done his best to reassure her but it was when she'd asked, *What do I call him?* that John had been stumped.

'You don't have to make up your mind now.'

Sitting opposite him at the kitchen table, she'd looked near to tears. 'I do.'

John had got up from his seat and, moving over to her, had taken her in his arms and made the decision for her. 'You should call him Karl for now.'

It was a Saturday and after an early dinner Bella took a belligerent Freddie (he wanted to stay home to see the other dad) to the fairground where he'd have a go on the push-penny machine, his favourite pastime at the fair and the only thing that opened in winter.

At one o'clock prompt John and Joy stood on the draughty platform as the electric train from Newcastle came into the station. Taking his daughter's hand in his, they watched as the train came to a halt. As doors opened and people alighted from the train, John spotted a man who must be Karl standing on the platform. Dressed in a rather shabby dark suit that looked a little tight on his square, bulky figure, and with brown eyes and hair, there was no mistaking him; his features were the double of Joy's.

John's heart sank.

Karl looked around, no doubt hoping to catch sight of the people who'd be meeting him.

John moved forward, pulling Joy by the hand, and caught Karl's attention.

'Welcome to South Shields,' John said. 'This is Joy.'

He felt her stiffen. Looking down, he saw her scuff the ground with the toe of her shoe.

Karl dropped on one knee and, smiling, told her, 'My children are shy at meeting new people too. I hope soon we won't be strangers.'

———

Later, in the front room, Joy and John sat united on the couch, Karl on a chair by the roaring fire, and the atmosphere was strained. The best china tea set and a plate of Jacob's assorted biscuits graced an occasional table, prepared earlier by Bella before she left.

Karl was saying to Joy, 'I had no doubts when I saw you because you have the Becker look.' His smile was infectious, his round face kindly and he had a German accent.

John sat up a little straighter. Had the man had doubts about Joy being his? The thought had never occurred to him before.

'I would have been in touch before if I'd known about you. It is so good to meet you,' Karl told Joy and John felt accused for not being in contact earlier. 'My wife, Jenny, sent a message to welcome you into our family.'

'You said in the letter you had family?' John felt excluded and wanted to be part of the conversation.

Karl's ruddy face beamed. 'Ja. Two boys, younger than you. Your brothers.' Addressing Joy, he spoke with a cheery voice.

John glanced at his daughter, who sat as stiff as a brush handle but her gaze never met the German's.

'I have brought a photo of my family for you to see. The boys look forward to meeting with you.'

John felt fidgety. He didn't want to be involved in looking at a happy family scene.

'I'll make a pot of tea.' He knew he was being churlish but couldn't help himself.

As he pushed himself up John noticed a look of consternation cross Joy's face.

'I won't be a tick,' he told her.

While he was in the kitchen pouring boiling water in the pot, muffled laughter could be heard through the wall.

This was all too congenial for John's liking, then he checked himself. For Joy's sake he should be happy. Karl was her father and for them to have a relationship was something Ethel would have wanted. John gave a tortured sigh. Lord help him, that's what his head said but unfortunately his heart hadn't caught up.

As he came back into the front room, teapot in hand, Joy was listening intently to Karl, face enraptured and smiling.

'Daddy, Karl has been telling me all about the farm and how his little boy, Hans, is frightened of the geese because they chase him.'

Karl nodded at her. 'You will come one day and see for yourself.'

A band of tightness grasped John around his chest.

The afternoon wore on, John being civil to Karl because, in different circumstances, he knew he'd have been drawn to the seemingly unaffected man who spoke openly about his life.

It was when he told Joy, 'I came to this country as a prisoner. Do you understand that, Joy?' that John's ears pricked up and he glanced down in concern to see Joy's reaction.

Joy gave an uncertain frown. 'A prisoner is someone who did something bad and got locked up.'

John jumped to Karl's defence. 'Sweetheart, Karl was a prisoner of war. That means a soldier who fought on a different side and was captured. It could have happened to me.'

As a look of puzzlement crossed Joy's face, Karl looked over towards John and gave a nod of appreciation.

'Jenny says I speak before I think. But I want to have no secrets from Joy.'

John helped by telling Joy, 'Karl was in a camp when he met Ethel. Remember I told you about Ethel and your mother working at Teviot Hall and becoming friends?'

Joy looked shyly at Karl. 'What was she like? She made me a memory quilt.'

She then turned to John, her expression unsure. He realised Joy was growing up and, being sensitive, she picked up on things, such as John's reluctance to face facts that he wasn't her real dad, and so Joy was nervous to broach the subject of Ethel being her mother.

'Tell you what' – he spoke in an overeager voice – 'how about I go and get the memory quilt so you can show Karl while he tells you about Ethel, your mother.'

Not wanting the others to see what those words cost him, John stumbled from the room.

———

He gave them time to be alone and when John returned to the front room, the colourful quilt in his hand, the atmosphere, heavy and somewhat uncomfortable, had changed.

'Here it is,' John declared over-brightly, taking in Joy's long face. 'Did you learn much about Ethel?'

'Joy is familiar with her mother's background thanks to you.' Though he spoke in a friendly manner, Karl's expression was one of deflation.

John, mystified as to what had happened, told Karl, 'It was Lily, my late wife, who told me about Ethel. I was simply the messenger passing the information on.'

Lily's voice came back to him: 'I want Joy to know what a wonderful person her mother was. That she loved her enough to give her up if needs be, so Joy could have a better life.'

'Your wife, Lily, sounds a...' Karl appeared to search for the word he wanted and finally said, 'a good woman to promise to bring up her friend's baby.'

John looked over to Joy and smiled. 'Lily loved her very much. We both do.'

The uncomfortable silence was back again and Karl fidgeted in his seat as if readying himself to say something.

'I understand why you didn't tell Joy about her true identity when she was young. My dear friend, you have done a good job of bringing Joy up but now things are different.' John stiffened, knowing something significant was to be said. 'I've asked Joy if she would come and live with me and my family. Not because of duty but because she is my daughter and her place is in my family. Jenny and I have spoken of this and we both agree. But the decision has to be Joy's.'

It was as though someone punched John in the chest and he slumped down on the arm of the couch. 'I don't know what to say, this is so unexpected.'

He looked over to Joy, who had a rather defiant look on her face.

John went on, even though his mouth was exceedingly dry, 'This is too sudden for Joy to deal—'

'I agree. I've told my daughter that we must get to know her a little more first.'

His daughter, John thought indignantly. Then conceded the man only spoke the truth, Joy was his daughter.

Karl looked over to Joy. 'Joy is a Becker, and knows her own mind.' He turned towards John. 'Her answer was a firm no.'

John's body sagged with relief but he didn't feel victorious as he saw the look of despondency on the other man's face.

What could he say? In an attempt to smooth things over, he held up the memory quilt. 'Joy, how about you show Karl the quilt your mother, Ethel, made?'

Joy came forward slowly and, taking the quilt from him, she moved over to Karl. Seeing them together, the resemblance they shared that he could never have, in that moment John accepted Joy wasn't rightfully his.

Meanwhile, Karl was looking equally downhearted staring at the quilt. Suddenly his demeanour changed and he sat upright.

His eyes rounded with surprise. 'My name is embroi—' He frowned in frustration as he searched for the correct word. 'Stitched on it. Proof to you that I am your daddy.'

His heart twisting unbearably, John needed a few moments to collect himself. Picking up the untouched tea in the pot, he told them, 'I'll make a fresh pot.'

When he returned, Joy, looking decidedly pensive, was now sitting on the couch beside Karl while he enquired about her school life.

The afternoon continued, talking about this and that, John helping out by asking about Karl's family, his life and work. Apparently, he was head man as the aged farmer who owned the place was retired and owned a purpose-built bungalow at the top of a hill looking down on the farm.

'He has a beautiful view but' – Karl laughed good-naturedly – 'he is never at home long enough to enjoy it as he is always checking up on the farm.'

John nodded. 'I have a boss just the same. Always checking up on my work. But the bloke's understanding about my gammy leg.'

'The war?' Karl exclaimed.

John nodded. 'Yes. A landmine.'

Karl wagged his head. 'Such madness, my friend. The warmongers never learn.'

The conversation dried up after that and John tried, in the agonising silence, to think of something to say. Then he noticed Karl, seemingly perfectly at ease, was content to sit quietly stealing glances at Joy.

Finally, Karl made a move to stand.

'I think it is best I go now. Jenny will be anxious if I am too late getting home.'

He moved over to John, who stood up and extended his arm. Karl gave him a firm handshake and, still holding hands, he met John's gaze – and John noticed the unshed tears glistening in the other man's eyes.

'We have both loved and lost.' Karl's voice was gruff with emotion.

Without another word, he loosened his grasp of John's hand and made for the door.

————

As John closed the front door and he and Joy made their way back to the front room, he put his arm lightly around her shoulders.

'Tell me, sweetheart, what did you say to your fath— Karl?'

'About what?' Joy made a dive for a biscuit on the plate.

'About you living with him on the farm.'

Joy frowned in concentration, remembering. 'I told him it would be fun seeing the farm. But when he said, "I'd like for you to live with your daddy and two brothers and my wife Jenny," I realised.'

'What did you realise?'

'That I didn't need a new daddy or brothers.' Her smile was like the sunrise. 'So, I told him, "No thank you, I've already got a daddy and little brother here at home."'

EPILOGUE

MAY 1954

The day was grey but thankfully the torrential rain of the recent days had kept away. As everyone walked to the church, taking in the scene, John considered himself a lucky man.

Karl had travelled up with his family especially for the occasion and they were staying for the weekend at Olcote, the three boys in one room in the double bed, Joy in a camp bed on the landing. She'd complained to John that it was hard and uncomfortable.

'You want to think yourself lucky,' Bella told her. 'When Lily and I were Lumberjills that's all we had.'

John's mum and Bella walked alongside each other, deep in conversation. John lagged behind with Joy and a disenchanted Freddie, who thought church services boring. John chuckled, knowing his nine-year-old son's problem was that he was peeved because he wasn't the centre of attention.

'How long will this confirming take?' Freddie wanted to know, dragging his heels.

'Confirmation,' Joy corrected. 'It's after the main service and there are a few of us.'

'We have to sit through a whole service first?' Freddie's incredulous voice was full of disgust. 'Nobody told me that. It'll take forever.'

'It wouldn't make any difference if someone did. You'd still have to attend. Wouldn't he, Daddy?'

John tousled Freddie's hair, adding to the lad's disgust. 'You sure would. Wait till sports day at school when we all have to watch you win everything you enter.'

Freddie was the athletic one, while Joy was more musically inclined. She'd joined the school choir and had just started learning to play the piano.

For weeks now John's daughter had been attending confirmation classes at the vicar's house and today was the big day of her confirmation. Bella had helped find her a suitable white dress, which John wasn't allowed to see as the two of them wanted it to be a surprise.

When John had suggested to Karl that their daughter should be confirmed, he'd agreed without objection.

Joy had got over her awkwardness about Karl when she and Freddie were invited to the farm over the Easter holidays. They'd talked of nothing else for weeks after. Since then, John had taken it upon himself, encouraged by Bella, to include Karl in all the decisions he made concerning Joy and the two men corresponded often by letter.

As the company walked up the sweeping St Michael's and All Angels' driveway, John glimpsed Lily's parents and Jean and Harry and their two boys waiting at the arched doorway.

Ida Armstrong looked up from straightening her grandson Stanley's tie and, seeing them, gave a wave.

All Lily's relatives now knew the situation of Joy's birth.

John, after he'd told Ida, felt absolved when she answered, 'I won't deny it's come as a shock but I know our Lily was desperate for a bairn.' Her eyes swam with tears. 'God love her, she wasn't herself for a time after she had those miscarriages.' She continued in a squeaky voice, 'Joy will always be our granddaughter, won't she, Arthur.'

Her husband, too emotional to speak, simply nodded.

As he reached the top of the church driveway, John called out to the others waiting, 'My, aren't we all smart, dressed up in our Sunday best.' Reaching young Stanley, he ruffled his hair. 'Especially you in a suit.'

The boy looked daggers at his mam. 'It's me da's trousers cut down to size.'

'Don't start him off, John.' Jean's face wore a harassed expression. 'I've bribed him with a Minchella's ice cream afterwards if he's a good lad and behaves during the service.'

Ida piped up, 'What that lad needs is a—'

'All present and correct,' John quickly put in.

'Except for those two buggers of mine.' Ida looked at Harry. 'I can't remember when Sam or Ian last set foot in church.'

Bella looked at John and he knew she was thinking the same thing. It was at their wedding at this very same church, eighteen months ago.

Others were now starting to turn up and enter the church.

John took his wife's hand and said to the others, 'We'd like a word with Joy before we go in.' He laid a hand on Freddie's shoulder. 'Son, you go in with Grandma.'

Freddie pulled a long face. 'Do I have to?'

'Yes, you do. We won't be long. Find a seat beside the aisle and then you can be first to leave when it's time.'

Freddie didn't need a second telling.

When everyone had disappeared through the church doorway, the three of them stood to one side.

'Bella and I want you to have this,' John told his daughter.

When they married, Bella insisted Joy and Freddie called her by her first name, knowing as she did so that Joy already had two mothers and didn't need the complication of another one.

Bringing a velvet box from his inside jacket pocket, John handed it to his daughter.

Opening the lid, Joy gasped, 'Oooh, it's a silver locket. I've always wanted one.'

'Open it up,' Bella told her and John could tell she couldn't wait to see Joy's reaction.

Joy took the heart-shaped necklace out of its box and, opening it, cried, 'It's got a picture of Mam inside.' Then looking at the other side of the locket, she asked, 'Who's this other lady?'

'Your mother, Ethel,' John told her. 'Thanks to Bella, who found a photograph of her.'

'When we thought of the idea of a locket and putting Lily in it,' Bella chipped in, 'I regretted there wasn't a photograph of Ethel. Then I remembered that when we were Lumberjills a girl called Vivian took a picture of the gang when we were working in the forest, and I managed to get in touch with her.' Her eyes held a faraway look as though she was remembering those days.

Joy touched with her forefinger the grainy black and white photograph of Ethel's face. 'It's my other mam Ethel.' Her tone was one of wonderment. 'I never thought I'd see her. Oh, thank you, Bella.' Joy wrapped her arms around Bella's enormous waistline.

'I think we'd better get a move on.' John hated to break up this moment but the last few stragglers were now entering the church.

Bella said, 'You go inside, John, and I'll wait while Joy takes off her coat. We want you to get a surprise when she walks down the aisle.'

———

Later, while they sat in one of the front pews, the church service nearly over and the young girls ready to walk down the aisle from the back of the church, John took Bella's hand.

He leant over and whispered, 'The next time we have a family occasion it'll be our baby's christening.' He eyed her swollen belly.

It was nearly her due date and Bella, with pink cheeks, thick glossy hair and sparkling eyes, looked the picture of health – but that didn't stop John from having the occasional gnawing worry.

'That's perfectly natural for any expecting husband,' Bella had assured him. 'John, even more so with your heartbreaking experience with Lily. But don't let fear spoil the excitement of the birth of our baby.'

As Lily was before her, Bella was always right and John cast out his doubts.

Though Bella and John had professed to never want to love again, they'd come to realise that was their heads speaking, while their hearts knew differently. Their friendship, over time, blossoming into love, John realised he couldn't bear the idea that she might one day go. What could he lose, he'd thought, by telling her so? The wonder was she confessed she'd been harbouring the same feelings. Despite their fears, especially John's about starting a family, the pair of them decided to live and love again.

Now, as the organ started up and filled the church to the high ornate rooftop, the congregation stood and began singing the last hymn. John, sitting at the end of the pew, was distracted when Bella prodded him in the ribs and then nodded towards the aisle.

Then he saw her: Joy. Dressed in a white knee-length frock with flared skirt, Peter Pan collar, puffed sleeves, and enormous bow tied at the back, she looked adorable. A tightening came into his throat and tears prickled the backs of his eyes.

As the choirboys' voices soared, Bella leaning towards him whispered in his ear, 'John, I can sense them... Lily and Ethel. I feel they're here watching and glowing with pride.'

———

A LETTER FROM SHIRLEY

Dear Reader,

First of all, I'd like to say a big thank you for choosing to purchase *The Orphan's Secret* and for your continued support. Writers depend on readers and there would be no book five without you lovely readers supporting me and reading my books. I'm truly grateful to all of you.

If you did enjoy *The Orphan's Secret* and would like to keep up with all my releases, just sign up at the following link. Your email address will never be shared and you can unsubscribe at any time.

www.bookouture.com/shirley-dickson

The inspiration for the book came from a chat with the fantastic Christina Demosthenous, who brought my attention to the idea of a memory quilt. The concept of how a memory quilt could represent someone's past and yet influence the future inspired me and the seeds of *The Orphan's Secret* were sown.

Before working in maternity as an auxiliary nurse, many years ago, I supposed getting pregnant and delivering a healthy baby was the norm. Later, I came to realise for some unfortunate women this was certainly not the case. And so – thinking about these brave women, the heartache, distress and suffering that miscarriages and stillbirths bring – Lily was conceived in my imagination.

While writing this book during Covid restrictions – cocooned in my office bedroom away from winter's icy blasts – the story couldn't have been more poignant as my granddaughter was expecting her second baby at the time. Thankfully, she went on to deliver a healthy baby.

The setting again starts in South Shields, my hometown, where the locals will realise I've taken liberties with street names and bombings, necessary for the sake of the story. The story travels to the beautiful Border country where I explore the arduous life of a Lumberjill. Although there are many beautiful stately homes in Scotland, unfortunately there is no Teviot Hall.

I was fascinated when researching and reading accounts of Lumberjills – known as Britain's forgotten army. Leaving the security and comforts of home to do gruelling and arduous work in wintry elements and living in appalling conditions in billets – though Lily was relatively lucky with hers. A book that helped enormously while researching *The Orphan's Secret* was *Lumberjills* by Joanna Foat.

It wasn't until more than sixty years later in 2007 that members of the Women's Timber Corps received their richly deserved first formal recognition for their war effort. A life-sized bronze sculpture of a Lumberjill was unveiled by the forestry commission in Scotland, dedicated to the members of the Women's Timber Corps.

If you enjoyed *The Orphan's Secret* and have time to leave a review, I would be most grateful. It makes such a difference to an author and I do love to hear what readers think. Thank you to those who mention my book to family and friends as it helps readers find me for the first time.

Also, I would love to hear from you on my author page or Twitter.

Take care and happy reading!

Shirley

facebook.com/shirley.dickson.714

twitter.com/ShirleyDWriter

ACKNOWLEDGEMENTS

Firstly, as always, thank you to Wal: you were always the believer, and see what you've helped me to achieve with your faith.

Then there's the behind-the-scenes cast – the wonderful Bookouture team who has helped me bring my publishing dreams to an amazing reality. Thank you, to every one of you hard-working people for your enthusiasm and support in getting *The Orphan's Secret* ready for publication. Huge thanks go to Vicky Blunden for your brilliant edits which have improved the book immensely – working with you is always a pleasure. Special thanks to Christina Demosthenous, for your continued encouragement and belief and for saying just the right thing when I need it most. I'm truly grateful for all that you do. And to Bookouture authors, a talented and supportive group, thank you. Being part of the Bookouture family is the icing on the cake.

Thank you to Rossi, who took the time in her busy life to talk me through pre-eclampsia, which was an enormous help but any errors are mine alone. And thank you to Mary for her great help with answering medical questions.

To my family, Tracy, Andrea, Joanne, Phil, Nick, Gary, Gemma, Dale, Robbie, Laura, Tom, Will and the recent delightful addition, Amelia, thanks for all you do. Life would never be the same without you lovely people in it. To Auriel, we missed you for the proofread but hopefully next time.

My thanks go out to all the wonderful reviewers and bloggers – I'm so grateful to you for taking the time.

Lastly, to readers, a heartfelt thank you. I couldn't do any of this without you.

Printed in Great Britain
by Amazon